THE
ELEMENTAL

SARA GALADARI

For Adnan

*In the limitlessness of space and the vastness of time, I am forever
elated to explore it with you*

CONTENTS

THE ELEMENTAL

Too often we wish for the power to alter the past and change our present
Rarely do we realize the power we have to alter the present and change our future

Sara Galadari

PROLOGUE

"They're here." Her voice trembled, drowned out by another deafening bang. She darted across the room, hastily stuffing her things, scattered across the table, into a small leather satchel.

Another loud bang crashed. She heard the door rattle on its hinges and stifled a gasp, pressing a closed fist to her mouth. She couldn't afford to panic now. She knew what she was getting herself into.

And she was ready.

She steadied herself, taking in a deep breath before flying into action, finishing packing her belongings and securing her satchel's clasp. She hugged her cloak tighter around her, taking care to tread lightly as she approached the small crib by her bed.

The outline of a small lump huddled beneath a

woolen blanket was just barely noticeable in the flickering candlelight. She placed a hand on the blanket, gently shaking the small lump.

"Mm?" a small voice murmured from the blankets.

"Shh," the woman breathed softly, rubbing the small child's back.

"Mama?" the child whispered, unaware of the terror lacing her parent's breaths. She peeked her head out of her blanket and reached a small hand out, sleepily holding her mother's cheek. "Mama, morning now?" she muttered, her voice thick with sleep.

The woman leaned into her little child's palm, cupped ever so gently on her face. Her hand was still warm from her disrupted slumber.

The little girl's obliviousness to her mother's panic soothed her some. She leaned in and wrapped her arms around her tiny girl, squeezing her tight.

For a moment, all was well.

The woman squeezed her eyes shut. She didn't want this moment to end.

She breathed, mustering the strength to let go of her little girl, and picked up a small cloak draped across the railing of her crib. She pulled back the blanket wrapped around the child and replaced it with the dark, silky blue cloak, fastening the clasp with a quiet *snap*.

"Helia, we're going to have to keep *very* quiet, okay?" she whispered, looking into her eyes, making sure she understood.

"Why, Mama?"

"The bad men." She could feel her heart split in two as she saw her daughter's face slowly twist with fear at her words.

"Bad men," the child repeated solemnly. She understood. The woman nodded.

"Come on, we have to go," she said, scooping her up in her arms. Making sure her satchel was in place, she pulled Helia's hood over her head before pulling up her own.

Helia clung to her mother, bouncing uncomfortably in her arms as she quietly hurried out of the room. The small torches mounted on either side of the hallway were unlit, leaving the two to continue in darkness. Soft moonlight trickled down a large crack in the wall, providing just enough light for the two to make their way out of the cottage.

If she could just make it to the castle's Grand Library...

She paused as she reached a large wooden door. This was going to be the risky part. This door separated them from the safety of her quarters and the open sky above the courtyard.

She would need to make it across the courtyard, up the staircase to the second level of the castle, through the rose garden and past the set of the heavy iron doors, continue down the hallway, and finally...

A loud bang interrupted the silent revision of her plan. She swiveled her head around, eyes slightly bulging out in her panic. The sound was close.

It didn't matter. She didn't have time to panic. She needed to make it. Everything was depending on this.

"Mama?" a small voice squeaked from beneath the hooded cloak in her arms.

"Shh, my love. It's okay," the woman whispered against the top of the toddler's head.

She took in a deep breath, slowly pushing the heavy wooden door ajar. Cool air softly blew through, sending a small shiver down her spine.

All seemed quiet.

She knew it wouldn't stay that way for long.

The once-bustling castle grounds were now eerily silent. Where guards normally stood and chattered away lay piles of rubble and shattered stone. The castle's once-pristine walls now stood battered; large stones were knocked out in a crumbly, decrepit mess, while other sections of the walls were completely obliterated.

She knew that coming back to the castle was dangerous.

She knew the risks she was taking by going back to the cottage within the castle grounds.

But it was their only chance left.

She couldn't lose their only chance.

The woman pushed the door open further, slipping silently across the courtyard. She breathed a sigh of relief as she realized that they were still alone.

Shallow breaths were drowned out by hastened footsteps over the cobbled pathway along the courtyard. The woman winced, feeling her thin shoes curl over a particularly jagged cobblestone and poking the sole of her foot. She stifled a small grunt of pain as she hurried up the steep steps, careful not to draw any further attention to herself. She could barely see. The night sky was suffocated in the thick, black smoke that poured out from the city beyond the castle grounds. Her calves screamed as she pushed herself higher and higher up the stairs, desperate to escape, the weight of Helia in her arms growing heavier by the second.

As she reached the top of the stairs, she turned her head to peer below. Her elbow struck against a loose stone from the crumbling wall beside her. She gasped loudly, watching the stone clatter against the cobbled steps, the sound thundering deafeningly amidst the silence she so desperately wanted to keep.

"Over there!" A gruff voice exclaimed. The sound of feet shuffling against the rugged floor sounded closer than ever.

Time was up.

The woman didn't have time to check how close the man was, or how many more there were. Ignoring Helia's frightened wails, she darted across the grounds and dove into the rose garden's overgrown, thorny, tangled midst, the prickly bushes brushing painfully against her body as she ran as fast as could, hoping that the thorny thicket would slow down her pursuers. She could feel her sleeves being torn to shreds as the thorns poked and scratched at her, and little rivulets of blood dripped down her arms. She winced as she felt a spiny branch scratch across her face.

"Mama," Helia yelled as a particularly sharp point poked at her back. "It hurts," she cried pathetically.

"I know, my love. Shh, we're almost there," she murmured against Helia's head, adjusting her arms to shield the tiny girl from the thorns and pulling the girl's cloak taut against her body, trying to protect her. Her muscles screamed with fatigue as they continued through the thicket, and she could feel herself beginning to slow down.

They were so close.

She could see the heavy iron doors ahead of her. Just

a few more paces…

"Don't let them get away," boomed a deep voice behind them. "Set it all on fire. They've got nowhere left to run."

The woman pushed her way through the last of the bristly shrubberies and ran towards the entrance, throwing her body at the heavy metal doors and bursting through.

The Grand Library stood as a shadow of its former self, with priceless old tomes strewn about, piles of books ripped apart and drenched in water or burned to a crisp, and bookshelves blasted into splintering messes. The ground was smeared with remaining soot from singed pages, obscuring the intricate etchings carved into the ancient marble floors.

The woman ran towards the center of the library and dropped to her knees, setting down Helia, who was now openly wailing in terror. Her heart broke all over again at the sight of her baby crying with such fright, and she knew she couldn't do any more to protect her.

"Helia, listen to me," she said, trying to steady her trembling voice. "You have to be brave, like we talked about. Can you do that? Can you be brave for Mama?" she uttered softly, wiping the tears off of Helia's face with both palms. She held back tears as she saw her own blood, still wet on her hands, streak against her daughter's cheeks.

Helia shook her head vehemently. "No, Mama. I don't wanna be brave," she sniffed, wiping her nose with her sleeve. "I wanna go ho-oo-oome," she wailed in between tears, crying hard. The woman felt her own tears flowing freely down her face.

"I know, love," she said. "You're going home now. Everything will be okay, I promise. Okay?"

Helia nodded, still crying.

Wiping her tears, the woman pulled a long chain from around her neck and fastened it around Helia, the heavy stone pendant hanging down to her navel. The woman picked up the pendant and began fiddling with it, murmuring under her breath as she struggled to concentrate.

The pendant began to faintly glow blue from in between her fingers as she twisted it, a faint clicking sound emitting from her ministrations.

"Listen here," she whispered, still carefully twisting the pendant around itself, the blue glow growing brighter and brighter. "You see Mama's bag?"

Helia nodded her head, still sniffling.

"Take Mama's bag—that's right, good girl. Don't you let go of the bag, all right? Whatever you do, don't let go of Mama's bag. Keep it safe with you."

"Okay, Mama," said Helia, clutching the satchel tightly. She closed her eyes as her mother pulled her hood over her head, pressing her lips to her forehead in a strong kiss.

BANG.

They were out of time.

The woman whirled around, throwing herself in front of Helia, shielding her from sight. She put both arms down, feeling the hilt of her daggers slide effortlessly into her hands from their concealed straps beneath her sleeves, facing her assailants. There were four young men standing at the foot of the Grand Library, its iron doors blown clean off its hinges and lay strewn on either side of the library's entrance. She wrapped her hands firmly around her weapons, her eyes darting from one opponent to the next.

One of the men looked down at her and sneered, his teeth glistening in the night. His eyes bulged in excitement, face twisting into a sinister smile at the thrill of the chase.

"Hand over the Elemental," one of the men commanded. His harsh voice boomed in Helia's ears, and she instinctively retreated behind her mother.

She knew that voice. She would never forget that voice.

"Mama," Helia squeaked in terror, clutching at her mother's cloak. She felt her heart pounding in her chest.

The pendant around Helia's neck flashed as bright as the moonlight pouring through the shattered windows of the library. Helia's mother grinned.

It worked. Her plan was complete.

There was no more running away.

"The Elemental," the man barked again.

"Over your dead body," she uttered, the sudden surge of relief at her plan succeeding fueling her with vigor. She narrowed her eyes and focused hard, drawing energy from the sheer adrenaline flowing through her veins. She could feel a rush of power burst through her.

She smiled.

Everything was clear now.

She drew her arm back, taking careful aim, and hurled a dagger towards the men. One of the men that was flanking to her right screamed and twisted in agony as the dagger's blade sank into his cheek.

She smirked as she hit her target.

He shrieked in pain, grasping at his face.

Before the man could retaliate, she flung another dagger towards the other two men, glaring as her attacks hit her targets.

She whirled around, eyeing the fourth man. She was out of weapons. She darted towards one of the injured assailants, her hand outstretched to yank her dagger back from its mark.

At the same time, her final opponent lurched forward, grabbing the woman roughly by the arm and wrenching her hard towards him, drawing his hand for his own weapon. The woman tried in vain to wrestle his arm away from his weapon.

"Mama!" Helia cried, falling to the ground, unable to tear her eyes away from the man holding her mother. The blue glow around Helia's neck grew brighter and brighter, growing hotter by the second.

The woman snapped her head in the direction of her child's voice. "Everything's going to be okay," the woman cried. "Go!"

The last thing Helia could see before the world whooshed and vanished around her was her mother being pushed to the ground and the man standing above her, his sword drawn high above her head. She felt warm liquid spray across her face as the blade slashed through her mother's torso. She shrieked in horror, wiping the liquid from her face instinctively, and looked down at her hand to find it covered in thick blood.

AN UNEXPECTED VISITOR

"Mama! Mama!" Helia wailed in fright as her surroundings dissolved into a kaleidoscope of shapes and colors. Slowly, her world stopped spinning, and she found herself underneath a brilliantly lit chandelier, its light bouncing off of the pristine marble floors and illuminating the room with an invitingly warm and comfortable air. "Mama! Mamaaaa!" Helia continued to cry in a panic.

"What the—" a deep voice yelled from behind her. Helia whirled around, tears streaming down her face as she stared up at a very startled man. He was sitting at a table nearby, a small lamp burning beside a very large stack of books towering over him. A small book lay open in front of him with his fervent scribbles scrawled into its pages, his pen in his mouth as he paused for inspiration on his next words—which were now long gone with the sudden apparition before him. He knocked over his book and ink pot in his surprise, sending them flying across the floor loudly and landing close to the toddler.

"Mama! Mama!" Helia chanted, squeezing her eyes shut and wishing hard that her Mama would appear in front of her and take her away.

"Who-wha-how?" the man stammered, adjusting his glasses as he rushed to his feet and drew nearer to the wailing toddler.

Helia warily stepped back, locking her eyes on the strange man through the blur of tears. "Mama," she cried pathetically.

"Uh. Um. Er—" the man spluttered, completely flabbergasted at the little girl in front of him. Why, she seemed to appear as if out of thin air!

"What is that sound?" hissed a young woman. "Noiro, the number one rule in a library is that you should remain quiet." She stomped her way towards him and stopped in her path as she took in the scene in front of her: a very stunned man stood in front of a screaming toddler shrouded in a hooded cloak that looked a little too big for her, the man faltering stupidly as he tried to find words to calm the little girl down. He looked up at the young woman.

"She just popped out of nowhere!" he stammered, gesturing wildly at the little girl.

"What?"

"She just…"—he pointed at the toddler—"appeared!"

"Mamaaa…" the toddler wailed, growing more agitated by the flummoxed man.

Noiro began patting his hands down his coat, frantically searching for something hidden in one of his pockets that might help quiet the child. He paused above his breast pocket and shoved his hand to retrieve the item, hastily presenting it to the toddler.

Helia, mid-wail, glanced at the object in front of her: a round, glistening piece of sugar-coated candy enclosed in a brightly colored wrapper. She tearfully eyed the candy, then slowly moved to stare at the man holding the wrapper, who seemed to breathe a giant sigh of relief at the momentary silence. "Here, take this. It's for you," he said, kneeling down to the toddler's level.

His words had the opposite effect he hoped for, and the toddler's eyes began to well up with more tears.

"M-Mama said 'm not supposed to have candy before dinner," Helia sniffed uncertainly, folding her arms and turning her head away from the man, her face still hidden amidst her cloak's hood. She began to cry louder.

Noiro sighed again, this time in defeat.

"You're right," chimed in the woman, still standing in her place. She walked over to the toddler, her boots smartly clipping against the marble floors. "Your Mama's smart, kid," she said, also kneeling down to Helia. "My name's Miela. Can you tell me your name?"

"H-Helia," she replied, sniffing as she wiped her cheeks and nose with the back of her hand. Her finger caught the hem of her hood, and it slid down her hair and around her shoulders, revealing her blood-splattered face.

Miela inhaled sharply.

"You're hurt." Her voice rose in alarm. She quickly turned the cloak over and examined the child's body, searching for signs of injury.

"Miela, I don't think that's her own blood," Noiro interrupted, gesturing at the splatters against her face. "And it's still wet. I think someone else—"

"Mama," Helia whined, beginning to cry once more as

she saw the adults in front of her panic.

"Helia, honey, I need you to tell me," Miela said, grasping both of Helia's arms tightly. "Is your Mama hurt? Where is she?"

Helia began to cry harder, jerking her arms away and pulling her hands up to her face, smearing the blood even more across her skin.

Miela cursed, her panic growing along with the child's wails.

"Hey, she's obviously scared," said Noiro, nudging his way past Miela and moving closer to the toddler.

"Noiro, someone's hurt! And with that amount on the child, the victim looks like they were hurt badly. We need to help—we need to find—"

"You're not going to get any answers by scaring her further," Noiro said firmly. "She's a child, not one of the criminals you normally deal with." He knelt down to the toddler.

"Okay, Helia," he said, grunting when he felt one of his knees creak as it rested against the marble floor. "We're going to help you find your Mama, but we need your help. Can you be brave and help us find your Mama?"

Helia's sobs quieted at his gentle tone. She nodded.

"I'm brave," she said quietly.

"Yes, you are," Noiro praised. "Now, Helia is a wonderful name, but I bet that's only what your Mama calls you. What do other people call you?"

"Helia," the toddler repeated, confused.

"It's a beautiful name." Noiro smiled. "My full name is Noiro Pollux. Do you know your full name?"

"Helia," she reiterated uncertainly. Noiro nodded. It was obvious she was overwhelmed.

13

"Okay, Helia," said Noiro. "Do you know your Mama's name?"

Helia nodded. "Mama."

Noiro and Miela sighed.

"I know it must be very scary," said Miela, trying to sound calm in front of the child. "I need you to think hard, okay? Where were you and your Mama before you got here?" asked Miela.

Helia gestured at her spot on the floor behind Noiro. "Right there."

"And what were you doing before you got here?"

"We runned. We runned all the way here."

"Running? Running from who?" Miela asked.

"From the bad men," Helia said slowly, her shoulders dropping as she recalled the sharp blades hurtling towards her mother. Tears began to leak out of the corners of her eyes. She whispered, "Mama…"

"We're gonna find your Mama, I promise," said Miela. "Can you describe the bad men?"

"They're big," Helia raised her arms up. "Very big men. And they like to burn stuff. And they have knives!" she cried. "They hurt Mama."

"Bad men?" asked Noiro, confused. "All that blood… I thought they were probably attacked by an animal…"

Miela didn't answer, focusing on the toddler in front of her. "Good, Helia," she said gently. They were getting some progress on information. "Can you tell me again, where did you come from?"

"Right there," Helia pointed again behind Noiro. "But it was night. And it was cold…"

Miela narrowed her eyes. "Cold?" she murmured to herself. They were in the middle of a summer heat wave.

"Cold?" Noiro echoed. "It's just past the Summer Solstice—"

"Helia, I'm going to take a quick look in your cloak. Are you okay with that?" Miela asked softly. Helia nodded hesitantly, watching Miela's hands slowly reach out and push aside Helia's woolen cloak to reveal thick cotton pajamas beneath, a large pendant on a long chain around her neck, and a large leather satchel tucked away at her side. Helia's hair stuck to her neck in a slight sweat, the heat from the thick summer air outside seeping into the library and making her pajamas and cloak hang heavier on her tiny frame.

"That's a pretty necklace," said Miela, trying to compliment the girl to set her at ease. Helia shifted uncomfortably. "Can I see what's in the bag, Helia?"

Helia shook her head and protectively clutched the satchel's strap in her hands. "Mama said not to let go."

"I'm sure she just didn't want you to lose it," Noiro chimed in soothingly. "She'll give it back, I promise."

Helia shook her head vehemently.

"No, Mama said not to let go," she repeated, her voice wobbling as she stood her ground against the two adults in front of her. "I want Mama."

"We're trying to help you find your Mama," said Miela, attempting to hide her frustration at the child. She knew she was nervous and scared, but the more time they spent coaxing the child, the more the child's mother was losing blood.

Miela wiped her hands on the back of her trousers, leaving crimson stains on her clothes. Her hands were bloody from just touching Helia's cloak. With that amount of blood, and the time they spent talking to the child and trying to figure out what was going on, Miela feared the mother may already be dead. She shook her head and pushed the thought to the back of her mind.

"You'll give it back?" asked Helia.

Miela nodded, holding out her palm.

Helia stretched out her hand and dropped the satchel's strap into Miela's grasp.

"Thank you," said Noiro, patting the girl's head reassuringly as he watched Miela sift through the satchel's contents.

"Nothing out of the ordinary," she murmured to herself. "This is a heavy bag for a child to carry! A couple of old books, some other junk…" Miela flipped through one of the books, squinting. "The handwriting in this is terrible. I can't make out a single word."

"Hold on," said Noiro. "Let me see."

Miela handed Noiro one of the battered books as she sifted through the contents of the bag. She let out a sigh, not finding any item that helped her identify the girl or her mother. She looked at Noiro to see if he had any luck. He stood still, frozen in his place as he held the book Miela handed him. His face was pale as he stared at the first page of the book.

"Is something wrong? Did you find something?" she asked quickly.

Helia looked up at the two adults as they pored over the book Noiro was holding, feeling very uneasy. They were taking too long with her Mama's books, and she briefly wondered if they were ever going to give her back the bag at all. Her stomach twisted in knots at the thought; her Mama told her to not let go.

"I don't understand," said Miela, looking at the book

and then back at Noiro. "What's the big deal?"

"Where did you get this book?" Noiro slowly uttered, staring at the toddler.

Helia looked up at the man and folded her arms. "It's Mama's," she said defensively. "Can I have it back, please?"

"Uh, just a moment," said Noiro, still staring at the first page of the book.

"Noiro, you've gotta say something," insisted Miela.

Noiro turned his head slowly to Miela, then to the child, his mind reeling.

"Well?" Miela pressed.

"Th-this is not her mother's," said Noiro quietly.

"How could you know that?" asked Miela. "It's just a book!"

"Because it's mine," he whispered, pointing at the messy words scrawled onto the weathered paper. "This is my book."

"What? How can she have something that's yours? Do you know her? Have you two met before? Does that mean you know her mother?" Miela fired, spurred by the possible lead they had.

He shook his head, handing Miela the book. "Never seen her before in my life…"

Noiro walked over to the desk he was sitting at right before Helia's apparition and bent over to pick up one of the books he had knocked over in his surprise. He flipped to the first page, murmuring to himself as he walked back over to Miela, turning the book around and showing her the first page.

"What?"

"Miela, look at my book here. They're identical!"

Miela looked at Noiro's clean, crisp book, and then looked at the battered book in her own hands. He was right; other than the state of the book, the two were identical.

"So," hummed Miela, crossing her arms and sneering, "you plagiarized from an old book?"

"No, seriously, Miela! Flip through the other pages! Look!" Noiro exclaimed, flipping through his own stack of papers. "Look, here on the fifth page. There's a giant ink stain from where my pen snapped last night. Check in that book. Is that there?"

Miela flipped through and scanned the page, her finger resting on an identical ink stain marring the paper. She looked up at Noiro, and then turned to look at Helia, who was still watching the two warily. "What are you proposing this means, exactly?"

Noiro shook his head.

"Well, for one thing, it looks like my research is… completed," he said slowly, flipping through the worn book's pages. "Which is impossible. I just started…"

"What do you mean?" Miela demanded, exasperated. "Explain."

Noiro sighed, putting a hand on the bridge of his nose as he tried to pull his thoughts together. "I've been working on a theory… but, no, it's just a theory. It can't be real. Can it? Did it happen?" He scanned the pages of the worn book and paused at a page, examining a detailed sketch.

"Noiro, I'm not following," Miela said. "What are you talking about?"

"I've been working on a theory," Noiro repeated. "It's just a theory, but… I only just started… But this kid has my completed work right there with her…"

"So you think that that *old* book," Miela pointed at the battered book in his hands, "is your *brand new* research?"

He frowned. Noiro's voice shook as he said, "Assuming my research came to fruition… that *is* my research."

"What? How's that possible?" asked Miela. "You say you've never met this kid before. How on earth can she have your research?"

"Because her mother must've given it to her," said Noiro, pushing his glasses up his nose. He pointed at the sketch he was examining in the weathered book. "That's my research." He shoved the book into Miela's hands.

She looked incredulously at her old friend, and then flipped the book open.

Sure enough, Noiro's name was etched into the front page as the author. She flipped through a few more pages, pausing when a large, colorful sketch caught her eye amidst the neat scribbles of text. She examined the sketch for a moment, thinking hard, and then glanced back at Helia.

"Helia, can I see your necklace for a moment?" she asked.

Helia shook her head no. "No, it's mine! Mama gived it to me," she said nervously, afraid that her necklace would be taken away from her by the two strangers, who seemed more preoccupied with her mother's books than helping her find her mother. She held the pendant protectively in both hands, glaring at the two.

"Impossible…" Noiro breathed. "It's just… impossible…"

"Noiro," Miela uttered, turning to him. "What was your research on?"

Noiro looked back at Miela. "Bending time," he stated.

"What?" Miela grew more confused.

"Time travel," Noiro explained. "It's... I've... I've been..."

"Time travel?" Miela repeated slowly, her jaw dropping.

The pair stared at each other, and then incredulously at the child.

"How?" Noiro whispered. "How?"

"Sorry! Sorry! I know I'm so late," a new voice said hurriedly, and a flustered woman swept in hastily, setting her bag down onto the nearby desk with a loud bang. "I needed to stop by-"

"MAMA!" Helia cried loudly, running towards the woman with her arms outstretched, her face filling with excitement and relief. "Mama! Mama!" she beamed up at the woman and stretched her arms up, waiting to be held.

"Oh! Who are—uh, guys? Who is this?" she asked uncertainly, hesitant to touch the sweaty, sticky child that clung to her. "You're hurt!" she gasped, staring in horror at the blood smeared across the toddler's face. "She's hurt!"

The woman looked at her friends, perplexed. Noiro and Miela were completely silent, staring at the pair in disbelief.

"No," Noiro breathed, his face twisting in anxiety.

"Hello?"

"Mama! Mama!" insisted Helia, desperately trying to get the woman's attention as she tugged on the bottom of her summer dress, leaving a sticky red handprint behind.

"Um… Elara," said Miela, looking at her childhood friend.

"Miela, what?" Elara scoffed. "Seriously. Who is she? Is she okay? She's covered in blood! Why are we not panicking? Why are we not taking her to the hospital? Why are—"

Noiro shook his head seriously, still stunned. "Elara," he uttered. "Elara, stop."

"Mama!" Helia repeated impatiently, tugging on Elara's dress again.

The two adults in front of her looked like they had seen a ghost. Noiro looked like he was going to be sick. Miela's face was pale, and completely stunned.

Elara frowned, confused. "What?"

REVELATIONS

"Mama," Helia pleaded, waiting for her mother to pick her up. Elara took pity on the girl and hesitantly lifted her up. She shifted uncomfortably with the weight of the unfamiliar child in her arms.

"She's covered in blood!" Elara repeated. She turned her attention to the sticky, sweaty, bloody child in alarm. "Are you okay? What happened?"

"'M okay, Mama." Helia nodded her head enthusiastically. "You okay, Mama? You okay?" She grabbed Elara's face with both of her tiny hands, looking intently at the woman.

"What? Oh, uh, yeah…" Elara trailed off, dazed.

The little girl in her arms took no notice of her bewilderment, and instead took comfort in her arms, nuzzling her little head against the woman's neck, sighing happily.

"Guys? An explanation?" Elara demanded, trying to

adjust the toddler into a more comfortable position.

Noiro nodded. "Let's put the kid down so we can talk."

"Uh, hey, do you wanna, uh… what do kids like to do?" Elara asked helplessly, struggling to find an excuse to put the child down and be preoccupied with something else.

"Hey, Helia, how about that sweet now? Your Mama doesn't mind, does she?" Noiro looked pointedly at her.

Helia turned her head to Elara, as if to ask for her permission.

"What? Um, yeah, that's fine," Elara spluttered, baffled.

"All right, enjoy the sweet at that table, all right? But don't touch any of my books!" said Noiro as he guided the toddler to his desk. Helia happily unwrapped the sweet he handed her and plopped it into her mouth, grinning from ear to ear. It was hard to believe that the toddler was the perfect picture of panic and despair just moments ago.

"Okay. What on Earth is going on?" Elara demanded, turning to her friends.

"Uh…" Norio glanced anxiously at Miela, his glasses sliding down his nose ever so slightly.

"How about you start off with telling me who that kid is." Elara gestured at the blood-smeared toddler smacking at the sweet as she absentmindedly examined the stack of books next to her.

"Well…she's yours," said Noiro firmly. "Or at least, we think she is. Or, she will be your kid." He sighed. "This is very confusing."

"What?" Elara's voice rose as she drew back, bewildered. She rambled, "I don't have a kid! Believe me, I'd know if I had a kid. And I definitely do not have a kid. She must be confusing me for someone else. She's—"

"Not many kids confuse their parent for someone else, Elara," Noiro interrupted. "At least, not like that. And... well, she had this." He handed her a tattered-looking book.

Elara frowned. "An old book?"

"Elara. Look at it. It's our research. Completed. Only... we only just started."

"That doesn't make any sense. How can she have our research if we haven't even finished with the first stages of it?" Elara took the book from Noiro's hands, scanning through its pages. "This book is in awful condition." She ran her finger down its spine. "It's almost falling apart at the seams."

"Yeah, that's because it's old," said Noiro. "Flip to the first page."

Elara almost dropped the book. There, on the first page, was her own name signed next to Noiro's as co-author. Noiro held his own book open to the same page. It was an identical copy, down to the small smudge of ink that she had left when her hand accidentally swiped over a part that was still drying.

"This doesn't prove anything," said Elara loudly, trying to convince herself more than anything else.

"Think about it, Elara," insisted Noiro. "What if... what if we were right?"

Elara blinked, thinking hard.

"We were right?"

He shrugged weakly.

"She was also wearing this," said Miela, walking over from Helia, holding up a long chain with the large pendant.

Elara examined the necklace, confused. "This means nothing to me," she said shortly.

Miela shrugged. "The kid said it was yours. Refused to hand it over until you showed up, too."

Elara studied the pendant closely. It was a dark, heavy stone. She frowned as she noticed the etchings on the stone. Elara held a hand up. "Our research, which we've only just started, is on bending time. This kid shows up, out of nowhere, and has our completed research with her."

Noiro nodded slowly.

Elara glanced at him and asked, "Did we prove that bending time can work? Moving completely through time—is that actually possible?"

"It must be," Noiro answered, although he sounded doubtful himself. "I mean, I guess we proved that it *is* possible, because otherwise, Helia wouldn't be here, would she?"

Elara blinked at the name. "Helia?" she echoed. "That's an unusual name…"

Miela stared at the child. "She does kind of look like you…"

Elara shook her head again as the two began to fill her in on how they stumbled across the toddler. This was too much to digest in such a short amount of time. She nibbled nervously at her lip.

"So…Helia is mine…from the future?" Elara's eyes were wide in disbelief. "Why did her mother—uh, *I*—send her back, then?"

"It sounds like you two were running from something—'bad men,' as Helia put it," said Noiro.

"Her description didn't give us much to go on, but they definitely sound like bad news," Miela added, "bad enough to scare you into sending your kid back in time. *Alone.*"

25

The three fell silent.

"Hold on," said Noiro suddenly. "Knowing Elara… you must have left us some clues in the bag." He gestured over to the satchel, which lay forgotten at the foot of the desk.

Elara's eyes travelled from the old, dirty satchel that lay on the floor, and then to the one that she had set upon the desk when she arrived.

That was her bag.

Could that be her child?

She felt sick.

"Where do we start?" asked Noiro, looking to Miela. "This is sort of your area of expertise."

Miela scoffed. "Yeah, as a Guardian, I come across time travelling tots all the time."

"You know what I mean," said Noiro. "You deal with criminal cases all the time. This is just one very unusual case."

Miela raised an eyebrow at Noiro. It was certainly an unusual case.

"Okay," she breathed deeply.

If she treated this like any other case she helped when tracking suspects…

"The blood," Miela said. "The kid's covered in blood. We can test it to identify its properties, and… well… see who it belongs to." She avoided Elara's gaze.

Noiro nodded and suddenly said, "Not here."

The three jumped, realizing that they were in a very public place. If Helia was running from someone, there was no telling who it was. The last thing they needed to do was draw attention to themselves, if they hadn't already with the toddler's previous wailing. Fortunately, the library was mostly empty as the day was almost over.

"We can go over to my place," offered Noiro.

The trio nodded, and quickly began to pack up their belongings from the table.

Noiro shrugged off his outer shirt and wrapped it around Helia's tiny frame. "The blood," he explained, quickly fastening the buttons over Helia's clothes. "We don't want to draw attention…"

Miela handed Elara the satchel that came with Helia. "I think you should carry this," she said.

Elara nodded, shouldering the bag that was identical to her own, save for the leather being more weathered with age.

Elara felt queasy as the group followed Noiro out of the library. She had no idea, when she started her day, that being late for a research session with Noiro would result in her suddenly having a toddler and a bag full of mysteries. "How are we going to explain the kid?" she hissed, holding Helia's hand in hers as they strolled through the pathway of a very prim and neatly kept rose garden.

"The best excuse I can think of to avoid any questions," Miela said immediately, "is that she's a witness in a case I'm handling. I'm sure I can pull that off—the Colonel's been on my case for taking on more civilian cases for a while now. He'll be happy about it, if anything."

"This way," said Noiro, turning up another pathway.

They could see a small stony cottage at the edge of the castle grounds at the end of the pathway. A stone sundial stood at the center of the cottage's front garden, with an intricate golden dial planted firmly at the sundial's base. A few feet away were a few vials, which were propped outside on a wooden bench, left to dry in the warm summer air. A soft breeze blew past, and the sound of wind chimes could be heard tinkling in the distance.

Elara loved the little cottage that she called home. It had been her home for as long as she could remember.

Often mistaken for Noiro's younger sibling, Noiro was, in fact, Elara's guardian. She was told that he found her abandoned at his doorstep as a baby, and couldn't find it in his heart to turn her away. Noiro, who was only twenty years-old himself at the time, raised her as his own, sacrificing a lot of his own personal endeavors for the sake of being a responsible, caring provider for his new charge.

Elara began to take after Noiro's interests as the years flew by. Her childhood was spent on the floor of his laboratory, watching him tinker away at his different research assignments. Being a special Scholar for the Royal Family, Noiro was given the privilege of living within the castle's grounds, and with it, all the security and provisions that came with it. Elara grew up comfortably under Noiro's guardianship, and blossomed into a young, erudite, insightful woman.

As Elara grew more interested in Noiro's research assignments, he began to include her in some of his work. He started her off with small tasks, like having her measure out the different substances he was examining in vials, or identifying different elements in certain research assignments. He could not help but beam with pride as she soon began to fly through the tasks and come up with her own theories during research assignments. Seeing her love grow for exploring different theories and drawing her own conclusions, Noiro went to great lengths to ensure she received the best education, and supported her with the resources she needed. As she grew more experienced, and even began to take on her own independent research assignments, Noiro sought to work together and push her to pursue more, with some assignments coming straight from the Royal Family themselves.

Elara looked at Noiro as he fumbled for his keys, stopping momentarily in front of the small, cozy stone cottage. She knew she was privileged to call Noiro's cottage her home. She was lucky to have Noiro as her guardian. Twenty years had passed since he found her and raised her as his own. To her, they were blissful, happy years. She wondered if he felt the same. Becoming a guardian overnight was certainly no easy feat, and he was only twenty then.

Did he feel the same, gnawing, unrelenting feeling of anxiety as she felt now, with Helia by their side?

She watched him, his brow furrowed in his worry as he finally unlocked his front door, eyes nervously darting to the small child that stood between the adults. He'd always had a soft heart, especially for children. She could tell that he was agitated.

Who wouldn't be? Elara bit her lip. A bloodied child, *her* child, appeared from the future. She could only assume that it was her own blood on the child.

Something terrible must have happened.

Elara glanced at the child, who was silently watching the man in front of them push the door open. As panicked as she was when she appeared, the toddler seemed to have completely forgotten her fright as soon as she laid eyes on Elara.

"Inside, make yourselves at home," said Noiro, ushering the group into his cottage, snapping Elara out of her thoughts. "Just don't touch anything."

29

He walked over to a nearby cupboard and rummaged through some bottles.

The group steered into the cozy cottage, standing awkwardly in the center.

As small as it looked from the outside, it was a rather spacious cottage. The doorway opened up into an airy seating area with comfy armchairs surrounding a dark-stained wooden table. The walls were lined with some old bookshelves that were built-in. Behind the seating area was a small laboratory, with high tables standing in each corner of the room, an organized mess of vials and containers scattered on each one. A book lay open on one of the tables, with a few notes hastily scrawled in.

"Here," said Noiro, handing Elara three thin vials. "You know what to do."

Elara glanced at the blood on the child and then back at Noiro, nodding.

Noiro, obviously flustered, turned quickly to offer Miela and Helia a seat at the seating area. "Please, sit. I'll get us some tea. And maybe something nutritious for the young lady." He flashed a small smile at Helia.

The toddler grinned cheerily back at him. She was about to sink into a plushy arm chair before Miela stopped her. "Hold on, kid." She gently held the child's arms. "Let's get you changed out of those dirty clothes."

Noiro nodded, leaving Miela to take care of Helia.

Elara walked over to the laboratory, setting the vials down. Taking one of the vials, she pricked the tip of her finger and dribbled in some of her blood into the long, thin glass. She was familiar with collecting blood samples from different animals and beings for their research projects, and was no stranger to the pricks and stings of the procedure.

Elara wrapped her finger with a small strip of gauze, placed the vial into a rack, and prepared the other vial to collect the blood samples from Helia's cloak and from Helia herself. Whoever's blood was soaked into Helia's cloak would help confirm their suspicions. According to Noiro and Miela, that blood was Helia's mother's. She needed to compare the blood sample to Helia's and her own blood to prove their hunch.

Elara paused for a moment, closing her eyes and taking in a deep breath. Was she ready to confirm Noiro's hunch? Was that little child truly her own? She wondered again how Noiro must have felt when he found a wailing baby at his doorstep.

"Elara? Everything all right in there?" Miela's voice called out from the sitting room.

Elara snapped her head towards the voice. "I'm fine! I'll just be a moment." Taking another deep breath, Elara walked back into the sitting room.

Miela and Noiro were sitting solemnly, perched at the edge of their seats. Three mugs of steaming tea were arranged neatly on the table in front of them, untouched, accompanied by a small plate of biscuits. Miela's leg hopped nervously as she spied the glass vials Elara brought with her, and she glanced at Helia. The little girl sat on the wooden floor, her legs splayed out in front of her as she happily munched on a large apple.

"I, uh... I moved her to the floor so she wouldn't stain the rugs or seats," said Miela. "Getting blood stains out is a pain." She unconsciously reached a hand to the hilt of her sword, which was fastened tightly to her back with leather straps. "Trust me."

Elara nodded silently.

"I tried to take her cloak, but she said her Mama would."

"Oh. Right. Okay, I'll get it," said Elara hesitantly, walking over to Helia.

"Mama! Mama, you hungry?" Helia grinned toothily through another bite of her apple, offering Elara a bite.

Elara forced a smile as she softly declined. "Helia," she said, testing the feel of the name on her lips. It seemed to roll off effortlessly, even though it sounded so foreign on her tongue. "Helia, I'll need to borrow your cloak."

Helia lifted her arms up automatically, and she cautiously undid the clasp of her cloak and slid it off her tiny shoulders. The dark material of her cloak hid the bloodstains well, but it soaked through to her pink cotton pajamas underneath, a deep, crimson stain marring the soft fabric. Helia appeared unbothered by the bloodstains, seemingly content now that her mother was back with her.

Elara, on the other hand, felt her throat close up at the sight of the blood.

Who knew there could be so much blood?

What horrors did this child go through?

"We need to get you cleaned up," she remarked softly, tucking a tendril of hair, crusted over with drying blood, behind Helia's ear.

"I'm sure I can find something for her to change into," said Noiro, handing Elara a damp cloth to wipe Helia's face.

Elara tried to ignore the sheer look of adoration on Helia as she dabbed at the toddler's face, wiping away some of the blood that had since dried.

Despite Elara's discomfort, she couldn't stop staring

at the child. Miela was right; she looked a little bit like her. Helia had her dimpled chin and olive skin. Her wavy hair, a deep brown, curled around her round cheeks. Her almond-shaped eyes crinkled as she cheerily grinned at Elara when she finished wiping her face.

Elara looked away.

"Let me take this," offered Miela, breaking Elara's deep train of thought and gently taking the bloody cloth from her hand. "I'll give it to Noiro so he can test it. For the time being, I think it'd be a good idea to get this kid into a bath."

"A bath?" Helia piped up distastefully. "But I don't wanna take a bath," she folded her arms.

"Think about how nice you'll feel in some clean, fresh clothes," said Noiro, walking back into the room with some clothes in his arms. "They're some of your old clothes—might be a tad too big for her, but I think they'll do for the time being." He smiled apologetically as he set the clothes down onto the couch.

"They'll do fine," Elara assured him gratefully.

Noiro nodded. "The bathroom's up the stairs, second door on your right."

With the toddler in hand, Miela and Elara trudged up the stairs and into the bathroom. Miela carefully pried off the bloody clothes while Elara began to fill the tub with warm water, dipping her hand into it to test its temperature. Miela sponged the blood off the child before putting her into the tub. Helia sighed contentedly in the warm water, despite her earlier protests against having a bath. Elara softly ran her fingers into Helia's hair and worked them up into a sudsy mess.

"See? Having a bath isn't so bad now, is it?" said Miela,

grinning at Helia.

She nodded vigorously, and happily splashed the water around.

"Oh wow, you have thick hair," said Elara, grunting as she tried to avoid the splashes while trying to untangle her fingers from the child's head.

"Do you have toys?" She looked up suddenly at the two women. "For the bath!"

"Uh, um… No, sorry," Elara answered.

"Okay." She shrugged nonchalantly. She was far too preoccupied with playing with the water.

"What toys do you like?" asked Miela, attempting to make conversation with Helia. She felt sorry for Elara. She could see how uncomfortable she was around the toddler, and couldn't blame her for feeling that way. Nonetheless, it was clear that Helia was comfortable, ecstatic, even, with Elara's presence. As far as the toddler was concerned, she was reunited with her mother, and all was well.

Miela couldn't help but take an immediate liking to the tot. She wondered if Helia remembered her from the future, somehow. She shuddered internally as she recalled the child just hours ago, bloodied, terrified, and wailing frantically for her mother only a few short hours ago. The toddler certainly seemed to calm down slightly when she began to interact with her. She frowned, dawning on a niggling thought.

If Helia had calmed down with Miela, why did Noiro not have the same effect?

"I like swords!" Helia yelled theatrically, pulling Miela out of her thoughts. She watched the toddler thrust her arm forward, brandishing an imaginary sword in her small fist.

"Oh?" Miela arched an eyebrow, impressed. "I like swords too. Wanna see mine?"

"YEAH!"

"Uh, Miela, maybe it's not a good idea to pull out something sharp near a child... in a place that's wet... and slippery... and covered in soap..."

"Good point," Miela agreed, grinning at Helia. She winked and said, "Later."

Helia nodded, winking back.

They finished up the toddler's bath and wrapped her up in a towel, drying her thoroughly before she dripped any more water outside of the tub. It seemed that most of the water had escaped the tub already.

"I think we can get you dressed over here," Elara said as she picked up the clothes Noiro handed her earlier, and quickly dressed the toddler.

"Ladies," Noiro greeted them cheerily as he sipped away at his cup of tea. "I hope you don't mind, I went ahead and drank some of my tea. It was getting cold."

"That's fine," said Elara, ignoring the knots in her stomach.

"Drink your tea," nudged Noiro.

Elara nodded, setting herself down and reaching for a mug as Noiro walked over to Helia, leading her to the laboratory.

Miela came in and sat next to her childhood friend, handing Elara the old satchel that Helia was carrying earlier. She said softly, "I put Helia's necklace in the bag. I didn't want to pry any further, in case there was something private."

Elara pressed her lips together and accepted the satchel. She glanced again at her own identical satchel, looking brand new, lying on one of the tables in Noiro's research laboratory. She already knew that the satchel she was holding and the satchel in the laboratory were one and the same. She was certain, regardless of the anxiety welling up in her chest, that the toddler happily chatting away to Noiro was hers.

"No use in hiding what's in the satchel," she said finally. She looked up as Noiro walked back into the room. "We need answers. Let's take a look at what's inside." She unfastened the clasp and turned the satchel over, dumping out its contents on the table. The three drew closer to the table, examining the objects that fell out.

In front of them lay two books: a tattered notebook, and their research journal; a large cloth that was wrapped around a jagged stone; Helia's necklace; and a ring.

Elara gingerly picked up the least formidable object to examine first: the ring. She stared at it in awe; it was a beautiful ring. It looked antique, made with platinum and twisted into an intricate floral weave, encircling a brilliant deep cut sapphire stone, set into the center of the ring. As much as she tried to convince herself that the ring could be any insignificant piece of jewelry, she was certain that it was her wedding ring. The wave of emotions made her stomach churn, and she put it back on the table.

Next, she examined the necklace. It was an unusual necklace; it seemed like it was crudely put together with very little attention to craftsmanship compared to the ring she had just examined. The platinum chain was long and thin, and the heavy, jagged, dark stone pendant had a hole messily carved into the top where the chain looped through it. The stone was warm and felt like it was pulsating in her hand. A shudder traveled through her as she held the stone, and she set it back down. Elara squinted at the stone. It looked as if it was carefully carved with symbols. Three rings of movable stone dials were engraved into the pendant, with small notches etched into the dials.

"I'm not familiar with this type of stone," she commented, looking at Noiro questioningly. "My first guess would be obsidian, or onyx. But... it's something I've never encountered before."

Noiro extended his hand in a silent request to examine the pendant, intrigued. It was not often that Elara struggled to identify an element. She handed the necklace to Noiro and turned her attention to the journal.

Elara flipped through the entries and furrowed her brow. None of the entries made any sense. The pages were mostly empty, with just a few lines of a sequence of numbers scribbled in the middle of each page. Her eyes flickered as she traced the ink with her finger; she'd recognize her own handwriting anywhere.

A piece of paper stuck out of the journal's pages, catching her eye; it was the only paper in the entire book that had any text written on it. Curious, she pulled the paper out—a newspaper clipping—and scanned the page, feeling the knot in her stomach twist tighter.

Tragedy in Polaris

10-11-9382. The once magnificent Kingdom of Polaris, named after the brightest star that shines in these heavenly skies, lies in ruins at the hands of another macabre massacre. The world mourns the great Kingdom of Polaris, reeling in loss at the gravity of last week's attack against Polaris Castle, which left the home of the beloved Royal

Family and their subjects completely destroyed. The terrible carnage took with it the lives of over two hundred Polarians, among them our beloved King Ami and Queen Violet. Guardians from the Investigators Unit report several accounts of organized troops outnumbering and overpowering the Castle's inhabitants, and are still laying siege. We all pray for an end to this endless war, but with the loss of our beloved haven, Polaris, now a ruined shell of its once magnificent entity, many members of the public wonder if anyone can find the strength to stand another day of violence, tragedy, and an ever-increasing death toll.

"Wha…" Miela breathed from over Elara's shoulder, snatching the paper away to read it again. Elara watched as the two scanned the newspaper clipping over. Miela's mouth dropped open in horror. Norio looked like he was going to be sick.

"9382… That's five years from now," said Noiro weakly, pointing at the date at the beginning of the article.

The three turned their heads to look over at the toddler, who remained oblivious to the adults huddled over the table, humming to herself while playing at the foot of the table.

What horrors had Helia seen?

"Right…" Noiro cleared his throat, dazed. A small bell rang in the distance, and he turned his head towards the library. "Uh… I'll be right back…" He blinked, his face pale. "I'll just check on the DNA samples." He excused himself and walked over to his research laboratory.

Elara and Miela remained silent as they waited for Noiro's return. Miela's eyes were hard, staring at the window outside and watching the moon appear brighter in the darkening sky. Elara followed her gaze, looking at the crescent moon. She could hear the friendly guffaw of laughter from a couple of guards as they passed the cottage's pathway on their rounds and a giggle from one of the cooks making her way with a giant tray of freshly baked bread. Outside of the cottage, the world was cheery and peaceful, and utterly unaware of the massacre that would destroy the castle and obliterate its inhabitants in just a few years. She wondered if the guards and cook who were loudly chatting outside would be one of the victims, and shook her head at having such a terrible thought.

"Elara," whispered Noiro, standing at the doorway of the laboratory, holding a vial. He opened his mouth to speak, hesitated, and then sighed heavily. "She's…"

"I know," said Elara. "I know that she's mine."

Noiro nodded.

The three sat in pregnant silence.

"Well… We finished step one of this mystery," Miela said finally, folding her arms. "And we know what to do next."

Noiro and Elara looked curiously at Miela.

"We're going to stop this."

THE GUARDIAN HEADQUARTERS

Elara stirred, groaning as the morning light flooded her bedroom and brought her out of her deep slumber. In the onslaught of information that she received the day before, she had forgotten to draw her curtains closed. She sat up sleepily, stretching her neck and letting out a yawn.

Thud.

Her eyes flew open at the sound. Elara turned her head towards the source of the sound and saw the journal lying on the ground. She sighed.

It must have slid off the bed when she moved. She stayed up quite late the night before, trying to make sense of the jumbled numbers scrawled on each page, to no avail. She leaned over and picked up the book, hesitant to leave the comfort of her bed yet. She looked over to her other side, watching a small mound breathing softly beneath her covers. Helia insisted on crawling into bed with her, and as much as Elara was uncomfortable with having the toddler snuggle up to her in the middle of the night, she hadn't the heart to tell Helia otherwise. She couldn't leave her alone in her guest bedroom, either.

Elara sighed again, leaning back in bed and glancing at the window, the sun beams gently filtering into her room. She still had a few hours left before she had to meet Miela and Noiro.

"Good morning," Elara greeted as she pushed Noiro's cottage door open.

"Good morning!" Helia echoed, excitedly pushing past Elara and peeking her head into the sitting room.

"Morning," Noiro returned, walking from the kitchen with a big plate of piping hot scrambled eggs. "How're you doing?"

"You're kidding, right?" replied Elara dejectedly as she took a seat in the sitting room.

Helia grinned at Noiro, and he smiled back, gesturing to a few scattered toys he set out on the rug. She skipped over to the toys, excited at the prospect of playing first thing in the morning.

Elara smiled at the toddler's glee. "Thank you for that," she said, gesturing at the toys that Helia was closely examining, beaming at each one as she set them down in a row.

"I knew we still had some of your old toys around," replied Noiro, staring at his plate of eggs for a moment, lost in thought. "I'm glad they're being used again. I set aside a few clothes for her as well, I think they should fit."

Elara smiled. "I didn't know you held onto them."

Noiro nodded, still looking at his plate. "Of course I did." He smiled, then cleared his throat as he felt a wave of emotion well up inside him. Eager to change the subject, he said, "How'd you sleep last night?"

Elara, seeing Noiro's demeanor shift, followed suit, replying, "I could barely sleep last night. I couldn't stop thinking about…"

"I know, me too," whispered Noiro. He set the plate down on the table. "Breakfast?"

"I'm good, thanks," she declined politely. "Where's Miela?"

"Running late, I reckon. She should be here any moment now."

"Do you think her superiors will have any issue with Miela taking on a confidential mission?" asked Elara, leaning back in her chair.

"I doubt it," he replied, digging into the plate of eggs. "From what she's been telling us, her superiors have been encouraging her to take a break from her higher profile cases. They need some more manpower on the civilian cases, I guess. With a minor involved, it'd make sense to keep the facts surrounding the case confidential, too. So she shouldn't get too many questions."

"Hmm."

"You don't seem too convinced," noted Noiro.

"I'm just worried, that's all," confessed Elara. "There's a lot we don't know. Why did I send a child—*my child*—alone through time? With what we know about bending time, it's risky… dangerous, even. What was I thinking?"

"If I know you well, and I do," Norio began, "I know that you had your reasons."

"I know… I'm hoping we'll find out more. Do you think we will?" asked Elara, her eyebrows furrowing with worry. "We have five years till the date of that…attack."

She waved away the thought, not wanting to dwell on the newspaper clipping they found tucked away in her journal. "That might seem like a lot of time, but it's really not."

"We'll need to brush up more on time bending theory, but from what I know, the future might already be altered," mused Noiro. "Remember the butterfly effect?"

Elara nodded. "It's the idea that a small event can have an impact on a larger series of events," she recited, having read hundreds of books during her research on time bending. "In theory, a butterfly flapping its wings in one place might influence the winds to shift into a destructive hurricane somewhere else."

"Exactly," agreed Noiro. "A seemingly tiny, insignificant event can be the catalyst that triggers a larger series of events. Helia merely being here, at this point in time, might alter our entire timeline. In fact, her own timeline may not even exist anymore. If Helia hadn't shown up when she did at the library yesterday, then you and I would have had a different day. Most probably, we might have spent the day writing this." Noiro held up the completed research book that was in Helia's satchel. "If Helia hadn't shown up yesterday, we would be in different places at this very moment. You might be in your kitchen at home, having breakfast. I might still been asleep in my room upstairs. Instead, as a result of Helia's coming to the library yesterday, we are here in my kitchen. Instead of spending this very moment wondering about what you're going to do today, you're researching material to help avoid a terrible event in the future.

"Helia's arrival is the catalyst that's triggering us to begin investigating an attack that hasn't happened yet."

Elara folded her arms, concentrating on Noiro's

explanation. They were delving into the very beginnings of time bending. It was a subject most could barely begin to wrap their head around, and researchers dedicated years to exploring the fabrics of time itself before entering into the theory of time bending. And yet, here they were, trying to do just that.

"Who knows, the attack might never happen at all, with the shift in events from Helia's original timeline," offered Noiro hopefully.

"Ever the optimist," Elara scoffed.

"It's a possibility," he returned. "Maybe her arrival itself altered the series of events that lead to the attack happening."

"Or we might have shortened the timespan of the attack," Elara pointed out.

"Ever the pessimist." Noiro smirked.

"I'm being realistic," grumbled Elara. "Following that logic, the date on that newspaper clipping might as well be an arbitrary one."

Noiro nodded. "You might be right, and you might be wrong. We'll have to brush up on more time theory before we can jump to any conclusions. Trying to guess the future's outcome... Well, your guess is as good as mine." He sighed. "Lucky for us, we already have one piece of the puzzle." Noiro pointed his chin towards the completed research book as he chewed on another mouthful of eggs. "Our timeline of completing our time bending research assignment just got a whole lot shorter."

Elara paused, thinking hard. "I... I think we should hold on to the research for ourselves for the time being," she said slowly. "That journal has valuable information that we need to look into. Not to mention, it was sent along with my journal. It has to be a clue."

Noiro nodded in agreement. "I think we should take a closer look at everything before turning in anything."

"Ready, guys? We're gonna be late," a voice called out from behind them. Noiro choked on his forkful of eggs in surprise as a pair of hard hands clapped against his shoulders.

"Miela! You're here!" Helia squeaked excitedly.

Elara smiled at the sight of her childhood friend walking over and leaning down to chat with Helia. Miela's tough exterior did little to deter Helia, and she had taken quite a liking to the Guardian. Miela was a force to be reckoned with; she was fierce and formidable, traits which helped her greatly as she climbed the Guardian ranks, making Captain before many of her more senior comrades. She was tough, yet fair, and gained much respect from her peers and superiors alike for being able to lead her division effectively and efficiently. She was as beautiful as she was brave; her honey blonde hair was pulled back in her usual thick braid that hung down to the middle of her back, with small curly tendrils hanging loosely around her face. Her green eyes crinkled as she laughed at something Helia said, and she ruffled the toddler's hair affectionately.

Elara cleared her throat, catching Miela's attention. "Ready to go, Miela?"

"Just about. I spoke with the Colonel. I have my clearance papers to handle a confidential civilian case, especially since it involves a toddler. We shouldn't have too many people poking their noses in." Miela straightened her posture as she looked up, interrupting her deep conversation with the toddler. "We just need to stop by my office in headquarters for the boss's signature."

"Damn bureaucracy," Noiro barked, wolfing down the last of his eggs. "A complete waste of time, if you ask me."

Miela shrugged. "No time to waste. Finish your eggs, and let's go."

The four set out to the city center of Polaris. The trek from Noiro's cottage, nestled in the grounds of Polaris Castle, to the Guardians' Headquarters was not long, but it felt like an eternity to little Helia, who insisted on walking rather than being carried. She defiantly stuffed her feet into her little shoes, let Miela quickly swap out her shoes so that they were each on the right foot, and stubbornly kept up her pace with the adults (who made sure to slow their pace to a gentle stroll).

"Are you sure people won't ask too many questions about Helia?" Elara asked, glancing at Miela worriedly as Helia clutched at her fingers.

"I think we'll be all right," Miela replied firmly. "The Guardian environment is all about military discipline. We've been trained not to ask questions. People see all sorts of unusual things. People *do* all sorts of unusual things. Some might be curious, but we already have our story straight. She's a witness in an investigation. That's all."

Elara sighed, feeling a little more at ease, and tried hard to ignore the knots in her stomach as she held onto Helia's hand while passing the gates towards the Guardians' Headquarters.

"Good morning, Luan," Miela greeted the security guard.

"Good morning, Captain Miela," the guard answered back, his tone clipped and short. "Credentials?"

"Of course." She pulled up the sleeve of her right

hand, flashing a tattoo on the inside of her wrist. Two crescent moons faced each other, framing the constellation of Polaris.

The symbol of the Guardians of Polaris.

It was a prestigious symbol, bestowed only to the elite members of the Guardians of Polaris. Miela beamed with pride as she held out her wrist for the guard to examine.

"Captain Miela Avon," she announced raptly. "I have three civilians with me."

The security guard saluted Miela as she passed by.

"Showoff," Elara teasingly whispered to Miela.

Miela chuckled.

It was strange to see her childhood friend, someone she had spent her years playing little games together and sharing silly jokes, be regarded with such authority in such a rigid establishment. Nonetheless, Elara could not help but be proud of her friend's achievements. It was no easy feat, enlisting as a Guardian. It was a difficult life to commit to, with years of combat training, mastering weapons, and honing on developing skills to enlist in the desired Guardian Divisions. Depending on what a Guardian worked towards, they could either enlist as an Amity Guardian, a division dedicated to spending long hours chasing after criminals and maintaining peace and order within the kingdom's limits; a Watch Guardian, which were specialized teams assembled to patrol the kingdom's boundaries and uphold border security; or an Imperial Guardian, an elite squad entrusted with safeguarding the Royal Family's protection and wellbeing.

Miela, a Captain in the Amity Guardian Division, sported an intricate wreath of olive branches on the back of her Captain's jacket, the emblem of the Amity

Guardians. She had worked hard to reach her position as the Captain, and had her sight set on climbing higher up on the ladder. Elara knew that she could, and there was little that could stand in her way once she set her mind to it.

The group followed Miela as she led the way into the main hall, nodding every now and then to passing comrades. They joined a small group of officials standing in line at the lift.

Helia glued herself to Elara as they waited in line. Elara and Noiro stood straight, although their posture was a slouchy mess compared to the rigid, disciplined, straight backs of the Guardians around them. Miela stood straight and tall, blending in with her fellow comrades. She looked smart in her Guardian uniform, which consisted of a structured pale blue jacket and stiff, pressed trousers, which were neatly stuffed into a shiny pair of black boots. She had her powder blue Captain's hat tucked under her arm, her hands donned in fitted white gloves.

Elara spied several Amity Guardians, noting the emblem emblazoned on the backs of their jackets, and two Watch Guardians, set apart by the emblem of a thick, ornate brass key on the backs of their uniform, standing attention at the entryway of the elevators, carefully eyeing the flow of people in the building. She scanned the crowd for any Imperial Guardians, searching for the telltale emblem of the crown, but to no avail. Imperial Guardians were an elusive squad, being comprised of the highest ranking elites amongst the Guardian ranks, rumored to be handpicked by the Royal Family themselves.

Elara felt out of place in her civilian clothing; she was wearing a fitted blue blouse, and long, white trousers that were cropped at her ankle. She brushed a lock of hair behind her ear and held Helia's hand tightly in her own. Helia was dressed in a faded pale green summer dress, which clashed oddly with her winter boots. Given it was only a day since Helia had stumbled into their lives, they hadn't had much choice with her footwear and opted to use the shoes that Helia came in from the future.

Miela was right about not worrying about too many questions. Helia received no extra attention aside from a few side glances.

A soft *ding* sounded, and the lift's doors opened. Elara held onto Helia's hand as they waited for the lift to clear before entering along with Miela and Noiro. Thankfully, they had the lift to themselves; the other officials had caught the adjacent lift that had arrived seconds before.

"Mama, can I press the button?" Helia asked excitedly. "I know which button to press!"

"Oh?" said Miela, her interest piqued. "Have you been here before?"

"Yeah! Lots of times! With you, Mama!" Helia beamed.

Elara exchanged curious glances with Miela and Noiro. She rarely visited the Guardians' Headquarters, especially since it was usually restricted to civilians such as herself.

"We're going to a different floor today," Elara admonished gently. Helia nodded, watching Miela press on one of the buttons. She beamed as she felt the elevator begin its ascent.

The lift doors came to a slow stop at one of the floors, and Elara held onto Helia's hand again. "Not this floor," she said softly, feeling the toddler move her body towards the door.

"But this is——" Helia began, and then stopped. A tall

man walked in, joining the four in the lift. He faced the lift's doors, holding a lieutenant's hat under his arm as he pressed one of the buttons with a gloved finger.

"Captain," the man saluted Miela as he entered.

Miela nodded in response. "Lieutenant."

The Lieutenant's eyes shifted to Noiro, his eyebrows subtly lifting up in surprise.

"Argon?" Noiro blurted out, surprised to see a familiar face at the Guardians' Headquarters. He hadn't seen the man in years. He felt his stomach churn; Noiro did not know Argon so well, but he was well-acquainted his father. The two did not get along as boys, and often found terrible ways to torment each other during their training. As adults, they were coldly polite towards each other at best. The animosity was passed down to his son, Argon, which was reciprocated right back. Much to Noiro's disdain, Argon had often extended his sour behavior to Elara, who had frequently interacted with Argon, given their close proximity in age. Noiro sourly pressed his lips together.

"Funny, I didn't know they let vermin in here," said Argon coldly, his back still turned.

Elara stared incredulously at the man, unimpressed with his unprovoked jab. Miela glared at the man, her eyebrows raised in contempt at her colleague. She was no stranger to his comments as well, having often brawled with him as a child during their school days after tormenting Elara. He managed to put aside his animosity towards Miela during their time training as Guardians, and opted for a more professional relationship with her, but that did not erase their sour past.

"I could say the same," replied Noiro, not missing a

beat, staring straight ahead.

Argon scoffed. "Be careful," said Argon coolly. "You're addressing a Lieutenant of the Amity Guardians."

"Am I?" Noiro sneered. "Whose uniform did you steal?"

Argon swiftly turned around, his nostrils flared and his lip curled as he faced his childhood nemesis, struggling to keep his cool. "I earned my place here, Noiro. Don't you dare undermine the efforts I made—"

"Efforts?" Noiro scorned. "Blackmail and bullying your way in, more like."

"Be careful of what you're accusing me of. If I didn't know any better, I'd think you were insinuating I bribed my way into being a Guardian."

Noiro folded his arms. "I know who you are."

"And I know who you are. Not all of us have their *connections* to smooth out any bumps on the road," Argon jeered. "I worked for what I have. And I don't have time to waste on the likes of you." He ran a hand through his short, curly black hair. "I'm already—"

At that moment, Helia turned her attention away from the glowing buttons on the elevator, to the strange man standing before them. Her face twisted into one of confusion, frowning for a moment, before completely melting away into pure delight and excitement. "DAD!"

Noiro, Miela, and Elara's mouths fell open as Helia hurtled towards the Lieutenant and wrapped her arms tightly around Argon's legs. "Dad! Dad! Dad, you're here! Dad!"

"Huh? What? Who the hell is this?" Argon exclaimed, wrinkling his nose in disdain at the small child.

"Dad! 'M Helia!" the toddler beamed at the man,

clutching at his pant leg. "It's me!" Helia looked almost giddy with joy. "You're back! Mama, look! Dad's back! He came back from the sky!"

"What? Ugh! Move, you little brat," Argon ordered harshly, roughly pushing the child's arms away from him.

"Helia, come here," ushered Miela. Her voice was calm, yet her eyes raged with fury at the way Argon spoke to the toddler. Elara lifted her hand out towards Helia, requesting her hand. Miela's cold glare never veered from Argon's face. Helia moved back towards Elara, tightly clutching at her fingers.

"This kid's with you, Captain?" asked Argon, turning to Miela, her title rolling off his tongue in a sneer, brushing the imaginary dirt from his pants.

"She's a witness in an ongoing investigation." Miela nodded curtly, her mind reeling as she raced to connect the dots. What had Helia just called the man?

Argon visibly shuddered as he eyed the toddler, who was looking at the man with a mixture of excitement, confusion, and hurt.

"Dad," Helia began, her voice small. "It's me—"

"Keep it away from me," Argon said coldly.

Elara stood frozen in her spot, horrified. She felt like she couldn't breathe.

"Argon?" Noiro uttered in disbelief, shocked as he stared at Helia, who couldn't tear her eyes away from the angry man. "There's no way…"

"Lieutenant Argon," Miela barked, interrupting him before he could say another word. He automatically snapped his heels together and raised his hand to the side of his temple in a salute to his commanding officer, a force of habit from his years of training. As much as he disliked

Miela for being affiliated with his childhood nemesis, he respected her rank, and the rules of the Guardians.

"Yes, Captain," replied Argon stiffly.

"You're coming with us," Miela said in a level voice, hiding the incredible speed at which the gears in her heads were turning.

"What? You're going to—"

"I said, you're coming with us. We need to talk."

"Excuse me?" Argon demanded loudly, outraged. Helia gulped and moved to hide herself behind Elara's legs. Elara's heart wrenched for the child, and she gently squeezed her hand.

"Are you defying your Captain, Lieutenant?" Miela challenged. He opened his mouth to protest, and then thought better of it, remaining silent. Miela winced internally. She hated pulling rank on her colleagues to have them follow her orders; she'd much rather their motivation be respect. But she didn't get to her position by rolling over to insubordinate comrades.

"No, Captain," said Argon, knowing full-well that he had crossed a line to make Miela resort to using her rank.

"Good. You've just become a serious part of our case, Lieutenant. Come with us."

Ding.

The lift's doors opened to Argon's intended floor. He looked at the open doors and remained in his place, resigning himself to following Miela's orders.

The group waited in silence as the lift brought them to Miela's floor, and they followed her as she led the group down to her office. Helia walked slowly, dejectedly glancing at Argon as they walked down the stark white hallway. Elara sighed sadly as she looked at the distraught toddler and rubbed her hand softly to try and reassure her. Helia squeezed her hand tightly, pouting.

"Please, sit." Miela offered the group a seat without looking at them, rummaging through some papers on her desk before pulling out one of the sheets. "I'll be back. Noiro, Elara, a word?" She pointed her head at the door.

Elara nodded and turned to the toddler. "Hey," Elara whispered, rummaging a hand through her satchel. "I'll be back before you know it." She attempted to comfort Helia, seeing the toddler's worried face at the thought of Elara leaving the room. "Why don't you take this paper and my special pen? Can you draw me a pretty picture?"

Helia slowly nodded, taking hold of the objects in Elara's hand and putting them on her lap.

Elara squeezed her shoulder sympathetically. "Good girl. I'll be right back, okay?"

She shot a glare at Argon, who sat with his arms folded and his head turned to the window, and followed Miela and Noiro outside the office.

"Argon, Elara? Argon? Are you kidding?" Miela whispered harshly.

"What? I'm just as revolted as you! Even more than you!" Elara snapped, her eyes bulging in fury.

"I just can't believe this," Noiro breathed angrily. "Argon? Out of every living organism on Earth, you chose—"

"*I* didn't choose anything," Elara interrupted vehemently, furious at the way her friends were reacting. She was just as shocked and horrified as they were at the revelation.

Noiro pinched the bridge of his nose, breathing deeply. "We can't fixate on this. We have to focus. We know what's riding on this." He adjusted his glasses, his eyes still closed as he tried to calm himself. "Miela? If that man is who Helia says he is, then he is a part of this investigation."

Miela nodded firmly. "As much as I don't like the guy, he's reliable. He follows rules, and he respects them, even when he doesn't want to."

Noiro scoffed. "That's hard to believe."

"Noiro, you can't let your grudge on him cloud your judgment," said Elara quietly. She turned to her friend. "Miela, if you say he's reliable, then I trust you. Do you believe we can count on him to keep this confidential?"

Miela nodded again.

Elara pressed her lips together. "Then that's enough for me. Norio?"

Noiro sighed, nodding as well. "Let's get started."

The three headed back into the office. Helia had her head bowed down close to the paper Elara handed her earlier, intently drawing. Argon sat in his seat, glaring at the child.

"Leaving me alone with the kid is your idea of a proper investigation?" Argon quipped, turning to look at the trio.

"Why? Are you afraid of her?" Elara shot back.

Argon glared at her.

"Everyone, stop it," Miela ordered, leaning against her desk and folding her arms. "Argon, Helia is an important part of the investigation, which is why she's here."

Helia's head snapped up at the mention of her name, and she smiled at Miela. Miela smiled back at the toddler, and watched as she went back to her drawing.

"Okay," said Argon slowly. "And what do I have to do with your investigation?"

"We believe that there's something suspicious going on. Something dangerous."

Argon leaned back in his chair, the anger dissipating from his face at Miela's words. "Something dangerous?"

"Yes. Before we begin, Lieutenant, you should know that this is strictly confidential. No one outside of this room can know what is about to be said. Your sworn silence is expected, and your cooperation would be appreciated," advised Miela.

Argon lifted an eyebrow. "My cooperation?" he echoed uncomfortably. "I have nothing to do with anything dangerous or suspicious, if that's what you're accusing me of."

"You're not being accused of anything...yet." Miela narrowed her eyes in suspicion at his quick move to defend himself.

Argon glowered at the group.

"We just need your help."

"And if I don't want to help?"

"Then we won't force you," said Miela. "But whether you like it or not, you're in the middle of this. So, you have two options, because of where you stand in this case." Miela held up one finger. "You can either join the investigation as one of our peers, and you'll be filled in on everything there is to know on this case, our theories, plans of action, and individuals of interest."

Argon remained still as a statue, staring at the three of them.

Miela held up a second finger and continued, "Or, you can remain in the position you are in now, which means I cannot and will not answer any questions you might have, and you'll be meeting with us at our beck and call to answer any of our questions, then be sent away with no explanation, until this case is marked closed."

Argon scowled at his superior officer. "That's not really much of an option. I'm still stuck in this either way," he said disdainfully.

"I'm not giving you these options to please you," said Miela. "Which will it be?"

Argon glared at the Captain and finally surrendered. "I'll help."

"You're agreeing to become an official part of our investigation?" Miela checked, waiting for Argon's confirmation.

"I agree." Argon looked away, his face hard. He did not like being forced. He gritted his teeth.

Miela looked at Noiro, silently requesting him to fill Argon in.

Noiro cleared his throat. "The truth is, we don't know how to tackle this case," he began.

Argon stifled a scoff. "Of course you wouldn't," he muttered to himself.

Noiro shot another glare at the man as he continued, "It's a complicated case."

"Well, how about start by telling me who this kid is?" Argon jerked his head towards Helia, who had finished her drawing and was now fiddling with her hair as she quietly hummed to herself.

Noiro sighed. "Well, she's actually where all of this begins." He looked at Elara pointedly, who took her cue.

"Argon," she said, looking at the man uncertainly as she placed a hand on Helia's back. "This... This is Helia."

Argon nodded at the child, who stole a glance at Argon and then looked back at Elara, who was still holding her back.

"Helia... Well, she's..." Elara paused, uncertain how to explain the peculiarity of it all. She changed her tactics. "How much do you know about the concept of bending time?"

Argon gave her a strange look.

"Bending time?"

"Time travel," Elara clarified. "Moving through time."

"In theory?" Argon paused. "Not much. I've heard of the theory of relativity, if that's what you mean," said Argon slowly, his demeanor shifting as his confusion began to take over.

"Beyond that," pressed Elara.

Argon shook his head no. "I know there are theories being developed, but I don't know much," he admitted, glancing sideways at Noiro. "All I know is that it's impossible. It's just a theory."

"Well, we believe that it *has* been successfully carried out. Or rather, it *will* be successfully carried out," uttered Elara, gesturing at Helia.

"You're telling me that you think this kid is going to crack the theory of bending time?" Argon snorted incredulously. "Is this a joke?"

Elara shook her head.

"No. And you're right, Helia isn't going to crack the theory of time bending. We believe that her mother helped crack it," Elara asserted. "When we found Helia, she came with this." She pulled out the completed research book from her satchel.

Argon inched closer, curiously taking in the tattered old volume in her hands. "What's this?" he asked. "An old book?"

Miela shook her head. "It's the complete theory of time bending."

Argon scoffed. "The complete theory? And it worked?" asked Argon disbelievingly.

Elara nodded. "It worked. From what we know, Helia comes from at least five years from now."

Argon's eyebrows shot up, his eyes growing wide. "What?"

"We know how this sounds," Noiro added. "But it isn't that far-fetched. You've obviously heard of these theories before. You know that this is something scholars have been trying to work on for a long time."

Miela continued, "From what we've discovered from Helia, she and her mother were running from something." She glanced at the small child, who was calmly sitting in her seat. It was hard to shake the image of the blood-soaked toddler from the day before. "Something bad."

"Something bad?" Argon frowned. "Like what?"

"We don't know, exactly. We're working on a few hunches. But we think it was some sort of a militarized force. We don't know much, other than that... And they were organized enough to successfully pull off an attack against Polaris," finished Miela.

Argon shook his head disbelievingly at this information. "Polaris is one of the most secure kingdoms in the world," he said apprehensively.

"Well, whoever they were, they were strong enough to break through the walls, and overthrow the Guardians' attempts at protecting the city and the castle," said Miela.

Argon shook his head again skeptically.

"Here," said Elara, pulling out the newspaper clipping from her satchel and handing it over to Argon. He reached for the paper with his hand, hesitantly drawing it closer to him.

The three of them watched as the color drained from his face while he scanned the piece of paper in his hands.

"What?" Argon uttered softly, looking back up at the trio in disbelief. "That can't be true... They breached the castle?"

"They destroyed it," Elara corrected. "Five years from now, Helia and her mother were escaping from...whoever these people were. We believe that Helia's mother sent her back in time here after being badly hurt, possibly fatally injured, to change the future. We think—"

"Wait." Argon crossed his arms. "You're making an awful lot of assumptions here. How can you possibly know, or even presume, what this woman's motives are?" he challenged.

Elara stared back at him, swallowing hard.

"Her mother..." she paused, locking eyes with Argon. "I'm her mother," she asserted, holding her head high, daring Argon to say otherwise. Elara felt unusually calm as she uttered those words. She felt her heart slow, and she realized it was the first time she outwardly referred to herself as Helia's mother.

It felt strange.

Argon's eyebrows shot up again in surprise. He had known Elara for a long time, despite their torrid relationship as children. It was certainly news to him that she had a child. "What? How—"

"I couldn't believe it myself at first," said Elara, shaking her head. "When she first saw me, she called me Mama. I thought she was mistaken. It had to be a mistake. But we had her blood tested against the blood we found from her clothes, and tested it against my own blood as well. It was a match."

Argon rubbed his head, trying to grasp the information. His mind was reeling. He looked up at her, still gripping at his head, his fingers raking messily through his hair. "So... Five years from now, you're dying, and you send your kid back here?" he summed up, his voice faltering as his eyes darted between the child and Elara.

"Yes." Elara pursed her lips.

"You all think that this kid was sent back here to save your life?" asked Argon.

"No, not just my life. Everyone's," she replied indignantly.

"And your life, as well," pressed Argon.

"Everyone's," Elara repeated, slamming the newspaper clipping onto the table. "Didn't you read this? It's not just a random, one-off attack. 'An end to this unending war.' It's not just an attack. It's a war. We think *this* is what we're meant to change." She pushed the newspaper clipping towards him, her eyes burning.

Argon felt sick. "And you think I know something about this? Do you think I'm a part of this attack? A part of this... militarized force?"

"Yes," Miela answered, her arms calmly folded across her chest.

Argon angrily opened his mouth to protest. How dare she accuse him of those atrocities? He was a loyal Guardian of Polaris. He dedicated his life to the kingdom. How dare she?

"But not attacking Polaris," Miela continued. "We think you were protecting Polaris."

"Of course I'd be protecting Polaris," roared Argon,

insulted that anything otherwise could be suggested. "Why else would I be a Guardian?"

"Being a Guardian doesn't necessarily mean that someone would remain noble and true. Mutiny and coups happens all the time," Miela pointed out, her eyes narrowed. "And whoever these people were, it sounds like they had the resources and power to overcome Polaris. Anyone could be a suspect."

"Then what makes you think that I'm not part of the enemy?"

Miela gestured to Helia, who was now staring at the adults in confusion and fear. Why were they all yelling? Her eyes nervously darted between Elara and Argon, and she fidgeted uncomfortably in her seat.

"She mentioned *me*?" Argon asked, eyeing the toddler skeptically.

"Sort of," said Elara. "See, well…" she looked anxiously at Miela, unable to bring herself to say the words.

"What?" Argon demanded. "Spit it out."

"We believe you're her father," Miela finished, her face remaining stoic. Noiro looked down.

Argon's mouth dropped open, his eyes locked on Miela as his blood began to boil. Did she truly not hear how ridiculous her words were?

Miela maintained her eye contact with Argon. "You heard me."

"And you believe I'm her father?" He gestured wildly at the toddler, who stared back at him, her heart sinking at his harsh voice. Helia blinked back tears; he sounded so angry. "Based on what grounds?" Argon's nostrils flared.

"In the elevator," Noiro answered. "When she saw you.

Do you remember what she called you?"

"Okay, this is enough," Argon said, roughly pushing his chair back. "You're all insane. I've never seen this kid before in my life! You're all crazy!" he shouted, jumping to his feet, his eyes wild and frenzied. "You're dragging me into this insane story you pulled out of your asses just because this twerp called me Dad? You all—"

"Lieutenant Argon, sit back down," Miela ordered, her voice rising as she rose to her feet as well.

"You're crazy if you think that I had a kid with *that* woman. I barely know her. I barely know any of you. How can you even think that I'd—"

"I assure you, you're no prize," Elara shot back, also rising to her feet.

"As much as we'd all like to believe it isn't true, I think it is," said Noiro, his voice still calm amidst all the yelling. He could see Helia sitting quietly in her chair, her eyes quickly darting between Elara, Argon, and Miela, looking terrified. In her eyes, her Mama and Dad were towering over her, spewing hatefully at each other. The confused child looked at the adults in the room helplessly as they continued to yell at each other.

"Prove it," Argon spat. "Prove that she's my kid."

"We will," said Noiro, still keeping his voice calm. "We're not just going to take Helia's word on it. We're taking the claim seriously. We'll need to have a sample from you as well to test, and we'll—"

"Does this mean anything to you? Do you recognize it?" Elara asked suddenly, pulling out a ring from her satchel. Argon stared at the ring for a moment, and then looked back at the woman holding it in her palm.

"Where did you get that?" he glowered, his voice

lowered as he gaped at the ring.

"So, you do recognize it?" Elara repeated tentatively, holding her voice steady as she watched the man in front of her wrestle with himself to answer. He didn't want to respond, but he couldn't help himself and burst out, "Yes, I do. It's mine. How did you get it?"

"It's not yours. It's mine," Elara replied firmly, closing her hand around the ring.

"Like hell," Argon roared. "That's mine. It was my grandmother's wedding ring. It's been passed down my family for generations. I don't know how you got your grubby little hands on it, but—"

"So, you were planning on giving this ring to your wife one day, right?" Noiro finished, folding his arms. Elara clenched her teeth together, struggling to keep her cool.

Argon nodded angrily. "Yes, that's the plan."

"That ring belongs to Elara. Helia had it in her mother's bag, which she brought with her from the future. It even has some of Elara's blood on it, still," explained Noiro.

"Which means that the ring you own is still wherever your family keeps it," finished Elara, sitting back down next to Helia. She felt a small pair of hands wrap around her arm, and she looked down at the child.

"Mama, you angry? Dad is angry?" Helia whispered anxiously. Elara realized how scared the toddler must be. From her point of view, all of the adults were angry, yelling and arguing with each other. She remembered that just a few seconds ago she was yelling, too. Her gut wrenched painfully inside her.

"Enough," she said, looking at everyone in the room. "We're all scaring Helia."

Argon began, "I don't—"

"Argon," Elara pleaded, softening her voice. "Just look at her. Look at the ring. Just… look."

Argon angrily glared at the toddler, who seemed to shrink further away.

Elara sighed, shaking her head. They were getting nowhere.

"Let's do the blood test," insisted Noiro. "It'll take a few minutes."

Argon sighed, defeated. "Fine."

"We can do the test in your laboratory," said Miela. "We need to keep everything as confidential as possible. That means no external parties."

Noiro nodded. "In the meantime, let's answer a few questions." He kneeled down to Helia. "Helia, is that okay with you?" he asked kindly.

Helia looked at Elara, who smiled back reassuringly, and then nodded at Noiro.

"Okay, Helia. Can you tell me who your Mama is?"

Helia nodded hesitantly, and turned to point at Elara. "Mama!"

"Good! And what's Mama's name?"

"Mama," Helia said confidently.

Argon rolled his eyes; Noiro glared at him. He continued, "Good, Helia. You call her Mama. But do you know what other people call her? Like what does your Dad call her?"

Helia paused for a moment, thinking. "El."

Elara smiled at Helia, and turned her head to catch Miela and Noiro's glance. It was more information that they were able to get out of her from the day before. But then again, the child was distraught, terrified, and covered in her mother's blood at the time.

"What about me, Helia? What's my name?" asked Miela.

"Auntie Miela," said Helia, beaming.

"Good job, Helia!" cheered Miela. "Do you know another name people, other grownups, call me?"

"Cap'n," replied Helia, pretending to salute.

Miela smiled, proud.

"Great job, Helia," Noiro praised. Helia beamed, getting the hang of the line of questioning.

Elara moved closer to her. "Helia, can you tell me about your Dad? Who is your Dad?"

Helia pointed at Argon. "That's Dad," she said, turning to face Argon.

Elara nodded, keeping her eyes trained on Helia. She could feel Argon's eyes boring into her. "And do you know what other people call him? What does Mama call Dad?"

"Argon," she replied.

"And do you know what other grownups call him?"

Helia looked up thoughtfully. "Uncle Noiro calls him a word I'm not allowed to use."

Miela stifled a giggle; Noiro cleared his throat uncomfortably.

"Er—good, Helia," praised Elara, fighting back a grin. "Anyone else?"

"Auntie Aurora calls him Aero," she offered.

"Aurora? I don't know an Aurora," Elara hummed, thinking. "Noiro, do you—"

"How do you know Aurora?" Argon said suddenly, his unexpected participation startling the room.

Norio looked excited at Argon's response, eager on

finding out more information. "Does that name mean anything to you?" he asked Argon.

Argon's gaze didn't waver from the toddler as he snapped at his childhood nemesis, "Shut up, Noiro. How do you know Aurora?"

"She's my Auntie," Helia said, as if stating an obvious fact. She was beginning to grow confused with this game they were playing. She wanted to go home and play. Perhaps get a snack.

"She's my sister," Argon explained to Miela, massaging the side of his head with one hand.

"Your sister?" asked Noiro, looking surprised. "I didn't know you had a sister."

"We don't get along," Argon snapped. "I haven't seen her in years."

"Mama. Are we finished?" Helia piped up hopefully with a pout adorning her face. "I wanna go home."

"We'll be home soon," Elara promised.

"With Dad?" she asked, her face lighting up at the very thought.

"Er—no," Elara replied uncomfortably. "Not with Dad."

Helia's face fell, her hopes dashed. She turned to Argon pleadingly. "Please. Please, Dad. Let's go home together. I'll be good, I promise," she beseeched.

Argon was silent, uncertain how to respond to the child. His discomfort grew when he watched the toddler's eyes fill with tears as she touched his arm. She couldn't understand why her father was so upset with her. He looked away, swallowing hard. It was difficult not to look at the toddler who was trying so desperately to connect with him.

Elara placed a comforting hand on Helia's shoulder. "Some other time, Helia." She sighed. "I think we've had enough for one day." She looked at Miela, who nodded in agreement.

"Thank you, Argon, for cooperating."

Elara scoffed at Miela's words. She wouldn't call Argon's behavior cooperation. It was far from it.

"You can leave for the day, if you want," Miela continued. She knew it was a lot of information to take in at once, and it was obviously hard on Helia as she adjusted to unfamiliar versions of people she once knew. "I'll show you out."

Elara watched as Miela and Argon walked out of the room, and locked her worried gaze with Noiro.

"We'll figure everything out," Noiro said reassuringly, although he looked like he needed some reassurance himself.

Outside of the room, Argon and Miela stood silently in front of one another, unsure of how to continue in light of the information they learned that day.

"It's a lot," Argon said suddenly, breaking the silence.

"I know. We're barely wrapping our heads around this ourselves. And imagine how difficult it must be for the kid. She's just a baby, you know," she said solemnly. "She can't be more than three."

Argon remained silent. He knew he acted cruelly towards the toddler in the room. A part of him knew he acted the way he did because he was scared and confused. But his being scared and confused certainly didn't excuse his nasty behavior. A small, gnawing feeling of guilt began to creep up his belly.

"It's gonna be tough," continued Miela, "but I'm still

expecting you to bring your best to the table while helping us pursue this case."

Argon nodded silently, albeit reluctantly.

"Take the day off and clear your head," said Miela. "It'll help."

"When are we meeting next?" asked Argon.

"Actually, we're planning on meeting tomorrow morning, at Noiro's."

Argon raised an eyebrow curiously. "Why not here, at headquarters?" he asked.

"Well, mainly we don't want to draw any more attention to Helia than necessary," she replied. "And we need to crack some codes. Noiro's personal library will come in handy."

"Codes?"

"Mm," Miela confirmed. "Helia showed up with a few other items from the future. Clues, we think. They'll be a little tricky to crack."

"Clues?" Argon echoed. "I don't get it. If Elara went through all that trouble to send Helia back from her time, why wouldn't she just clearly write down everything?"

Miela shrugged. "I'm guessing it was coded in case they fell into the wrong hands. We don't know exactly who we're up against."

Argon nodded, frowning. This case was getting bigger and bigger the more he learned about it. He looked over his shoulder and back towards Miela's office.

"Argon?"

"I'll be there," Argon said firmly, turning back to look at Miela.

"Okay. I'll write down the location—"

"I know where Noiro lives," Argon interrupted. "He

and I, we go way back."

Miela nodded knowingly.

Argon took his cue, saluted, and left.

Miela sighed, turning back to enter her office where Elara and Noiro sat. Helia was leaning into Elara's side, her eyes beginning to droop shut. She let out a small yawn.

"That went well," said Elara miserably, glancing up at Miela as she walked back in. Her throat felt scratchy from the shouting match. She couldn't help but feel disappointed. Everyone had behaved so poorly. But try as she might, she couldn't bring herself to blame anyone for their reactions. It was a lot to take in.

"I think we need to take a break," murmured Miela, repeating the advice she gave Argon moments ago. "Clear our heads. We'll be no use to anyone if we continue the way we are and get wrapped up in our heads."

"You're right," Noiro agreed, rubbing the back of his neck.

"Helia also looks like she's had enough," said Elara, wrapping her arm around the toddler who was now dozing off beside her. "I'll take her home so she can get some sleep. I think it might be around her naptime…" Elara trailed off, wondering how on earth could she serve as a responsible parent to a toddler who came into her life less than twenty-four hours ago.

"All right, it's settled," said Miela. "Get some rest, all of you. We'll meet tomorrow morning at Noiro's."

TIME THEORY

Elara tapped her foot anxiously as she prepared a set of vials in Noiro's lab. She slept well the night before, albeit having woken up a few times; she was still getting used to having someone in bed with her. Helia kept snuggling up next to her beneath her covers, making her unbearably hot in the summer night.

Nonetheless, she found that she enjoyed spending time with the toddler. Helia was an inquisitive child and took it upon herself to examine every nook and cranny of her house to find the best spot to play in. Elara also noticed that she had an affinity for drawing, and helped her set up a small corner with some of her old art supplies that she'd managed to scrounge up for the toddler to play with.

Reminiscing on her day with Helia helped calm her down, and Elara slowed her tapping foot as she finished setting up the last of her vials. She could hear Noiro and Miela in the sitting room next door, casually chatting away.

A calm breeze wafted through the cottage. The air was still cool in the early morning hours. She walked into the sitting room to join her friends as they waited for Argon to arrive.

Just as she'd entered into the room, a sharp knock sounded against the front door.

"Ah, that must be him," said Noiro, getting up to his feet to answer the door.

Argon stood rigidly at the doorway, glancing at Noiro uncomfortably as he waved him in. He walked into the sitting room, where Helia was splayed out on the floor with a handful of toys, lost in her make-believe world. To Argon's surprise, Miela was kneeling down on the floor with her, speaking in a silly voice as she moved one of the dolls towards Helia's toy. He felt the beginnings of a grin tugging at his lips; he was certainly not used to seeing this side of Captain Miela.

"You can follow Elara to the laboratory, she'll just do a quick blood test," explained Noiro, gesturing towards the laboratory.

Elara nodded at him, hiding her discomfort with a solemn expression. The prospect of spending a few solitary moments with the man who had been so hostile towards them the day before made her shudder.

Argon followed Elara to the laboratory, silent in his discomfort as well. He had not taken the news very well in Miela's office, and he knew it. He felt a twinge of guilt as he watched Helia warily glance at him before returning to her conversation with Miela and her dolls. He hadn't meant to be cruel to the toddler either.

"You'll just feel a quick prick," said Elara, holding up a thin syringe.

Argon nodded, rolling up his sleeve and offering her

his arm. She tapped on a vein, humming to herself as she watched it pop out against his arm. Argon closed his eyes, trying to ignore the syringe. He wasn't a fan of needles, especially with the several medical checkups he had to endure when he was first enlisting as a Guardian.

"There," muttered Elara, pressing a small bandage to his arm where she had collected the blood.

Argon watched her as she emptied the syringe out into a series of vials she had in front of her. He saw some vials further down the table marked with the letter *H*. "Helia's?" he asked curiously. He was lousy at creating small talk, but the uncomfortable silence was more than he could bear.

"Hmm?" Elara turned her head. "Oh, those. Yes, I had some collected last night."

They sat for a moment in silence as Elara tinkered with the vials and shuffled some papers around.

"The results will be ready soon," Elara said finally. She gestured at door. "We can join the others in the sitting room. We set out some tea for you as well."

Argon nodded his thanks and followed her out of the laboratory.

"Finished?" asked Noiro, eyeing the small bandage on Argon's arm.

"Yes. We'll know the results soon," assured Elara, taking a seat in one of the plush chairs and sinking into it. Helia scooted closer to her mother, still playing on the floor. Elara smiled warmly at the toddler.

"So… what now?" asked Argon. He looked at the stack of books on the table in the middle of the room. "Research?" He should have known. Research was Noiro's forte.

Noiro hummed and pushed his glasses up the bridge of

his nose. "We have a few puzzle pieces we need to put together."

"I see," mused Argon.

Noiro turned his attention to the table. "Helia had some items hidden away in her mother's satchel. We'll start with this," he said, picking up Helia's necklace. The jagged stone pendant swung in the air as he held it up for the group to take a closer look at it.

"Whose is it?" asked Argon as he examined the pendant.

"It's Helia's," replied Noiro. "She was wearing it when she first arrived."

"What's so special about the necklace, though?" Argon probed curiously.

"That's what we need to find out," admitted Noiro. "I've been doing some reading, and I have a theory." Noiro paused. "I think it's the key to how Helia got here."

"What?" Miela leaned closer to the pendant.

"It's a reach, I know," Noiro began, "but Elara and I have been doing our own research on time travel. And the completed research journal that Helia showed up with held some answers too.

"In theory, time travel is possible. A number of theories by other scientists support the idea. For example, we know from the theory of relativity that time can be affected by a number of factors." Noiro set the necklace down onto the desk, looking at Elara.

"Right. Like speed, or gravity," Elara interjected.

Noiro nodded. "Exactly. But it's a little more complicated than that. You see, while most people think of time as a constant, some scholars demonstrated that time is actually a subjective illusion.

"Speed affects time. Time can speed up or slow down, depending on how fast an object, or in our case, a person, is moving.

"Gravity can also bend time; the heavier a mass is, the greater its gravity. The greater its gravity, the greater is its ability to bend the fabric of space-time, therefore, time is experienced at a different rate in correlation to gravity's extent."

"But this is all *in theory*," observed Miela, leaning forward as she concentrated on Noiro's explanation.

"Yes," Noiro agreed. "Time travel has only ever existed *in theory*. It's been proven, *in theory*. But it's never actually been carried out. Moving through time—that's a huge area of debate amongst scholars.

"You see, people assume that you can travel through time. But that's making the assumption that time is a medium that one can travel through. The theory that Elara and I are working on is called *bending* time." Noiro paused, pulling out a sheet of paper and drawing a line across it, with two points labeled A and B on either side of the line. "Imagine that this line"—he pointed at the line he drew— "is a timeline. We know that time moves forward; thus, we know that we *will* move from point A to point B.

"But what if I wanted to travel from this point in time"—he gestured to point B—"back to *this* point in time," he said, gesturing to point A.

Silence hung in the air.

"You following?" Noiro checked in with the group.

They nodded.

"Here is where we bring in Newton's First Law," Noiro continued. "An object in motion will stay in motion until a force is acted upon it." He gestured to the line once again. "Time, in this case, is an object in motion. And it will remain in motion, until a force is acted upon it. Now, how do we move from point B to point A?" Noiro folded the paper in half.

The group stared, awaiting his response.

"We enact a force onto time," Noiro stated, slowly folding the paper to make points A and B on either side of the line meet. "That's what Helia did when she got back here. She was at point B. She enacted a force onto time, and effectively bent time to come back to our point in time: point A."

Noiro set the piece of paper down.

"So, we're trying to figure out what was the force Helia used," Argon finished.

Noiro nodded. "Exactly. That's the key we're looking for." He gestured to the completed research journal he placed on the table earlier. "I was taking a look through our research—our completed research journal from the future—and I think this might be the force used to bend time." He reached for the research journal and flipped through the pages, finally coming to a page in the middle of the book, and turned it around for the others to see.

A roughly sketched-out diagram of a stone was on the page, with a few scribbles beneath. Elara could vaguely make out one of the words written beneath the sketch: *Aether*. She frowned. Where had she heard that word before?

"That stone"—Noiro pointed at the diagram—"is the pendant on Helia's necklace." He picked the necklace back up from the table, holding it up for the group to see. Sure enough, the rough sketch of the stone matched the jagged stone pendant hanging on the necklace

"What is it, exactly?" asked Elara, intrigued.

"I'll get to that," Noiro assured her. "But before we get there, do we have any questions?"

"I do." Miela raised her hand. "Is bending time dangerous?"

"Extremely," Noiro replied seriously. "Not to mention it can open up a whole world of paradoxes. For example, let's say a person went back in time and accidentally killed himself in the past—perhaps he might've accidentally triggered a series of events that led to his death before he ever had the chance of bending time in the future. Well, it would be a mess, wouldn't it? Because of his untimely death in the past, he would have never made it to the point in the future where he made the decision to bend time and go back to himself in the past. Er, does that make sense?" asked Noiro, realizing that he had a set of blank faces staring back at him. "Basically, bending time could have drastic consequences on the future if there were any changes made in the past. It's dangerous to play with time."

"So that's where the butterfly effect comes into play," said Elara thoughtfully. "With the very act of time travelling, you can argue that *any* changes made in the past can have an impact on the future. Accidentally tripping someone could potentially trigger a series of events that could change that course of history. Even stepping on a stray ant could somehow result in an accident that wouldn't have happened otherwise."

Miela added, "In other words, who knows how much we might've changed already by just being here, discussing time bending in Noiro's cottage, instead of doing whatever we were doing at this day and time during the timeline where Helia never came back in time to us."

"Yes—which brings me to my next point: trying to change the future can potentially be dangerous as well. Too many unforeseen consequences. Suppose you were trying to prevent an accident from happening that fatally injured a family member of yours, and you went back in time to try and stop it from ever happening. Let's say you saved your family member, and went back to your current timeline, only to find that somehow, you accidentally triggered a series of events that resulted in killing your entire family instead." Noiro sighed. "We can't control the future's events by simply changing the past. We could stop one thing, but it could trigger a whole other set of problems in its stead."

"But that's what we're trying to do, right?" said Miela. "We're trying to alter the future. We're trying to stop that war. We're damned if we do, damned if we don't."

"Unfortunately, yes," Noiro uttered. "But like Elara said, we've already altered the timeline, and potentially the future. Helia coming back to our point in time has already triggered a change in events."

"So, *how* did Helia bend time?" asked Argon.

"Ah, well, we're back to the necklace," said Noiro, holding up the necklace, the jagged stone pendant swinging slightly from his grasp.

"In order to bend time, we need a force. Now, Helia didn't just go back a few seconds into the past, let alone a few days. She jumped back *five years*. You need an incredible amount of force to pull that off," said Noiro. "Planets ten times larger than the size of Saturn don't have enough gravity to bend time to that extent."

"Saturn? We're talking about planets, now?" asked

Argon incredulously.

"Yes. But we don't have to look any farther than our own planet." Noiro smiled. "Our planet is ruled by four elements: Water, Earth, Air, and Fire. But there is a fifth element." Noiro pointed to the stone pendant. "Aether."

"Aether?" Miela echoed.

"Wait, I'm confused. Fifth element?" Argon furrowed his brow. "What do the elements have to do with bending time?"

"It has everything to do with time," said Noiro. "We know the four elements that rule our planet. But what about elements *outside* of our planet? An element that exists within the universe?" Noiro folded his arms. "The element that existed before our planet came into existence. The element that existed before Water, Earth, Air, and Fire. Scholars as early as Plato and Aristotle refer to it in early texts when describing the world's elements: Aether. The first element.

"Scholars across the ages cite the element of Aether when describing arcane, seemingly supernatural phenomena. Unexplained blips in gravity, or inconsistent tales around speed. Have you ever picked up an object you've held a thousand times, only to find that this time, it was much lighter than you anticipated? Have you ever walked the same long path you've walked a thousand times, only to find that this time, you reached in the blink of an eye? Strange, unexplainable singularities that you simply couldn't rationalize?

"It's because of Aether. The element is a force that directly impacts gravity and speed. We experience its effects all the time, without ever even realizing it." Noiro took in a deep breath. "And what other object do we know is impacted by gravity and speed?"

Elara looked up at Noiro excitedly. "Time!"

"Exactly." Noiro nodded. He held up the necklace once more, tracing his fingers against the dials carved into the stone pendant.

"I don't know how we did it. I don't know how we managed to capture the essence of Aether in its physical form. But I believe that sometime in the future, we managed to do just that. And we used it to bend time. And that's how Helia got here," Noiro concluded his explanation. He was breathless yet giddy, his mind racing as he stared at the stone pendant. He whispered, "It's groundbreaking, really."

"And dangerous," Elara added. "How could we have been so *stupid*? Bending time is dangerous. How could we have been okay with actually bending time, let alone bending time with a *baby*?"

"We must have been desperate," mused Miela. "Judging by the state that Helia was in when she arrived, with all that blood, it looked like you didn't make it." Miela felt a shiver run up her spine as she recalled Helia screaming and crying in the library, and the shock as she took in her blood-soaked clothes and blood-spattered face.

Noiro gulped.

"I have a hunch that none of us made it, if Helia was the one who was sent back. She came from a dark world. You were trying to change it," said Miela.

"What's done is done. We need to focus on how to move forward the best we can," Argon uttered quietly.

Elara sighed, nodding.

"It's a stroke of genius, using Aether to bend time," admitted Noiro, examining the stone in his hand. "I wonder how we found it…"

"What does it matter? At least we have it now, and the research behind it," Miela pointed out.

"Perhaps…"

"Well, we have the stone and necklace figured out," said Argon. "What's the last piece of the puzzle?"

Elara picked up one of the books laying on the table. "This. I've been looking at this for the last couple of days, and I can't seem to figure out what it means."

"What is it?" he asked, eyeing the book in her hands.

"It's a journal," she replied. "My journal. It was packed in Helia's bag. But it's coded." Elara flipped through the pages to show the group. "Instead of normal entries, each page has a sequence of numbers. I think it might have ties to our time bending research. I looked up certain key-phrases to try and see if the numbers corresponded with that, but no luck."

"What about equations?" suggested Noiro.

Elara shook her head. "I tried everything. I can't make heads or tails with it."

"Is it possible to ask a Scholar?" asked Miela, putting a finger on her chin as she thought aloud.

Elara pondered at the proposal. The Scholars of Polaris were part of an ancient society that went back as far as history itself. They held troves of knowledge and hidden wonders within their depths, spending their lives working to preserve accounts of lost societies and civilizations, and working to bring humanity further through their research and technology. Not anyone could set off to become a Scholar; it took a certain level of circumspection and prudence, and was surprisingly made up of unpleasant, wary, cagy, and sometimes downright sinister individuals.

Nevertheless, they were a highly respected faction of society, revered by even the King himself.

Elara rubbed her forehead. It would be risky, bringing it to the Scholars. Their own guarded motives could derail the entire investigation.

But, did they have many other options?

More importantly, did they have enough time?

Elara sighed. "They might know something more."

"That's an idea," Noiro said slowly. "But I'd be cautious bringing it up with someone outside of this room. We don't know who was involved in the war in the future. What if we reveal something that leads to Helia being found out? Or something that could put us all in danger?"

"We need to go to someone we can trust," said Miela firmly. "There's a lot at stake."

The group fell into a spell of silence as they thought hard. Miela was right. If they were going to consult someone else, it needed to be someone they trusted.

"What about Professor Neptune?" Noiro pondered aloud. "He's one of the leading Scholars of Polaris. He even gets called upon by the Royal Family from time to time."

"Professor Neptune?" Miela repeated doubtfully. Professor Neptune was a notorious Scholar of Polaris, albeit a powerful one; he seemed to have a hand in almost every organization within the city, from schools and universities to ministries and royal affairs. He even sometimes appeared as a guest lecturer in some tactical seminars during her early training days as a Guardian.

As esteemed as Professor Neptune was, he was infamous for dabbling in unethical matters as well. He had his fair share of run-ins with the law; the Guardians were often called on cases involving mysterious injuries or disappearances, which were somehow oddly linked to Professor Neptune. However, they never could find a solid piece of evidence to tie it to him—it always seemed like he left *just enough* evidence to suggest his involvement, but not enough to actually indict him with anything. Miela shuddered, recalling a few of her own altercations with the Professor in her line of work. He always seemed to sport a smug, knowing smile as the Guardians tried to link him to their cases, as if he knew that he would escape unscathed.

And he always did.

To say Miela was suspicious was an understatement.

"Professor Neptune…" Argon paused, sharing a doubtful look with Miela. As a Guardian, he was quite familiar with him as well. "I don't know."

"I trust him," Noiro vouched. "I know he's a little eccentric…"

Miela scoffed loudly at Noiro's choice of words.

Noiro continued, "He's just misunderstood He's an old mentor of mine, and an old friend."

Elara sighed. "It's not like we have other choices for help. She turned to the group. "But we can't tell him everything. We just need his insight on the codes."

"Agreed."

"How can you bring up the codes in the journal without actually showing him the journal?" inquired Argon.

"Maybe we could just write down a few of the numbers on a separate sheet of paper and show him," Miela suggested. "Bring it up that way?"

"That's a good idea."

"When do you think you can meet with Neptune?"

asked Elara. She knew Professor Neptune well. As a child, she watched Noiro host him as a guest at his cottage quite frequently. Professor Neptune was one of Noiro's oldest friends, and an even older mentor. He was an ambitious man, and took every advantage he could get to advance his research studies. Ambition often clouded the Professor's judgment, and it was not unusual for his research methods to err on the immoral side. In fact, most of his research methods were highly controversial. He was notorious for using human subjects in his experiments, and exposed many of his research subjects to terrible, horrific stimuli, all in the name of science.

Professor Neptune was a powerful man. He certainly faced many Guardians who were sent after him, yet he hardly ever emerged with anything more than a mere slap on the wrist. He was charismatic, well-liked, and well-connected, and was certainly no stranger to using his connections to get him out of several sticky situations.

Elara was not fond of him.

"Hmm," Noiro thought, glancing at the window, "I'm supposed to meet with him this weekend to drop off some research logs. Perhaps we can pay him a visit then."

"We? Are we coming with you?" asked Elara, raising an eyebrow.

Noiro nodded. "If you want to."

Elara bit her lip. She knew Professor Neptune frequented Noiro's cottage, but it was seldom that she ever visited the Professor.

But this wouldn't be a regular visit. There was too much at stake. Try as they might, they couldn't figure out the codes before them.

They needed help.

Elara's eyes fell on Helia, who was still sprawled out on the ground, concentrating hard as she slowly scribbled onto a piece of paper. Noticing Elara's gaze, the toddler looked up and grinned toothily at her mother. "Look, Mama! It's us," she said, beaming at Elara as she held up a slightly crumpled up paper.

It was a messily-drawn picture of herself and Helia, sprawled out on a bed together and sleeping, like they were last night.

Elara's breath caught in her throat. Something stirred in her stomach as she looked at the toddler, who was so enamored by her. "It's lovely," she whispered, smiling softly at the toddler.

Helia drew her attention back to the paper, carefully scrawling away again.

How could she deny a potential lead in their search for answers? Especially if it meant sparing Helia from suffering the trauma she went through in the future... Elara turned her head back to Noiro.

"Let's go to Neptune."

"It's cold," Miela muttered, pulling her coat close against herself as they trekked down a long set of stony stairs. She squinted, her eyes struggling to adjust to the dimming light as they went further down the stairs, and away from the sunlight at the cave's entrance.

Argon muttered in agreement. The shift from the warm summer breeze into the cool, chilled air that blew through the cave's entrance left him uncomfortably cold. He frowned, sighing deeply as he followed the group down the stairs.

A lot weighed on his mind since the last time the

group had met in Noiro's cottage. Before all of this, he was just a carefree man, minding his own business and climbing his way up the ranks as a Guardian of Polaris. Until that moment, he could kid himself and tell himself that he didn't really belong in this situation which he was dragged into, and that it was all a big mistake.

But everything changed with Helia's arrival in his life. Helia was his. And the test which Noiro ran proved it.

Suddenly, everything was cemented in reality.

He thought hard to himself, the fear beginning to churn his stomach as he thought back to all of the information that Elara, Noiro, and Miela pushed onto him. Terrible thoughts about how the future would turn out. Argon closed his eyes.

He was still processing the news of becoming a father overnight. He was still getting used to working so closely alongside people he disliked for most of his life. He wondered how his father might have reacted to the news of his son partnering up with his old arch nemesis, had he still been alive. Argon looked up, watching the back of Noiro's head as they trudged down the endless flight of stairs into the inky darkness below.

"I told you it would be cold," Noiro's voice drifted to Argon's ears, pulling him out of his thoughts. Noiro confidently led the way, feeling perfectly comfortable in his thick cloak. "It's always cooler underground."

Noiro knew each and every step that was carved into the deep stone caverns, having made many a trip down into the Old Archive—his first one being a tour with his father when he was just a boy. His father would often bring Noiro along with him to many important meetings held amongst other prominent Scholars. Unlike other children, who would have moaned and groaned about spending time listening to old men chatter away about theories and scholarly research, Noiro thrived on it. As a young boy, he'd often sit quietly in the corner, a small notebook in hand as he jotted down notes. As he grew older, he began to venture down on his own, often making the long trip from his hometown to the Old Archive in hopes of gaining his own recognition and credibility, and perhaps one day being accepted as a Scholar himself.

Noiro turned into a tunneled pathway, lit by small lanterns which hung from either side of the walls, and to a large, iron door. He pulled a large brass key from his pocket, turning the lock with a series of loud clicks and clacks, and finally pushed the heavy door open.

Elara watched in amusement as Miela and Argon gaped at the wondrous halls of the Old Archive. The walls were lined with marble bookshelves, each holding a massive spread of tomes. The books' spines glittered under the warm light of the antique crystal chandeliers, each with engravings that detailed its land's origins. The ceiling was inscribed with calligraphy written in the world's different languages, all weaving together to form an intricate geometric pattern, crisscrossing its way across the vast stony structure. The air was calm, with a few groups of scholars wandering about, idly chatting away.

"This way," said Noiro, ignoring his fellow group members' awe as he walked smartly across the magnificent floors, leading them towards a set of doors at lined up at the side of the hall. He knocked on the door in the middle, waited a few seconds, and then pushed the door open.

Inside was a cozy office, with a hand-woven carpet lining the floor depicting the night sky and its constellations. A sturdy mahogany desk stood at the head of the room, and a handful of soft leather chairs arranged in a semicircle to face the desk. A celestial dial sat in one corner of the office, the gears inside the dial softly whirring away as it showed the planetary movement patterns.

"Take a seat," Noiro offered, closing the door behind them. "I'm sure Professor Neptune will be here any moment."

The group followed his instructions, each taking a seat on one of the chairs.

"Why is the Old Archive underground in this dingy cave, instead of up at the Grand Library in the castle grounds?" Miela asked, settling uncomfortably into her seat. She gazed up at the different instruments, each of which was carefully perched on different shelves and cabinets. She had never seen such apparatuses before; some were colorful dials with smooth, fluid movements, while others were mechanical, rigid, and dull. She could hear a distant ticking noise from somewhere in the room. She wondered if some of these instruments were of the Professor's own inventions.

"The most important rule in the scholarly world is to protect knowledge," answered Noiro, settling into his seat beside Miela.

"So what's the library in the castle grounds for, then?" asked Argon pointedly. "Isn't the Grand Library one of the most extensive libraries? And the most protected, with it being located within the grounds of Polaris Castle."

"The Grand Library is *one* of the most extensive libraries," Noiro pointed out, smiling. "But the Old Archive down here has every single book and tome ever produced in recorded history. Some of them are so old that the outside temperature and moisture could damage the books kept in here." Noiro gestured at the books lining the countless shelves. "There are books in here that survived wars, genocides, and the extinction of several civilizations. Priceless pieces of information and knowledge that would've otherwise been lost, had it not been protected and hidden away in within these walls."

"Wars?" Elara folded her arms curiously. "Why would books be affected by war?"

Noiro leaned back in his chair. "If you think about it, wouldn't you agree that knowledge is one of the pillars that supports a thriving civilization?" He looked at the stack of books lying on the desk in front of them. "With knowledge comes power. With knowledge, you have doctors, engineers, teachers, artists, scientists… You take that knowledge away, then you take that power away."

"Targeting scholars, libraries, and schools is a common tactical move in the military to bring a civilization down to its knees," Miela added, her voice hard. As a seasoned Guardian, she was well-versed in calculated attacks against civilizations. "Destroying knowledge rips away the identity and strength of its beholder. Languages have been lost that way. Technology. Culture. Progression. By targeting scholars, you can set back an entire civilization hundreds of years. By erasing knowledge, you can ultimately erase that civilization. It's an awful tactic, but an effective one."

"It's been done before?" Elara asked, horrified.

A deep voice chuckled from behind them. "Thousands of times."

The group turned around, startled at the unfamiliar voice that intruded on their conversation. An older man stood at the doorway, his dark, thick hair curled ever so slightly around his forehead and over his small eyes. He was wearing a set of deep velvet robes of that draped across his shoulders. A heavy brass chain hung around his shoulders and draped across his torso, with a heavy metal plate resting in the center of his chest emblazoned with the emblem of Polaris: the constellation of Polaris, encased by two crescent moons facing opposite each other.

"Professor Neptune," Elara began, her eyes wide as she stared at the man who stood confidentially in the doorway.

The man strode in, his small, beady eyes twinkling as he took a seat at his desk.

"Have you heard of the House of Wisdom?" the Professor asked. He continued before the group even had a chance to open their mouths to respond: "It was one of the world's most magnificent libraries during its time. Located in the heart of ancient Babylon, it was the city's own Grand Library. Think of it as an ancient predecessor of the Grand Library of Polaris."

"What happened to it?"

"It was destroyed," Professor Neptune answered simply. "You see, the House of Wisdom wasn't *just* a library. It was a center of knowledge. It had a society of scientists, academics, translators, researchers, poets, alchemists, astronomers… They hailed from all over the ancient empires, overcoming and rising above political differences to form a society of knowledge. They worked together to preserve knowledge.

"Babylon was the center of knowledge and wisdom in its era," Neptune continued. "It was what made them one of the most powerful and strategic civilizations at that time. People travelled from all over to seek the highest quality of education. They even had translated works from ancient scholars: Pythagaros, Plato, Aristotle, Apollonius, Archimedes, Euclid, Ptolemy and many more. It was a scholarly haven.

"Unfortunately, that is what made the House of Wisdom the perfect target to take down Babylon. The library was destroyed, and all of the books and records, all of which were so meticulously preserved and recorded, were destroyed. The fall of Babylon was cemented when those books were heaved in into rivers, and its scholars ruthlessly slaughtered. The waters of Babylon ran black with ink, and its soil stained deep with blood."

"That's horrible," uttered Miela.

"Not all was lost," said Professor Neptune, lifting a finger in the air. "Miraculously, some of those tomes survived. In fact, we have the surviving records stored here, right in this very cavern."

The Professor gestured at the walls around him. "History is unkind, and has a tendency to repeat itself. Polaris learned from the plight of Babylon, as well as previous civilizations before them," he said. "The founders of the Old Archive vowed to take every precaution to protect knowledge. Yes, we have the Grand Library of Polaris, and yes, it's protected by the castle guards, and the entire force of the Guardians of Polaris. But as we know, castles, cities, and civilizations eventually fall.

"That is why we keep the very root of our knowledge, our city's wealth, our source of prosperity, hidden away within these walls. Hidden away within the bowels of the Earth, safe from harm." The Professor stretched his mouth into a small smile as he looked at his captivated audience. "Any questions?"

PROFESSOR NEPTUNE

"Neptune!" Noiro got up to his feet to greet his mentor. Elara watched as the men embraced each other affectionately, chuckling lightly as they did so. She smiled at Neptune.

"Do you have what I asked for?" Neptune grinned at Noiro.

Noiro nodded, pulling out an envelope from his coat.

The Professor sifted through its contents, rifling his fingers through a stack of old, withered papers, humming in satisfaction. "Perfect." He beamed at Noiro. "This will help a lot."

He turned his attention to the group, his eyes briefly pausing when he noticed the small tattoo on Miela and Argon's wrists peeking out from beneath their sleeves; their Guardian's mark. He seemed slightly wary at the sight of Miela and Argon, but said nothing of it.

"You've brought guests," said Professor Neptune,

smiling at the group. His smile did not quite reach his eyes, and he raised an eyebrow inquisitively at Noiro.

"Yes." Noiro cleared his throat. "We were hoping you could help us."

"Oh?" Professor Neptune's interest was piqued. "The great Noiro needs my help?"

Elara was not quite sure if she detected a hint of sarcasm in his voice. Or perhaps, disdain? There were certainly many scholars who were envious of Noiro's proximity to the Royal Family, and it was no secret that there were many who believed he was undeserving of the privileges the Royal Family afforded him.

Noiro, oblivious to the Professor's tone, pulled out another envelope from his coat and slipped out a few sheets of paper. On each sheet was a jumble of numbers scrawled onto it that he had copied down from the journal earlier. He hadn't bothered to make a copy of each page; rather, he and Elara figured that having a few pages for Neptune to look over could give enough insight to point them in the right direction. "We were wondering if these numbers meant anything to you," he said slowly, handing the papers over to him.

Elara watched Neptune's face for any reaction, and felt a small knot in her stomach as she saw Neptune's face darken in concentration as he studied the papers.

"Where did you find these?" asked Neptune casually, turning over one of the sheets to look at the numbers.

"Er—in an old book," Noiro uttered quickly. "A personal side project, really."

"Mmm-hmm," Neptune hummed, tapping a finger to his chin. He took out a scroll from his desk, and began scribbling down the sequence of numbers. Elara felt uncomfortable at the thought of there being another copy of the codes.

She could feel Noiro tense up beside her as they watched Professor Neptune scrawl out more of the codes onto his own scroll.

"What are you doing?" Miela asked loudly, her voice echoing Elara's uneasiness.

"Hmm? Oh, I was trying to move the numbers around. Maybe they're a part of an equation," said Neptune, thinking aloud.

Noiro nodded. "That's the same conclusion we came to. But we're stuck."

Neptune hummed to himself, and then began to write down the sequence of numbers again. He paused, murmuring victoriously to himself, and then looked up at Noiro.

"Did you figure it out?" asked Noiro eagerly. He definitely caught the shift in his old friend's demeanor.

"Have you considered Pi?" Neptune tilted his head, his eyes twinkling as he glanced up at the curious entourage before him.

"Pie?" Miela repeated, befuddled. "Why would we consider pie?"

"Not pie. Although, it's never a bad time to think about pie." The Professor chuckled. "I meant Pi. Mathematical Pi."

"No, not more math," Miela groaned.

"Pi is more than just math, and it's more than just diagrams of circles. You have to look deeper," said Neptune knowingly. "Pi opens up the world to an endless realm of possibilities. Its numbers are endless. It's all encompassing; it has every single number arranged in every combination imaginable. You"—Neptune pointed at Argon, who was closely examining an apparatus in the corner of his office, fascinated.

He snapped his head towards Neptune.

"Yes. You. Pick a sequence of five numbers," said Neptune.

Argon looked displeased at being involved with more mathematics and reluctantly replied, "one, two, three, four, five."

"That specific sequence of numbers occurs twice in Pi." Neptune smiled. "In fact, that string occurs over two thousand times in the first two hundred million digits of Pi."

Argon remained stoic, seemingly unimpressed.

Neptune narrowed his eyes at Argon, displeased at his lack of enthusiasm. "Another example, let's say we wanted to search for the year we're in now, 9377. That would be close to the three thousandth position in Pi," he said, watching Argon turn his attention back to him. "Or look at five years from now, 9382. That would be close to the four thousandth position of Pi."

The group simultaneously took a sharp breath at Neptune's choice of words. 9382. The year Polaris was destroyed.

Noiro looked deep in thought, an inkling of realization dawning on his face.

Elara frowned at Neptune, suspicious.

"Oh?" said Miela, also struggling to maintain a neutral face as the Professor mentioned the very year of the attack that they were trying to prevent.

Did he know something?

Miela glanced at Neptune, who was smiling, satisfied

that he managed to capture his audience's attention. He chuckled lightly at their serious faces. "I'm just saying, the possibility of Pi is endless. Maybe you should try looking there for your answers."

"Do you think that dates have a correlation with the numbers?" asked Noiro.

Neptune shrugged. "Maybe. Maybe not. I'm not going to spoon-feed you the answers, Noiro. You should know that by now," he said, a hint of mirth playing in his voice.

Noiro grunted, but respected Neptune's method.

"But that's the dilemma with looking at Pi. Anything is possible. There could be ties, and there could just be coincidences," Neptune continued. "What did you say this was for, again?"

"A side project," Noiro asserted. "I also just wanted another excuse to see you again."

Neptune smiled at Noiro.

"Ah. It's nice to know that you still enjoy the company of an old man like me, Noiro," Neptune chuckled. "Now, tell me, how is your current assignment for the Royal Family going? I dare say, your subject of choice has me absolutely captivated."

"Thank you, Neptune." Noiro smiled sheepishly. "Elara and I are actually working on it together." He gestured to Elara, who sat perched at the edge of her seat.

"We're still at the very beginning," assured Elara firmly, pushing the thought of the completed research book from the future to the back of her mind.

Professor Neptune nodded.

The group stared at the man as he sat in his seat, his head lifted up towards the ceiling, deep in thought.

The sound of gears suddenly shifting into place and clicking fervently pierced through the silence. Elara tilted her head towards the source of the sound, which seemed to be coming from the apparatus Argon was examining earlier.

Argon had his hands up at chest level, as if to prove he hadn't touched the delicate device. "I don't know what happened," he blurted out over the growing clicking noise emitting from the device. "I was watching the movement, and suddenly..."

Neptune smiled. "That's one of my own inventions."

"What is it?" asked Argon.

"It's an Element Dial. Still a work in progress, really." Professor Neptune proudly strode over to the device, gently nudging a piece of wood back into place. "I'm working on developing a model to track movements of elemental energy."

"Elemental energy?" echoed Noiro, intrigued.

"Yes," said Neptune. "You see, we have sundials placed all over Polaris, which gives us a way to keep track of time using shadows cast by the dial. We also have the lesser known moon dials, which tracks planetary movements. Both useful, but quite predictable after you track patterns and movements long enough.

"I realized that while we have dials to track objects moving in space, we don't have any dials in place to track objects on Earth." Professor Neptune smiled. "Even more so, how amazing would it be to track the energy of the elements? To predict the patterns of elements? Their movements? What if we could push the boundaries of energy further? Think of the power we could harness..." the Professor trailed off in his wonderment. "I want to push the boundaries of what we know about the Earth's power." He paused, waiting for someone to prompt him to continue speaking. He seemed to rather enjoy the attention he was getting from the group.

"Marvelous work," Noiro remarked, examining the dial closely.

Neptune chortled, satisfied that he had the prompt he was looking for.

"I've managed to come up with a way to identify elemental energy, but I can't figure out a way to measure its movements," admitted Neptune. "I'm sure I'll figure it out, though."

"You always do," Noiro assured him.

The Professor smiled at Noiro, and then turned to Argon, gazing at him curiously. "It's strange," he murmured. "It's never done that before. You sure you didn't touch it?"

Argon raised an eyebrow at the Professor's fixated gaze.

Professor Neptune narrowed his eyes, and then turned away, looking back at the Elemental Dial. It was a delicately designed model, with metal crafted so finely that it looked like gleaming strands of thread that held up the models of elemental bodies: a deep green emerald encased in a layer of clay, a sparkling sapphire suspended in a shallow glass sphere of water, a small diamond balanced perfectly on a thin stand, and a raw, uncut ruby embedded into a glowing ember. The four stones, once solitary and immobile, were slowly pulsating, as if they were almost vibrating, yet their movements were so fluid that it was difficult to believe that it was a simple model constructed out of wood and stone. At the base of the model was a large, thin marble slab, with measurements and plot lines carved delicately into its surface.

"Why is it going off like that?" asked Elara curiously. "Are you sure it's never done that before?"

"Never," Professor Neptune shook his head. "It's curious. I'll need to take a closer look later." He glanced at Argon again, furrowing his brow.

"It's marvelous," said Noiro, still examining the device. "I'm sure this is something the Royal Family would be quite interested in. What do you think, Elara?"

"I think so," Elara agreed, "It would definitely be a useful—"

"I've just remembered," Neptune interrupted the two uneasily. "I have to start to leave for an engagement." He moved himself in between Noiro and the dial, blocking it from his view.

Noiro folded his arms hesitantly. The shift in his old friend's demeanor had certainly caught him off guard. "We have to get going as well." He stood up, taking the hint. "Thank you for your time, Professor."

"Any time," Neptune chirped, clapping a hefty hand against Noiro's back. "Bye, now!" All traces of his friendly manner were wiped clean off his face, and he ushered them quickly out the door.

"Well. That was odd," said Miela, wiping her forehead as they clambered out of the cavern's steps. Elara nodded in agreement.

"Ah, it's natural of him to be wary of prying eyes," said Noiro. "Scholars are usually quite protective of their work, especially when they're still in the process of researching something new. If he makes a breakthrough,

I'm sure he wouldn't want to share credit with anyone else, nor risk someone else claiming that his work was their own."

"Hmm," Elara murmured. As curious as their visit was, she could understand why Professor Neptune was held with such high respect. She thought back to his explanation on the House of Wisdom, and his leading them through their conversation to draw connections between knowledge, civilization, and power. The significance of the Old Archive seemed more momentous now. She turned her head back to the cavern's entrance, the gravity of the world's knowledge encapsulated in the Earth's belly almost drawing her back in.

Indeed, Professor Neptune was a thought-provoking scholar. She could have never imagined herself be so engaged in a conversation about Pi, and yet, the Professor gripped them into a captivating lecture surrounding Pi and its mysteries.

She turned her attention to Noiro.

"Insightful visit," remarked Noiro as he clambered out behind the group. He slipped on the last step, almost knocking his head onto the stony platform. Argon, who had emerged just seconds before, turned instinctively and grabbed Noiro's arm, stopping him from hitting the floor. "Thank you," Noiro grunted, rubbing the back of his head sheepishly. Argon inclined his head at the man, saying nothing.

The group stood at the mouth of the cavern. The wind whistled through the rocks, ringing in Elara's ears.

Elara gasped suddenly. "The codes!" She whipped her head around back to the cavern's opening. "We left the copy of the codes with the Professor!"

"It's okay," Noiro reassured. "We can go get them back—"

"What if he figures it out? What if—"

"That's why we went down there to begin with," Noiro argued gently. "Besides, wouldn't it be a good thing if he figured them out? We can't seem to make any sense of them, ourselves."

"I think he'll have a hard time figuring the codes out," said Miela with a smirk. She gestured her head towards the path, silently ushering the group towards the pathway leading back towards the city. "I swiped them off of his desk."

Elara breathed a sigh of relief as Miela flashed them a handful of crumpled up papers from her pocket. "You're brilliant, Miela," she said, beaming at her friend. Even though they visited Professor Neptune for his help with the codes, the thought of having a copy of the codes with someone else made her stomach squirm.

"I *am* brilliant." Miela chuckled. "Come on. Let's go back to Noiro's."

The group walked along the pathway, following the way back to the heart of Polaris. Elara welcomed the growing warmth around her, which was far more comfortable than the chilly air that blew through the Old Archive caves.

The caves were well-hidden, almost impossible to find if one didn't know what to look for. Hidden in the outskirts of the coast, at the edge of a thick forest that surrounded the city of Polaris, the caves of the Old Archive were quite a trek from the main city's entrance. The pathway from the forest was covered in small shrubberies and lined with thick, leafy trees, their branches growing and interlocking with one another, blocking out the sunlight the deeper the path went into the forest. Eventually the trees cleared, and the forest's path turned from dirt to stony rubble and beach sand. High cliffs lined the coastline, and cold, icy winds gusted across the grey, foamy sea. The cave's entrance was etched into the side of one of the cliffs, shrouded by overgrown bushes and thick, long grass which blew in the wind, and further camouflaged by large stones and rocks. To the untrained eye, the cave's entrance appeared to be a shallow nook etched into the cliff's side. The only indicator that marked the cave's presence was the small symbol of Polaris etched into a stone in the center of the cave's entrance.

A few paces into the cavern, cloaked in the dark depths of the cavern's walls, stood a tall stone figure of a woman. The statue was weathered with age, and the carefully carved features were faded and smooth. The woman's long hair seeped from her head and into the rocky wall, and her flowing, stone dress was swept behind her. Her hands, stretched out before her and cupped together, cradled something in her grasp that was no longer there; her empty hands now caught the water droplets that dripped from the cave's ceiling, wearing away at her palms. On the floor, beneath the woman's feet, was an etched script that had eroded away with time. Elara could only ever make out the letter L.

Elara's mind wandered as she walked along the pathway. She wondered how Helia was doing. She couldn't take Helia along with them on their trek to the Old Archive, lest they draw more attention to the toddler. Elara bit her lip, remembering her struggle earlier that morning; she couldn't very well leave the toddler by herself at home, and she couldn't bring the toddler out with her, either. Although they faced little inquiry about Helia during their time at the Guardians' Headquarters, she did not want to take any chances and risk exposing Helia to any unwanted attention.

Miela suggested they leave Helia with their old friend, Tami Nassah, assuring Elara that Helia would be in the best care possible while they were on their mission.

Tami was a gentle soul, yet fierce with determination. As one of Polaris's renowned medics, she was held with the highest regards in medical circles. She also happened to have two adorable little puppies, which had the initially hesitant Helia, reluctant to leave her mother's side, delightfully bounding away with Tami's puppies, her anxiety about being without her mother for a few hours completely forgotten.

Elara was glad that Helia had her own ways of having fun, and hadn't seemed to pay much attention to the changes around her world, compared to what her world in the future must have been like. Elara wondered what her own life looked like during Helia's time.

She sighed.

There was no way to tell exactly what had happened in the future. She wished that Helia was old enough to recount her tale, or that her future self had written down clear, regular journal entries, instead of a series of codes.

"Here we are," said Noiro, interrupting Elara's thoughts. They had arrived at their home earlier than she had expected. Noiro pushed open his cottage's door, letting the group in.

"I'm famished," Miela stated, rubbing her belly as she walked in. "All those stairs…"

"I think I have some sandwiches in the kitchen," commented Noiro, leading the way to the kitchen. Miela followed, her stomach rumbling loudly.

With Miela and Noiro gone, Argon stood awkwardly in the middle of the cottage. Other than spending most of their childhood tormenting each other, he had rarely interacted with Elara before. He glanced at her, watching as she walked over to the sitting room, plopping herself down onto one of the chairs.

Argon frowned. He could hear Noiro and Miela chatter away in the kitchen. Elara was reaching for a book, paying no heed to the man standing in the middle of the house.

What was he doing here?

Argon walked over to one of the couches, setting himself down.

Here he was, involved in an intense case with people he was unfamiliar with, and even more so, quite not fond of. He toyed with the thought of making up an excuse to leave, and save himself from an evening of forced conversations and small talk.

"You can leave, you know," murmured Elara, not unkindly. She could only begin to understand the predicament he was in, and knew that if the roles were reversed somehow, and she were the one in a house with people she either disliked, or didn't know very well, that she would also be uncomfortable and awkward.

Argon shook his head. "We need to figure out those codes," he said. "What can I do to help?"

Elara looked at him contemplatively. Compared to the way he initially reacted when they revealed Helia and his adamant denial, he seemed completely invested in their tasks at hand. "Well, we're stuck on the codes for now," admitted Elara, "so until we crack the codes and figure out what they mean, let's try and gather every piece of information that we know so far."

"My thoughts exactly," agreed Noiro, walking back into the sitting room with a plate of stacked sandwiches, followed by Miela, who was contentedly munching away on her own sandwich. He set the plate down onto the table. "It'll be helpful to have everything we know in one place. Hold on, let me get some materials that might help us… Miela, could you give me a hand?"

Noiro and Miela trudged up the stairs, leaving Elara and Argon alone in the sitting room once again. It was quiet, save for the small sound of Noiro scuffling about on the second floor.

"I'd like to apologize," Argon blurted, breaking the silence.

Elara tilted her head curiously at the man, who was looking intently at her. "Apologize?" she repeated, surprised.

Argon nodded, looking down at his lap for a moment. "I was…unkind earlier," he acknowledged frankly, "when we met at the Guardians' Headquarters. It was uncalled for. I'd like to apologize for my behavior."

Elara was silent.

He continued, unwilling to carry on with the room's silence. "And the kid…Helia," he uttered, saying her name for the first time, "I regret the way I handled, well, everything. I've always been told that I don't take surprises very well. I guess it's true." He rubbed the back of his head in defeat.

"Being surprised doesn't give you a free pass to act

however you like," Elara scolded. She hadn't forgotten the look on Helia's face as Argon spewed angrily at them in Miela's office. "She's a child, you know."

"I know," Argon countered, his voice hardening. "And I'm trying to apologize."

"Does it matter? You shouldn't treat people like that." Her tone was sharp. She knew that he was trying to apologize, but her mind kept going back to his angry face, and then to Helia's heartbroken one. Anger ignited inside her, and her blood boiled. "And not just Helia. Look at the way you've treated me, ever since we were kids! You tormented me. You were cruel. How am I supposed to respect someone who thinks it's okay to treat people like that?"

"You're holding my behavior towards you when we were children against me?" Argon demanded, bewildered and angry. "We were kids! Kids fight all the time!"

"You haven't changed one bit." Elara scoffed. "You still just stand there in the corner, sulking away like a little boy."

"You haven't changed either," Argon shot back. "You're still a stubborn, insufferable know-it-all."

"I see you're both getting along swimmingly, as usual," Miela interrupted dryly as she descended the stairs, lugging along a large tray of books balanced on a giant board. Noiro trailed behind her, carrying an armful of books.

"He's unbearable," Elara huffed, turning around and crossing her arms disdainfully.

"Yeah, you're no walk in the park, either," spat Argon angrily.

"Fighting like this isn't doing anything to help,"

Noiro chastised, raising his voice over the bickering. "Grow up, the two of you. We have some work to do." He set down the books he was carrying on the table in the sitting room.

The two begrudgingly turned their attention to Noiro as he began to organize their materials. Noiro set up a large chalkboard at the head of the room. He drew a long line, marked with some points along the line's axis. Underneath each point, he stuck a few blank notes stacked underneath.

"This is the timeline," stated Noiro, pointing to the long line. "And these points represent points in time." He pointed to the marks he drew along the line.

Everyone nodded.

"All right, we'll start with the very basics," said Noiro. "What do we know?"

"We've learned quite a bit from what we could gather from Helia," provided Elara, cupping her chin as she thought. "We know she comes from at least five years from the future, 9382…"

Noiro nodded, jotting down the year at the endpoint of the timeline, and scribbling Helia's name underneath.

"What else?"

"We know we're her parents," Elara continued, avoiding Argon's gaze.

Argon nodded.

Noiro hummed softly as he scribbled down the note onto the timeline. "What else do we know?"

"Well…We know that you died," Argon remarked solemnly as he turned to face Elara.

She nodded. "With the amount of blood—*my* blood—that we found on Helia when she first showed up... I think that's a safe bet to make." Elara shuddered at the thought of her bloody demise. From the way blood was sprayed and splattered on Helia and her clothes, it looked like Elara was slaughtered in front of the toddler.

"Not just you, Argon, too," Noiro voiced softly. He turned to the Lieutenant. "You didn't catch what Helia said when she first saw you?"

Argon shook his head. "I barely registered anything when she first saw me," he admitted. "All I remember was a random child pointing and yelling at me. The next thing I knew, I was hauled off to my commanding officer's office, and sworn to secrecy over a future war we're trying to prevent."

Noiro couldn't help but feel slightly ashamed as he listened to Argon's recount of how he was introduced to the entire ordeal. He remembered how, in the heat of the moment, they quickly pounced on the Lieutenant when they met in the Guardians' Headquarters. No wonder Argon had been so defensive and wary of them.

"What *did* Helia say? I didn't catch it either," asked Elara, snapping Noiro out of his train of thought.

"Er, she said that her dad was back...from the sky. Could she have meant heaven? I'm guessing that means that somewhere down the line, Argon, you died," he finished simply.

"Oh." Argon blinked. He glanced sideways at Elara, who he knew had suffered a bloody death. How did he die? Was it painful? Was it peaceful? Or was it violent? A dozen questions flooded into his head as the thought of his own demise manifested.

Argon saw Noiro and Elara continue speaking, but he couldn't concentrate. He noticed Miela leaning into the conversation, pulling out a large map and pointing to different areas. Their voices faded to a soft buzz in the background as he withdrew internally.

As a Guardian, Argon was an experienced combatant. He was used to facing potentially lethal conditions, and had faced many close calls in the past. Even still, the idea of his own mortality never seemed tangible, and he rarely ever dwelled on it.

And yet, there they were, discussing his death as a real event that took place in the future.

Five years. Perhaps even less than that. That was all he had left.

Argon thought hard. Could their efforts in changing the future also change his death? Was he being selfish for wondering about his own death? Argon winced internally. Guilt gnawed at his belly as he thought about the several thousands of lives also resting on the decisions they were making at this very moment to try and prevent the upcoming war, and yet, here he was, wondering about his own death.

For the first time, Argon felt scared.

"Oh my God." Miela's voice pierced Argon's thoughts. He lifted his head to see Miela staring at the map she laid out on the table, her eyes wide.

"Miela?" Elara snapped her head towards her friend.

"I know what they are," Miela repeated, her voice low. She looked up at the group, her face brightening up.

"What are you talking about?" asked Noiro. "What do you know?"

"The codes!" Miela exclaimed, waving her arms frantically. "I know what the codes are!"

"What?" Elara's mouth fell open. "How? What is it?"

"Coordinates," Miela blurted quickly. "They're not codes. They're coordinates."

SHADOWS OF TIME

"They're coordinates!" Miela repeated frantically. She pulled out a couple of crumpled up balls of paper from her pocket and smoothed it out over the table. The paper was the one she swiped earlier from Professor Neptune's office, which had one of the codes from Elara's journal copied onto it. She pulled it close to the map on the table, which was lined with grids.

"Look, over here," Miela pointed excitedly to one of the grid's squares. "By Polaris Castle. This grid, here."

"It's Noiro's cottage," remarked Elara, examining the map's grid.

"Yes, but look," insisted Miela, tapping her finger at the edges of the map. "See how there are numbers at the beginning of each notch of the grid? The numbers that mark the vertical lines of the grid make up the longitude, and the ones on the horizontal lines make up the latitude." She put a finger on the map, pointing at Noiro's cottage.

"Take this point for example. Follow the vertical and horizontal line back to the numbers at the edge, and there you have it! You have your coordinates!"

The group looked at her.

She pointed to the code from Elara's journal. "The codes are coordinates!" Miela's eyes gleamed in excitement. Sure enough, the coordinates of Noiro's cottage matched the exact sequence of numbers that made up the code.

"Of course!" Noiro's jaw dropped. "How could we have missed that?"

"I'm a genius," Miela exhaled, grinning as she folded her arms proudly.

"I'm betting that the future Elara figured that you would know what these numbers were." Noiro beamed proudly at Miela. "Well done!"

"Miela, you're brilliant," Elara admired.

"And look!" Miela continued, pointing to the continuing sequence of numbers on the page. "Each page is dated, so we know that the date on this page, July 2nd, 9377, with the coordinates of Noiro's cottage…"

"That must mean that something significant happened over here," mused Noiro.

"It had to be significant enough for you to note it down. And July 2, that's only a few days away," remarked Elara.

"It looks like we have our starting point for the timeline," said Noiro, turning his attention back to his chalkboard. He marked the starting point of the line with the date.

Elara frowned. If that was the starting point, then that meant they only had a few days until the first significant event happened that would trigger the beginning of the end.

They didn't have much time.

"So, what now?" asked Argon, who had been quiet throughout the commotion.

The excitement in the room died down at Argon's words. Sure, they figured out the codes. But what was next?

"Are we just supposed to wait and see what happens on July 2nd?" Elara wondered out loud. "That seems counterintuitive. Especially if we're meant to change the future events."

"I don't think we're supposed to wait," said Noiro, shaking his head. "Besides, with the butterfly effect, that date is now arbitrary."

Elara let out a frustrated sigh. "Well, then what?"

The group sat in silence for a moment, racking their brains.

"Hold on," murmured Noiro. He stood up and walked over to the research laboratory.

The group waited in silence.

Noiro emerged seconds later, carrying Helia's necklace. "Helia used this to bend time," he reminded them, holding up the necklace. "What if we can use it the same way she did?" Noiro glanced at the room's occupants, and then back at the pendant. "Look at the notches and dials embedded into the Aether pendant. They're numbered."

"The codes?" Elara suggested, raising an eyebrow.

Noiro nodded. "What if we input the codes into the Aether Stone?"

"You're not suggesting that we travel back in time ourselves...?" Elara was alarmed. "We don't even know how to use that thing!"

"Also," Miela added incredulously, "what about the butterfly effect that you keep rambling on about? What if we go into the future and, I dunno, step on a bug by accident, and change everything again?"

"Bending time doesn't necessarily mean travelling through time," explained Noiro thoughtfully. He picked up the completed research journal from the future and flipped through the pages. Noiro topped at a chapter and turned it around for the group to see.

"Shadows of Time," Elara read aloud. She looked up at Noiro, the gears in her head turning. She gaped at him. "We were right?"

He nodded, smiling.

Miela shook her head, still confused. "What do you mean?"

"It's one of the theories Elara and I have been working on," Noiro elaborated. "Creating a shadow of time. A way to bend time without actually travelling to it."

"Is that even possible?" asked Miela incredulously.

"Well, it *was* just a theory. You see, instead of bending time and traveling through it, the idea is to bend time *just enough* for that point in time to cast a shadow. That way, we can view events in time, but without actually moving through time ourselves," Noiro clarified. "I think we must have figured it out in the future, because the completed chapter is here in the research journal. A marvelous stroke of luck."

Elara smiled.

Noiro furrowed his brow as he scanned through the chapter, his glasses slipping down the bridge of his nose as he leaned his head close to the book. He trailed his finger down one of the pages, slowly coming to a stop as a huge grin broke across his face.

"What?" wondered Elara, looking at Noiro.

He looked up, turning the book around to show her. "According to our book, all we need is the Aether Stone…and a sundial."

"Well, I'll be damned," she gasped incredulously and looked up at Noiro. "It's that simple?"

"Most inventions have to be simple so that they can be used effectively," Noiro pointed out with a grin adorning his face.

"You see the dials on the Aether Stone?" asked Noiro, holding the pendant up again.

Elara examined the three dials that encircled the stone. Upon closer inspection, she noticed tiny numbers inscribed on top of each notch around the dials. "Hmm…"

"The dials act like a combination code. If we enter in the codes from the journal, we should be able to use the Aether Stone to navigate to that point in time," Noiro gushed eagerly. "When bending time, one would wear the pendant, spin the dials to match the sequence of coordinates, date, and time, and the wearer would be transported."

"But we're not moving through time," Miela repeated.

Noiro nodded. "We're going to cast a shadow of time," he clarified once again. "Argon, I need a hand with bringing the sundial in."

Argon nodded, and the two men quickly went outside to haul the large, stone sundial back into the house.

"We designed the Aether Stone to fit the tools we already have," Noiro recognized, carefully twisting the dials around the Aether Stone. With the last number from the code in place, Noiro set the Aether Stone in the center on the sundial.

Just as soon as he did so, the room flashed around them. Elara felt dizzy as she watched the bright swirls of colors whizzing by and spinning about. Just as suddenly as it began, it stopped. Elara looked around her to see that the room looked exactly the same, except darker.

"What...what are we?" Argon stuttered, blinking as he tried to steady himself.

"Ah!" Miela cried in surprise as a woman walked right through her. "What the—"

"That's me," Elara gasped, pointing at the woman who strolled into the laboratory and began stacking up some books onto one of the desks, her telltale satchel lying on the chair beside her.

"It worked," Noiro breathed, gaping at his surroundings.

The visiting Elara walked over to future Elara, examining her closely. "So that's what my hair looks like," she hummed.

"Noiro! Elara! I'm here," a voice called. The visiting group turned around to see future Miela striding into the cottage. "I picked up some dinner for us. I figured you'd be hungry."

They watched as future Elara, Noiro, and Miela gathered around the sitting room table.

"So, what are we supposed to do? Just watch?" asked the visiting Argon.

"I guess so." The visiting Noiro shrugged. "Keep your eyes peeled for anything that sticks out to you as odd."

As soon as he said that, a loud knock rapped against

the cottage's front door. Future Noiro looked up in surprise.

"Are you expecting anyone?" asked future Miela.

Future Noiro shook his head. "Argon?" he said in surprise. Future Argon looked hesitant as he stood in front of the door. He was dressed in a casual pair of trousers and loose-fitted shirt, a stark difference from his usual Guardian uniform. "Can I help you?" Noiro asked uncertainly.

Future Argon opened his mouth to say something, and then paused. Argon was a proud man, and facing Noiro, a man he severely disliked, was conflicting. The internal battle that raged inside him was apparent on his face.

"Argon?" Noiro repeated.

"I'm looking for Captain Miela," said future Argon finally, his voice hard and his posture straight and official. "Is she here?"

"Lieutenant?" Future Miela gently pushed her way past Noiro. "Is something the matter? Am I needed back at headquarters?"

Future Argon glared, his teeth gritted together as he shook his head no. The smell of their dinner from inside wafted through, and future Argon faltered.

"I apologize, Captain. I see I've interrupted—"

"Lieutenant. You're here already. If you have something to say, then say it." Miela folded her arms. Argon nodded.

"This is…This is about something personal, Captain," said Argon stiffly. "I need to talk. Privately."

"And it couldn't wait until tomorrow, when we're back at headquarters?" Miela raised an eyebrow curiously.

Argon shook his head. He looked hesitant to say

anything else, his eyes darting to Noiro, who was still standing at the doorway.

"I'll step outside then," offered Miela, sensing his apprehension.

"No, please." Noiro held his hands up. "It's too hot outside. Come in. You two can use my office."

Argon followed Miela as she led the way into Noiro's cottage. Future Elara looked up from her seat at the table, curious. Her eyes widened in surprise as she recognized her old childhood rival solemnly following Miela into Noiro's private office.

The visiting group scrambled to get into the door, eager to hear what future Argon needed to say.

Future Miela was leaning her hips against the table, watching Argon as he stood facing her. He looked wary, and his eyes seemed tired, as if he hadn't slept for a long time.

Future Miela seemed to notice his demeanor. Concern flitted across her face, and she folded her arms.

"So, Lieutenant. What's going on?" asked Miela.

Argon began to slowly pace back and forth. His face twisted, as if he were in pain. Finally, he spoke. "I was attacked."

"Attacked?" Miela repeated in alarm. "By who? Are you okay? What happened?"

"No... I... No," Argon admitted, embarrassed. "I'm not sure what happened, exactly."

"Tell me everything you can," Miela urged. She leaned forward, watching Argon.

"I was out with some friends last night," he began. "We were celebrating Yun Zeru's promotion."

"Yun Zeru?" asked Miela, surprised. Argon nodded.

"Who's Yun Zeru?" hissed the visiting Elara, her eyes still trained on the pair conversing before her.

"You don't know who he is?" The visiting Noiro sounded surprised. "Everyone knows who he is! He used to be the Queen's Advisor."

"He resigned after the coup," the visiting Miela added. "He enlisted as a Guardian. Pretty high up, actually."

"Really?"

"Pay attention to what they're saying!" Noiro hissed at the two women. "We might miss something important."

The group turned their attention back to the future Miela and Argon.

"Yes. He just made General, and he invited some of us out to celebrate," future Argon continued. "I left earlier than everyone else, since I was supposed to get up early for a drill. And I…" Argon stopped pacing, standing near the edge of the study's desk and resting his palm on the wooden surface. "I was just walking down the road. And… I don't know what happened next." Argon put a hand to his forehead. "I woke up at home. My body was covered in bruises…" Argon paused, looking at the floor. "Whoever it was, they knew where I lived. They took me to my home… They beat me…" Argon lifted his sleeve, revealing trails of angry, blistering welts that travelled up his arm.

"You weren't just beaten," the future Miela gawked at the gashes in his arm. "You were burned!"

Argon nodded, pulling his sleeve back down. "That's not all," he said. "My home was ransacked. All of the furniture was knocked over, and my family pictures were removed from their frames. We can't find them anywhere; I think they took it with them. The doors and windows were left wide open, too. My mother's jewels were also taken."

Miela remained silent as she listened to Argon recount his experience. "I'm sorry, Lieutenant," she whispered. "I'll send a team down to check it out. We'll get to the bottom of this."

Argon shook his head, exhaling angrily. "That's not the worst of it," he said. "There was also a message. Written in blood."

"What?"

"It was written in blood," Argon repeated. "It covered my entire bedroom wall, floor to ceiling. '*We know*' in blood."

Miela furrowed her brow. "What do you think they mean?"

Argon shrugged, shaking his head. "I don't know."

Miela sighed. "Argon, I'm really sorry this happened." She paused. "Hold on…You said the writing took up the whole wall?"

Argon nodded. "Floor to ceiling."

"There's no way that much blood could be used…unless someone was…"

"Harmed. Or dead," Argon finished.

"This is…I can't…" Miela exhaled, closing her eyes. "Lieutenant, I understand your need for discretion around your case, given your circumstances. But you know very well that if there's a case involving murder, it will be difficult to—"

"Captain, there's a reason why I'm coming straight to you instead of reporting it to the other authorities. I think… I think we *need* to keep this quiet," he said. "Not just for my sake."

Miela was silent.

"Think about this," he urged. "I'm a Lieutenant with the Guardians. I was with a bunch of royal officials last night. Not many people are that closely connected with them. If word got out that I was attacked…"

"They might take it as a message against the Guardians, or worse, the Royal Family," finished Miela, a far off look in her eye. "Especially with Yun Zeru in the mix…"

"It's not easy to break into my house to begin with," continued Argon.

Miela nodded in agreement. Being a Guardian, his house should have been well warded. "Do you know anyone who would try to scare you? Someone resentful, maybe? Maybe someone who wants to get into Yun Zeru's inner circle?"

Argon shrugged. "I'm not sure. Not many people know I'm affiliated with Yun Zeru." He began to pace again. "Even you weren't aware, and you're my commanding officer."

Miela nodded.

"I don't know," sighed Argon. "Being a Guardian, I know I've made some enemies. But I don't know *anyone* who would do something like that."

"All right, Lieutenant. I'll check it out, and I'll keep it low profile," Miela assured the distraught man. "But I'll need to put together a task force."

"People you trust to keep this case confidential, I hope." Argon crossed his arms, his eyebrows pulled together in worry.

"Sargent Esen and Detective Vega," Miela suggested. "They're one of our best."

"All right. Do we need any consultants?"

"Maybe," hummed Miela. "Elara's been brought on a few of our more recent cases as a junior consultant. She doesn't have much experience under her belt, but you can trust her."

Argon nodded, silently giving his consent. He wasn't fond of his childhood rival, but he could not argue with her intellect.

"Let's go," said Miela, hastily walking out of the room. Argon turned foot and followed.

"What's the next code sequence?" whispered the visiting Noiro.

The visiting Elara jerked in surprise at his voice, pulling her out of the conversation that she was so immersed in. Elara showed Noiro the next page, and he spun the Aether Stone's dials to the next code. The visiting group gasped as the world around them suddenly changed.

"What just happened?" cried the visiting Miela, alarmed.

"We're moving onto the next code sequence from the journal. A different day," Elara explained. Argon nodded, his alarm apparent as well at the sudden change.

The group turned their attention to future Elara, who was fumbling with a set of keys as she tried to open up a locked door, balancing a stack of books and papers in her other arm.

"Where are we?" asked Elara.

"Guardian Headquarters," Miela whispered, eyeing the rows of marble bookshelves carved into the wall. She pointed to her new Guardian uniform. "You're a consultant."

"Elara!" a voice called out from the other end of the hallway. Some Guardians looked disapprovingly as a tall uniform-clad man ran down the otherwise silent hall.

"Elara, have you seen Captain Miela anywhere?" the man asked.

Elara let out a small, triumphant exhale as she finally fit the right key into the door. She gestured for the man to follow her into the room. "I'm supposed to meet her in an hour," Elara said, dropping the stack of books onto her table with a loud thud. "Why?"

"It's urgent," the man insisted. "I need to speak to her now."

"Oh no." Elara's face fell. "Vega, what is it?"

The Detective sighed, shaking his head. "It's the Erifs," he muttered darkly.

Elara gasped and covered her mouth. "The Erifs? Did they find her body?"

"Inana? No." Vega shook his head. "It's her parents. Mr. and Mrs. Erif. They're dead."

Elara gasped, and sat down slowly in her chair. "How?"

"It looks like a double suicide," Vega mumbled. "It started off like any other call. One of the neighbors called in a welfare check on the Erifs. The front door had been left open for a couple of days. When I got there… Oh, God, the stench. I knew we were too late." Vega closed his eyes, shuddering at the memory of the two bodies strewn across the living room carpet.

"Suicide?" Elara whispered, horrified. "Do you think that maybe…losing Inana…?"

Vega shook his head again. "Maybe. I don't know. I don't think it's a suicide. It sure looks like it, though. But something's off."

"What makes you think that?"

Vega shrugged. "There was still some food on the

table. Half eaten. It was covered in flies by the time we got there, given the door was open for a few days. But who would commit suicide in the middle of having dinner?" Vega put his hands on his side. "There was no sign of a struggle, either, which is strange. If an intruder had come in, I'm sure there would have been some signs of resistance. You know what Mr. Erif is like. He's a big man; he'd fight back."

Elara nodded. She had known the Erifs for a long time, and it was certainly unlike Mr. Erif not to engage in a scuffle had an intruder broken in.

"They also had some suitcases packed, as if they were ready to leave," continued Detective Vega.

"Leave? Elara asked, putting a hand to her chin.

Vega nodded. "Most of their clothes were packed. Some valuables, too. A lot of money. It looked like they were going to leave for good."

"Something must've scared them off. They were still waiting to hear any news about Inana," said Elara, frowning.

"I know. It doesn't make sense. But the lead officer responding to the call was adamant about reporting it as a suicide. Everything's off about this," he confessed. "That's why I need to meet with Captain Miela. She'll be upset if this case goes to anyone else. She's been trying to find Inana for months now."

Elara got up from her chair. "You're right," she agreed. Miela had been looking for Inana for the last five months; she would definitely want to know. Elara bit her lip. She knew the chances of finding Inana alive were slim to none. But her parents never lost hope, clinging to any bit of information they could get their hands on regarding their daughter's whereabouts.

"Five months," the visiting Elara murmured, her thoughts focused on what her future self said about Inana.

"December," the visiting Noiro remarked quietly. He held up Elara's journal. "The journal was marked December."

Noiro glanced at Argon, whose face was dark with horror and fear. Inana had been a close friend of Argon's. "We were neighbors back in Ursa Isles when we were growing up," the visiting Argon uttered softly. "She was my friend."

"We're going to stop this," the visiting Miela asserted.

Argon nodded, his resolve burning inside him.

"It's been five months since the attack on Argon," the visiting Elara noted. "Five months since Argon's attack, and five months since Inana went missing. And the future Elara mentioned that she assumed Inana was already dead. Could Inana's blood be the one found in Argon's room?"

Argon grew even more worried at Elara's words. Her conclusion certainly made sense. Could it be?

The group stood still as the world shifted around them again. Elara looked up to see that future Elara, Noiro, Miela, and Argon were on a small boat, floating through a deep, serene ocean. Miela and Argon sat at the head of the boat, while Noiro and Elara sat in the rear. Future Miela grunted lightly as she heaved an oar into the water, steering the boat through a collection of small islands and sandbars. Argon rowed in unison, expertly navigating through the area.

"Where are we?" the visiting Elara asked.

"Ursa Isles," murmured the visiting Argon. He was definitely familiar with his hometown, although it had been years since he had last gone back.

"Stop your whining," future Elara laughed, catching the visiting group's attention. "It's a beautiful day for being out at sea. And it's the first lead we've had in ages."

"I'm not complaining," future Argon grumbled, although there was a hint of mirth in his tone. "I just don't understand why *I* have to come, too."

"You know exactly why," future Elara chided. "Except for you, we've all never been to Ursa Isles before. Besides, your sister isn't exactly going to give up information so easily to a bunch of strangers."

"Yeah, yeah," future Argon muttered, steering the boat forward. Elara nudged him, smirking. He smiled at Elara, nudging her back.

"Y'know, I'm not so sure why *you're* here, either," Argon continued teasingly. "I thought only Guardians were involved in solving cases."

Elara scoffed. "After being involved for over a year now, I think I'm pretty much a Guardian." She grinned. "Besides, there's not much to it. Just snap my feet together when someone walks by and look serious." She pulled together a solemn look, which quickly broke out into laughter.

"Hey! You got him to smile!" Miela chuckled, turning her head. "He's been groaning and moaning all day about this call."

They drew closer to a small island, and Miela and Argon landed the boat onto its sandy shores. The group clambered out of the boat, helping to push it further up the beach and clear out of the tide's reach.

They turned and walked up the beach, following Argon as he led them up a sandy pathway through the island's vegetation.

The small tropical forest cleared, and the visiting Elara could make out houses beginning to dot the horizon.

"This way," said future Argon as he led them up another pathway. Even though it had been years since he had last been here, his body moved automatically towards his old childhood home.

The group followed Argon to a small, yellow house at the end of the pathway. A few palm trees stood at either side of the house's entrance, and some small, red flowers crept up the sides of the fence.

"This it?" inquired future Miela, looking at Argon.

He nodded in response, looking at his sister's house. His grin slipped away from his face, suddenly feeling guilty. He couldn't remember the last time he had visited her.

"All right. Argon, do you mind starting us off? I need to find my notebook," Miela trailed off as she dug around in her satchel.

Argon nodded and lifted his hand to knock on the door, pulling himself into a dignified, disciplined stance. Elara fought back the urge to laugh; she had seen Argon slip in and out of his military-trained stance a thousand times, and it always entertained her.

He rapped his knuckles on the door. A small shuffling noise sounded from behind the door, followed by a small click as a lock slid out of its place.

Elara smiled cheerily as a tall woman with short, curly black hair answered the door.

Argon stared, stunned at the familiar face staring back at him.

Elara looked at Argon, waiting for him to speak. He

looked perplexed, frowning as he stared at his sister. The woman stared back at him, her eyes almost blank.

Something was not right.

Elara, growing more uncomfortable with the prolonged silence, stepped forward towards the woman.

"Estelle Tawer," she greeted, extending her arm out to shake her hand as she smiled warmly. "I'm Elara Jove. I believe we—"

"ELARA!"

The visiting group were stunned by the sudden action of future Argon. From where they stood, it looked like a cordial greeting, and were shocked by future Argon's shout and the way he shoved future Elara roughly to the ground. But nothing shocked them more than the sudden shriek from the older woman as she charged towards them, a sharp knife drawn. The woman fell to the floor, missing her target, her knife still clutched tightly in her fist. She lifted her head, her short, curly hair tumbling over her face, her wild eyes darting fervently back and forth from beneath her messy locks. She yanked herself up and lunged again, this time towards future Argon, the point of the knife aimed directly at his face.

Future Noiro moved quickly, ramming his body into her from the side and intercepting the crazed woman's attack. She fell to the floor once more, whimpering as Noiro held her head with one hand and the knife in the other. Estelle glanced desperately at the door to her house, and then back down the road away from it. The internal battle the woman was fighting was apparent: should she make a run for it?

The door to her house creaked ajar.

"There's someone in there!" future Miela yelled, and

ran into the house in pursuit of the hidden offender, leaving Estelle on the ground, with Noiro still on top of her, attempting to hold her down.

Estelle let out a terrified wail at the sight of the door moving. A sudden surge of adrenaline rushed through her, and she flipped over Noiro, grabbing the knife away from him. In one swift motion, Estelle plunged the sharp blade into her neck and ripped it open.

The visiting and future onlookers watched in horror as Estelle Tawer gurgled and choked on her own blood, her body twitching horribly as a deep crimson stain rapidly grew larger on her blue cotton dress.

"Damn it," future Argon cursed loudly. He frantically moved towards his sister, quickly turning her over and pressing his hands to the wound on her neck, applying pressure. Her head slumped over lifelessly, and his hands slipped over the blood. "Elara, get something to stop the bleeding!"

"It's no use," future Elara cried, scrambling for a piece of cloth and pressing it to the woman's neck. "She hit the jugular vein. She's dead."

"We have to try!" Argon pleaded, gawping at his dying sister. He lay her flat on the ground and began to perform chest compressions, trying to revive her heart. Tears gathered in the corner of his eyes as her body jerked lifelessly underneath the pressure of his palms.

Noiro was still frozen to his spot on the ground next to him, eyes glued on Estelle.

Argon let out a frustrated growl as his efforts to revive her were clearly failing. A loud snap sounded from her chest, and Argon froze. "Her rib," he moaned in horror. He moved away from the body, suddenly afraid to touch her. Her head lolled lifelessly to the side.

There was no point in continuing the resuscitation. She was dead.

Elara moved a hand onto Argon's arm. Her hands were slippery with blood. He put a hand over hers, squeezing it tightly as he stared blankly at his sister's dead body.

A scream ripped through the house.

"Miela!" future Noiro yelled. The three sprang into action, racing towards the source of the scream.

The visiting group held their breath as they watched their future selves run full-tilt through the house, anxiety coursing through their veins as they craned their necks to see what happened next. Before they could see what happened inside the house, the world changed around them again.

"No! Damn it! What happened?" Elara demanded, whirling around to look at Noiro, who was twisting the Aether stone to the next page in the journal.

"Damn it!" she cursed again, turning away from Noiro.

"Easy, El," Miela murmured, her voice wobbling. The tremble in her voice was barely there.

"Miela? Miela!" Elara's voice interrupted the outburst amongst the visiting group, and they turned their attention back to the new scene materializing in front of them.

"You're okay," the visiting Noiro breathed in relief, looking at future Miela walking down a hallway.

Future Elara was running through a long, narrow hallway, her footsteps thundering as she raced to catch up with the tall, blonde woman in the crisp Celestial Forces uniform.

"Miela! What is it? Is everything alright? I got your message. Did something—"

"We have to go," future Miela urged, her face pale with panic.

Future Elara's breath caught in her throat at her friend's stance. It usually meant one of two things: someone was in trouble, or dead.

She dreaded either.

"Miela? What happened?"

"I'll explain on the way. Let's go."

"Just tell me," Elara pleaded desperately. "Who? Who is it this time?"

Miela gritted her teeth, turning to look at Elara. "We just got the call. The Tawers."

"No!" Elara's breath caught in her throat as the blood drained from her face. "Argon?"

"I don't know, yet," Miela faltered.

Elara gulped hard.

"Wear your armor, and don't leave my side," said Miela, shoving a bag into Elara's hands.

Future Miela and Elara raced into the next room, and the visiting observers watched as the world changed around them again.

It was the same night. Future Miela and Elara were sprinting across a lawn and leapt over a small fence, both clad in a thin, flexible, metallic armor. Miela's Captain insignia flashed in the moonlight as they swept through the grounds. The house that once stood in the center of the grounds now lay in ruins. The visiting Elara glanced back at the visiting Argon, anxiously inspecting his reaction at seeing his home destroyed. Indeed, Argon looked like he was going to be sick.

"Are there any survivors? Do we know who is in there?" future Miela barked at one of the moving officers combing through the scene. The officer glanced at a body a few feet away, lying face down. The remains of a pale pink night dress was draped over the body's thin frame, and an unruly mop of familiar curly black hair spread across the floor. A small pool of blood trickled out from beneath the body. Future Elara looked away. She didn't need to see any more to know who it was.

The visiting Argon's blood ran cold as he stared at the remains of his mother's body. He took a step forward, and then hesitated. He felt like he was going to be sick.

"Nothing happened yet," the visiting Elara reminded him gently. "We're going to prevent all of this."

The visiting Argon showed no signs of acknowledgement, his face stoic.

"Sweep the area," future Miela commanded. "Look for any other bodies."

Future Elara glued herself to Miela's side as they moved to examine another section of the house.

"Over there!" future Miela yelled, pointing to a pale hand that was sticking out from beneath some debris. The two women heaved their bodies against the wooden structure, trying to move it off of the body beneath.

There, lying on his side, was Argon Tawer. Elara knelt near his head and placed her fingers on the pulse point on his neck, tears welling up in her eyes.

The visiting Elara's eyes were tearing up in the same way, completely immersed in the scene before them. She looked over at the visiting Argon, who was staring at his own body, completely numb.

"Oh God," future Elara breathed shakily. "Oh God…"

"Is he…?"

Future Elara's body shook as she stared at the still body

before her. "We promised him we'd protect him. We said we would… Damn it! Why didn't he leave? He should have left! Damn it, Argon!"

"We couldn't make him leave Polaris," Miela replied quietly. "He wouldn't go. He wouldn't abandon—"

"He should have!" Elara cried.

"This isn't right," whispered the visiting Elara.

"This shouldn't happen," the visiting Miela agreed. "How did—"

"No, I mean this isn't it. This isn't right," said the visiting Elara seriously. "Argon can't be dead. You're not dead. You can't be; we haven't seen Helia yet. You can't be dead."

The visiting Argon, Noiro, and Miela looked at each other and nodded gratefully at the visiting Elara for the reminder. She was right.

"Elara… I still have to…" future Miela began uneasily, kneeling beside the visiting Elara.

"I know," future Elara answered, her eyes glued to Argon. "Do what you have to do. I'll stay here."

"I'll send someone to…"

"Just go, Miela," Elara cried. Miela nodded silently. She squeezed her shoulder, and then quickly got up to search for any more bodies in the house.

Elara looked back down at Argon and scooted closer, turning him over so he was lying on his back. His eyes were still open, and his arm landed on the floor with a thud. She pressed her palm over his eyes, closing them shut. His mouth was still slightly ajar. If she didn't know any better, she would have guessed that he was sleeping.

"I'm sorry," she murmured sorrowfully, turning her head away from his body. She couldn't bear to look at him like that anymore. She inhaled deeply, tears falling freely down her face. She moved to get up, and paused as she heard the faint sound of glass tinkling against the floor. Her head snapped down towards the sound, curiosity momentarily overshadowing her grief as her eyes fell upon an object that rolled out of Argon's fingers.

"There. What's that?" The visiting Miela pointed.

"A vial. It's empty," the visiting Elara remarked, kneeling down next to her future self. "The label's scratched off here a bit…" She frowned, and then her face brightened up with realization. "It's from Noiro's laboratory!"

Future Elara studied the vial, frowning as she recognized the vial as one of Noiro's vials. She ran her finger over the scratched label and then uncorked the vial, lifting it to her nose. She scrunched up her face sourly as a strong, bitter smell wafted into her nostrils, and she exhaled in distaste. Elara furrowed her brow, thinking hard.

Suddenly, she dropped the bottle and pulled herself closer to Argon's head, gently pulling back his eyelids.

"What's happening?" the visiting Argon demanded. "What is she doing? What are you doing?"

"I'm not sure," the visiting Elara replied. "I think she must've figured out something—"

Future Elara gasped and shot up to her feet.

"Miela. Miela! His eyes! His pupils! Call Noiro! Call Noiro now!" Future Elara's voice drowned out the visiting one as she took off after future Miela.

"What? What?" Future Miela whirled around, two other officers nearby watching Elara as she ran towards them.

"Call Noiro," she said, panting. "Ask him to check his vials."

"His what?"

"His vials!" future Elara repeated frantically. "Are any of them missing? Ask him which one. Quickly!"

Future Miela moved hastily, pulling out a small phone from her pocket and punched in Noiro's number.

Elara watched as Miela quickly relayed what she was just told, nodding as she listened intently. Elara could hear Noiro's voice trickling out from the receiver, and Miela nodded again, watching her frantic friend.

"You're right," Miela confirmed. "A few vials are missing, actually. Why? Wh—"

Elara snatched the phone away from Miela and pressed it to her ear. "Noiro. Which ones are missing?"

"Elara?" Noiro's worried voice trickled into her ear.

"Which ones? Quick, Noiro!"

"Er, a few vials of nitric acid, celestial essence, atropine, and a couple of vials of pilocarpine," Noiro's voice crackled through the phone.

"I knew it," she hissed excitedly. "Thank you, Noiro!" She tossed the phone back to Miela and took off running back to future Argon's body.

She dropped to her knees, beginning to desperately search around Argon. The visiting group anxiously peered over future Elara's shoulder as she continued her search. Finding nothing, she turned her attention to the body.

"Come on, come on," she muttered to herself as she patted anxiously at Argon's pockets. She stopped at his breast pocket and quickly stuck her hand in to pull something out. There, in her fist, was another vial.

"Good work, Tawer," Elara breathed quietly, grasping

the vial in her hand.

"What are you doing?" asked future Miela, who tailed her childhood friend back to Argon.

Elara didn't answer. She examined the vial closely.

"Atropine. He took atropine," said the visiting Elara as she watched her future self urgently pull at the second vial's cork with her teeth. "It slows your body functions down; your heart rate, your breathing, everything. It's highly unstable. Too much of it could kill you."

"That's what she meant when she was talking about his pupils earlier," explained the visiting Noiro. "One of the telltale signs of atropine poisoning is dilated pupils."

"What is she doing, then?" the visiting Miela repeated Argon's earlier question.

"Using the antidote, I think," mused the visiting Elara. "Argon must have stashed the antidote in his pocket."

Indeed, future Elara popped open the vial's stopper, and drew closer to Argon. "You'd better hope this works," she whispered to the man lying on the floor, trying to steady her hands as she lifted the vial to his mouth, slowly drizzling the liquid down his throat. She lifted his head, trying to help the liquid go down.

Come on, Argon, she pleaded internally as she pressed her fingers against his neck, praying for any sign of a pulse. *Please...*

The observers, both visiting and future ones, held their breaths in anticipation, watching. Even though the visitors knew that future Argon would survive the atropine poisoning, they couldn't help but worry as they watched the man lie lifelessly before them.

A wave of excitement flooded into future Elara when she felt a faint flutter beneath his skin as his heart beat a little stronger. She poured a little more of the liquid antidote into future Argon's mouth, tipping his head back and pressing her finger down onto his tongue. He made a small gagging noise, and the liquid drained down into his throat. A chuckle punctuated a small sob as future Elara saw future Argon's face regain some color.

"Good... Argon, one more..."

She poured down the rest of the liquid into his mouth, watching in relief as he gagged and swallowed. She took a step back and watched anxiously. Future Miela put a hand on her friend's shoulder. Elara put her hand on top of Miela's and squeezed, holding her breath.

Future Argon suddenly gasped, taking in a deep breath. His eyes were still shut.

"Argon?" Elara called, shaking his shoulder softly.

Nothing.

"Argon? Argon, wake up." Her voice rose as panic began to set in once more. She shook him a little harder. Her heart thundered in her ears as she repeated, "Wake up."

The man lay motionless.

"Get up, Argon," she commanded, tapping his shoulder. "Argon. Argon, get up, damn it!"

Argon raggedly breathed in again, and let out a small groan.

"Wake up," Elara ordered shakily, her eyes raw as tears blurred her vision once more. "Wake up!" she shook him harder. Miela held her breath.

The man stirred, groaning again. His eyes weakly fluttered open. He turned his head slowly to the side, and Elara dropped her head into her hands and began to cry, overwhelmed with relief and joy.

"Elara?" future Argon croaked.

She sniffed, lifting her head from her hands, and chuckled blearily, wiping her nose with her sleeve. He smiled weakly back.

"You... You idiot!" Her relief suddenly disappeared, replaced with a small wave of anger. "What were you thinking? Atropine? You could've died!"

Argon, stunned at her unexpected reaction, glanced nervously at Miela, who was still standing beside her. Miela shrugged, a small smile dancing on her lips as she watched Elara angrily berate the man.

"Elara..."

"Answer me, damn it!" she fumed, steaming. "Do you know what you did? How you made me feel? I thought you were dead!"

"I thought I was going to die," future Argon uttered softly, closing his eyes. He was exhausted. Every muscle in his body felt like it was on fire but limp at the same time. "They were too fast. I couldn't get away. It was ten to one. I thought I was going to die...so I took the poison. Just enough to make it look like I was already dead." Argon grimaced as he slowly stretched his neck, still too weak to move.

"It could've killed you! Atropine is highly unstable! You know that!"

"I know, but I had to risk it. If they found me, I would've been killed for sure. They might've even had a go at torturing me first, like the others. The poison gave me a chance of surviving," Argon rationalized. He smiled. "And I was right; my plan worked."

"I thought you were dead," Elara repeated. "I thought you were dead... If anyone else found you...you could have been buried alive."

"Which is why I was hoping that you'd be the one to find me," Argon replied earnestly.

Elara paused.

He didn't understand. To him, it sounded simple. Logical. He could see that she was distraught, but he didn't understand the depth of it all.

"Never again, Argon Tawer. You hear me?" she uttered ominously. "Don't you dare do anything like that ever again. You can't do that to me again."

"Elara?" Argon shifted uncomfortably under her gaze.

"You can't do that to me again," she repeated urgently. "Never again."

Argon locked his eyes with hers, and pushed himself to sit up. He felt overwhelmed; overcome with waves of anxiety, exhaustion, fear, relief, joy. She moved closer, tipping her head forward and resting her forehead against his, exhausted and drained. "Never again," he agreed, his voice soft yet firm. His heart raced as he felt her breath against his cheeks. Argon closed his eyes as he leaned into her, the tumbling waves of emotions coming to a halt as everything slowed down in his head.

He loved her.

The visiting Argon and Elara looked up at each other, uncomfortable and dazed. It didn't make any sense. But looking at where their journeys had led, for their future selves, it made all the sense in the world.

"Nothing."

The visiting group looked around as the scene around the materialized into the familiar sitting room of Noiro's cottage. The future Miela was standing at the coffee table, while the rest of the room's occupants stood around, watching Miela as she stared at the large map rolled out in front of them. The room was crowded, with some people standing around the edges while others huddled together onto the couches. Elara noted that there were a few more arm chairs added to Noiro's sitting room. It seemed that having more visitors at the cottage was becoming frequent enough for him to expand the seating options.

Future Noiro was standing at future Miela's side, gazing intently at the map before them and jotting down a few notes. Future Elara was sitting on the other side of Miela, with Argon next to her.

The visiting Elara recognized some familiar faces gathered around as well; Tami Nassah, Meer Nima-al, Araceli Sora, Altair Aquila, Astra Otthild, Venus Wolf, Imine Erela, Kalani Leo, and other Guardians she didn't recognize.

The visiting group's attention was distracted by a sudden outburst from future Miela as she slammed her palm against the table.

"We have nothing! No leads, no clues, nothing! All of the attacks over the last two years... Nothing!"

"We've been getting more reports of refugees being driven to Polaris for protection," said Elara.

"How many?" Miela demanded in frustration, pushing some of her hair away from her face. Her usual long braid was no longer there; her hair was cropped short, falling right at her chin. Her eyes looked hard, like she hadn't slept in weeks.

The visiting Elara glanced at everyone else. They all looked the same. Her future self looked more weathered and exhausted, her long hair messily pulled back with a ribbon. Future Argon's dark hair had a few white streaks in it, and his beard was on the verge of being messy and unkempt. Future Noiro's hair had turned completely silver, his face ragged and anxious.

"About three million more people, by last week's count," reported future Noiro. "I think it's now a total of ten million since the King died. All of the reports are the same. Houses are being broken into, artifacts stolen, unexplained suicides. There've even been reports of schools from some outer cities having mass suicides. But nothing about who is behind it all. Nothing left behind at any of the scenes. Nothing."

"It's maddening. How can we have mass evacuations from cities, hundreds, if not thousands of attacks, and not one person's seen what's behind the destruction? How can we fight against something if we don't even know what it is?" Miela gripped the side of the table, frustrated.

"We know that they're looking for something, whoever they are," said Elara. "They've been ransacking homes and museums. The list of items stolen are all the same: they're some sort of gems or family heirlooms. They have to be looking for something. And none of them turned up on the black market, either, which rules out the theory of them being stolen for money or funds."

"But we don't know what they're after," the future Miela griped. "What could be so important that it's worth killing people over?"

"The deaths were all ruled as suicides—"

"I know what they were ruled as," Miela quipped irately. "But we know they're not suicides. There's no way…"

"We're going around in circles," the visiting Miela

remarked, watching her future self flustered and frustrated as she marked off evacuated cities on the map.

"Noiro, take a look at this," the visiting Miela pointed at the cities. "Could be useful for us to know."

The visiting Noiro walked over and stood beside his future self, quickly noting down the affected cities. "Wow... I didn't know things would be this bad," he murmured, his face twisting with worry as he examined the charts, the little scratches over the evacuated city names marring the map.

"When is this?" the visiting Argon asked suddenly. "I've lost track of time."

"A little over a year after the attack on your home," Noiro replied, finishing jotting down the last of the cities on his notebook. Argon nodded, his stomach in knots.

The scene changed around the visiting group again.

This time, they saw future Elara running through the forest. She looked behind her, eyes wild with fear as they scanned the dark trees around her, fervently searching for whatever it was that she was running from.

She tripped over some uneven ground, grunting as she hit the floor. She hoisted herself up, her lip bleeding and her palms caked in mud, and kept running. She seemed to be counting under her breath as she ran, her eyes focused on the trees.

The group followed her as she suddenly stopped in her tracks and her counting ceased. She turned, touching one of the trees, and then ducked into it.

The visiting Elara blinked as she watched herself disappear into a tree. "Where did she go? Where are we?"

"I don't recognize the area," murmured Miela, looking around. They were deep into a forest. A soft glow was in the distance, and the sound of two sets of footsteps echoed through the thicket.

Noiro watched closely. "She disappeared into a tree. It is hollowed out!"

The group watched as future Elara tried to calm her erratic breathing and pressed herself into the tree's trunk. She shivered, the insects brushing against her ear as she burrowed into the tree's rotting hollow. She held one of her muddy palms to her mouth, stifling her breaths.

A faint rustling sound began to grow louder and nearer. Future Elara peered out from a crack in the rotting hollowed out tree, watching for what was coming. The group turned their attention to the sound.

"Any sign of her?" a gruff voice quietly called out.

"No. But she was headed this way," another deep voice answered.

The two men were clad in blue Guardian uniforms, with hoods that shrouded their faces from view. The visiting Miela frowned. The voices were unfamiliar.

"We can't let her escape. She might've seen something…"

"Did you get an ID on her?"

"Not really," scoffed one of the men. "But I've seen her before. She's part of the resistance."

The other man nodded. "A definite target, then."

"Should we alert the Yun Zeru that we found one on the run?"

The man guffawed. "And let him know that she got away? He'll have your head."

The visiting group gasped along with future Elara. Yun Zeru?

"What does Yun Zeru have to do with any of this?"

questioned Miela. "He's a Guardian. A General! And those two men are Guardians as well. Why is she running from them? Why are they after her?"

Future Elara held her mouth with both hands again, pressing them tight against her face and hoping that the men hadn't heard her gasp. Her eyes bulged out of her head slightly as she tried to hold her breath.

"Did you hear something?" The two men froze, straining their ears. Future Elara, cold and covered in sweat, desperate and terrified, closed her eyes. She crouched down slowly, her hand trembling as it closed down on a small stone. She took a deep breath, and then threw it further ahead into the forest.

The men's heads snapped up at the sound.

"She's moved ahead! Keep searching," ordered one of the men. "She can't have gotten far."

Future Elara sighed in relief as the sound of their footsteps drew further and further away from her. she peeked through a slit from the tree trunk, watching to see if there was anyone else lying in wait. A few silent moments passed before she took off running once again. The group watched her as she fought her way through the forest's overgrown shrubberies and trees, finally making it to a large, stone wall.

Without hesitation, she stuck her feet into the crevices of the stones and hoisted herself up. The group watched as she scaled the wall, her fingers bleeding and slipping with the mud caked onto her palms. After what seemed like ages, she made it over the wall and dropped to her feet on the other side, wincing as she felt the shock of her landing travel through her legs and up her spine.

"It's the forest behind Polaris Castle!" the visiting

Noiro exclaimed, pointing at future Elara as she ran through the castle grounds. "She was in the forest behind the castle!"

Future Elara burst through the doors to Noiro's cottage, where future Noiro, Argon, and Miela were seated quietly at the table. They looked up, alarmed at the sudden outburst.

A filthy, muddy woman stood at the door, panting hard. Her hair was matted, and tear stains streaked through the dirt cakes onto her face.

"Elara!" Argon yelled, recognizing her. He clambered clumsily towards her and fiercely grabbed her, pulling her into a tight hug. His fists were closed tightly on her coat, not caring as the dirt rubbed off onto him. She hugged him back tightly, burying her face into the crook of his neck. She held back tears as she felt him hug her tighter. He suddenly pulled away, holding her at an arm's length, seething through clenched teeth at her.

"God, Elara. Do you have any idea...?" Future Argon was shaking, fear flashing in his eyes as he looked at her. His eyes looked hollow; she knew he hadn't been sleeping. "Three days, Elara. Three days! Meer got back on Tuesday! You've been missing for three days! We've been going mad! Three days!"

"Damn it, El. Where have you been?" Future Miela pushed her way past the man and squeezed Elara tightly. "If I weren't so happy to see you, I'd kill you!"

Elara shivered as she looked at Miela and Argon, the cold setting into her bones as water and mud dried on her skin. It was clear that their overjoyed relief was short-lived, melting away into raging fury.

"Where were you?" future Miela demanded, folding her

arms and gritting her teeth.

Future Argon took her hand and brought her into the sitting room, sitting down next to her. He wouldn't let go.

"We're married," the visiting Elara remarked, glancing at the platinum wedding band flashing on Argon's finger as he held Elara. She spied the sapphire wedding ring on her finger as well. "I wonder how long it's been."

Future Elara glanced at future Noiro as she sat down, still shivering. Noiro quickly ran over with a thick woolen blanket, throwing it over her shoulders. She nodded her thanks.

Miela sat down across from her. "I'm waiting, Elara."

Elara frowned as she gathered her thoughts. "You said Meer made it back? What about Venus? Did she get back okay?"

Noiro glared at the table. "Venus is dead," he said flatly.

"W-what?" Elara stammered. "No, she can't be! I saw her! I saw her leave with Meer. They got away…"

"She's dead," Miela confirmed solemnly. "What happened to you? Meer said that they ran, and they also saw you leave. But then you disappeared—"

"For three days," Argon growled again, fuming at her. He squeezed her hand tighter, his worry and relief mixing together as he felt her leaning into him. She held his cheek, her remorse and guilt weighing her down like a ton of bricks flung onto her chest.

"The mission wasn't over," Elara said firmly, her eyes burning determinedly. "We were on our way back from getting some supplies. And then we stumbled upon a group of…*them*."

"What? You saw them?" Miela demanded.

Elara nodded. "There were about twelve of them. Looked like they were on a patrol. But I couldn't see who they were," she said, looking down and staring at her knees. "I knew we had to find out more. It was a chance I couldn't pass up. So I tailed them. I saw Meer and Venus leave, but I had to continue. I had to find out."

"Alone?" Argon raged. "You followed them alone? You could've been—"

"I know," Elara snapped angrily, another wave of guilt washing over her. "But I had to. I saw an opportunity that I needed to take. We needed to know."

"Did you learn anything?" Miela demanded. "What did you see?"

Elara shook her head. "They saw me. I'm not sure if they know who I am, or if they recognized me. But they saw me."

"Elara!" Miela gasped. "You could've been—"

"I know," she snapped bitterly. "I was careless."

"We need to leave," Noiro declared. "We all have to leave. And we need to have everyone else leave as well."

"I'm sorry," wailed Elara. "I'm—"

"It's okay," said Miela. "It was only a matter of time before they realized…"

"That's not all," whispered Elara. "The attacks. We've had it wrong the whole time."

"What do you mean?"

"It's the Guardians. They're the ones behind this."

"The Guardians?" Miela repeated in disbelief. "No. No way. No, you must have seen it wrong—"

"I know what I saw," Elara snapped again. "It's the Guardians."

Miela and Argon both shook their heads. "No way,"

Argon declared. His mind flew back to the comrades he spent so long with. He made it his life's mission to join the Guardians to fight and protect. She had to be wrong. "You're wrong."

"Argon and I are Guardians. How can you think that the Guardians are part of the attacks? Are you saying Argon and I are part of the attacks, too?" Miela demanded.

"Of course not," Elara shot back. "But I didn't want to jump to conclusions, either. That's why I needed to stay and tail them. I didn't know I'd take that long to get away... I kept trying to make a break for it, but every time an opportunity presented itself, I had another discovery about the attacks."

"And?"

"It's not all of the Guardians. Just the ones under Yun Zeru."

"General Yun Zeru?" Argon's mouth dropped.

"But...what?" Noiro stammered, completely flabbergasted.

Elara sighed. "They call themselves the Elites," she explained. "And they're looking for power."

"Power? They want to rule Polaris?"

"No." Elara shook her head. "They're looking for physical power. They're looking for something called an Elemental."

"What?" Noiro leaned forward in his seat. "An Elemental? But that's a myth. How do they—"

"Hold on," said Argon, interrupting Noiro's rant. "What is an Elemental?"

Noiro sighed, pushing his glasses up the bridge of his nose. "It's not what," he said. "It's who. An Elemental is someone who has the power to control the elements.

Water, Earth, Fire, Air… But it's a myth. It's not real."

"Of course it's not real," scoffed Argon. "That stuff is just… myths!"

"So… Yun Zeru is tearing the world apart… looking for a myth? A person?" Noiro rubbed his temples, his white hair falling onto his forehead.

"He thinks that the Elemental is the key to giving him power," said Elara dismally.

"So he wants to, what? Destroy everything? There'll be nothing left to rule," muttered Miela bitterly.

"That's not entirely true," corrected Noiro. "Think about it. The attacks on that scale… He can't carry those out alone. He must have supporters."

The scene before them changed once again.

"Miela! MIELA!"

The visiting group turned their attention to future Elara as she screamed, her feet thumping against the floor as she ran towards Miela, throwing her arms around her.

The visiting Elara didn't recognize the place they were in. The walls were dark, and there was very little light. She peered out of one of the windows to see a beach. The waves crashed angrily against the shoreline, spitting and spraying frothy sea foam into the air. She looked at the visiting group questioningly, and they all shook their heads. None of them recognized the house or the area.

"Elara," future Miela cried, holding her. Her face was bloody, her hair matted with blood and dirt.

"Miela…"

"I'm safe. I'm okay," she panted, tears streaming down her face, disappearing into the blood caked onto her face.

"You're pregnant," Noiro gaped, pointing at future

Elara's visibly swollen belly.

"Oh God," future Elara gasped, looking at future Miela.

Miela glanced down at herself and realized how terrifying she must have looked. Her clothes were ripped in several places, and her face was beginning to grow sticky from all of the blood. "I'm fine," she reassured Elara, wiping the blood off her face. "It's not mine."

"Where are the others? Argon?"

"He's okay. They're on their way," Miela said firmly, avoiding Elara's gaze.

"Who?" Elara demanded, following her friend as she walked into the house and stripped off her outer layers, wincing as she peeled off part of her clothes that was stuck to her arm.

"We don't know yet," Miela admitted. She looked angry. "I... I couldn't help everyone. I barely made it out myself..."

The scene swirled around them once more.

They were in the same house, but this time, it was almost dawn. Future Elara was sitting down on a sofa in a loose cotton dress, cradling a bundle of blankets in her arms. She tapped her foot anxiously as she slowly adjusted the blankets in her arms.

"Helia," the visiting Norio murmured, taking a few steps closer to the bundle of blankets. A small, round face poked out from the blankets.

Future Elara sighed anxiously, mumbling to herself as she glanced at the door every few minutes.

"She's waiting," said the visiting Elara, watching herself. "She's waiting for someone."

She watched her future self as she sniffed tiredly, glancing at the door once more, her eyes swollen and bloodshot. Her ears perked up at the sound of the doorknob turning, and she slowly rose to her feet.

"Argon?" she called out tentatively.

"Elara," a disheveled man came in, almost stumbling as he practically ran towards her. Elara squeaked, tears of relief streaming down her face as her husband embraced her.

"How did—what—are you—"Elara stammered, her words tumbling out faster than she could manage as she stared at her bloodied husband. He was covered in dust and debris, and his armor was ripped into shreds. A few scratches peeked from beneath his clothes, a considerable gash on his side peeking out.

"I'm okay," he murmured reassuringly.

"What are you doing up?" Argon asked, concerned. "Is the baby okay?"

Elara nodded, sniffing. "The baby's fine. Helia couldn't sleep…" she uttered softly. "Are you…"

"I'm fine," he said, putting his arm around her.

"You were gone for so long, Argon. I was so worried," she whispered, her eyes brimming over with tears again.

"I know," he said sorrowfully. "Here, let me put her down."

"Argon," Elara pleaded.

"I'll be back, I promise," he vowed, scooping the baby into his arms.

Elara nibbled at her lip, watching his retreating back. She knew that he was just a few feet away, but she couldn't bear it. Not after spending all night worrying and wondering if he was alive or not.

Argon returned, sitting down softly next to his wife. He opened his mouth to say something, and then hesitated. She squeezed his knee supportively, watching him as he stared blankly at the ground.

"They took the bait," he began, his voice flat and emotionless as he stared ahead. "They came, just like we expected they would... But we weren't ready." He couldn't look at her as he recounted the night's events; it would make it feel too real.

Elara felt her heart break for him.

"We fought. We fought hard," he said determinedly. "But we weren't ready... There were too many of them. They were just too many..."

"What happened?" Her breath gripped in her throat.

"They seized every Guardian and lined them up outside, almost as if it was a drill. And they asked them to pledge allegiance to the Elites."

"They're not hiding anymore," Elara recognized.

Argon stared blankly ahead. "No, they're not."

"And?"

"And they killed everyone who refused. No prisoners. No hesitation."

Elara held his hand, squeezing hard.

"It was horrible, El," Argon's voice broke. He looked up at her, the pain in his eyes piercing her heart. "They... they didn't just kill everyone. They demolished the entire headquarters. They destroyed everything and killed everyone."

"No," Elara gasped sorrowfully.

"We weren't ready." He turned his head to look at her, tears brimming over.

"Argon?" She held his face softly. He leaned into her

palm, closing his eyes as a tear rolled down his cheek.

"We couldn't find the bodies," he continued, swallowing hard. "We fought. And we lost. We couldn't find…"

"Who?" Elara urged, feeling sick. "Oh God, who?"

"Araceli. Altair. Kalani…" Argon faltered, his voice catching in his throat as he looked at his wife. "Miela. Miela…didn't make it. And there are more…"

Elara felt her blood run cold at the sound of Miela's name. She turned to him, her eyes wide in horror, his words replaying in her head and driving into her heart like knives. "No…" she moaned, a sob escaping her chest.

Argon hung his head mournfully. Of everyone in the war they had lost, the news of Miela hit the hardest. She was one of her oldest friends. Her supporter. Her comrade. Her confidante. They shared countless memories, celebrated so many birthdays and holidays. They fought so hard beside each other for so long. It hurt. There was no other way to describe how she felt. It just hurt.

The visiting Miela looked pale as she heard her own name mentioned amongst the dead. Her eyes were wide and unblinking. Her throat was suddenly dry.

"We're not going to let this happen," the visiting Noiro murmured to her. "We won't let any of this happen."

The world changed around them once more.

They were in the same house, but this time, it was crowded to the brim. The visiting Elara glimpsed a few familiar faces, and many unfamiliar ones. Her heart pained as Miela's usual place beside her was empty.

Future Noiro was staring intently at a map, gesturing to

different groups. It looked like they were planning some sort of strategy.

Suddenly, a woman burst through the front door, panting hard. "Polaris Castle is under attack."

The visitors were thrown into the same panic that the future group was in, as everyone scrambled towards the door.

"I'm going," future Argon stated determinedly, his heart pounding loudly in his chest. Cold sweat broke out across his forehead as he reached for his weapons.

"I'm going too." Elara edged towards the door.

Argon turned around, holding her arms gently, yet firmly. "You know the rules," he said softly. "One of us stays with Helia."

Elara paused. He was right; they established those rules when she was still pregnant with Helia. They knew they were fighting a war. They knew the risks and possible sacrifices they would have to make. She bit her lip, looking up at Argon anxiously, the thought of him going into another battle so soon wrecking her internally. But she knew that every person counted. Every person who was fighting against the Elites was needed.

But she still didn't want him to go.

"Just...please be careful," she said finally. Her heart pounded as she watched him suit up into his armor and head for the door.

"This is it," said the visiting Noiro, watching the scene intently. "This must be the attack we read about in the article."

The visiting Miela nodded, concentrating on the events unfolding before them.

Future Elara shifted anxiously in her spot while she

watched the front door swing back and forth in the wind as the last of the crowd in the house left for battle. She closed the door softly, turning the lock with a loud click.

She couldn't bear to stay in the house while her family and friends were out defending the castle.

She heard Helia begin to stir, and then gurgle.

"Mama?" a child's voice called out.

She turned her head and began to walk towards the voice. "I'm coming, Helia," she called back. She opened the door, plastering a small smile on her face. A small toddler stared back at her. She looked like she was almost two.

"Mama!" Helia lifted her arms up, indicating she wanted to be picked up. Elara knelt down, swooping her up in her arms and resting her head onto hers, closing her eyes.

She couldn't leave Helia alone.

"Elara! Elara, we need you!" a voice called from outside of the room. She ducked her head out to see future Tami scurrying about, poking her head in each room and searching frantically for something.

"I'm here." Elara ran out, Helia still in her arms.

"We need you," Tami repeated. She ducked into a room and emerged quickly, holding a bag of supplies.

"Medical assistance. We need to be out there," she said firmly. She glanced at Helia, wrapped up in her mother's arms, and then back at Elara. She looked torn; she didn't want to ask her to go to the battlefield while Helia was left in her care. She knew the rules: one parent with each child at all times.

But they were desperate.

Elara looked down helplessly at the child in her arms.

"Elara, please," begged Tami. "We need you."

"But Helia…"

The world changed around them again.

Horror met their eyes.

They were in front of the castle grounds, the outer walls completely desecrated and reduced to rubble. In the distance, they could see the castle engulfed in flames. Blood trickled down the cracks in the ground between the cobbled path. The smell of burning flesh filled their nostrils, and the thick smoke swirled into their eyes, hot and heavy. Elara began to cough, feeling the ashy heat burn the back of her throat.

"Where's Helia?" the visiting Noiro demanded.

"Mama," a tiny voice bleated. The visiting Noiro glanced down to see a small hooded figure beside future Elara, clutching her hand.

"How could she—how could *I* have brought a child to a battlefield?" the visiting Elara demanded, infuriated. "What was I thinking?"

"It looks like you didn't have much of a choice," said the visiting Miela sadly.

She was right. There weren't many choices when fighting a war.

The visiting group stared at the once magnificent castle, a symbol of peace and prosperity, now reduced to rubble. Screams pierced the cold night sky as the flames licked at the structure, and they could see the shadows of soldiers diving into the castle. They couldn't tell who was a friend who a foe. The screams from those being swallowed by fierce flames melted into the screams of those being slaughtered.

Utter chaos.

Blasts of white, hot fire were blazed across the fields, and they caught a glimpse of bodies battling each other.

Future Elara led future Tami and Helia down a path, away from the castle, and under the ruins of a small house. "We can set up over here," she said firmly, dropping her bag and unraveling its contents. Tami and Elara worked quickly, setting up their supplies into a makeshift medical center. A loud blast rattled the ground beneath them, and Helia let out a loud whimper as she felt the ground shake under the blast's force.

"Helia, baby." Elara knelt down to her child. Her heart broke as she saw fear flashing in the toddler's eyes, and she brought her hands up to her ears to block out the sounds of the blasts. "Mama needs you to be brave. We're okay over here. Okay?" She tried to keep her voice steady but despite her efforts, it was high and strained as she lied through her teeth.

The toddler looked hesitantly at her mother, nodding. She brought up her thumb to her mouth, and Elara gently pushed her hand away. "You're a big girl, right, Helia? Big girls don't suck their thumb."

The toddler nodded once again, silently bringing her hand down to her side.

Elara's heart broke.

"I'm heading out to find any casualties," Tami called out, getting ready to dart out.

Elara nodded. "I'm ready."

Suddenly, the world around them went dark.

"What happened?" the visiting Elara cried, startled. She felt Miela and Argon beside her, turning their heads around in alarm as the vision before them disappeared. Their eyes adjusted to Noiro, standing by the sundial, his hand wrapped around the Aether stone.

"The sun's going down," Noiro murmured softly as he gently picked the stone up. "We need sunlight to make the Aether Stone reveal the time's shadows. Without it, I'm afraid we might actually be pulled through time itself."

Elara opened her mouth, then closed it again.

"We can't risk it. We don't know enough about the Aether Stone and how it works to risk anything yet," he said.

"We've seen enough for now," Miela agreed.

The four stood in the middle of the cottage, looking back and forth at each other, and then down and away, their own thoughts flooding their heads as they each digested what they saw.

"We won't let any of this happen. We're gonna stop this. We're gonna fix this," Miela declared fiercely.

"We will," Elara said determinedly.

She lowered her head as she stared at the ground. She would do everything in her power to stop this.

FAMILY TIES

"Star! Come back here!"

Elara smiled as she saw a fluffy little fur ball bounce happily towards her, and she knelt down to pet the dog, scratching fondly behind its ears. The dog greeted her with a very wet lick against her cheek, and she crinkled her nose as she felt the tongue swipe over her face.

"I see Star hasn't completely covered you in his slobber, yet," a woman called out from the front door of her house, leaning against the doorway and smiling back at Elara. She brushed her long, chestnut brown hair behind her ear, her locks falling in soft waves down her back. She waved happily at Elara as she drew nearer.

"Not quite." Elara grinned at her old friend. Star padded alongside her, wagging her tail hard at the prospect of a new friend.

"I hope your business matter went all right," said Tami as she led Elara into her house. She could smell a

160

wonderfully delicious scent wafting in from the kitchen, and realized that she hadn't eaten in a while.

Elara winced internally as her belly let out a loud rumble.

"You're welcome to stay for dinner," Tami offered, grinning warmly at her friend. She giggled as she heard Elara's stomach growl once more. "Food's just about done."

Elara smiled sheepishly as she rested a hand on her belly. "I was hoping you wouldn't hear that," she said, giggling. She looked at Tami, feeling rather unsettled as the things she had seen and heard while using the Aether stone mulled over in her head. It was strange to stand and chat with her friend who, not so long ago, she had seen terrified and scared while setting up a makeshift medical tent by a battlefield. "It's okay, though. It's late, and I'm sure Helia is almost ready for bed."

Tami nodded in understanding, unconsciously bending down to pet Star as she sniffed around at her feet. "Of course! But I'll pack you some to go—you can't say no," Tami said sternly, wagging her finger at her old friend. "I've made far too much, and it'll all go to waste, anyhow."

Elara smiled gratefully. She was exhausted from the day's events, and the thought of having to prepare dinner at the end of the day was weighing on her. Elara glanced around. "Where's Helia? I hope she wasn't too much trouble."

Tami waved and said, "Nonsense, it was a pleasure having her." She walked into her kitchen and reached for a ladle. Tami lifted the lid off of a bright red pot on the burner and inhaled deeply, closing her eyes in delight and satisfaction as the aroma of her cooking drifted through the kitchen. "She was an immense help in making sure the puppies had enough exercise and playtime today."

Elara laughed as Tami scooped a generous portion of the pot's contents into a container.

"She's an intelligent child, that one. I hope you find her parents soon…"

Elara felt a knot in her stomach at her words. Miela and Elara agreed on sticking to their original story: Helia was a witness in a case they were trying to solve, and her parents were missing. Elara was taking her in for the time being.

They couldn't tell Tami the truth, bizarre as it was. There was still so much for them to figure out. And for the sake of maintaining everyone's safety, at least for the time being, they had to keep everything under wraps. It was for the best.

But still, she couldn't help but feel like a fraud.

"Helia's wonderful," Elara agreed.

"How does it feel, being a guardian for the time being?" asked Tami.

Elara shrugged, unsure of how to answer. She was still digesting the fact that she was now a guardian. A parent. She bit her lip, wondering how she would do in raising a child that fell unexpectedly into her lap. "It's great," said Elara, not untruthfully. "She's a sweet kid. I'm still adjusting to having someone around the house, but she definitely livens up my day."

"She's brilliant," remarked Tami. "A bit shy, though."

Elara herself hadn't really had a hand in raising Helia. It was her future self.

It was jarring to watch herself in the future; the future Elara was someone she didn't really know, who shared a life with Helia and Argon, two people that she didn't really know either.

She shuddered internally, recalling the tiny Helia standing by her mother at the mouth of a raging battlefield. She certainly wasn't proud of her future self for that decision, even though she had no other choice.

As painful as it was to watch the future events unfold, she was grateful for her glimpses at the future. She felt like she could understand Helia a little better. Watching the world around them that shaped her life gave her so much more insight, not just on her child, but on herself as well.

Elara glanced at Tami, wondering how she would react seeing herself play out her roles in the war she saw in the future.

"Would you mind going out to the backyard and calling in the other puppy and Helia?" Tami asked, pulling Elara out of her thoughts. "I just need to find a lid for this container."

"Sure," said Elara. She walked out to the back of the house, poking her head out through a large window.

Helia was running wildly, giggling hard as a small shaggy puppy ran at her heels.

"Helia," Elara called.

The toddler snapped her head up excitedly at her mother's voice, and turned her course to run straight towards the window. "Mama!" she cried happily, bounding towards her.

Elara couldn't help but giggle as the puppy behind the toddler stumbled over its feet and knocked its head softly into Helia's legs.

"Atlas," Helia chided, giggling at the puppy. "Watch out, silly!"

"It's time to go, love," she told her.

Helia let out a long groan. "But Mama," she protested, "we just started playing!"

"It's late," Elara said firmly. "And we want the puppies to get their rest too and grow up to be big, strong dogs. Right?"

Helia nodded dejectedly. "Okay, Mama," walking back into the house.

"We'd love to have her over again to play," said Tami as she handed Elara a bag. It was warm, and the scent of its contents made Elara's mouth water.

"Thank you for watching her," Elara said again.

Tami put up her hand. "It's no trouble at all, really," she chirped. "Since I've moved my practice back to my own house, I'm basically around all day."

Elara hugged her old friend, grateful for her support. She knew she was a busy medic in Polaris, and yet she was ready to support her in a heartbeat.

Tami squeezed back tightly.

"All right." Elara looked at Helia, who was standing in between the two women. Atlas licked her feet, and she chuckled at the puppy, patting its head with her small hand. "Ready to go?"

Helia nodded. Elara scooped the toddler up in her arms, the bag of food hanging from the crook of her arm as she made her way out the door.

Tami ruffled Helia's hair from behind, smiling affectionately at the child.

"Bye, Auntie Tami!" Helia waved from her mother's arms.

The walk home was a short one, and the two were home in no time. Elara placed Helia on the floor, silently missing the growing familiarity of having her in her arms. She stretched out her arms in front of her; her muscles were still getting used to carrying the toddler around.

"Time for explorin'!" Helia cried happily.

"Time for your bath," Elara corrected, chuckling at Helia's nightly ritual of wanting to explore her house. "But you can go *explore* for a few minutes."

Helia walked around the small living room, as was her nightly tradition. She walked along the perimeter of the walls, knocking on the paneling every few paces and pressing her ear against the wall, concentrating hard. She told Elara that she was sure that every house had some treasure hidden behind walls, and made it her own mission to locate every bit of treasure she could find.

Elara giggled at the toddler and walked over to the kitchen, placing the container of food from Tami on the counter.

Helia peered underneath one of the couches, grinning as she fished out a silver coin, wiping it clean and pocketing it. She then wandered over to Elara in the kitchen, poking around until she found a cabinet filled with snacks. After receiving permission to take a piece of candy, she made her way down one of the hallways leading deeper into the house and poked her head into the bathroom.

"Ready for your bath? Then we can have some yummy dinner that Auntie Tami made," Elara said softly, following Helia into the bathroom and rolling up her sleeves. After a small debate around which scent her soap was, a lot of splashing and suds, and a few tears after some soap splashed into the toddler's eye, a thoroughly scrubbed and clean Helia strolled out of the bathroom, clad in a large, soft, cotton shirt. Elara wiped her forehead, looking down at her own soaked self in the bath's aftermath.

Getting Helia to take a bath certainly took a high level of effort.

"Hungry?" she asked Helia, leading the toddler into the kitchen.

Helia nodded, rubbing her belly exaggeratedly. "Mama, where are my pajamas?" she asked, looking down at her large shirt.

Elara bit her lip guiltily: with not many options, Elara put Helia in one of her own shirts for the night. "We'll go shopping soon," she promised. "Uncle Noiro packed you some clothes too, but we definitely have to go get some more."

"I like the clothes from Uncle Noiro," said Helia.

Elara chuckled. "I'm glad you do."

"They're little, like me!"

"Well," Elara paused, unsure how to respond. She began to set the kitchen table for their dinner. Helia hopped up onto a seat, settling in front of her plate as she watched Elara intently, waiting for an answer. "They were mine. A long time ago."

"Yours?" Helia gaped.

Elara nodded.

"But you're so big!"

"There was a time when I was little, like you," said Elara with a chuckle. "Uncle Noiro took care of me when I was little."

"Really?" Helia asked excitedly. "Is Uncle Noiro your Dad?"

"In a way," Elara replied, biting a forkful of food. "I don't know who my Mom or Dad is. So Uncle Noiro took care of me."

"Oh." Helia looked down at her plate.

Elara smiled. "Eat your dinner, baby, it's getting cold."

Helia nodded, taking a big bite from her plate. She clumsily dropped a few morsels around her. "How did Dad get back?" she asked suddenly. "I thought you can't come back from the sky."

"Er... Dad found a way."

"He must've missed me," said Helia as a matter of fact, taking another bite of her food.

Elara smiled again. "Yes. He did. Very much."

The two continued their dinner, Elara listening to Helia telling her about her day with the puppies. She hoped that the toddler couldn't tell she was only half-listening as she watched Helia chatter away excitedly. The toddler was certainly talkative. She studied Helia's eyes, noting how they were remarkably like her own. She had short, black hair, a trait she seemingly inherited from Argon, although it wasn't quite as curly, falling in soft, messy waves around her face. The way Helia's mouth turned when she spoke was in the same way hers did.

Helia yawned halfway through her speech, drawing Elara's attention to the time. "Oh! It's past your bedtime!"

"But 'm not tired," Helia insisted, pouting.

"You look tired," Elara said pointedly as Helia let out another big yawn, reaching her hand out to hold hers. "I know I need to rest, too."

Elara led Helia to her bedroom.

"I like the big bed," Helia said, throwing herself onto Elara's large mattress and sinking into the covers.

"Me too." Elara chuckled, walking closer to the bed and arranging the covers around Helia's little body. "We'll get you a good Helia-sized bed, soon. But in the meantime, you'll have to snuggle up with me."

"Yay," Helia murmured sleepily, her head slowly sinking into the pillow, curls splayed out across the soft linens.

"Sleep well, kid," Elara said softly, running her fingers through her soft hair.

Helia sighed, half asleep, and leaned into her palm. "Mama sleep with me now?"

"In a bit," said Elara. Her clothes were still wet from Helia's bath, and she still needed to clear the kitchen table. Helia sighed sleepily, turning as she fell asleep, and Elara left the room quietly.

She returned to the living room and sat down for a moment on the couch, dropping her head into her hands. It was the first time that day that she finally got to sit down. She sighed, the weight of everything she saw that day settling onto her shoulders.

There was so much to do, and her head was filled with so many thoughts that were all jumbled up together. She also needed to sort out Helia's affairs; getting clothes, toys, food…

Her mind turned back to the Aether Stone. She wondered how much potential damage she and her friends were doing by peeking into the future.

From what she knew from her own research on time bending, timelines change all the time compared to the present's events.

The future certainly must have changed tremendously since Helia's arrival spun things into motion. Elara sighed again, her mind wandering to her future as a Guardian.

She had never envisioned herself pursuing a career as a

Guardian, but she had certainly helped Miela out in the past by consulting on a few cases.

Elara thought back to the thick research journal in her satchel from the future. The book which held so many answers.

A loud knock sounded at the door, interrupting her thoughts. Elara turned her head curiously. It was late, and she certainly wasn't expecting a visitor at this hour. Her mind jumped to the future's events, and she froze, nervous.

Did someone find something out?

She thought quickly about Helia, who was slumbering away in her room. She internally reprimanded herself for being so careless and bringing the toddler out in public; had someone seen Helia and started asking questions? Or did someone find something out about the Aether Stone? Elara's stomach turned, remembering the series of terrible events she witnessed just a few hours ago. The images of lifeless, battered, bloodied bodies filled her mind's eye, and she felt her blood run cold.

Another knock sounded against the door, this time, a little louder. Elara felt a cold sweat break out across her forehead, and she silently inched towards the door, trying not to make a sound. She knew it looked like she was home; her kitchen and living room lights were still on, and the glow from her little house's windows definitely gave her away.

She held her breath, her fingers trembling as she reached for the curtains beside the front door, trying to catch a peek at the late night visitor.

A tall, muscular man stood in the darkness, tapping his foot as he raised his hand to knock once again. He nervously shuffled his feet together. She couldn't make his face out in the darkness. She squinted, studying the man. The man knocked once more, seeming frustrated at the lack of response. He took his hat off to ruffle a hand through his hair

A light went off in Elara's head as she saw the outline of the man's thick mop of curly hair. After today, she would recognize that mop of hair anywhere.

"Argon," Elara greeted, opening the front door.

"Uh, hello," Argon said stiffly, looking uncertain. "I hope I'm not intruding…"

"You're not," said Elara. "But it *is* late."

"I… I know," Argon admitted, looking down. "I wanted to speak with you."

Elara shifted uncertainly.

Argon noticed her apprehension, and asked, "Do you mind if I come in? It should only take a moment."

"Sure."

Elara opened the door wider, letting him in. She tried to compose herself into a confident and relaxed stance, but the unusually high pitch her voice took belied her attempt to appear natural and at ease. She showed Argon to the living room and watched him sit down. He was still dressed in his Guardian uniform.

Elara glanced down at herself and groaned internally. Her shirt had mostly dried from Helia's bath, but the outline of the water stain was still fairly visible. Her hair was messily pulled back into a loose bun at the top of her head. She was pretty sure that she smelled a little, as she had yet to take a bath herself. She was definitely not prepared to accept company in this state.

She closed her eyes, irritated when she caught herself

mulling over how she looked. She shouldn't have felt the need to dress up for anyone, let alone Argon. Besides, he was the one who had stopped by so late in the evening, completely unannounced. Elara hadn't even realized that he knew where she lived. In fact, she wondered how he'd managed to find out.

"So," Argon spoke, inclining his head. Elara's thoughts stopped abruptly at his voice, and she realized that they had been in silence for the past few minutes. She was still standing in her spot, while Argon was seated stiffly on her couch.

"How was your day?" Elara asked, wincing at her question. She already knew how his day went; they had spent the majority of it with the Aether Stone. But she didn't know what else to say to the man sitting in her living room.

"It was fine," Argon replied politely. He felt awkward. "How was yours?"

"It was fine…"

"So, where's Helia?" Argon asked, attempting to pull them into a casual conversation.

"She's sleeping," Elara replied. A small smile pulled at the corner of her mouth. "The kid was completely wiped out after dinner."

"She must've had a long day," Argon said. He chuckled lightly. "I know we had a long day ourselves."

"Yeah," Elara agreed, feeling herself relax a little. "So…um…you wanted to speak to me about something?"

Argon nodded. "Helia," he said seriously. "I want to see her."

Elara felt her neck tense up with anxiety, and her mouth suddenly felt dry. She looked back at him for a moment. "I don't know… I don't think it's a good idea."

"No, not now," Argon explained quickly, putting his hands up. "I don't want you to wake her up. I meant—"

"I know," Elara interrupted softly. "I know what you meant. I just…don't think it's a good idea right now."

"But I'm her father," Argon uttered, his voice turning hard.

"I know," whispered Elara. "But not exactly. You're not the person she knows as 'Dad.'"

"You're not the person she knows as 'Mama,'" Argon shot back.

"I know, but I'm what she has right now."

"I'm trying to also—"

"I know," Elara repeated. "And I appreciate that. But she's confused. She was asking earlier about… well… She needs a constant—"

"I want to be a constant," Argon demanded. "Don't you think she's going to start having questions? Don't you think she's already confused?"

"She is confused," Elara confirmed. "But she's adapting. She has no choice. And I don't want to make it any harder on her than it has to be. God knows what effect the war had on her already. She needs consistency in her life. Safety. And I know she can find that with me," Elara explained, her voice rising.

"But not with me," Argon said.

"No," she said honestly. "I want her to. I know she misses you. But it's not *you* she misses. You're not the same man we saw through the Aether Stone. You're not who—"

"You don't know anything about me."

"I know," said Elara. "That's exactly it. I don't know

anything about you. That's why I'm so uncomfortable with your getting involved."

"I'm her father," Argon argued.

"You are," agreed Elara. "That's why this is serious. You're not just anyone to her. You're her dad. This isn't some toy you can just come in and decide you don't want anything to do with one day, and want to be involved with the next. This is her life."

"How can you keep judging me for my initial reaction?" Argon thundered. "You can't keep throwing that in my face to justify every point."

"You didn't see the way she looked when you were basically spitting at the idea of being her father," Elara interrupted, her nostrils flaring. "She didn't understand what was going on, but she understood enough to know you didn't want her."

Argon faltered, his face twisting with guilt. "It was a mistake," he admitted angrily. "But she's my kid. You all took great lengths to prove it. Why don't you want me to be a part of her life?"

"How do I know that you won't just walk out?" Elara demanded. "You don't know me. You don't like my friends. You don't like the people in Helia's life. How do you think it could be good for her to see her parents constantly at each other's throats?"

"You're the one constantly coming at mine!" Argon yelled.

"Quiet, or you'll wake her up," Elara ordered fiercely.

"I hope I do," Argon sneered. "It might be the only way I get to see her!"

"How do you think you could be a parent to her if you don't even care about her sleep? Or how she feels?"

"How can you be a parent to her if you deny her her right to know her father?"

"Are you ready to admit that you're her father? Are you ready to take her home and show her to your mother? Your sister? Your family? Are you ready for everyone to know that she's your child, and that I'm her mother? Being a parent, a committed parent, is a lot bigger than you think," she said furiously, her lip curled.

"You're preaching about parenting when you've only had a couple days' worth of experience?" Argon snorted. "You're carting her off to be watched by friends half the time because you don't have time to watch her."

"It's not a bad thing to ask for help," argued Elara defensively, her own guilt apparent on her face.

"I'm offering to be that help. Isn't her father a better option than someone else?" Argon crossed his arms.

Elara sunk down onto the sofa across from him, taking a deep breath as angry tears filled and blurred her vision. Helia needed a mother who would always be there to protect her and take care of her, and she was committed to being that. Her future self entrusted her with that responsibility.

But Argon also had a point.

"Mama?" a small voice called. The two adults snapped their heads at the hallway, where the small child they were arguing over huddled in the corner, rubbing her eyes sleepily.

Argon moved to get up from his seat, but Elara was faster, and moved towards the girl protectively to lead her back to her room, tucking her back into bed. The small girl murmured peacefully, rolling to her side and falling back into a deep slumber. Elara pressed a soft kiss against her forehead, softly brushing her hair away from her face.

Something stirred inside her as she watched the toddler sleep. The child had seen so much horror, and lived through so much trauma during her short time on Earth. But looking at her softly snoring away, no one would have ever known. She deserved a peaceful life.

And Elara was determined to give her one.

She slowly crept out of her room and back to Argon in the living room, where he was still seated.

"Can you take some time to think about this? Please?" Argon whispered.

Elara nodded.

Satisfied with her response, Argon saw himself out. Elara sat still, exhausted, overwhelmed, and confused. She closed her eyes as she heard the door shut behind Argon, taking a few steadying breaths before moving to get ready for bed.

VICTIMS OF WAR

"Are we all ready?" Noiro sat down on his usual spot, nursing a cup of hot tea.

Miela, Elara, and Argon looked back at him from their seats. Elara rubbed her temples, closing her eyes and letting out a sigh. Try as she might, she had barely gotten any sleep the night before as anxiety riddled her mind at the thought of having to face more of what the Aether stone would reveal.

A small noise caught her attention, and she turned her head towards the sound. "I'll check on Helia before we begin," said Elara, excusing herself from the sitting room. Noiro nodded and gestured towards the stairs, where Helia was napping away in her old room upstairs.

"Have you found out anything back from headquarters?" Noiro asked Miela, attempting to break the tension in the room. No one was looking forward to using the Aether Stone again.

Miela shook her head. "Not much so far. But I haven't really had time to properly check through any open cases over the past few days," she replied with a sigh. "Argon, any luck on your end?"

He shook his head. "I've been hearing some buzz about Yun Zeru's ranking as a Guardian, though."

Miela nodded. "That's to be expected. We know he gets promoted to General—at least in the timeline we're looking at."

"She's still asleep," Elara announced softly, coming down the stairs. "Are you sure we won't wake her with the Aether Stone, Noiro?"

Noiro nodded. "The time shadows should remain contained to the room the sundial is in. We'll be fine. We just have to take care not to go past dark."

"Good thing we're starting off early, then," said Argon, casting a look outside the window. The sun was still rising in the cool morning air, and was barely peeking over the high castle walls around them. He could hear a bird tittering outside.

"Indeed," agreed Noiro, walking over to the sundial's podium, Elara's coded journal in hand. "Shall we?"

Elara watched as he twisted the dials on the Aether Stone, each click ringing ominously in her ears as he slowly entered in the next code.

The room flashed around them, and the group took a moment to view their surroundings.

They were in a small bedroom. It was dark, and they could just barely make out the shape of a person lying in a large bed, tossing and turning every few moments beneath the covers. A few inches away lay the tense form of another person, stiff and unmoving, buried beneath the thick blanket.

A sudden loud bang startled the visiting group, followed by rough, menacing laughter from somewhere in the house.

The couple jolted awake, shooting up in a panic at the sound echoing through their home.

"Oh, God. They're here!" future Elara breathed in horror, throwing the covers off of her and leaping off the bed.

Future Argon flew across the room, racing towards a small crib a few feet away. "I'll get Helia! Get the bag! We need to get out!" Argon ordered, his voice rough with fitful sleep. He leaned over the crib and pulled a small bundle of blankets wrapped around the small child. He looked back at Elara.

"Go! I'll follow," Elara urged, her eyes wild with fright.

Argon paused, looking down at the bundle in his arms, which began to stir.

"Go, Argon!"

He nodded firmly, turning to run out the door.

Elara ducked her head under the bed and yanked out a large duffle bag, pulling the strap over her head and securing it around her shoulder.

The visiting Elara felt her heart thunder in her chest as she watched her small family scramble fearfully for their lives. She knew that the future scenes she would see today would be intense, but she wasn't prepared for this. She didn't know if she could ever be prepared to watch herself and her family run for their lives.

The visiting Elara heard heavy footsteps behind her, and looked over her shoulder to find a massive hooded figure running right at future Elara, who was still by the bed. She whirled around, her mouth parted open in shock. She was cornered.

Future Elara moved quickly. She could feel the adrenaline rippling beneath her skin. She charged towards him, pulling out a small knife from the side of the bag, and sank it into his flesh. The man screamed, stumbling as he gawped at the blade sticking out of his belly. Elara took her chance and ran past him, shoving him to the side. She could hear another round of laughter in the house as furniture and glass shattered and smashed against each other, the assailants wreaking havoc in their home.

She raced towards the bathroom, closing the door behind her and tracing her hands down the tiles, silently counting. She paused, knocking against one of the tiles. Hearing a hollow sound echoing beneath the tile, she pressed her hand firmly against the cool ceramic and stepped back.

The tile sank into the wall to reveal a panel, which slid roughly against the stone foundation to reveal a small, narrow passageway.

"What the—" the visiting Elara's mouth dropped open. "How?"

"It's an escape route," explained the visiting Argon. "Every Guardian's home has some sort of escape route built in."

"For good reason," the visiting Miela chimed. "Doing what we do, we don't exactly make a lot of friends."

"This isn't my home, though," said the visiting Argon, examining the room they were in. Everything was covered in a thick layer of dust and grime. There were a few bottles lying on the ground, and some shattered glass in the bathtub.

"Judging from what we last saw, we must already be on the run," mused the visiting Elara. "It looks like we're... squatting in another Guardian's home."

"Abandoned home, by the looks of it," uttered the visiting Noiro, studying his surroundings.

Future Elara threw her bag in and clambered into the small hole. Breathing heavily, she felt around her in the dark, her palm closing around a small panel beside her. Her breath caught in her throat as footsteps drew near the bathroom's entrance, and she pressed hard against the panel.

The tile slowly slid back in place, enveloping her in the darkness. Turning away, she crawled deeper into the passageway.

The world twisted around the visitors, and they were suddenly transported to a jagged, rocky terrain nestled at the base of a cliff. The sea roared angrily at the other side, and the wind pierced their bones with its icy chill.

"Argon! ARGON!" Elara yelled, her voice almost drowned out by the wind.

"In here!" Argon shouted, his voice barely discernible over the howling wind. His voice was followed by the terrified wails of a small child.

Elara looked up, spying a dark hole in the side of the cliff a few meters off the ground. She scrambled up the rocks, slipping occasionally as the ground crumbled beneath her feet while she climbed her way to her small family.

"Argon?" Elara's voice echoed through the cave.

"I'm here," his voice called back to her.

Elara felt her way through the cold, rocky interior and squeezed herself through the tight gap in the rock, a small glow growing brighter as she drew nearer towards Argon's voice. Her eyes adjusted in the dark cave, and she saw a man with curly black hair holding a crying child in his arms.

He stood in the middle of the cave, a small lantern burning at his feet with the smallest flame it could possibly muster. His body was shaking, his chest rising and falling as he panted deeply, staring at her as if she were the only thing that mattered.

"Argon," Elara sobbed, relief flooding through her as she stumbled towards him, arms outstretched to embrace him and her petrified child. He pulled her close with his free arm, Helia pressed in between the two, still wailing in fright. She struggled to keep her voice hushed. "Are you two okay?"

"We're okay," Argon answered, his voice breaking. "Are you?"

The visiting Elara and Argon glanced uncomfortably at each other as they watched their future selves huddle close together.

"I'm okay." Future Elara shuddered as a cold bead of water dripped onto her head. "Everything happened so fast."

"I don't know," Argon admitted, his heart racing. "What matters for now is that we're safe."

With their fear and adrenaline subsiding at the faint glimmer of a safe night, Helia's wails grew more apparent. Elara turned her attention to her child. "Shh... it's okay, baby." She raised her shaky hand and gently stroked Helia's damp hair.

"I wanna go home," Helia cried miserably, wiping her eyes as more tears spilled out across her round cheeks.

"I'm sorry, baby," Elara uttered mournfully, pressing a kiss to the back of her tiny hand. "We can't go home now. Not tonight. But we're here together."

"We'll have fun," Argon added, forcing his voice to sound cheerful. "We're going camping. Isn't that fun?"

"N-no," Helia pouted, burying her head in Argon's neck. "I wanna go home…"

"But why go home when we can have fun over here?" Argon stretched his mouth into a smile. "Mama made sure to pack a lot of stuff for us. You see Mama's bag? Do you wanna see the cool beds she has for us tonight?"

Helia tentatively lifted her head to look at Elara. Elara smiled, relieved to see that the fear and terror in the child's eyes was slowly beginning to slip away as curiosity took over. She peered at her mother, who began to dig out some rolled up sleeping bags.

"See what Mama brought for us? Show us, Mama," Argon urged. Her heart felt heavy as she plastered on a smile for Helia, feeling her own tears ready to take over as they tried to convince their little girl that everything was okay, when it was far from it.

"Let's set up our beds." He knelt down and gently placed Helia on the floor. "Pull that side there—yes, exactly. You're such a smart girl," he praised, his rambling calming Helia down as she began to grow preoccupied with the sleeping bag and soon became fixated on fiddling with the zipper.

The visiting Noiro leaned closer, examining Helia. "She looks about the same age as she is now," he said, looking at the toddler. "Perhaps a few months apart?"

"You know, I think I have a treat for such a smart little girl," future Elara said, cutting off the visiting Noiro's question. She pulled out a small parcel of biscuits from her bag.

"Oooh," future Argon said playfully. "Mama has biscuits! Did you see that, Helia? Mama brought us biscuits for our night camping!"

Elara reached out and placed a small biscuit in the child's expectant little hand, and she happily unwrapped the biscuit and took a large bite out of it. Elara lifted another parcel and silently asked Argon if he wanted one as well. His fake smile fell as Helia munched away, lifting his hand as he politely declined. His stomach twisted with the thought of the intruders violating his home. His family's safety. They were on the run for so long, he had forgotten what it felt like to go through a day without looking over his shoulder.

"The others…" Elara whispered, her voice trembling as she held back tears. "Are they safe?"

"We don't know, yet." Argon shook his head dismally. "But we can't go back yet."

Elara groaned. Her head was suddenly pounding, and she closed her eyes, bringing her hands up to her temples.

"Please, you have to rest," Argon murmured, holding his wife's arm gently.

Elara shook her head. There was no way she could sleep.

"For Helia," he pleaded.

She bit her lip, looking down at their child, who was still sniffling beside Argon.

"Please," Argon softly urged.

Elara nodded. She slowly crawled into her sleeping bag, its flimsy material rubbing against her legs as she slid in. Their sleeping bags were right next to each other, Helia snuggling in her father's sleeping bag and nestling comfortably between her parents, Argon's arm draped over the toddler protectively. Elara pulled herself closer to her small family. A wave of fatigue washed over her, and she sank deeper into their makeshift bed, grateful that the two people who had come to mean more than anything to her in the world were safe. She gently reached her hand out to hold Argon's, and he squeezed her hand tight in his.

The world shifted around them once again.

The visiting group found themselves in a small tent. Future Elara was seated on the floor, her legs crossed as she leaned forward, watching future Noiro intently as he spoke. Beside her sat Argon, Detective Vega, Sargent Esen, Tami, Meer, and Astra. It looked like they were in the middle of a discussion.

The visiting Elara casted a glance at future Helia, who was tucked away in the corner of the tent, her legs splayed out in front of her as she played quietly with a few pebbles. Her hair face was smudged with dirt, and her hair was a little messy. Elara looked back at the group of adults who were huddled around, deep in discussion. They all seemed dirtier and more disheveled than their usual state. She spied a few white strands of hair running through her future self's head, and her face was hard, eyes punctuated with dark purple bags. A deep scar marred the side of her cheek, and another small one was on her lip.

War had not been kind to them.

"We can't continue like this," Vega uttered dejectedly. "We just can't. How is he always one step ahead? Yun Zeru's forces grow stronger by the day. It takes so long to track him, and we're always confronted by his team before we can even catch a glimpse of him."

"It feels like he's taunting us," Meer spat. "He isn't even trying to hide his efforts anymore. He's always just out of reach. It's like trying to catch smoke with our bare hands."

"He's won," croaked Astra.

"No," growled future Noiro. "No. We can't let him win. We can't just let ourselves be hunted down like animals. We're the last ones, damn it!" He slammed his fist onto the ground, his eyes burning with fury. "We need to change our tactics. We can't go after them anymore. We make the monster come after us."

"They already are after us," future Elara pointed out. "His army tracked down our last hideout—"

"No. Not the army. Yun Zeru," Noiro said firmly. "We draw *him* out."

"How?" asked Elara.

"By using his weaknesses against him. His pride. We taunt him." Noiro's voice was hard. His tired shoulders were pulled back with determination, and his weary body stood strong as he spoke with resolve. "If we can destroy him, we might just have a shot at surviving this war."

The visiting Noiro looked at the future group, shaking his head sorrowfully. "He's deluded," he uttered sadly, pointing to his future self. "We're down to eight people. That's it. How can he possibly think that eight people can take down an army?"

The visiting Miela folded her arms. "Hope can drive people to do incredible things."

"Or desperation," countered the visiting Noiro, staring at the future group.

"I can't ask all of you to risk your lives for this,"

continued future Noiro. "You know what the risks are."

"We know what we signed up for," said Vega. "And we have nothing left to lose."

"There's nothing more dangerous than facing someone who has nothing left to lose," Meer chimed in determinedly. Noiro nodded.

"Yun Zeru has taken so much of my family away from me," Argon growled.

Elara nodded in agreement. "I'm in. Till the very end."

The visiting Miela turned around and looked at the visiting Noiro. "What are you planning? What are they planning to do? They're crazy!"

"I don't know," said the visiting Noiro defensively, putting his hands up. "This is the future. I don't know what I—*he* planned."

"Taunting a man like Yun Zeru… What on Earth are you all thinking? How can you all agree to something like that? You all should run! Survive! Not…this!" the visiting Miela's fumed. "How could you? How could you agree to this? And Helia! What did you plan for her? Did you even think about her? How could—"

"Miela, none of this has happened yet," interrupted Elara. "And we won't let it happen. This is why we're watching this. We're not going to let this happen."

The world faded around them as the Aether Stone shifted them to a different point in time.

The world came back into focus, and the group of adults who were once huddled in the tent together were now at the base of the ruined Polaris Castle.

It was daylight. The air was cold around them, and future Elara could see her quick, nervous breaths fogging the air in front of her as she tried to quell her thundering heart.

"Are we all clear on the plan?" asked future Noiro. The group nodded in unison.

"Mama? Mama, where we goin'?" Helia's small voice piped up from the bundle of blankets in Elara's arms.

"We brought Helia?" the visiting Argon drew his breath in sharply. "How could we—"

"Mama and Dad have some work to do," future Elara told her daughter gently.

"No! No more work!" Helia protested, shaking her head vehemently. "No!"

"Hey, we'll be right back," said Argon softly, placing his large palm on her forehead. His voice shook, betraying his fear.

"No, Dad. Don't go..." Helia's lips trembled as she stared at her father. "Please."

Elara could feel Helia sensing the tension and fear that hung heavy between the adults. She had seen too much. She knew too much.

"We'll be back together soon, I promise," Argon reassured her. "Before you'll even notice."

"Really?" Helia looked doubtful.

Argon nodded. "Really. You'll see. You hold on to Mama, okay?"

Helia nodded, leaning into her mother's chest as she hugged her tight.

"We'll be back together soon," Argon repeated, this time, looking at Elara. "Right?"

"We will," she said forcefully. She grasped his hand tightly in hers.

Noiro cleared his throat. "Are we ready?"

The group of adults nodded. Argon squeezed Elara's hand before slowly letting go, his hand stiffly moving to his side. It took everything in his power to let her go.

"Let's go."

Elara took off running, Helia wrapped up in her arms. The castle ruins were deserted, and her footsteps seemed too loud amidst the eerie silence. It was strange; there were no guards, no military activity, nothing. It was almost as if Yun Zeru had forsaken the Polaris Castle entirely, driving the message in that the Polaris Empire was over. Their history didn't matter anymore. Their very presence didn't matter. The castle was left to crumble away, a shell of its former glory.

She ran towards the western quarter of the castle's ruins, watching fervently for any signs of movement. It was risky, making their move in daylight.

But they wanted to draw Yun Zeru out. They wanted to hit him where it truly hurt. They needed to be bold. They needed to hurt his pride and his perception of his strength and power over the sieged city.

Argon took off to the other side of the castle. Nature had already began to try and reclaim the rubble, with small shoots of greenery beginning to sprout from the cracks in the wall. He cast a worried glance in his wife and child's direction, their figures growing smaller and smaller as they moved towards opposite ends of the castle. He loathed the fact that he could not be with them. That he could not protect them.

The last remains of his family.

But he needed to end this. He needed to play his part to end the war.

Noiro ran through the remains of the iron gate and

towards the center of the castle. He hoisted himself up, scaling the crumbling walls, his hands trembling as he searched for his next foothold. His heart roared in his ears, and his mind was eerily blank; it was almost as if someone else were controlling his body, and he was just part of the audience. He reached the top of the archway, and rested for a moment at the foot of the long iron flagpole that sat at the highest point of the arch. He narrowed his eyes as he turned his attention to the field. He saw the last bit of resistance against Yun Zeru, eight adults and a single child, get into position. That was all that was left of the last stand against the bloodiest battle Polaris had ever known.

He turned his attention back to the flagpole, unraveling his knapsack and pulling out a large cloth, throwing it out in front of him. The Polaris insignia shone bright against the dark fabric. Noiro fastened the cloth onto the flagpole and hoisted it up, watching the flag fly higher and higher, waving magnificently and proudly against the early morning sky. He watched as the rest of his group scattered across the high points on the castle grounds as they unraveled the Polaris banners.

It was a bold move. In the middle of the day, no less. The flag and banners being displayed proudly across the Polaris castle was the biggest insult to Yun Zeru. It was a stain against his victory against Polaris, a stark reminder that not everyone bowed before him.

Proof that he had still not won yet.

He had to come.

The visiting group waited, watching intently as their future selves poised themselves for battle.

"What's that sound?" The visiting Miela swiveled her head, looking for the source of a faint chiming sound.

"Bells," the visiting Noiro remarked, frowning as he strained his ears. "I think it's an alarm."

Sure enough, the chiming sound grew louder and louder, and future Elara could feel her ears ring as the sound swelled, enveloping the air around her. Hooded figures began to swarm towards the Polaris Castle, clad in the same blue uniform that she had spied in the forest. They came to a halt at the gates, and the crowd began to part, carving a clear path through. A lone figure walked steadily through the crowd, neither wearing the uniform nor a hood. He wore a thick, black coat, with a blood red cape draped over his right shoulder. A thick scar ran across the left side of his face, cutting through his eyebrow and the center of his eye. His scarred eye's unseeing pupil shone a cloudy grey, a stark difference between his other coal black eye. His silver hair was slicked back, accentuating his sharp, hawkish features. His boots clipped against the cobbled ground as he walked ominously towards the gate.

There was no doubt that they were face to face with Yun Zeru.

Future Elara's breath caught in her throat as she stared at the man from her hiding place, pressing her body against the wall. She squeezed Helia tight against her, holding a hand softly to her lips to quell any noise the child might have made.

Yun Zeru examined the banners fluttering in the wind, his lip slightly curled in disgust.

"Looks like we have some survivors here," Yun Zeru's voice boomed. The sound of his voice shook Elara to her core. "Not for long."

His voice didn't seem like it belonged to someone who

encouraged so much bloodshed and turmoil. He sounded... normal. And that was what scared her. She had built Yun Zeru up in her mind to be this big, scary monster of a man.

Yet, there he stood, looking like any other man she might have passed on a peaceful day in the city.

"NOW," Noiro yelled.

A series of explosions shattered the ground beneath Yun Zeru's army. Some fell to the floor, shaken as the Earth trembled beneath their feet. The future Elara breathed heavily, her hand poised over the second detonator as she waited for the army to move. She needed to aim for Yun Zeru...

A hand suddenly grabbed at her, and she drew in a deep breath, driven by instinct as her lungs expanded, getting ready to scream. The hand pressed hard against her mouth. Her mind raced as she struggled.

"Shh, it's me, El," a familiar voice whispered raggedly. Her eyes widened.

"Argon?" her voice was muffled beneath his hand. He nodded, dropping his hand. "I couldn't leave you two alone."

Elara wanted to berate the man she loved for abandoning his post. But she couldn't.

How could she, when the very sight of him quashed her fears of facing their enemy?

"We stay together," he said.

Elara nodded.

"Let's destroy this monster," uttered Argon. He pressed the detonator firmly, bracing himself around his family as the ground trembled with the force of the blast.

"No!" Yun Zeru's voice roared over the explosion.

"The Elemental!" He ushered to his men beside him, waving them into the castle.

"The Elemental?" Elara frowned. "Why is he—?"

"Doesn't matter," Argon yelled as he pulled her up to her feet. "We have to go!"

Together, they ran through the ruined castle.

The once pristine halls were now disheveled skeletons. Empty lanterns hung on either side of the remaining thick, stone walls. Lush, rich, thick tapestries were ripped into shreds, hanging in their tattered remains. Crushed glass littered the floor, and mirrors were smashed and shattered into sharp, thin slivers.

The little family ran past one of the larger halls, where one giant tapestry hung from one wall to the other, miraculously still intact. Elara turned her head towards it as she continued to run, taking in its ornate embroidery.

In the center, the figure of a young woman was meticulously stitched into the fabric. A crown sat in her raven hair, with stitched beams of light embroidered around the crown. The woman was looking down into her hands, which were clasped above her chest. In her grasp, a precious black stone peeked from between her fingers.

A mix of leaves and vines branched out from around the stone's borders, each leaf's tendril delicately stitched into the fabric. Gusts of wind blowing around the leaves were etched into the fabric, with beams of fiery light swirling around the branched out greenery. Rivers and streams of deep blue waters were intertwined throughout the carpet, with each wave carefully mapped out within the streams.

The four elements.

Elara's eyes narrowed.

Elara halted suddenly, pulling Argon's hand to stop him in his tracks. "We have to go back," she said urgently, her eyes shining.

"Are you insane?" Argon yelled. "Yun Zeru's hell hounds are coming after us. We have to keep moving!"

"Trust me," Elara asserted. She grabbed his hand, pulling her husband and child into the depths of the castle. She ran down the staircase, turning down another hallway.

"Where are we going?" asked Argon, Helia bouncing in his arms as he ran with his wife through the ruins.

"The Queen's quarters. I have a hunch," Elara called back.

The visiting Elara watched as her small family raced into the Queen's wing of the castle, finally making it towards a set of heavy doors. She raced towards the door, its hinges rusted shut.

"We need to get in," yelled future Elara. "Help me!"

Argon and Elara heaved their bodies against the door. Sure enough, their weight pushed the heavy wood open, and Helia watched as her parents broke into the room.

There, in the middle of the floor, lay the Queen's decaying remains. Elara fought back the urge to heave, the smell of her rotting corpse overwhelming her senses, as she rushed over to the Queen's side. A few inches away from her head lay an ornate platinum Diadem. It was a beautiful piece of royal jewelry; heavy set emeralds, rubies, sapphires, and diamonds were encrusted into the base, and the twines of the Diadem rose in small, delicate points, with platinum vines twisted around the tips of the Diadem. At the very back of the Diadem lay a shiny black stone, brilliantly carved into a multi-faceted gem.

Elara closed her hand around the Diadem, staring at

the coveted royal artifact in disbelief.

"Let's get out of here," said Argon, helping her up. "Before they make it—"

A loud snarl ripped through the room, cutting Argon's words off. They spun around and saw three large, hooded men, each of them wielding a broadsword and pointing it at them.

"They're trapped," the visiting Miela whispered, horrified.

She was right. They were cornered in the Queen's quarters, with nothing between them except the rotting carcass of the Queen.

Future Argon brandished his own sword, and pulled out her daggers. Immediately flying into action, she hurled one of them at the men, hitting him directly in the eye. He screamed, blood spurting out from between his fingers as he held his eyes.

"Helia! Take her! Go!" she yelled desperately.

Argon raced towards the screaming toddler, grabbing her and pushing through the other two men, holding his child in his arms as he raced down the hallway. Elara chased after the two men, who turned their attention to Argon.

"RUN!"

Elara's breath caught in her throat as her whole world shattered before her eyes. One of the men lunged at Argon, his sharp sword swinging in one clean arc. She screamed, watching as his body staggered forwards before dropping to the ground face-first. His neck was sliced clean through, blood billowing out of the gash and all over the toddler who was still in his arms. Her heart pounded in her chest, her body moving of its own accord as she threw a dagger at the man who snatched her husband's life away from her, the blade digging deep into the center of his back. In a blind range, she threw herself on top of the last man, wrapping her hands around his neck, and squeezed as hard as she could, watching as the man began to slowly choke, clawing at the woman's hands wrapped fiercely around his throat. Her knees were soaked in blood, and her eyes drifted to her husband's body, the blood spilling out from him and pooling around where she knelt. She squeezed harder, watching as the life began to fade from the man's bloodshot, bulging eyes, his voice catching in his throat as he struggled to draw in air, and his hands desperately clawed at her, growing weaker with every passing second. Elara screamed ferociously, digging her nails into his throat as he breathed his last breath.

Helia's screams continued as Elara ripped the small girl from under her father's body, tears streaming down her face as she ran.

The visiting Elara felt as though someone punched her hard in her gut. She couldn't breathe as she watched the blood-soaked toddler screaming in her mother's arms. The visiting Argon's face echoed her own.

Future Elara ran as fast she could. She passed a window and quickly snuck a peek out of it. To her horror, each of her friends were lined up in front of Yun Zeru in the court yard, their hands and feet bound tightly. It seemed that his troops succeeded in finding the last members of his resistance. She watched in terror as Yun Zeru bellowed at them, pressing Helia's face into her chest to muffle the child, her heart breaking as she felt the toddler's shoulders shake in her grasp.

Noiro lifted his head up defiantly at Yun, spitting in his

direction. Yun Zeru's face twisted in disgust, and nodded his head at one of his troops. A man walked towards the future Noiro, carrying a torch.

Elara howled mournfully as she watched the man lower the torch to Noiro's feet, his body slowly igniting. His screams pierced her ears, the smell of burning flesh and hair reached even to where she stood. Yun Zeru stared at the burning corpse, unfazed.

She wanted to help. She needed to save them.

She glanced down at her baby wailing desolately in her arms.

She had no choice. She had to keep Helia alive.

Elara held Helia tight against her body, her mind spinning as she ran towards the back of the castle.

"Where is she going?" asked the visiting Elara, watching herself.

"I don't know," the visiting Noiro murmured softly. He felt sick to his stomach, his own screams still echoing in his head as his future self slowly perished in the flames.

"She's going to hide," said the visiting Miela, watching her friend run.

Sure enough, Miela was right.

The future Elara ducked into the kitchens, throwing open one of the cabinets and crawling in with Helia.

The world swirled around the visiting group once again.

Future Elara sat in a small, dark room, concentrating as she fiddled with something in her hands. She hissed suddenly, bringing a finger to her mouth and sucking on it, dropping the blade that she was using. On the table, lay a small, battered journal, and the remnants of the Diadem, now shattered into countless pieces of platinum and precious stones.

"The Diadem," the visiting Miela gasped in shock, pointing at the broken royal artifact. "She broke it? Why would she break it?"

The vising Elara peered closely at the black stone nestled in her future self's hands, eyes lighting up as she recognized the familiar markings. "The Aether Stone!"

"How did she find the Aether Stone?" asked the visiting Argon, pointing at future Elara as she continued to carve her blade into the stone.

"Did we miss something?" the visiting Miela echoed. She edged towards the sundial, where the visiting Noiro stood. "Did we miss a code from the journal?"

"This is it," said the visiting Noiro. He drew close to the future Elara and examined the journal. "She's writing down the number sequences in the journal, and carving the dials into the stone."

Future Elara finished making one more carving in the stone and pulled out a long chain, looping it through the new hole she had etched into the stone, fashioning a crude necklace. She quickly gathered her things and trudged carefully around the shattered mounds of glass and splintered messes of wood. The ruined remains of what was once Noiro's cottage.

She made her way up the stairs and into one of the rooms. She set the journal and stone onto the small table which stood at the side, and finally sat down on the bed, glancing over at the crib, where a small mess of blankets lay. Elara could hear the soft, familiar snore as Helia slumbered fitfully.

BANG.

"They're here," she whispered, her voice trembling as she quickly shoved the items she had placed down only a moment ago into an old, leather satchel.

The visitors observed silently as future Elara picked up Helia from the crib, murmuring softly against her head as she soothed her child. She fastened a small cloak around the toddler's shoulders and quietly snuck out of the cottage.

The visiting group watched in dismay as two hooded men tailed after the fleeing pair, yelling at each other to pursue the woman and child. Future Elara raced through the thicket of overgrown rose bushes, finally making it to the Great Library. Several more men ran after her, but she bought herself a few moments alone with Helia. She pulled the necklace out and put it over Helia's head.

The pendant began to faintly glow blue as Elara twisted the dials, a faint clicking sound echoing through the empty library.

"Listen here, Helia," she whispered, pulling her satchel's handle over her toddler's head. "You see Mama's bag?"

Helia nodded her head, still sniffling.

"Take Mama's bag—that's right, good girl. Don't you let go of the bag, all right? Whatever you do, don't let go of Mama's bag. Keep it safe with you."

"Okay, Mama," said Helia, clutching the satchel tightly. She closed her eyes as her mother pulled her hood over her head, pressing her lips to her forehead in a strong kiss.

BANG.

The visitors watched as future Elara whirled around, throwing herself in front of Helia and facing her assailants.

The moonlight poured in from the doorway, illuminating four young men standing before her.

"Hand over the Elemental," one of the men barked.

"Mama," Helia squeaked. The pendant around Helia's neck flashed bright. Elara grinned.

"She's sending Helia back," remarked the visiting Noiro.

Elara flew as she attacked the men, holding them off from her daughter. She turned her head to glance at Helia, making sure she was okay. At that moment, one of the men swung his sword against her chest, and blood sprayed across the floor, and all over Helia.

"No! Mama!"

Elara wheezed, blood bubbling in her chest as she tried to draw in air. She refused to take her eyes off of her baby until she was sure her plan had worked.

The pendant around Helia shone bright, enveloping the toddler in a blue flash. When the light disappeared, so did all traces of Helia.

The future Elara breathed a sigh of relief, and turned to her assailants, staggering as another blast hit her.

Her clothes clung to her as blood billowed out from her wounds and soaked through. She wheezed, her breathing sounding wet and garbled as more blood spilled from her lips. Elara fell to the floor, her body hitting the marble with a loud thud, and she breathed her last.

The world vanished around the visitors for the last time.

They were left sitting in Noiro's calm, comfortable cottage.

It was over.

The four adults sat silently, each of them lost in a

swirl of thoughts and emotions at the events that they witnessed.

Elara stood slowly, knees trembling beneath her as she tried to pull herself together. "I'll get us some water," she said blankly.

Miela nodded robotically. Argon sat, still as a statue as he replayed the scenes in his mind. Noiro fought back the urge to dry heave, and he stared intently at the ground.

Elara wandered to the kitchen in a daze, pausing in the middle of the dining table as she stared out the window, the warm, comforting rays of the sun shining against her face. The weight of all of what she had witnessed hit her full force, and she let out a quiet sob as she fell to her knees beneath the burden of it all.

THE HISTORIAN

"Elara?" Noiro called uncertainly, his ears picking up the small sob from the kitchen. He stood up from his seat, making his way to the kitchen. He walked slowly over to where she knelt.

Her head was bent over, and her fists were curled up on her knees as she cried.

"Are you okay?" Argon whispered. He immediately regretted the question; of course she was not okay. No one was.

Elara nodded, sniffing as she wiped her cheek. "I'm okay," she said. "It's...it's just a lot to take in."

"I know," said Noiro sadly.

"How could we have done that?" Elara uttered mournfully. "All of that. How could we?"

Elara's question caught Noiro by surprise.

"She was a coward," she continued, recalling her future self's actions. "She watched you all die. She was the last one left, and she couldn't do anything to save you. I watched all of you…"

Argon's head snapped up from the sitting room as Elara's voice reached his ears, and he concentrated as he tried to listen closely to the rest of the conversation.

"Elara, what are you saying? She did everything you could. Anyone would have made the same decisions she made."

"She could have stopped Yun Zeru. She had weapons—I could've—"

"Done what, exactly?" Noiro interrupted her. "Put Helia up to the same fate? She was protecting her. She was protecting all of us. Nothing was her fault. And nothing is your fault. You don't have anything to do with this."

"Noiro, *she* is me," Elara reminded him.

"Yes, she is. But you're not her. You didn't make any of those decisions. And even if you did, so what? Your decisions led Helia back to us to stop all of this. Without you, we would have never known any of this. No one will have to die. We're going to stop this."

Elara nodded. Another tear rolled down her cheek.

"No, don't just nod your head. I want you to say it. I want you to believe it. We're going to stop this," Noiro pressed.

"We're going to stop this," Elara repeated. She wiped her face again. "You don't have to… Go back to the sitting room. I'll get us some water—"

"No. You go back. I'll get the water," Noiro said firmly. Elara opened her mouth to argue, and then decided against it. She was exhausted.

She made her way back to the sitting room, where Argon and Miela were still seated.

Miela still looked shaken, although she said nothing. Elara squeezed her shoulder comfortingly, and Miela put a hand over Elara's.

"Drink up. I also brought us some fruit," Noiro said, bringing in a tray into the sitting room. He set down the tray and pushed an apple into Argon's hands. "Eat."

Miela reached out for a banana, quickly peeling it before Noiro shoved another piece of fruit at one of them. Noiro was like that; he pushed food towards people when he didn't know what else to do. She recalled him trying to push a sweet into Helia's hand when they first met at the library.

The same library where Helia saw Elara murdered a few mere feet away from her.

No wonder Helia was in hysterics when she had first appeared. She vowed once again to keep the little tyke safe.

"Okay. Where do we begin?" Miela asked, leaning forward.

"Inana," Argon answered swiftly. "If our assumption is correct on Inana being the one who was the first casualty in all of this, and it was her blood on my wall when I was attacked, then she was the first confirmed victim in this whole bloodbath."

"I think you're right," agreed Miela. "She's the first piece of the puzzle. And according to the timeline we saw, the attack that happened isn't very long from now."

"We need to figure out why she was targeted, though," said Noiro. He looked at Argon curiously. "How close are you to Inana? And her family?"

"We've been friends since we were kids," Argon replied. "We're still good friends, but we don't really have time to see each other as much as we used to compared to when we were little. Why?"

"Do you think anyone would want to hurt her to get to you?" asked Elara.

Argon shook his head. "If someone wanted to get to me, they would go after my mother, or sister." He frowned for a moment. "I wonder if Inana's attack was meant to hurt her parents. They're an old Polarian family, and they're...comfortable."

"What? Comfortable?"

"They're wealthy," Argon clarified. "Extremely. And closely tied to the Royal Family. I wonder if they were being blackmailed?"

Elara folded her arms. "It's a plausible assumption, especially since Inana's parents were attacked months after her disappearance. It can't be a coincidence."

"Do you think you could speak to Inana?" asked Miela, looking at Argon.

"I was supposed to have dinner with her the other week, but we cancelled. I could ask her this week."

"Good," Miela said, satisfied. "But be careful. We can't reveal—"

"I know, Captain," Argon interrupted. "It's confidential. I know."

"Good." Miela smiled. "Okay, so Argon will talk to Inana. What's next?"

"Estelle," Elara chimed. "In the future, she was so scared that she was almost deranged. Something was definitely not right."

Miela nodded. "You're right. She looked terrified."

"I haven't spoken to her in years," muttered Argon tentatively, "but I know that that was not my sister. I mean, she *is* my sister. But what we saw... That was not her."

"I wonder why we were going to see her in the first place," mused Elara. "I remember us talking about getting some information... Information about what, though?"

"I don't know," Miela admitted. "But we do know that she was targeted for something. Maybe about something she knew. She looked scared. Like she was being watched."

"She was so scared that she slit her own throat than chance facing whatever it was behind the door," added Elara.

"Do you think it's possible that she found out something? Or could it be that she is also linked to Argon's attack, as well? You said that if someone wanted to hurt you, they'd go after your mother and sister. They were both attacked in the future," observed Noiro, looking at Argon.

"I think we should go talk to her. We should find out what she's been up to," suggested Miela, rubbing her temples. "It's possible that nothing's happened yet. But I don't like how little time we have until the first attack on Inana. We need to move quickly."

"We can go tomorrow," proposed Noiro.

Argon raised an eyebrow. "Tomorrow?"

Noiro nodded. "The sooner we move, the better. If something already happened, she may already be spooked. And she never came to us for help in the future," Noiro pointed out. "She might have been feeling threatened, scared, alone."

Argon fell silent, a feeling of guilt creeping over him. How could he have abandoned his sister in the future? He couldn't even remember what their falling out was over; it was so long ago.

"What about Yun Zeru?" Elara asked suddenly, breaking Argon out of his thoughts. He shuddered at the thought of the man; he had never seen anyone so ruthless before. He couldn't erase the image of him burning Noiro out of his mind, the screams etched into his memory forever.

He never wanted to hear another sound like that again.

Miela turned her attention to Argon. "You were celebrating with him the night of your attack," she said. "You seem to be the common connection here with Inana, your sister Estelle, and Yun Zeru."

Argon shrugged. "I mean, he's approached me a few times..." he trailed off thoughtfully.

"Most of the men he's approached seem to have risen incredibly fast in their military career," Miela said pointedly. "If he's approaching you, it means he's interested in you."

"Do you think he's recruiting?" asked Argon, his eyebrows pulled together in worry.

Miela shrugged. "It's possible. To pull off something that big, he's had to be planning it for a long time."

"Let's see if we can use that to our advantage," Noiro suggested. "If you start acting differently now, anyway, something might tip him off. It's best to remain neutral for now."

"Agreed," Miela said. "Okay. Let's get to work."

Elara stood in front of her mirror, brushing her hair to the side with a small clip. She examined herself for a moment before shaking her head and pulling the clip out. She sighed, giving up experimenting with her hair, settling on pulling it back into a high ponytail.

A soft knock rapped against her front door, and she headed towards the main entrance, peeking through the window to catch a glimpse of who was at her door.

"Hello," she chimed cheerfully.

"Good morning, Elara," Noiro greeted. "Am I the first one here?"

"Yep. Argon and Miela should be here soon," Elara said, leading Noiro into her home. "I just dropped off Helia at Tami's. She's delighted with the puppies there."

"Hello," Miela called out from the front door, letting herself in. Argon nodded in greeting as he followed.

"We stopped by the office before coming here," Miela explained, lifting a small book in her hand. "I wanted to dig for any more information on the Erifs before Argon's dinner with Inana this week."

"Did you find anything interesting?" asked Elara, showing Miela and Argon into the sitting room. She avoided Argon's gaze as she offered him a seat. She still felt a little uneasy after all that they had seen from the future.

Elara felt confused. There was no other way to describe what she felt when she looked at Argon. To see their future together, watching the two of them fall in love in the midst of wars and battles, raising a child together while on the run, watching him risk his life to save their child... The loss she felt when she watched him die. She never imagined herself being able to love like that, or to have someone love her like that.

Looking at him now, she felt baffled. She did not know him. She knew the man she saw in the future, but Argon was not that man right now.

She recalled Argon's initial reaction to Helia, and how horrid he was to her at first. A small, sudden wave of rage washed over her as she remembered his first words to her child, *"Move, you little brat."*

Her mind flipped back to the scene of Argon's retreating back as he raced through Polaris Castle, with Helia wailing in his arms as he raced to protect her. How the blood spilled from his body after he was brutally slaughtered while shielding his daughter.

It was unsettling, to say the least, to watch him be so devoted to her and Helia. She wondered how he felt. After all, he had seen the same things she did. He saw Helia's unconditional love for him. He saw her own devotion to him in the future.

He watched himself die protecting his family.

"We didn't find much," Miela admitted, pulling Elara away from her internal reflections. "Only one thing: Inana's father had his home broken into a few months ago."

"I remember Inana telling me about that," said Argon pensively. "It was a while ago, though."

Miela pressed her lips together. "I was looking through any reports that mentioned the Erifs. Mr. Erif's home was broken into around four months ago. Nothing was taken, but Mr. Erif reported that the intruder turned their house completely upside down, and his dog was slaughtered on his doorstep. He came in completely distraught, demanding that the intruder be caught and put away. Two days later, he came in and retracted his report, dropping all the charges."

"Why would he drop the charges?" Elara questioned.

"He said he was overreacting," Argon replied, recalling

his conversation with Mr. Erif. "Strange. I didn't know his dog was killed, too."

"It's all here in the report," said Miela.

"It sounds like he's being threatened," added Noiro thoughtfully.

"That's what I think," agreed Miela. "But why?"

"That's what I'll find out when I see Inana for dinner tomorrow," vowed Argon. "I know she was pretty shaken up about the break in."

"Okay, that sounds good," approved Miela. "Now, for our task today: Are we ready to see Estelle?"

The group stood up, feeling a little uneasy as they prepared to leave Elara's home. Elara felt a sinking feeling in her gut; they were attacked the last time she saw Estelle. And they never found out who was watching Estelle, or why she was driven to taking her own life in front of them.

It was a lengthy trip to Estelle's house, seeing as they needed to take a boat out to reach the Ursa Isles. Their trip was rather silent, each of them concentrating on their own thoughts. Argon felt his stomach twist as they drew nearer to his sister's home. It had been years since they last spoke.

"We're here," Argon announced, coming to a stop in front of the familiar little house. He led the group down the pathway and towards the front door.

"Ready?" Miela asked firmly. She couldn't help but feel the tension in the air. Unlike herself in the future, she kept a focused gaze on the door in front of them, watching vigilantly for any signs of danger. Argon nodded, and rapped his knuckles sharply against the door.

The group could hear a small shuffle of footsteps. There was a small pause before the door opened, and a tall woman poked her head out of the door. Estelle looked much younger than the version they had seen in the future, and much more at ease. Her face broke out into a smile as her eyes met Argon, and she pulled him in for a hug.

"Argon!" she cried happily. Argon stiffened uncomfortably, confused. Had she forgotten their grudge? He slowly moved his hands to hug his sister back.

"Er—Hello, Estelle," Argon greeted solemnly. "How have you been?"

"Great! And you?" Estelle beamed, taking a step back to look at her brother. "It's been a long time."

"It has," Argon admitted, the twinge of guilt twisting tighter in his stomach. Yet his lips curved into a small smile as Estelle grinned, clearly elated at his appearance. "I'm doing well. It's good to see you."

"It is!" And you've brought friends?" She boldly turned her head to Miela, Elara, and Norio, curiously, yet not impolitely.

"Uh, they're…yes," Argon faltered, turning to the group behind them. Could he call them friends? They certainly did not hold the same animosity they shared as children anymore. In fact, he began to find himself looking forward to their meetings. Noiro was an insightful, curious fellow, who almost always steered their conversations to interesting discussions. Miela was spunky, lively, spontaneous, and fun to be around. He glanced at Elara, feeling his face grow hot. Elara was… Well, he was not entirely sure what he could call her. They were growing to be friends, indeed. But he couldn't shake off what he had seen through the Aether Stone: their future together, their life together.

Miela stepped forward with her hand outstretched, glancing perplexedly at Argon as he fell silent. "I'm Miela.

And this is Elara and Noiro."

"You're a Guardian," Estelle noted coolly, her eyes glancing at the small tattoo on Miela's wrist.

"Yes... Captain, actually," Miela said with a smile.

Estelle smiled back, although this time, it did not quite reach her eyes. She shook Miela's hand. "Very nice to meet you, Captain. Please, come in," she urged, moving aside to let the group in. If Estelle was surprised at the visit, she hid it well. She graciously led the foursome into her home and into her main sitting room.

"May I offer you something to drink?" she asked, gesturing at the four to take their seats.

"Oh, it's okay," Miela declined. "This is just meant to be a short visit."

"I insist," Estelle said firmly, and quickly rushed over to her kitchen. She appeared back with a tea tray, smiling at the group as she set it down onto the table in the middle of the sitting room.

The group had some tea.

"So, what brings you here today?" Estelle asked pleasantly. "Is this about the complaint I filed a few days ago?"

"Complaint?" Miela echoed curiously, exchanging a look with her friends. "Er—frankly, no. But I'd be happy to address it."

Estelle smiled. "I'd appreciate that. But we can get to that in a bit," she said. The woman looked at the group seated in her sitting room. "So, if you're not here for my complaint, then what is it you're here for, exactly?"

"Well," Miela began, her host's boldness taking her by surprise. Although Estelle's cheeriness was a stark contrast to her brother's solemnness, their brashness was something they apparently shared. "We were hoping you could help us. We're working on a case."

"Oh?" Estelle raised an eyebrow, intrigued.

"We were wondering if you had seen anything suspicious take place around here, lately?" Estelle inquired apprehensively, unsure of what exactly to ask her. She had been so nervous about coming to visit Estelle, especially after watching what had happened in the future, that she hadn't had time to really prepare her line of questions.

Estelle leaned back in her chair, bemused at the question. "Around the neighborhood? No, not really," she answered thoughtfully. "I mean, the neighbor's boys keep pestering me with their incessant noise they make at all hours of the night. You'd think they'd get tired of playing whatever games they've been tinkering around with, but no." She shook her head, slightly amused. "They're going to be my students next year."

"Students? You're teaching?" asked Argon, surprised.

Estelle beamed, nodding.

"Estelle is a historian," Argon explained to the group.

Estelle nodded proudly. "Not much else to do around here for a historian. More opportunities in Polaris, I guess," mused Estelle.

"Why don't you come to Polaris, then?" asked Elara. "I know that the Old Archive are always looking for historians."

"I don't really want to leave the Ursa Isles," Estelle admitted, sighing wistfully. She looked around her home, a small smile playing on her lips. "It's my family's home... We—I could never leave here."

She glanced at Argon. He looked away.

"Besides, I'm teaching at the local school. History, of

course," Estelle said with a grin, turning her head back to the group.

Miela smiled at Estelle. "I'm sure your students love your class." She paused, turning back to her original question. "So, other than the neighbors, notice anything unusual?"

Estelle shook her head again. "Nothing. It's a quiet little neighborhood," she replied thoughtfully. "Not much happens around here."

Miela nodded, crossing her arms as she thought.

"I'm sorry," Estelle sighed. "I don't seem to be much help…"

"No, it's okay." Miela waved her hands. "It's actually a relief."

"Is there something wrong?" Estelle asked, concerned. "Do I need to be on the lookout for something?"

"No," Miela repeated firmly. "Nothing to worry about… But if you do see something, please get in touch with us."

"All right," replied Estelle, looking unconvinced. "Is there anything I can help you with?"

"No—"

"Actually," Argon interrupted, "there is something."

"Oh?" Estelle looked at Argon expectantly.

"It's a little random, really. But I was wondering if you could tell us about the Queen's Diadem."

Estelle looked surprised at the question. To her, it definitely appeared to be a random request. However, to Miela, Elara, and Noiro, the question was a brilliant stroke of genius. There was little they knew about the Diadem, other than the fact that they risked their lives in the future to get it.

"The Queen's Diadem?" Estelle echoed pensively. "Sure. Let me think… It's a beautiful piece of royal jewelry, passed down to the royal descendants for generations. Is there anything specific that you'd like to know about?"

Argon shook his head. "Nothing specific. I'm not sure exactly what I'm asking for either," he admitted, feeling rather silly.

"That's all right," she said with a wave. She looked delighted at the chance to give a history lesson. "I'll just tell you what I know, and if anything comes to mind, you can stop me and ask questions."

Argon smiled.

"The Queen's Diadem… It's a unique piece, really. It has four sets of sapphires, rubies, emeralds, and diamonds embedded into the Diadem itself. The choice of gem is very intentional. Each gem represents the Earth's elements: sapphire for water, rubies for fire, emeralds for earth, and diamonds for air."

Elara frowned. Again, the mention of the Elements.

Estelle noticed Elara's fixation and continued: "You see, the royals pay a heavy tribute to the Earth's Elements, with each descendant claiming to possess an affinity for a specific element."

"An affinity?" Noiro repeated. "So, they're claiming to be Elementals?"

Estelle shrugged. "Not really. The royals *claim* they're connected to the elements, but they don't exactly have the power to influence the elements. There've been a lot of claims of Elementals popping up in their bloodline every few generations, but they're all unsubstantiated." She shook her head. "By my mark, they're not Elementals. But being able to make those claims certainly gave the Royal Family their foundation for power and legitimized their rule over the lands."

"But they're not Elementals?"

"Not quite," Estelle said firmly. "But the Royal Family is certainly quite captivated by the elements. Which is why the Queen's Diadem was fashioned in that way, to pay tribute to the terrestrial elements."

"What makes the Diadem so special?" asked Miela curiously.

"Well, it's certainly valuable," Estelle replied with a smirk. "I guess you could ask why anyone would covet a piece of royal treasure. It's a symbol of power. It's a symbol of royalty. Authority."

Miela tilted her head. "Hmm. I guess you're right."

Elara frowned. In the future, she'd found the Queen's Diadem in the castle. She remembered the beautiful stones encrusted into the Diadem, and the pure disbelief she felt as she grasped the royal artifact in her hand. An inkling of realization surfaced in her mind, and she looked curiously at the enthusiastic historian. "Estelle," she said. "What do you mean when you say stones in the Diadem were very intentional?"

"The Diadem's design itself is a tribute to the elements. It tells a story—hold on…" Estelle pushed herself off of her seat and hastily left the sitting room. The group exchanged curious glances at each other once again, before Estelle scurried back into the sitting room, a large book in hand.

She flipped through the pages, licking her fingers as she turned the pages, and paused for a moment, her eyes studying the pages before her. She turned the book around, showing the visiting group before her what she found.

A detailed painting of an intricate ornate platinum Diadem was spread across the book's pages. It was just as they saw it in the future: large emeralds, rubies, sapphires, and diamonds lined the Diadem's base. A platinum vine swirled around each gem, wrapping around each other into an intricate tangle that met in the center of the Diadem.

"The Queen's Diadem," said Estelle, pointing at the painting. "Each gem is connected; the diamonds, the emeralds, the rubies, and the sapphires are all intertwined with each other to signify how the elements of the world are connected to each other."

"I see."

"I can do some more digging on the Diadem, if you'd like," offered Estelle. "I have to admit, it's been a very long time since I studied up on royal artifacts."

Elara smiled gratefully. "I'd appreciate that."

Estelle smiled back. "It's no trouble. It's not often I come across someone so interested in history." She reached out for her cup of tea, which, until that moment, sat forgotten on the table between them. "Is there anything else I can help you with?"

"Er, no, thank you," Miela replied. "I appreciate the time you took to answer our questions. We'd best be going now" She stood up, nodding at her friends.

"Oh, Captain?" chirped Estelle. "Would you mind taking a report of my complaint?"

"Yes! Of course," said Miela smacking her forehead. "Thank you for reminding me. I'll just take a few notes…" She pulled out her notebook and began jotting down a few points as Estelle spoke.

The group began to gather their things as they got ready to leave Estelle's residence. Elara glanced at Noiro and Argon, eager to discuss her theory. She straightened out her blouse and turned to Miela and Estelle as they finished speaking.

"Thank you for the history lesson," said Elara gratefully, shaking Estelle's hand firmly. "Don't be surprised if I stop by again for another lesson."

"Please, do!" Estelle beamed. "It's a nice change from my students who look bored to tears." She turned to Argon. "Argon, please, don't be a stranger."

Argon nodded solemnly, a small smile gracing his face as he looked back at his sister.

Estelle walked with the group as they made their way to the front door, showing them out.

"Oh, one more thing," said Estelle thoughtfully as she leaned against the doorway. "Argon, can you please do me a favor?"

Argon turned around.

"Would you mind holding onto this for me?" asked Estelle. She quickly backed into the sitting room, rummaging about for a moment before returning with a sealed package. It looked rather thick, and was neatly wrapped up in some sturdy brown paper.

"Oh?" Argon hummed. "No problem, I can do that for you.

Estelle beamed gratefully. "Thank you so much," she said, handing the package over with a small chuckle. "Although, you should be thanking me for holding onto it for so long. It's yours, you know."

"What is it?"

"A book," Estelle replied simply.

"A book?" Miela raised an eyebrow.

Estelle nodded. "One of a kind. It's an old family heirloom from my grandfather's own personal library." She turned to Argon. "Dad left it to you when he died. You never came to pick it up from our library, though. It's rightfully yours."

"Oh," Argon murmured, letting out a breath he wasn't aware he was holding in.

"Keep it safe," Estelle urged, placing a hand on the package. "It's a part of our history. It's a part of us."

"I will," Argon promised.

Estelle nodded gratefully.

They bid each other farewell, and the group parted ways from Estelle's house.

As soon as they were out of earshot, Noiro let out a whistle. "That was quite an informative trip," he said.

Elara scoffed. "That's an understatement. Argon, that was a good move, asking her about the Diadem. I wouldn't have even thought of asking her about that!"

Argon nodded. "She's a history nut. Our whole family is, actually. I used to tease her about it when we were kids, but it turned out to be pretty useful today."

Miela sighed, rubbing her temples. "All right, let's start at the beginning," she muttered, trying to organize her thoughts. "We know we risked our lives to get our hands on that Diadem in the future on one of the last missions. Why? And why do the elements keep popping up in our search?"

"Well… The Royal Family's claim to the throne is based on the attribution of Elementals in their bloodline," said Noiro. "It makes sense that they've embedded that lore within their own narrative."

"But they're not Elementals," Miela pointed out.

"No, they're not," agreed Noiro. "Like Estelle said, there have been claims of Elementals popping up in their bloodline… But they're not verified claims. But if we want to explore the reason why, then we have to go to the root of the issue."

"And what's the root of the issue?" asked Miela.

"The beginning. We need to trace back where Elementals begin to pop up in their narrative," Noiro said firmly. "I have a few books on the royal history back in my cottage. I can do some reading and see what I can find."

"That sounds like a good plan," Miela noted. "Maybe we can find out what's so special about that Diadem."

Argon, who had been quiet for most of the conversation, softly cleared his throat. "I think we need to keep our voices down," he whispered. "We might be overheard."

"You're right," agreed Miela. "We can get into it more in Noiro's cottage. I assume that's where we're headed?"

Noiro nodded.

Elara lowered her voice as they clambered back onto their boat. "Miela, what did Estelle say her complaint was about?"

"That's what I actually wanted to bring up when we left her house," said Miela. "It was about the package she gave Argon. Someone tried to break into her house, and her library was ransacked. She thinks they were after that book."

"A break-in…for a book?" Elara frowned. Miela nodded. "Is it valuable?"

"It's one of a kind," murmured Argon, echoing what Estelle had said to him earlier.

"What's in that book that would be worth breaking into someone's house for?" Miela pondered.

"There's only one way we'll find out what they were after," said Elara, reaching for the package. "We need to open it."

"Not here!" Argon yelped, his eyes darting around. "Once we get back to Noiro's."

"Fine," Elara sighed.

Miela shuddered. "Whatever it is, I have a feeling Yun Zeru is involved."

"That makes me wonder," Noiro began, scratching his head. "When we visited Estelle in the future, there was someone in her house. Someone who scared her enough to try and kill us, and so terrified when she failed that she slit her own throat."

"You don't think…" Argon trailed off, his eyes widening, heart beating faster as he saw his sister, lying face down in a pool of her own blood, bright and clear in his mind's eye. "You don't think that Yun Zeru himself was there in the future, do you? Do you think he might be after the book?"

Noiro looked at Argon. "It's possible. In the timeline that we saw, we never showed up to Estelle's house to ask her questions in the beginning. If we had never shown up, then she would have never been able to pass the book along to Argon."

"And with the conversation around the Queen's Diadem… Do you think that that's what Yun Zeru was after? The Diadem?" Elara asked.

"I don't think so," replied Noiro. "In the future, he kept demanding for 'the Elemental.' It sounded like he was after a person."

"Strange," Miela hummed. "Especially when there aren't any Elementals... At least, none that we know of."

Elara sighed. She was relieved that they were making progress with understanding the upcoming war. But the more they learned about the future and what it held, the more questions she had.

The elements certainly popped up frequently enough in their mission's research. Why was it important? Why was the Aether Stone so important? What did Yun Zeru want with an Elemental?

The sun was setting as they neared Noiro's cottage. She looked at the silhouette of Polaris Castle, shining brightly amidst the clouds which were painted in an array of light pastels as the sun slowly descended in the sky. It was difficult to imagine the magnificent castle, standing in all its glory before her, be the burial grounds for everyone around her.

Out of everyone in that horrible war, the sole survivor was a three year-old.

"Oh," Elara breathed suddenly. "I have to pick up Helia!"

"It is getting late." Noiro nodded understandingly. "There's only so much playing a toddler can do with a handful of puppies."

"I can't believe I almost forgot," Elara said in dismay, stopping in her tracks. She fumbled with her satchel, flustered as she tried to consolidate her plans. "I'll pick her up, and then I can—oh, wait, I promised Helia that I'd..." Elara pinched the bridge of her nose as she mumbled to herself. "I can come after I—"

"Elara. Go," insisted Miela. She squeezed Elara's arm. "You're doing the best you can. Go."

"It's best we all take a break, anyhow," Noiro agreed. "We can meet up later this week. That way, I'll have some time to do some extra reading on the Royal Family."

"I'll also be meeting Inana for dinner this week," Argon reminded them. "I can update you on what I find out when we meet next."

"And the package?"

"I'll hold on to the package for now," said Argon, tucking it under his arm. "We can open it together when we meet next."

"All right," Elara said, smiling gratefully at her friends. "I've gotta go!" She hastily waved goodbye, and quickly turned around and set her course for Tami's house.

Elara's mind raced as she sped away. Trying to balance Helia along with her other duties was difficult. She bit her lip guiltily at the thought. She couldn't help but feel like a bad parent.

Helia turning up out of the blue had certainly turned everyone's lives upside down; trying to stop an impending war was only the cherry on top.

"Elara! Elara, wait!"

Elara snapped her head around at the sound of her name. Argon jogged lightly behind her, trying to catch up with the woman's hastened steps. She paused, politely waiting for the man to reach her where she stood.

"I was hoping I could join you," Argon said, coming to a stop as he reached her.

"Oh," Elara's breath caught in her throat.

Argon shook his head, his cheeks turning pink. "Er—I mean, I wanted to see Helia," he explained quickly. "I wanted to join you and see Helia."

Elara nodded, smiling faintly at Argon. "Sure."

The two continued their path, Argon matching Elara's quickened pace. It felt odd, having to walk with him without Miela and Noiro to break the tension. She peeked at him through the corner of her eyes, wondering if he felt the same way. She noticed that he was doing the same to her, his eyes quickly snapping back to the road ahead.

As they walked, Elara's mind drifted to Helia. She wondered how the little girl would feel, seeing both of her parents coming to pick her up together.

A family.

Elara didn't have much of a family. In fact, the only family she really had was Noiro and Miela.

She recalled Helia's face once again, smeared in her father's blood, screaming and crying horribly in her arms. She wondered if the little girl could fully comprehend the loss she felt as her father was snatched away from her, and then her mother.

Helia deserved a stable, happy family.

She looked at Argon again, and then cleared her throat. "Argon," Elara began. He turned his head towards her, a small curl falling onto his forehead as the wind began to pick up. "I was wondering what your plans were tomorrow."

"Tomorrow?" Argon thought for a moment. "I have a day off, tomorrow. I'll probably be running a few errands... There's a crack in my window that I need to replace." Argon stopped himself, wincing internally. Why was he bringing up something so mundane? He was certain she didn't care to hear about his errands.

"I was thinking about our conversation the other day," Elara said. "About Helia."

Argon felt his heart beat quicker.

"I was wondering what you were doing, because I wondered if you might like to join me and Helia for dinner."

Argon tilted his chin, surprised.

"If you still want to see Helia, that is," Elara added quickly, uncertainty beginning to creep up as he remained silent.

Argon snapped out of his silent daze, nodding eagerly. "Yes. Of course I want to see her." He leaned in, breaking out into a smile.

"A little bit after sunset," Elara suggested. "Does that work?"

"Yes." Argon nodded. "I'd like that very much."

"You can come over a bit earlier, if you'd like," Elara offered. "You can spend some more time with her before dinner."

Argon smiled. "I'll be there."

DINNER

"Is Dad here? Is Dad here yet, Mama?" Helia asked eagerly, trailing behind her mother.

"Not yet," Elara answered in amused exasperation, carefully slicing a strawberry.

"Now? Is he here now?"

"In a few minutes," Elara replied, finishing up the last of the strawberries and carefully placing them onto the cake. She licked some icing off from her thumb, and then bent down to brush her daughter's hair back with her fingers. "Why don't you go and wash up while I fix my hair?"

Helia stifled a giggle. "Your hair has custard!"

Elara gasped, quickly feeling around her head for some custard. She winced as her fingers sank into some soft mush, and quickly ran over to the bathroom to get a better look in the mirror. Sure enough, a decent-sized glob of bright yellow custard sat on a lock of her hair.

"Oh no," Elara muttered in dismay as she quickly ran some water over the custard to get it out. She had been nervous when she first asked Argon to come to her house for dinner, but her anxiety continued to climb all throughout the next day as dinnertime drew closer.

She toyed with the idea of trying to dress up, but quickly berated herself for thinking of it. After all, Argon's intent to come for dinner was to spend time with Helia, not with her. There was no need to try to impress him.

But, then again, she was the one to invite him over, and she certainly wanted to be a good host. She shook her head again, reminding herself that Argon was visiting Helia, not her. Besides, she wouldn't put in any extra effort for Noiro or Miela.

Elara looked over at herself, making sure there was no more custard on any of her clothes or hair. She wore a simple pair of white trousers, and a soft blue blouse. She smoothed her hands over her blouse, peering closer at herself. Her clothes would have to do, and she refused to put in extra effort to impress his company any more than she would for Miela or Noiro. His visit had nothing to do with her.

But she could at least do something with her hair?

She quickly pulled it to the side, her long, wavy hair tousling down her shoulder and hanging just above her midriff. She ran her fingers through her locks and nodded at herself in the mirror, satisfied.

"Is he here now, Mama?" Helia peered into the bathroom.

"No," Elara sighed. "Soon—" before she even finished, Helia had run out back to the kitchen. She was excited, and it made her nervous.

She wasn't sure what to expect. Helia was beyond ecstatic that her father was coming over especially to see her, but Elara was afraid that perhaps she might be disappointed.

She closed her eyes.

Knock. Knock. Knock.

"DAD'S HERE!" Helia shouted, running into the sitting room and jumping by the door. Elara inhaled deeply, following after Helia.

Putting on a smile, she turned the handle and opened the door.

"Dad! Dad!" Helia pushed past Elara and threw herself at him, squeezing his legs tight.

Argon's mouth was pulled into a small smile, and he gently touched the toddler's head as she hugged him even tighter. Helia looked up at him, beaming.

"You look nice, Dad. You look nice!" Helia said, clutching at Argon's trousers. Argon was dressed quite casually, with a crisp, charcoal button-down shirt, some black trousers, and leather shoes. His curly hair was neatly combed back, with a small, stubborn curl resting out of place on the side of his forehead. "Do I look nice, Dad?"

Helia stepped back to show off her outfit. Elara bit her lip, feeling self-conscious. She hadn't had time to go shopping for some more clothes for Helia, and rummaged up what she could find from Noiro's old storage. Helia didn't mind, however, and proudly showed off her pale yellow cotton overalls and a cropped white t-shirt.

"They were Mama's. You like them? You like them, Dad?" Helia babbled happily.

"It's very nice," Argon remarked, smiling at the toddler. "You look lovely."

"Please, come in," Elara said, gesturing at the man. Argon nodded politely and followed them in. Helia grabbed his hand, happily wrapping her hand around his, and led the way into the sitting room.

"What's that, Dad?" Helia asked, pointing to a bag in Argon's hand.

"I have something for you," Argon told her, looking up at Elara to make sure that it was all right with her. She looked curious and sported a small smile.

Good.

Argon retrieved a small package from the bag and handed it to Helia. The package was wrapped in brightly colored paper, with a small pink ribbon tied to the side. "Here you go."

Helia clutched at the package and quickly ran over to her mother. "A present! Dad got me a present!" Helia squealed, excitedly shoving the bag towards Elara.

"How nice!" Elara squeaked, grinning at the toddler's excitement and attempting to match it. "What do you say?"

"Can I open it?"

Elara chuckled. "First, say thank you."

"Thank you!" Helia piped. "Can I open it?"

Argon smiled. "Go ahead."

The little girl sat down onto the floor in the middle of the room and tore open the package. "A doll!" she gasped, clutching a rather large porcelain doll in her hands. It was slightly bigger than her torso, and had thick, chestnut brown hair that fell in waves, deep brown eyes, rosy cheeks, and a velvet red dress with a matching headband. Helia turned the doll over in awe, marveling at it before giving it a hug. "Mama, look!"

"It's beautiful," Elara breathed. She leaned forward, examining the delicate doll. "What do you say to Dad?"

Helia ran over to her father, throwing her arm around him while clutching at the doll with the other. "Thank you, Dad."

"You're welcome," Argon replied with a smile, hugging the little girl. As a Guardian, he spent a lot of time around sullen-faced military men and a handful of grim case files to solve. This much emotion and affection was new, but he certainly enjoyed it.

Elara chuckled. "I'll leave you two together. I need to check on dinner. It should be ready soon."

Seeing Helia so happy with her father warmed Elara's heart, and she smiled as she saw the same emotion dancing behind Argon's usually solemn eyes. Even though Argon hadn't spent much time with the toddler in their current timeline, their bond had somehow managed to span back across to them from the future.

"Wait," Argon said abruptly, looking up. "I brought this for you."

Elara's mouth parted open in surprise and anxiety as Argon reached into the bag, pulling out a small bouquet of flowers. She stared at the flowers, and then back at him, completely taken aback. She hadn't expected this.

"I wasn't sure which flowers you liked," he said, rubbing the back of his head. Her reaction, or lack thereof, was making him more nervous. His throat suddenly grew dry. "I saw these, and they reminded me of you." Argon gently pushed the bouquet of lilies forward.

Elara, shaking herself out of her stupor, nodded and accepted it with a blush creeping up her cheeks.

She felt silly. Argon was quite the gentleman. Bringing

a gift for the host was polite. It was simply what one did whenever visiting someone else's house. She had rarely been to a formal gathering where a gift would be given, and she hadn't perceived their dinner such an occasion. It was a play date with Helia.

Elara quickly glanced down at herself, wondering if she should have put a little more effort into her appearance. She looked at the flowers, the lilies' delicate scent wafting up towards her nose. They really were beautiful. Her cheeks grew warm as she remembered that he mentioned that they reminded him of her.

She suddenly realized that she was standing there, looking at the flowers, and still hadn't uttered a single word. She mentally kicked herself, feeling like an idiot. "Thank you," she blurted, feeling her ears growing hot. "They're beautiful."

Argon smiled nervously, now uncertain if he had overstepped his bounds.

"I love them," said Elara, looking up at him. "I'll go put these in some water."

"Mama? What's that smell?"

"Hmm—OH!" Elara darted towards the kitchen, the smell of something burning suddenly registering to her.

Elara breathed a sigh of relief as she peeked into the pot. The food was only slightly singed. She quickly removed the pot from the heat, saving the rest of their dinner from being burnt.

With the food scooped up onto the serving trays, she took a step back, looking over their dinner once more. Satisfied that the presentation was suitable, she sighed. She leaned on the counter, bending over and resting her head in her hands. She felt she had made a fool of herself, and her nerves were tingling with anxiety as she replayed the scene in her head. So far, she was far from a graceful host; she felt like an idiot.

Ugh.

It was, nonetheless, comforting to think that Argon had probably felt as uncertain as she did. She wondered if he had been debating about the same things she had been. Did he wonder about whether or not to bring her something? Had he spent time thinking about what to wear?

Probably not. He always looked nice.

Elara sighed again.

She had to go back out there.

She balanced the tray of food in her arms and walked slowly over to the dining table, setting them down gently. She went back into the kitchen, rummaging through the cupboards until she found a vase, filled it with water, and gingerly transferred the lilies into the vase. She put them in the center of the dining table, running her finger over one of the petals.

After a moment, she went back into the sitting room, watching as Helia avidly chattered away to Argon, who was listening intently to the toddler. She smiled at the two.

"Dinner's ready," she announced. "I hope you're hungry."

"But Mama! We haven't finished playing!" Helia objected.

"You can continue playing after dinner," said Elara firmly, watching pointedly as she trudged towards her seat at the dining table.

"Dad, you sit here." The toddler pointed at the seat next to her.

Argon sat down, pulling his seat closer to the table and placing a napkin across his lap. He looked at the lilies at the center of the table, and then back at Elara, a small, unconscious, lopsided smile splaying across his face.

Elara sat down as well, across from Helia and Argon. "Please, help yourself," she urged, oblivious to his smile.

"It looks delicious," said Argon, reaching towards one of the serving spoons. A decadent roasted herbed chicken sat on a large plate, with wedges of lemon, garlic, and tomatoes wedged beneath the poultry. Beside it sat a large bowl of crushed, buttery roasted potatoes, and another bowl of freshly chopped cucumber and mint salad.

"It's chicken," said Helia, beaming. "You like chicken, Dad?"

"My favorite," remarked Argon, heaping a large serving from each tray onto his plate.

"I'm glad," Elara smiled, plating the food for Helia before filling her own plate.

A few silent moments passed, and Argon felt obliged to say something. But he wasn't sure what to say. Finally, he uttered, "So, what did you do today?"

Elara looked at him curiously, chewing a bite of potatoes.

"I was all over the place today," she admitted, swallowing the lump of potatoes quickly, trying not to choke as it almost slid into her windpipe instead. She reached for her glass of water. "I met up with Noiro to drop off some books I managed to get from the Grand Library. We're trying to get some more information on the Diadem.

"After that, we went into the market to get some groceries, and stopped by a few stores to get some measurements for Helia. We're working on building her a wardrobe."

"The lady measured my belly," Helia giggled. "But she didn't want to measure my bellybutton."

"Helia was quite disappointed about her bellybutton not being measured," Elara chuckled. "So we measured it when we got home."

"We get to pick dresses tomorrow!" said Helia excitedly, waving her fork around. A small piece of chicken went flying from her utensil, and the two adults watched the morsel sail through the air and land gracefully into Elara's cup of water with a small plop.

Elara burst out into laughter, and Argon chuckled along with her. He couldn't help but notice how her nose crinkled up as she laughed, and her cheeks were rosy in the pale light. Her hair fell to the side as she giggled, and she unconsciously brushed a lock of hair behind her ear.

She was cute.

"I'll get a new glass," Elara chuckled, getting up from the table. She came back with a new glass and a big pitcher of iced water, pouring some into Argon's glass.

"Thank you," said Argon, lifting his glass.

"So what about you?" asked Elara. "How was your day today?"

"It was fine," said Argon. "I moved my dinner with Inana to breakfast today. It was... Well, we should probably discuss it at another time. But it was good to catch up with her; I haven't seen her in a while."

"Are you two close?"

"Kind of. We've known each other forever. Now that we're older and a lot more busy, we don't usually have the time to see each other as often as we used to when we were kids. But it's also the kind of friendship where when you finally do meet each other, it's like no time has passed at all."

"I know what you mean," said Elara. "Miela and I were joined at the hip when we were kids. Nowadays, with balancing work and other activities, it's difficult to meet up as often."

"Really?" Argon asked, surprised. "I was under the impression that you two still regularly saw each other."

"We do. But we're also meeting up more, now that we're working on the case," Elara said, carefully slicing into her chicken.

"I guess that's the silver lining to this case," Argon mused.

"I guess so." She chuckled. Elara hesitated, then asked, "So… does your family know you're here?"

Argon shook his head. "I told my mother I was going out to dinner. She lives with me here, in Polaris. She couldn't stand to stay in Ursa Isles since my father passed… And my sister, well, as you saw, she's still out in Ursa Isles. We don't really keep in touch that much."

"I see."

They fell into silence again, and Elara took another long sip of water from her glass to hide her discomfort in the long moment of silence.

"Are you going to tell your family about Helia?" she finally asked.

Argon looked taken aback by her blunt question. The dinner conversation seemed to take a turn from friendly, polite exchange to a direct, double edged inquiry. He would not let that affect his answer, though.

"No," he answered honestly. "At least, not right now. I

don't know how I'd explain it, and especially since we agreed to keep this a confidential case, I don't really see how I could disclose any information around Helia. And I...I want to keep her safe."

Elara nodded, taking another sip of water. Argon looked at her. She seemed satisfied with his answer.

"What about you?" asked Argon. "Are you going to tell your family?"

"Well...my family already knows about her."

Argon raised his eyebrow in surprise. "Really?"

"Yeah," said Elara. "Noiro is my family. At least, that's the only family I've ever known."

"Oh." Argon nodded, feeling like he had stepped into a sensitive topic.

"I don't know who my parents are," Elara confessed. "Noiro told me he had found me at his doorstep when I was a baby. He was kind enough to take me in, and I guess the rest is history."

Argon smiled sadly.

Elara noticed his empty plate, and gestured at the trays of food in front of them. "Please, don't be shy," she said. "I've made tons of food."

Argon grinned, placing a hand on his belly. "I'm stuffed, thanks."

"Finished, Mama!" Helia announced, eager to join in on their conversation. So far, the adults only seemed to talk about boring, grown up stuff. She stood up on her chair and lifted her plate up proudly for her mother to see. "Can we play now?"

Elara looked at Argon, noting the keenness in his eyes. "Yes, you can play with Dad for some time. You two go, I'll get dessert ready," she stated with a smile.

Argon nodded, standing up and following Helia into the sitting room.

Elara cleared up dinner, giving some time for the two to play together, and set out some new plates for dessert. She filled their glasses with some fresh mint lemonade and went out to the sitting room to find Helia and Argon splayed out on the floor, deep into a session of playing pretend. She handed a glass to Argon, who accepted it distractedly as he was deep in the throes of embodying an evil dragon. Elara sat back in her chair, watching the two amusedly.

"The dragon is coming after the beautiful princess!" Argon said in a gruff, dragon-like voice. Helia pretended to gather up the skirt of a heavy ball gown and run away.

After some time of playing pretend, Helia decided she wanted to play with her doll, leaving the two adults to sit together as the toddler examined her doll's dress. The two chatted together, and Elara found herself rather enjoying the conversation that seemed to flow naturally between them. Argon found himself constantly chuckling at things she said, and his cheeks soon began to hurt from laughing and smiling. He hadn't felt this comfortable in someone else's presence in a long time, and felt himself relaxing more into his seat.

Helia's loud yawn suddenly caught their attention, and the two looked down at the toddler. Elara glanced at the clock and gasped. "Is that really the time?" She looked down at Helia, who was blearily rubbing her eyes. "Goodness, no wonder Helia's wiped out!"

Argon looked at the clock as well, surprised that it had become so late. He hadn't felt the time pass, and felt a slight pit in his stomach as he realized that the evening was soon coming to an end.

"I'll put Helia to bed," said Elara, scooping up the sleepy toddler.

"But I'm not tired," Helia insisted, yawning once again.

"Yes you are," Elara retorted. "You've had a long day, and you need your rest."

"I want Dad," Helia murmured, leaning over to her father. "Will you read a story?"

"What?" Argon's eyebrows shot up, taken aback. He looked panicked. He had no trouble playing pretend, but telling bedtime stories was new territory for him.

"Please, Dad," Helia pleaded, her sleepy eyes staring adoringly into his. "The princess story."

"I...I don't think I remember that one," Argon stuttered nervously. Princess stories? He hadn't an inkling of what princess story she was talking about.

"I'm not sure if Dad can tell a story tonight," Elara said gently, coming to Argon's aid.

"No, I can," Argon said defiantly, looking at Elara. He felt like she was evaluating him, and he wanted to prove himself. He wasn't sure if Elara perceived the task as a test, but he certainly did not want to let either of the girls down. "I can tell you a story about a goblin. How's that?"

"I want the princess story," Helia maintained, her voice turning to a whiny tone. "The one you always tell."

Argon looked lost. He had no clue what she was talking about. It was obviously some story he had told her in the future, but he hadn't an inkling on what the story was.

"We'll have none of that, now," Elara asserted firmly. "You can choose between the goblin story, or no story."

"Okay," Helia surrendered sleepily. "Goblin." She leaned towards Argon, and he picked her up in his arms.

He was pleasantly surprised at how easily she fit into his arms, and snuggled closer to the child.

They went over to the couch, Elara watching Argon gently place Helia down. She noticed how unnerved he was, and couldn't understand his sudden determination. Did he feel he had something to prove?

She noticed Argon stiffly try to come up with a story about a goblin, his eyes constantly darting self-consciously at her. Elara smiled, understanding his bashfulness at his storytelling. She excused herself from the room to allow the man to finish his bedtime story privately.

After a while, Elara returned to find her daughter leaning against her father. Her eyelids fluttered closed, and she snored softly into his chest.

"I'll put her to bed," she said, smiling fondly at the slumbering child. She picked up the little girl, walking over to her bedroom.

"I should…uh…" Argon began, standing up from the couch. He paused. "Should I go?"

"Um. I'd like to talk to you for a moment. Is that all right?" Elara asked.

Argon nodded, sitting back down.

Elara disappeared down the hall with the toddler, and he could hear the child softly mumbling. Argon's sweaty hands shook, and he smoothed his trousers as he waited.

Was this it? Was he being evaluated? Was she grading him on how he was as a parent? Argon frowned at the thought. Anxiety tugged at his heart, and he shook his head. Why was he suddenly vying for her approval? He wanted to see Helia, and be a part of her life, but he shouldn't need to prove himself in order to be there.

Maybe… Maybe he wanted her approval for more than

just to see Helia?

Argon shook his head again.

This was about Helia. This was *solely* about Helia.

He couldn't ignore his pounding heart as Elara emerged from the hallway. She mirrored his nervousness, and her hands trembled slightly as she sat down across from the man.

"It's too bad we didn't get to dessert," Elara said, a hint of a smile flashing across her lips. "Helia was looking forward to that all day."

"It's all right," said Argon, smiling back.

"Can I get you a slice of cake? It's strawberry and custard."

"Sure." His stomach churned, and he didn't really feel like having dessert. But he also didn't want the evening to end.

Elara inhaled deeply, trying to calm her anxiety as she retrieved two small plates of cake, handing him one of the plates before taking a seat near him.

Argon politely took a bite and set his fork down, waiting. "So..."

"I don't know what to say, really," Elara said honestly, her eyes trained at the floor. She knew that they needed to talk, but she wasn't sure what to tell him, exactly. She turned to look at him. "I just need to know..."

"Go on," he urged softly.

"What is she to you? I mean, I know that she's your daughter. Biologically. But what does that mean to you?"

Argon looked her in the eye. He could see the apprehension and concern, and he could feel it reflected in himself too. It felt strange to look at her like that. He wasn't sure if he had ever really looked at her like that.

"She's my daughter," he replied simply.

"I know," said Elara. "But what does that mean? Do you want to be involved in her life? Do you want to support her? Do you want to be a bystander?"

"I want to be a part of her life," Argon said earnestly. His voice was strong and sure. "I'm not sure what you're asking me. What is she to you?"

Elara considered the question, looking down at her lap. A soft smile broke across her face, and she answered, "She is mine. She's my daughter." She turned to look at Argon, realizing what a difficult question it was. "She was sent to me, by me… the future me… and trusted that I could take care of her. She is a part of me. She's…she's mine."

"Do you love her?" Argon asked suddenly. His question surprised even him.

Elara answered quicker than she realized she could. "Yes."

She had only had Helia in her life for such a short time, and the toddler had thrown so much of her life out of balance. But she could not deny it to herself. She loved her. She loved her so much that her heart ached.

"That's why this is important to me," she confessed. "That's why I need to know what this means to you. I understand why I am a part of her life. Why I want to be a part of her life. But why do you?"

Argon looked away, his mind drifting into his thoughts as he searched for the words to reflect what he felt. She was honest with him. Raw. Vulnerable. And it was terrifying to reveal the same to her. But he had to.

He needed to.

"I'm not going to lie. I was unsettled when I first saw her. I was dragged away into an office, was held there with no explanation, and was told that I had a daughter. I was, well, stunned. I didn't know what to think. I didn't want to see her, either," he admitted, a sliver of shame lacing his words. "It scared me. And it was unnerving to see how she was so thrilled to see me. How she stared at me. How excited she was. After watching the time shadows, though… Watching what she went through… What *we* went through… I can't bear the thought of Helia wondering why I'm not around, or what happened to me. I can't stand letting her down. She's mine…"

Elara sat in silence, absorbing what he'd just divulged to her.

Truthfully, Argon hadn't expected to share so much of what was burning inside him. Admitting those feelings to someone he was just getting to know was disconcerting to say the least. But it felt so easy with her. It felt natural. He looked up at her, locking his gaze with hers.

Elara nodded simply. She understood his feelings; they mirrored her own initial feelings.

Argon's eyes found hers again. "I want to see her again. Please."

Elara gave a small nod, her feelings softening.

"When?" Argon asked, his heart growing lighter. A small tug of desperation and excitement pulled at his stomach as he waited for her response.

"When would you like to see her next?" Elara whispered. How involved did he want to be in her life? Did Argon want to see Helia once a week? More? She bit her lip.

"Whenever you'll let me," Argon answered quickly. He felt his lips moving before he knew what he was saying: "Tomorrow." He couldn't wrap his mind around what he was saying. What he was doing. He couldn't understand himself, or what he was feeling. Right now, he knew that he wanted more.

"We're going to get Helia some more clothes tomorrow," Elara informed him. She wasn't sure how she felt about his joining them in such a public setting. It felt… intimate. Unsettling.

Argon was a natural with Helia. And she had honestly found herself naturally flowing with him.

"Okay."

Argon's breath caught in his throat, and stared at her with his mouth ajar. He felt stunned and relieved at the same time.

"Does the morning work for you?" she asked tentatively.

"Yes. I'll be there." Argon stood up.

Elara stood up as well, knowing that the evening was over. They gazed at each other, uncertain of what to say. Elara's head was swimming. Argon's stomach churned. Their emotions had taken a rollercoaster ride, and each of them wasn't sure how much more they could take for one evening.

"Thank you for dinner," Argon blurted finally. "Everything was delicious."

"Thank you for coming." Elara nodded, tucking a lock of hair behind her ear. "Um… I guess I'll see you…"

"I'm looking forward to it," Argon said sincerely, his voice deep as he looked at her.

Elara nodded. Looking at him and the way he was that evening, Elara glimpsed a little bit of the man she married in the future.

That thought scared her.

The events they witnessed through the Aether Stone would not play out the same way. She was not the woman she saw in the time shadows. And he was not the man she saw.

Right?

Elara nibbled her lip, and her heart flip-flopped as Argon looked intently at her.

"Tomorrow," he said. Try as he might, he could not fight off the smile that broke out across his face.

"Tomorrow," Elara echoed, smiling as well.

With that, Argon turned and walked out the door.

THE ANCIENT PRINCESS

Noiro huffed, looking around the table. Elara, Miela, and Argon sat around the table in Noiro's sitting room, while Helia sat nearby, playing with her doll. The three adults grinned sheepishly at the exasperated man. They had agreed to meet earlier in the day, but each member of the group had to reschedule.

Elara asked to meet a few hours later than originally planned, since she was running behind on getting some more clothes and toys for Helia. Miela was called away for an important meeting with her superiors, as they were working on upgrading the city's defenses. Argon had some reason he needed to reschedule, but seemed mighty secretive to the reason why.

Noiro sighed. Argon had dropped off the package to his house, deeming it a safer option to hide the book for now. Having the sealed package from Estelle kept hidden away in one of his drawers was driving him insane with curiosity.

Whatever was in that package, if Yun Zeru was keen to get his hands on it, it must be important.

Could that book be an instrumental key to the future's war?

Noiro desperately wanted to have a quick peek, and it took every bit of self-control he could muster to hold himself back. The package now sat innocently in the center of the table, and the four stared peculiarly at it.

"Alright, let's get started," Miela declared, leaning forward. Noiro nodded, and pulled the package closer to him. He slowly moved his hands, delicately unraveling the packaging. He did not want to risk damaging the contents of the parcel.

The brown packaging pulled away to reveal a small, old leather bound book. The pages looked yellow and worn-out, yet the binding and cover looked very well preserved. The title's lettering looked slightly faded with age. Elara frowned as she examined the book.

"Fital's Tales," she read the title of the book aloud, curious. "What is this?"

Argon looked incredulously at the book. "It's a children's storybook," he said. "My mother used to read it to us."

"Why would Yun Zeru want a children's storybook?" Miela frowned. "There must be thousands of copies of this book, anyhow. Why would he need it from Estelle?"

Argon shook his head. "This book was never officially published. There is only this copy." He pulled the book closer to him, his fingers gingerly resting on the thick leather. "Fital wrote it himself, for his family. It's been in my family for generations. Fital, the author, was my mother's ancestor."

"Is there something special about this book?"

Argon shrugged. "There's nothing special about it. It's just a book of bedtime stories."

"It's strange," said Noiro. "I've never heard of Fital."

"Well, Fital wasn't really a storyteller," clarified Argon. "He was a historian, like Estelle. My family comes from a long line of historians."

"Do you think there's a message hidden inside?" asked Elara. "Let's take a look."

The four adults pored over the old tome, scouring its pages for anything peculiar that caught their attention. Each page was carefully handwritten, with colorful illustrations painted next to each new title. It truly was a beautiful book.

To their disappointment, nothing seemed out of the ordinary. Like Argon had said, it was just a book of stories.

"I don't understand," said Noiro, shaking his head. "What is so important about this book?"

"Hold on," Elara thought for a moment, and then flipped back a few pages. She tilted her head towards Helia, who was deep in conversation with her doll.

"The princess story," Elara murmured to herself. She turned back to her friends, the gears turning in her head.

"What is it?" Her friends looked back at her curiously.

"She wanted you to read the princess story to her last night," she recalled, looking at Argon. Miela quirked an eyebrow. Elara ignored her, looking pointedly at Argon.

Argon reached for the book, flipping through the pages before landing on one towards the end of the book.

"This is the only princess story," he said, showing the group the book. "The Ballad of the Ancient Princess."

Elara studied the first page, and then shifted her eyes to the illustration. She narrowed her eyes, and then gasped. "Look!" Elara squeaked, pointing frantically at the illustration. "Do you recognize that?"

"What? What?"

"That painting! I've seen it before!"

"That's impossible," Argon raised an eyebrow. "If you've never seen this book before, there's no way you could've ever seen this painting."

"I'm telling you, I've seen it before!" Elara insisted.

"Fital painted this himself." Argon pointed to the illustration. "This is the only copy in existence. Unless you've seen this book before, there's no way you could've seen it."

"The tapestry in Polaris Castle," said Elara. "From the time shadows!"

The group leaned in to examine the painted illustration. Sure enough, Elara was right.

An image of a young woman clad in a loose, flowing white gown was in the center of the page, with a magnificent crown shining on top of her raven hair. Her hands were clasped above her chest, grasping a precious black stone. Just like the tapestry, which hung magnificently in Polaris Castle, the elements emerging from the woman's hands closed around the stone: a mix of leaves and vines branching out from around the stone, gusts of wind, beams of fiery light, and streams of deep blue waters.

"What is Fital's painting doing in Polaris Castle?" Miela wondered. "Was Fital affiliated with the Royal Family?"

Argon shook his head. "I don't know. I don't think so. He was just an old historian."

"Curious," Noiro murmured. "This can't be a coincidence."

"But that tapestry was up there in the castle for anyone to see," said Miela. "Perhaps Fital had copied the images from the tapestry into his book?"

"Maybe," Argon hummed, although he looked quite uncertain.

"The answer has to be in the story," said Elara.

"I'll read it," Argon offered, turning the book around. He looked up at the group, clearing his throat. He couldn't help but feel slightly self-conscious as he began to read.

"A hundred years ago, no one quite knows why,
The waters of the Earth began to run dry.
With people turning desperate to find water to seize,
Humanity was soon brought down to its knees.
For you see, without the tides to fill our chalice,
The Earth's elements were thrown out of balance.
Soils turned to dust, and fires burned through ashy, parched lands,
Suffocating winds blew so fierce, nary a soul could withstand.

At the Northern mouth, at the edge of death's threshold,
Lay the Ancient Princess, her breaths numbered and cold.
Yearning for her final moments to be in peace,
She waited for the moment her hunger would cease.
As her body crawled across the jagged floor,
A stone shook loose, and fell with a thundering roar.
She watched the stone fracture in two,

Just small enough pieces for her to bite into.
Hunger roared inside her,
And her vision started to blur,
So she reached desperately for the stone,
And swallowed it whole.

The Ancient Princess closed her eyes, believing death had come,
But warmth radiated through her, and energy began to drum.
Her palms touched the floor as she pushed herself off the land,
And watched in shock as the ground cracked beneath her hand.
She dug her fingers into the cracks and pulled it apart,
And the Earth gave way to fresh water spilling out.

It was that day humanity was brought back,
With people flocking for salvation from the Earth's crack.
Under the Ancient Princess's watchful eyes,
Her empire prospered under peaceful skies.
As the Ancient Princess regained her strength,
She noticed some changes, which grew to be immense.
She found water would bow to her every command,
And fire could appear in the palm of her hand.
The Earth's bowels moved at her every whim,
And winds howled with a movement of her limb.
Baffled by the Elements' emergence within,
She called for the brightest minds to explore the origin.

Unbeknownst to the Ancient Princess, on that fateful

day,
It was no ordinary stone that fell in her way.
For she had consumed the First,
The key to the Elements in which she was immersed.

Mystified by the First and its power,
She feared what might happen with hands that went sour.
Plagued with fears of her prospering empire falling once more,
She set out to secure the world as her existence's core.

With one half of the First lying in the depths of her belly,
She hid the other amongst diamond, emerald, sapphire, and ruby."

Argon closed the book softly, looking up at the group in front of him. Noiro crossed his arms, thinking hard.

"So, let me get this straight," said Miela, frowning. "Yun Zeru's going through all this trouble to get his hands on a story about someone who ate a stone?"

Noiro, however, looked excited. "I wonder," he uttered, his eyes sparkling. He turned to Argon. "It seems that Fital might have stuck to his historian roots when writing this story."

"How?"

"Think of the first verse of the ballad," said Noiro. "*'The waters of the Earth began to run dry.'* I think it's referring to the War of Waters."

"The War of Waters?"

Noiro nodded. "There is a theory among archeologists

that in every new era, the Earth experiences some catastrophic event that aids in wiping out the existing population, and a new civilization is born in its stead.

"A long time ago, the world was running out of fresh water. Wars had always been waged over land, religion, resources…but war over water was new territory."

"I didn't know there was a war over water," Argon mused.

"It was one of the most catastrophic events to ever happen in human history. During that time, the Earth's climate was shifting rapidly, unpredictably. Weather patterns began to change immensely, and it affected the world's atmosphere in the worst ways," explained Noiro.

"How?" asked Elara.

He glanced at her. "Well, for example, a few centuries ago, the Earth had large deserts of ice and snow at its poles."

"What?" Miela interrupted in awe. "Deserts of ice and snow? How is that possible?"

"It was possible," asserted Noiro. "There were massive glaciers and ice at the North and South Poles."

"What? Land? Over there? There's nothing there, now." Elara frowned. "It's just ocean."

"We're talking about a long time ago," reminded Noiro. "Those glaciers were responsible for holding the majority of the world's fresh water supply. But because of the rapidly changing climates at the time, they deteriorated, and eventually melted into the ocean. Sea levels rose, and the oceans grew more turbulent each year. Eventually, the oceans overtook most of the Earth's landscape."

"What do you mean?" Argon asked.

"A long time ago, there was much more land above the

ocean than there is now," sighed Noiro. "There used to be mountains, which once touched the clouds, that are now mostly submerged and are mere rocky islands. Entire cities and civilizations were swallowed beneath the depths of the sea. Rains were scarce, but when it did finally fall, it was destructive. The world's existing fresh water turned sour with acid, and people were dropping like flies from lack of clean water and dehydration. And so, they fought over the last remaining reserves of water left in the world.

"It was a brutal war. People resorted to any possible venue for a sip of water: the ocean, polluted rivers…even blood." Noiro shuddered. "Humanity was on the brink of extinction. You see, we can go weeks without food, but only days without water."

"How did it end?" asked Elara.

Noiro shook his head. "The accounts are hazy. It makes sense; chaos reigned during that time, and it was impossible to keep track of what was happening. But this ballad does support one of the leading theories." Noiro rested a finger on his chin. "A newly discovered water source supplied the new wave of civilization. Some say it was the result of a sudden flood. Another theory is that enough people died that the Earth had time to heal and regenerate its resources. But no one knows for sure…"

"According to this ballad, though," Argon interrupted as he opened the book back to the page, "the princess tore the Earth open with her hands and brought forth water… Tore the Earth open? After eating a stone?"

Noiro smiled. "Not just any stone. The ballad referred to the stone as The First." He stood up, went over to his laboratory, and came back holding Helia's necklace. "What if it meant the *first element*?"

"The Aether Stone!" Elara cried, shooting up to her feet.

"Exactly!" Noiro exclaimed. "By consuming the Aether Stone, the Ancient Princess gained the ability to control the elements, making her an Elemental."

"That's what Yun Zeru must be after, then," Elara gasped. "The Aether Stone."

"He might be after more than that," said Noiro. "He might not know the Aether Stone's significance in all of this... And we saw what he was after in the future."

"He kept demanding we give him the Elemental," recalled Elara.

"Exactly," said Noiro. "He's after power. He wants to be an Elemental."

"But that's impossible," scoffed Miela. "You said it yourself, there is no such thing as an Elemental. This is just a children's storybook."

"But, assuming there *is* truth to the ballad... The Ancient Princess consumed the Aether Stone," said Elara. "That's how she became an Elemental."

"Only half of it, remember? The stone cracked in two."

"That's right. And she hid the other half."

"So, then, Yun Zeru must be after the Aether Stone," Elara repeated her earlier deduction. "He needs to consume the Aether Stone to control the elements."

Noiro shook his head again. "I don't think that's what he's after. Otherwise, he would have been asking for the stone in the future," he reminded her. "Remember, he kept asking for the Elemental."

"So he thinks that there is an Elemental out there?"

Noiro nodded.

"How did Yun Zeru even know about this book's

existence?" Miela sighed. She looked at Argon. "Your sister mentioned it's a family heirloom."

"I don't know." Argon turned his head away. "It's an old book that's been passed down for generations… She's also a proud historian. She might have showed it to her class? I don't think she saw the harm in sharing it with others."

Miela frowned. "Argon," she said slowly. "Your sister said that you inherited the book after your father passed."

Argon nodded. "That's right."

"In the time shadows, you were attacked. Your house was ransacked." She bit her lip. "Do you think whoever attacked you was looking for the book? They might've not known the book was still at your sister's."

Argon shifted uncomfortably. It made sense. Everything that happened in the time shadows was somehow tied to him and his family, and a big part of the mystery was *why*.

Argon felt a deep pit in his stomach. Was his family the reason for Yun Zeru's malevolent descent into chaos and massacres? The image of his sister slitting her own throat floated to the front of his mind. He shook his head vehemently, trying to get the image out of his head. Instead, he saw his own mother, slain and covered in blood in their own home. His blood boiled, and anger overtook him. He gripped the edge of the table, his knuckles turning white as his head hung low.

"Hey," Elara said softly, putting her hand on his arm. She could see him fighting internally, and could only guess what was going through his mind. "We've already stopped so much of what was supposed to happen."

Argon sighed.

"Yun Zeru will never see this," she said firmly. "We'll make sure of it."

He nodded, putting his hand on top of hers, squeezing hard. He was scared. There was no denying it. He squeezed her hand again. "We need to warn Estelle," he whispered. "She was killed in the future, remember?"

"You're right," agreed Noiro. "We need to go, now."

"Are you sure she'll be up now? It's late," whispered Miela as the group slowly trudged through a small pathway.

"We'll wake her up, then," Argon replied, his voice hushed as they turned a corner. "Here we are."

The group came to a stop in front of Estelle's home, standing by the fence.

Argon frowned. "The door's open," he muttered, his heart sinking. Were they too late? He lurched forward, but was stopped by Miela's sturdy arm holding him back.

"Lieutenant," she uttered. "Remember protocol. We don't know what's waiting for us behind that door."

"It's my sister," Argon said through gritted teeth, fiercely shaking her arm away.

"I know," she replied calmly. She drew out her sword, and Argon did the same. "But we follow protocol. We move together. Let's go."

Argon and Miela led the way, moving cautiously toward the front door. Noiro walked carefully behind them, anxious as they drew closer. Had Yun Zeru figured something out? Had he already made a move?

"Hello?" Argon called out, slowly pushing the door open wider. The lights were off, and he could barely make out what was past the entryway.

Silence greeted them, and his voice echoed against the

walls.

"Estelle?" Argon's voice rose as his heart pounded in his chest. He felt cold sweat break across his forehead as he walked into the house. Framed pictures of him and his sister were hung onto the wall beside the door, staring silently at the group who followed the man into his childhood home.

"I'm going to check the—" Miela began, but the sound of a startled scream drowned out the rest of her sentence. She whirled around, her sword brandished before her, ready to strike.

"Don't hurt me!" Estelle squealed, her arms thrown up in defense, a large fire iron clattering to the ground as it fell out of her grasp.

"Estelle!" Argon pushed past Miela, throwing his arms around her. "I thought something had happened! The door was open—"

"I heard a noise," Estelle cried. "I came down to investigate."

Miela's eyes flashed. "The door was open."

"What?" Estelle shivered, her voice sharply dropping to a whisper. "Do you think someone is in here?"

"I'll take a look," Miela assured, creeping past them.

"I'll take the first floor," Noiro asserted. Miela nodded and threw him a dagger. He caught it by the hilt, ready to investigate.

Estelle gawped at the group, flabbergasted. "What on Earth is going on?" she demanded. "You all scared me half to death!"

"Your door was open," Argon repeated. "We had to make sure you were okay."

"What are you all even doing here?" Estelle asked

incredulously. "I've seen you more this week than I've seen you in the past couple of years!"

"It's all clear," Miela called out, her boots thumping against the wooden steps as she made her way back down to the main sitting room.

"All clear here, too," said Noiro, emerging from one of the other rooms.

"Put down the weapons," Estelle ordered. "Honestly! What is going on? I have to be up early tomorrow, and—"

"Estelle, we have some more questions to ask," Noiro interrupted.

"Can't it wait until morning? It's late."

"Estelle," Argon implored, his eyes deep with concern. "It's important."

Estelle looked at her brother, and then sighed. "You owe me," she told him, folding her arms.

Argon nodded.

"I need some caffeine," Estelle muttered, going over to the kitchen. She certainly did not take kindly to her sleep being disrupted. "Tea, anyone?"

"I'll have a cup," said Miela. Estelle nodded, setting out another mug. She carried the tray out to the sitting room, and sat across from her unexpected guests. They sat in silence, each of them not knowing how to start. Miela sipped loudly on her tea, wincing as the hot liquid scalded her tongue.

"Where's Elara?" Estelle asked, breaking the silence.

"She's at home," Noiro replied simply. As much as Elara wanted to come with the group to Estelle's, she needed to stay back with Helia. It was far too late in the evening to impose on Tami again, and Helia was beginning to grow anxious when she saw the adults around her move about urgently as they were preparing to leave. The energy around them seemed familiar to the chaos Helia had grown up in, and no doubt it triggered some of the anxiety and stress in the child.

She needed her mother.

"Okay," Estelle nodded. She took a sip of her tea, waiting for one of her visitors to speak.

"It's about the book," Noiro began.

"What?" Estelle frowned.

"The book," Noiro repeated. "The one in the package you gave us."

"Okay..." Estelle nodded, growing more confused. "What is this about?"

"Estelle, how much do you know about that book?" asked Noiro.

Estelle turned to him curiously. "I know the book by heart," she replied. "It's a book our parents used to read to us when we were children."

"We have a few questions. About one of the stories," Noiro clarified.

"Questions so important that you had to come in the middle of the night?" Estelle said sardonically, raising an eyebrow.

Noiro looked at her seriously. "Yes."

Estelle felt her shoulders tense up as she took in the apprehensive trio before her. "Okay," she sighed, taking another sip of her tea. "Ask away."

Noiro cleared his throat. "The Ballad of the Ancient Princess."

"Ah, my favorite story from Fital's collection." Estelle smiled. "What about it?"

"Is it real?"

Estelle frowned, confused. "I'm not following you. Are you asking if the ballad's real?"

"The story it tells," Noiro asserted. "Is there any truth to it? We noticed some overlap with some historical events, and we wondered..."

Estelle shifted in her seat. "You must be referring to the War of Waters."

Noiro nodded.

"Well, every story is based on some truth," said Estelle thoughtfully. "According to my understanding, that ballad was supposed to be the story of Polaris's beginning."

"Really?" Noiro leaned forward, intrigued.

Estelle nodded. "For example, Fital refers to 'the Northern mouth,' in one of the verses. It's a reference to Polaris."

"Polaris is also the name of the North Star," Miela chimed in. "Of course!"

Estelle smiled at Miela. "According to legend, the Ancient Princess's connection to the elements saved humanity from going extinct," she continued. "With her ability to influence the elements, she was able to bring forth fresh water, and built her empire, Polaris, around it."

"So, she was an Elemental?" asked Miela.

"Technically, yes," said Estelle.

"This Ancient Princess—was she a real person? Or was she fictional?"

Estelle laughed. "Well, it's funny you ask that," she said. "Fital's stories were written as bedtime stories for his children, so they're easy to dismiss as just that: a story. But as a historian, I can't help but draw further conclusions."

"And those are?"

"My conclusions? Well..." Estelle crossed her legs. "I

believe the Ancient Princess's story might be based on Princess Laelia."

"Princess Laelia?"

Estelle nodded. "Much of the Royal Family's history is well documented. She's one who certainly had some strange accounts recorded about her. A lot of unexplained phenomena are tied to her time. Floods. Earthquakes. Hurricanes. Magma eruptions…"

"In other words, strange events tied to the elements," said Noiro.

Estelle nodded in agreement. "Exactly. If she truly was an Elemental, I reckon that she might have had trouble controlling the elements in the beginning. Or, perhaps, throughout her entire life."

"Princess Laelia…" Noiro frowned. "Why does that name sound familiar?"

Estelle looked at him curiously. "Have you not visited the Old Archive before?"

Noiro looked taken aback by the question. "I'm a researcher for the Royal Family," he said, almost defensively. "Of course I've been to the Old Archive."

"I don't mean to offend you," Estelle responded, putting her hands up apologetically. "I'm just surprised."

"About what?"

"Princess Laelia," she said. "She's the founder of the Old Archive. I thought you knew."

Noiro's eyes widened. "The statue by the entrance!" he gasped. "How did you know?"

"I'm a historian." Estelle smiled. "And I come from a long line of historians who dedicated their lives to preserving Polaris's history."

"Noiro, you did say that we needed to go back to the

roots of the Elementals in Polaris history," Argon said contemplatively. He turned to Estelle. "Are the elements mentioned before Princess Laelia's time?"

Estelle thought for a moment. "I don't believe so," she murmured. "If you're looking for the starting point of the elements in the Royal Family history, then Princess Laelia is it. She's even named her children after the elements."

"Oh?"

"She had four heirs," said Estelle. "And each were named after the elements: Prince Air, Princess Water, Princess Earth, and Prince Fire. Princess Laelia sent them out to the four corners of Polaris to watch over the lands and take care of the people, while Princess Laelia would rule from the center of Polaris. According to legend, each heir was bestowed the attribute of one of the Earth's four elements, and their reigning territory would reflect the ruling heir's element.

"Prince Air's lands, the Mizar Cliffs, reflected the element of air. As you know, their lands are built on high cliffs that tower above the sea, and they built high towers from which they built their livelihoods in.

"Princess Water's lands, the Ursa Isles, were a collection of small islands. Her people were one with the water, using the ocean's tides to bring power to the realm, and reaping their harvests from the ocean's depths.

"Princess Earth's lands are in the Cepheus Forests, where ancient trees possessed trunks as thick and wide as small villages, and the tips of the trees touched the sky's clouds. Princess Earth's subjects lived in harmony with the trees, carving their homes and building communities within the forest's massive trunks.

"Prince Fire's people settled near the Drako Volcanoes,

long dormant. They tapped into the magma that flowed beneath the Earth, harnessing its energy to melt down the Earth's resources and provide useful materials for Polaris."

Noiro leaned forward, thinking hard. "Estelle, if the Ballad of the Ancient Princess is, in fact, based on real people and real events"—he looked at Argon and Miela— "why did Fital hide the story in a children's storybook? Why is this not captured in a history book?"

Estelle shifted uncomfortably and said, "Fital was a strange man."

Argon narrowed his eyes, staring at his sister.

"Tell me more about Fital," pressed Noiro. "He was your ancestor, according to Argon."

Estelle chewed her lip nervously. "Yes," she answered shortly.

"What else can you tell me about him?" Noiro probed.

"It's getting late," Estelle said abruptly, getting up. "I really must ask you to leave."

Argon stood up. "Estelle," he said, "answer the question."

Estelle glared at him defiantly, her voice hard. "*You* would be able to answer the question, if you only stayed here."

"Don't change the subject, Estelle," Argon uttered. "It's important."

Estelle shook her head. "You don't understand."

"It's important," Argon repeated.

"Why? Why should I answer anything, when you won't even tell me why is it so important."

"Because *you* don't understand," Argon growled. "Your life depends on it. All of our lives depend on it."

Estelle's face drained. "What? What do you mean?"

Miela put her hand on Argon's shoulder. "You've said too much, Lieutenant," she hissed.

Argon ignored her, staring at his sister. "Please, Estelle."

"Tell me what's going on," she demanded. "I have a right to know."

Argon turned to Noiro and Miela. "She's right," he agreed. "She has a right to know."

"To know what?" Estelle asked.

"Are you sure?" Miela turned her attention to Argon. "You know what's at stake, Lieutenant. It's your sister. It's your call."

"She can help us," Argon asserted.

Miela sighed, then nodded. She turned to Noiro, who gave a curt nod.

"Tell me," Estelle ordered, her voice faltering as she saw the solemn exchange between the three. Argon sighed, and then began to fill her in.

Estelle's face contorted in horror as she learned about Helia's appearance, covered in her mother's blood, the Aether Stone, the horrible events which unfolded in the time shadows, and Yun Zeru's part in all of it.

"I...I die?" Estelle murmured blankly. "We...We all die?"

"Yes," Argon said shortly. "But it's bigger than that."

"'*Mystified by the First and its power, She feared what might happen with hands that went sour,*'" Estelle recited, her voice now a faint whisper. "Yun Zeru is after the Aether Stone?"

Noiro shook his head. "We don't know if he knows about the Aether Stone, yet," he said. "He was after 'the Elemental,' in the future."

Estelle nodded, silent.

"What is it?" Argon tilted his head towards his sister.

"I know why," Estelle murmured to herself. She lifted her head up to the three before her. "I think I know why our family was targeted in the future."

"Why?"

"Think about it. You were the first victim in this whole venture," she said, looking at Argon. "Your attack. And then I... I died. And then the attack against you and Mom at your home in Polaris. And then they were chasing after...your daughter." The words sounded foreign in her mouth; she couldn't wrap her head around her brother having a daughter.

"Yun Zeru is after our family?" Argon asked in disbelief. "What's so special about our family?"

"You'd know if you stayed here," Estelle repeated, tears welling up in her eyes. "If only you'd stayed..."

"Fital?" Noiro gasped suddenly.

Estelle nodded.

"What does Fital have to do with any of this?" Argon asked, his heart racing. "He's just... He's just an old historian."

"Fital..." Estelle began, and then faltered. "Fital was Princess Water's son. The Ancient Princess's grandson."

"Wh-what?" Argon's mouth dropped open.

"It's why our family is filled with historians," Estelle explained, her voice thick with emotion as everything began connecting in her mind to make sense. "Princess Laelia wanted to hide away the knowledge of the Elementals. She wanted to destroy it. But Fital didn't want the knowledge to get lost."

"So he hid it in stories for his children," Noiro finished.

"It's why our family never leaves the Ursa Isles," Estelle whispered and dipped her head down. "Once we learn the truth... If the knowledge, if the *power*, fell into the wrong hands..."

The group remained silent, taking it all in.

Estelle turned to her brother, a tear falling from her eye. "You didn't want to follow in the family's footsteps. You wanted to be a Guardian. You left..."

Argon's guts wrenched with guilt as he watched Estelle slowly become wracked with a flood of emotions. He remembered how he felt when he had first learned of everything. Of the time shadows. Of his death. Of Elara. Of Helia.

Helia.

Something suddenly clicked in his head.

"Hold on... Our family was targeted because we are descendants of the Ancient Princess, right? And you said that there were claims of Elementals popping up along the Ancient Princess's bloodline..." He looked out the window, pondering. "I know I'm not an Elemental. Neither are you, nor Mom."

"Hold on," Noiro said, getting up and reaching for Miela's cup of tea, which was now ice cold. He shoved it towards Argon. "Try."

"Try what?"

"I don't know. You're a descendant from Princess Water. Do something with water."

Argon, feeling silly, took the cup of tea in his hands. Concentrating on the liquid, he stared at it hard. His heart pounded in his chest. He wasn't sure what to expect.

Nothing happened.

He pushed the cup to Estelle, who did the same.

Again, nothing.

"You said there were claims of Elementals popping up between generations, right?" he asked Estelle.

She nodded.

Argon turned to look at Noiro and Miela, sharing a look of concern and excitement.

"I think I understand why Helia was sent back from the future," Noiro uttered.

Argon's eyes widened.

Was Yun Zeru after Helia?

Was Helia an Elemental?

"Estelle." Argon held his sister by the shoulders. "This is very important. Did you tell anyone about the book?"

Estelle bit her lip. "Um…"

Elara's eyes fluttered open, a soft, persistent snoring notching its way through her deep slumber. She grunted sleepily, turning to her side and throwing the covers over her head. She was determined to get some more sleep.

Alas, after a few more minutes of tossing and turning, she gave up. She could hear Helia stirring beside her. She turned her head to the tiny tot, who was sprawled out next to her. Her hair had a life of its own, splayed all over her pillow in messy waves, and her hand was thrown over one side of her face as she snored softly.

Elara smiled, gently pressing her lips onto her forehead, and swiping her hair away from her face.

Her stomach growled, and she pressed a hand to her belly. "I need a snack," she murmured to herself, and slowly slid out of bed, careful not to wake up the toddler.

She wandered about in the pantry, lighting a small lantern to illuminate the small kitchen, and eventually found herself some fruit. She rinsed some berries and arranged it into a bowl, and settled herself at the kitchen table.

As she began to dig into her late-night snack, her mind drifted to the night before.

Noiro had come by late after their visit to Estelle to fill her in on what they had learned. The normally placid, solemn man was jittery and jumpy as he recounted to her what they had learned from Estelle, and her mind reeled as she heard their theories on the Ancient Princess and the Aether Stone.

And Helia.

Elara looked up as she absentmindedly reached for another piece of fruit, thinking hard.

Helia, an Elemental?

She frowned, thinking back to her time with the toddler. She hadn't noticed anything odd about the tot, other than the fact that she had successfully travelled back in time. And the toddler absolutely hated baths, or any encounter with water, which made her affinity for being a Water Elemental highly doubtful.

But still, if Argon's family are descendants of Princess Water...

They spent the entire day testing Helia with small bowls and cups of water. They weren't sure what they were looking for, but as far as they could tell, nothing out of the ordinary occurred. Helia seemed rather perplexed with the whole ordeal, but soon grew fidgety and fussy as the hours passed by. Finally, Elara called an end to the day; she could see the toddler was overwhelmed with the anxious adults staring at her, pushing larger and larger vessels of water toward her.

Eventually exhausted, they all turned away for the evening. Argon hung back for another few hours, cradling and soothing his daughter into a lulled slumber. She insisted for her princess story, to which Argon contentedly complied.

The two spent the remaining time together, talking into the wee hours of the evening, their voices shushed as their daughter slept soundly on the couch between them. Despite the turmoil-filled days that passed since working on the Aether Stone, Elara felt cheerful as she chatted away with Argon. His usual solemn façade melted away into a wide, warm smile as he listened to her speak, and enthusiastically conversed with her, and before they knew it, it was close to midnight. Her heart thumped loudly in her chest as it was time for him to go. He lingered by the door, reluctant to end the evening.

Elara fought back a smile as she reminisced their evening. It felt strange to feel so alive and happy; it wasn't that she was unhappy before, but feeling that exciting spark was new. She hadn't felt that before Argon and Helia had come along into her life.

Helia…

Elara spent a lot of time thinking about her. She felt guilty for having to send her away to be babysat so often. Sure, she saw her in the mornings and evenings, but it was rare that they had ever had a day to spend entirely together. She owed it to Helia to spend time with her. She needed her. They needed each other.

Her work wasn't going to end anytime soon, but she was determined to set time for just her and Helia.

Turning to look at an old, leather book on the table, she sighed as she flipped it over. Fital's Tales. Argon had forgotten it; he must have left it there after Helia had fallen asleep.

She finished the last of her fruit, wiping her hands on her pants as she reached out for the book. She pulled it closer to her, and flipped it back open to the Ballad of the Ancient Princess, careful not to ruin the pages with any residual moisture from her fruity breakfast.

She reread the verses again, furrowing her brow as she concentrated. "This last verse," she thought aloud, resting her finger on the final sentence of the ballad. "*With one half of the First lying in the depths of her belly, she hid the other amongst diamond, emerald, sapphire, and ruby.'* " She closed her eyes, pondering.

She remembered towards the end of viewing the time shadows with the Aether Stone, there were massive waves of refugees being driven to Polaris for protection. And each of them had something in common: they had gems and family heirloom jewelry stolen. Museums were also hit, with precious stones and artifacts being taken away. She thought back to the attack on Argon in the future.

My home was ransacked. All of the furniture was knocked over, and my family pictures were removed from their frames. We can't find them anywhere; I think they took it with them. The doors and windows were left wide open, too. My mother's jewels were also taken...

That's not the worst of it. There was also a message. Written in blood.

'We know'... In blood.

His mother's jewels were also taken.

Diamond, emerald, sapphire, and ruby.

Elara frowned. What could that mean?

She turned her attention back to the book. She knew

that they had the Aether Stone safely hidden away with them, but that stone was from the future. In their current timeline, however, the Aether Stone was still hidden away somewhere.

She exhaled heavily, leaning back in her chair and closing her eyes.

Diamond, emerald, sapphire, and ruby.

In the time shadows, they never saw how exactly how they got the Aether Stone. The last scene they saw before she had the Aether Stone was her looking for the Diadem.

Her eyes flew open.

The Diadem which was set with diamonds, emeralds, sapphires, and rubies.

Of course.

Elara jolted up from her chair.

"It's been under our noses the entire time," she uttered in disbelief. "But that's impossible… I've seen the Diadem before…"

She looked at the illustration beside the Ballad of the Ancient Princess, scrutinizing the depiction of the Diadem. There were *only* diamonds, emeralds, sapphires, and rubies.

No Aether Stone.

"It must be hidden somewhere in the Diadem," she mumbled to herself. If the Ancient Princess was going to hide the Aether Stone in plain sight, she certainly wasn't going to simply set the Aether Stone into the Diadem, as plain as day for anyone to see.

She needed to get her hands on the Diadem.

A soft noise caught her attention, and her ears pricked. She turned her head towards it.

Nothing seemed out of the ordinary.

Perhaps it was Helia shifting in her sleep. She stood up,

slowly creeping up to the room, careful not to wake the little girl. Peering into her bedroom, she saw that the toddler had now taken over the entire bed, her limbs stretched out into a starfish position. Elara smiled softly, closing the door behind her.

No sooner had the door had latched shut than a loud crash reverberated through the house. Elara whirled around, her eyes wide and her heart pounding.

"Guard the exits. I don't want her to run."

Elara paled instantly as the voice reached her ears, her blood draining away from her face in horror. The voice was unmistakable. She heard it echo through her ears in her nightmares, and it followed her throughout her journey in the time shadows.

Yun Zeru was in her house. And he wasn't alone.

"Mama?" Helia's small voice called out sleepily from the room.

With a speed she had never known, Elara flew into action. She threw the door open, dashing to the bed and snatching Helia up. She turned to her bedside table, yanking out the dagger Miela had given her, stashing it in the waistband of her pants.

She heard heavy footsteps draw closer.

She had nowhere to run.

But they could hide.

In one swift movement, she pulled Helia to her chest and slid beneath the bed.

"Ma—"

"Shh," Elara hushed her instantly. Taking no chances, she pressed her hand against her daughter's mouth.

She stared down at her terrified daughter, desperately wracking her brain for an escape plan, but to no avail. She was panicking. She couldn't think straight. All she could do was run through the same thoughts, over and over again.

Come on, Elara. Think.

Elara's panic grew as she grew more aware of the situation. She didn't know how many intruders were there. Yun Zeru had given orders to someone to guard the exits, which meant that there were at least two people. She was outnumbered already. Were there more waiting outside?

She took a deep, shaky breath. She needed to calm down. She needed to think.

She hadn't heard glass when the intruders crashed in. They must have burst their way in through the door. She glanced at the windowsill of her bedroom.

The window.

Their only way out.

"Mm—" Helia resisted against Elara. She held her tightly, fear gripping her muscles in a tight spasm.

"The bad men are here," she whispered to the quivering girl. "We have to be quiet. We have to hide." Elara curled her body protectively over her.

Elara's breath caught in her throat as she saw shadows moving beneath the door. They paused, and then walked further away. She let go of her breath, her eyes locked onto the window.

They had to jump.

Slowly, she scooted herself and Helia out from under the bed. Setting the toddler down, she crept quietly to the window, peering outside.

No one was out there.

Elara slowly unlatched the window, trying to quietly slide it open. She leaned over the window. It looked like a long drop. Elara's breath escaped her lips in rapid, convulsing gasps as fear set in.

A loud, deep *thunk* sounded, and Elara froze in horror as she realized the dagger had slipped out from her waistband, clanking loudly onto the floor.

She squeezed her eyes shut, praying that the noise fell on deaf ears.

It hadn't.

"I heard something," a gruff voice yelled. "Over there!" The sound of heavy boots drew closer as the intruders returned to the bedroom door.

It was happening so fast.

Too fast.

She was still by the windowsill, with Helia wrapped up in her arms.

Knowing it was too late to jump, she shoved herself and Helia back beneath the bed, yanking the bedskirt down to hide them away, out of sight. Elara reached out from beneath the bed, quickly pulling the dagger to her. She pressed herself into the shadows, hoping blindly it would be enough to mask their presence.

The door swung open.

Elara held her breath.

"There's no one here," a tall, stocky man grunted as he lazily scanned the room.

"Of course she's here," Yun Zeru sneered, waltzing arrogantly into the room. "Aren't you, Elara?"

Elara's blood froze as she heard her name roll off the sinister man's tongue. She could feel Helia quaking beneath her, her entire body twitching with fear. She saw three pairs of heavy boots clomping closer.

Yun Zeru turned his head slowly as he surveyed the room.

He paused, a slight tremble of the bed sheets hanging over the bed catching his eye.

"Aren't you?"

There was a sudden lapse of silence, and then some creaking as the bed groaned beneath the man's weight.

Elara strained her ears as she tried to listen closer, her body hunching over Helia defensively, shielding her against the pressure of the bedsprings.

Without warning, there was a sharp sound of fabric ripping and tearing, and a sudden, blinding pain seared through her. She tried her best to remain silent, but a mix between a groan and shriek escaped her. She shook as she turned her head to the side to see the middle of a sword rip through the mattress above her and sinking into her shoulder, the tip of the blade embedded into her skin.

"That's what I thought," Yun Zeru sniggered darkly. "A coward, hiding under the bed *like a child.*"

Elara could feel Helia screaming against her hand, which was somehow still pressed firmly against her mouth. She was wailing and shaking in terror.

How do I get us out of this?

She looked just ahead of her; lying a few feet away was her dagger. She hadn't realized until that moment that it left her hand. How could she have let it go? She realized that both of her arms were wrapped tightly around her daughter, protecting her from the attack. She shifted Helia's body beneath her, gritting her teeth. The toddler was okay. Her own body had taken the hit, but Helia was okay.

She fought back against another scream as the blade ripped out from her shoulder, and she could feel warm liquid oozing out from her back and quickly turning cold as it seeped into her clothes.

"You have something that I want." Yun Zeru's voice sent shivers down her spine. Or was that the shock setting in?

A large hand reached beneath the bed and closed around her skull, yanking her from beneath the bed. Elara let go of Helia as she was dragged away, determined to keep her hidden. She grunted as the man pulled her up by her hair, her feet dangling an inch above the floor, her toes stretching to find the ground. She reached her hands up to the fists clenched around locks of her hair, digging her nails deep into the man's flesh. He grunted in pain, and let go of her in reflex.

Elara dropped down to the ground, landing on her knees. She lifted her head up.

Yun Zeru's eyes met hers, and he smiled icily.

"You have something I want," he repeated. "Give it to me, and I'll make this quick." He lifted his sword. Thick, dark liquid was dripping down the blade and onto his hand.

Elara didn't speak. What did he want? Did he know about Helia?

"Stubborn," Yun Zeru remarked coldly. "You won't be for much longer. Where are you hiding it?"

Helia felt her knees shake beneath her as she struggled to stand upright.

"Silent? Answer me." Yun Zeru drew his hand back and struck her across the face.

Elara gasped sharply, her head thrown back with the weight of his blow. In her daze, her eyes wildly searched for Helia. Was she okay?

Yun Zeru froze, his eyes scrutinizing her. She realized

what she had done, and snapped her gaze back at him.

But it was too late.

His face slowly melted into a menacing smile, and he turned his head, following her line of sight to beneath the bed.

Elara lurched forwards instinctively, all the while mentally berating herself for giving herself away. Yun Zeru yanked her arm, roughly holding her back.

"You"— he jerked his head at one of the men— "Check under the bed."

The man immediately scrambled to follow Yun Zeru's orders, and felt around beneath the bed. Elara could hear Helia scooting further away, but a few seconds later, the man closed his fist around a handful of hair. Helia's screeching wail resounded against the bedroom walls.

"NO! PLEASE! STOP!" Elara screeched, struggling to reach any bit of Helia that she could, but Yun Zeru's vice grip around her arm held her back. "No! Let her go! Helia!"

"A child?" Yun Zeru questioned suspiciously, perplexed. The man shrugged his shoulders, equally confused.

"A child…"

"PLEASE. Let her go," Elara pleaded. "Please."

"Well, look at that," Yun Zeru chuckled, smiling wickedly. "She speaks."

"Mama! Mama!" Helia cried, squirming against the grasp of the man who held her.

Yun Zeru raised a thin eyebrow. "*Your* child."

"Mama!"

"Shut up, you disgusting little imp," Yun Zeru ordered, roughly letting go of Elara and striding toward the child.

Elara lunged forward again, trying to grab her child, but Yun Zeru threw her back roughly. Her skull smashed against the wall behind her, and lights flashed in her eyes, momentarily throwing her into a blind fit.

He whacked the child on the head, shaking her hard. Helia wailed loudly, chanting, "Mama," over and over again.

"Please, don't hurt her… Please…"

"Give me what I want," Yun Zeru demanded, "and I'll consider your request." He turned to the child, speaking in a mocking baby voice as he shook the child, her feet hanging and rattling against the bedside table.

"Mama!"

"Your Mama has something of mine, an old book—"

"Yun Zeru," one of the men interrupted flatly.

"What?" Yun Zeru snapped. The man pointed silently at the bedside table. The top drawer had shaken open slightly with Helia's dangling feet. Elara shook her head, trying to clear her vision as she followed their gaze to where the man was pointing.

A ring.

Elara bit her lip in dismay.

Her wedding ring from the future.

Yun Zeru's eyes widened, his face darkening as he stared at the ring. He dropped the child, who scrambled towards her mother immediately. The man kicked the little girl down, and she fell with a cry.

"NO! *Please*," Elara cried with the child.

Yun Zeru, turning a blind eye, reached slowly for the ring, examining it closely. Tawer…" he uttered. His head whipped back towards Elara, and then at the little girl, who was on the floor.

"Mama," Helia moaned.

"Another Tawer?" Yun Zeru's eyes darted back and forth between Helia and Elara, his mind racing.

Could it be?

"Who are you?" Yun Zeru demanded, his voice thundering as he turned back to the child and shaking her. "Stop sniveling and tell me, you brat."

Helia, frightened, cried even harder. Her head snapped back suddenly as Yun Zeru struck her small cheek with his hand. "Mama," Helia cried pathetically, "*MAMA!*"

Elara desperately broke through the hold that the other man had her in and snatched up the girl, only to be separated once again by the sinister Guardian. He picked up the little girl by her neck and began to squeeze. Helia's voice began to gurgle as her windpipe was slowly crushed.

Elara had never felt so helpless.

Suddenly, the ground trembled beneath their feet. Elara felt the tremors run up her legs and looked around, confused. Yun Zeru and his goons had a similar, puzzled look on their faces as they felt the ground shake beneath them. Water spilled out of the ground and rushed around Yun Zeru's feet, powerfully swirling around his legs and throwing him off balance. He whipped his head to look at Elara, and then back at Helia.

The toddler's face was blood-red, and her eyes were rolled back in her head. Yun Zeru dropped the child in shock. "An... An Elemental? It's true?"

Elara took her chance and dove forward, scooping her comatose daughter from the floor. She bent over and dashed towards the open window, and throwing herself out of it, Helia grasped tightly in her arms. She fell flat on her back, bracing herself for the impact and cushioning

Helia from the fall. She wheezed and groaned as the wind was knocked out of her lungs.

"Get them! Get the Elemental!" a voice called from the window above her.

Elara mustered up every bit of strength she had left and pulled herself off the ground. Without casting a second look behind her, she ran as fast as her legs could carry her.

THE ELEMENTAL

Elara staggered towards the thick, wooden door, her injured shoulder screaming with the weight of Helia in her arms. She banged on the front door, sobbing with a mixture of relief and pain as her knees crashed against the stone floor. Tears flowed freely down her cheeks, and Helia bawled loudly, her cries piercing the early morning sky.

The door swung open, and Elara looked up to see Noiro staring down at the two of them in horror.

"Elara!"

"Get her inside," Elara panted, desperately pushing the toddler across the threshold.

Noiro moved quickly, kneeling down and scooping up the crying toddler.

"Help me," she uttered weakly, reaching for Noiro's

arms as he hoisted her up to her feet and brought her inside. He locked the doors and windows, scrambling across his cottage in a frenzied panic.

"What happened?" Noiro's voice shook. "Where? Tell me." With the blood soaking through her shirt, he couldn't tell where the wound was.

"Yun Zeru," Elara sobbed, answering his first question.

"What?"

"He broke in… He… I…" Elara couldn't hold it in any longer, falling to pieces as she wept uncontrollably. Her head whooshed as she cried, and she felt lightheaded. It felt like a white hot iron was lodged in her shoulder, and she pressed her hand to it.

"We need to get you looked at," Noiro said worriedly. "We need to go to a Medic—"

"No," Elara's face paled. "No. They'll take a report. It'll raise red flags. We can't tell them what happened… Yun Zeru…" Elara's voice was beginning to sound delirious as the shock began to take over her body.

"What happened?" Noiro asked again. He led her to the couch, gently pushing her to lie down.

"Bad…men…" Helia managed to gurgle between shuddering wails.

"He had others with him. I counted at least two." Elara shuddered. "We have to hide. What if I led him here?"

She tried to get up, but he pushed her firmly back down. "Lie down," he said softly.

Tears rolled down her cheeks. "It's not safe."

"We need to take care of you first. I… I don't know much beyond first aid."

"Tami," said Elara. "She can help us."

"Dad," Helia whimpered. "I want Dad."

"Okay. Okay." Noiro moved quickly to his office. "I'll have them over."

He emerged with a small first aid kit, and pressed some gauze to Elara's shoulder. The bleeding had already slowed, but they needed to treat it properly and address the extent of the damage. Elara winced, hissing as the gauze pressed hard onto her wound.

She lay there, shivering under the blanket that Noiro had brought her, Helia still crying beside her in fright. Her eyelids fluttered, and she felt very sleepy as the adrenaline began to fade from her body. She groaned in pain, the impact her injuries becoming more potent as the time passed.

After some time, she could hear muffled voices drawing closer to her.

"Elara? What happened?"

She turned her head towards the voice, and squinted through blurry eyes to see Tami standing there with her eyes wide and panicked.

"Elara! Helia!"

"DAD!"

Elara heard Argon's footsteps thundering towards her, bursting through Noiro's front door. He raced to their sides, collapsing to his knees, encircling his arms around them both.

"Move, I have to check her," Tami ordered, pushing past Argon.

"Check Helia," Elara croaked, her throat dry as she tried to sit up.

"Of course I'll take a look at her. But you're much worse off right now," she said softly. "Let's take a look."

Helia clung tightly to the safety of her father's arms as

he reluctantly moved away from Elara, giving the medic room to examine her.

He whirled around to face Noiro, Helia tucked in his arms, his eyes blazing furiously. "What happened?" he demanded again.

"I'm not sure," Noiro said, feeling completely at a loss. "They showed up like this. Yun Zeru, and at least two others—they broke into her place."

"Oh God, El." Argon's face contorted with fear and concern.

"We need to gather everyone. We're not safe... Helia..." Elara uttered, wincing as Tami began disinfecting her wound.

Just as she spoke, she heard Miela's thick boots clomping against the floor as she ran into the house. "Elara!"

"They were attacked," Argon explained shortly, shifting Helia's weight in his arms. "Yun Zeru."

"What?"

"They were—"

"I heard you." Miela's nostrils flared as anger flooded through her. She put her hand on her sword. "We need to go and—"

"No," Elara said heatedly. "No one is going anywhere. We need to discuss—"

"The time for discussing is over, Elara," Miela fumed. "You could have been killed. And it's apparent that he's not afraid. But he's not powerful, yet. We can—"

"I know what he's after," said Elara. She grimaced as Tami attended to her wound.

Tami turned her head around, her hands still focused on Elara. "You're all going to have to wait," she told them.

THE ELEMENTAL

"I need to bring her in. We need to stitch her up."

"No." Elara shook her head. "No. You don't understand, Tami. We can't. They'll be looking for us…"

"You need—"

"Please, Tami. Just do what you can," she begged. Tami looked at her old friend, her eyes meeting defiant, tear-filled ones. "Please."

"Okay… But this is going to hurt," she said. "I can give you something for the pain."

"No," Elara said quietly. "I need to stay clear-headed. I need to talk, still. I can't forget anything."

"It's going to hurt," Tami repeated.

"I don't care," she whimpered.

Tami pursed her lips, concerned, but began to work on her shoulder.

Argon peered over Tami's shoulder, staring at Elara's battered and bloodied face. He felt sick, his gut lurching inside him.

"You were stabbed… How did this happen?" Tami asked, trying hard to keep her voice steady. She was a seasoned medic in Polaris, and was used to seeing patients in dire conditions. But it was different, working on her friend.

It hit too close to home.

"A sword," Elara uttered, breathing hard through the pain as Tami cauterized her wound.

"What happened?"

"I… I hid," Elara answered, feeling childish and cowardly as she heard her answer out loud. "When I heard them, I panicked. I was going to escape from the window with Helia, but everything happened so fast. Too fast. They heard us. I grabbed Helia and hid under the bed. I

284

hoped they wouldn't find us…" Elara breathed in sharply as Tami continued to attend to her wound. "He knew we were there. Or at least, he guessed. He stuck his sword through the mattress and it went through my shoulder."

"Helia?" Tami worried. "Is she—?"

"I had her under me." Elara's heart ached as she recalled how Helia shook with fear beneath her.

Argon held Helia closer to him, his eyes locked on Elara. *You're incredible.*

"Yun Zeru didn't know she was there. He wanted the book. He didn't know about Helia until he saw her…" Elara couldn't bear to speak of it. Her voice wavered as she continued: "He snatched her from me. I held onto her the best I could… Helia was so scared. I tried so hard to get her back… She was so scared…"

"Oh, Elara," Tami consoled, brushing her hair back softly.

More tears spilled over. Elara wondered how she still had any more tears left to cry. "She kept calling out to me," she wept, her face screwing up as she remembered Helia's confused cries. "She kept calling out, 'Mama, Mama.' She couldn't understand why I was letting that man hurt her. She couldn't understand why I wasn't stopping him. I tried… I couldn't…"

"You did all you could," Argon told her.

"I know." Elara closed her eyes mournfully. "But I don't think she understands…"

"Helia is a smart little girl," Tami said firmly. "I think she understands better than you give her credit for. She might've not understood what was happening, but she knows that you would never want any of that to happen."

Elara's stomach twisted, unconvinced of her words. It

wasn't what she had seen, at all. She noticed Helia's wary glances towards her, and turning away to cling tightly to Argon. It hurt. It stung. She wondered if Helia could ever trust her again. It pained her to even think about.

"He knows that Helia is a Tawer," Elara said, her eyes meeting Argon's. "He had no doubt that she was mine. He was going to hurt Helia to make me tell him everything… But then he saw the ring…"

Elara bit her lip. She wasn't sure why she had held onto the ring, instead of keeping it with Miela or Noiro, along with the rest of the artifacts they found with Helia.

"The family ring," Argon murmured.

Elara nodded. "He got distracted. He took Helia and kept shaking her, hurting her, asking her who she was. He looked confused."

"Confused?"

"He said something to himself. 'Another Tawer,' he said," Elara recalled.

Argon frowned.

"It looks like he's been keeping track of your family members," Noiro posited, looking at Helia. Elara nodded. "I think so too. He…. He tried to… He hurt her. He began choking her… And I couldn't…" Elara's voice trembled. She turned her head to the side, ashamed. She failed to protect her daughter.

"How did you get away?" asked Noiro.

"Helia," Elara uttered, tears squeezing out the side of her eyes. "Helia saved us."

"Helia?" Miela was quiet until then. "How?"

"I… I'm not sure." Elara's eyes darted quickly to Tami. She didn't want to reveal what she had seen. She closed her eyes.

Tami had been by her side in the future. She risked her life to help save people during the war. And she had already learned too much while listening to their conversation.

And with Yun Zeru's attack… It was only a matter of time.

She had to know.

Elara opened her eyes.

"Helia's eyes rolled back in her head. I thought it was from being strangled… I was so scared, but then…" Elara looked at Helia, who was clutching at Argon's neck, her wailing slowly ceasing to soft hiccups as he comforted her. "She made water appear."

"What?"

"Water. It came out from the ground and threw Yun Zeru off balance. I took my chance and grabbed her away from him. We ran… and came here." She looked at Noiro, grunting in pain as Tami finishing stitching her shoulder. "It was the first place I could think of."

Noiro didn't know how to respond.

Water appeared? He looked at Helia warily, and then to Argon, who looked equally shocked. Miela seemed to want to say something, but looked hesitantly at Tami.

They would have time to talk more about that later.

Right now, Elara needed to rest.

He looked back at her. She looked so small, and her body was battered and bruised. It hurt to see her that way. He had raised Elara as a little girl. He was her family. He held her hand tightly, thankful that she was all right. That Helia was all right.

Tami finished bandaging her shoulder and then moved to examine Helia. Thankfully, she escaped with only a few bruises, although they looked like nasty ones. Her windpipe was bruised as well, with the force Yun Zeru used against the toddler. Helia's voice was a little hoarse, but with some more time to rest, she would make a full recovery.

"All right," Tami sighed, tidying up her kit. "I've taken care of the wounds I can see. Is there anything else that hurts?" Her worried eyes looked over her old friend.

"My muscles… and my head," Elara managed.

Tami nodded. "It's no surprise. You've suffered major trauma," she said sadly. "Please, I can give you something for the pain. You need to rest."

"Leave it here, I'll take it later," Elara answered.

Tami nodded, taking out a small bottle and leaving it on the table.

"I'll help you get cleaned up," Miela offered, moving towards Elara and helping her stand up. "We need to get this blood off you."

Elara struggled to get to her feet, looking down at herself. Her shirt was now stiff with dried blood, and she could feel it sticking to her skin. She felt her stomach lurch as she reassessed how much blood she'd lost. She didn't know she had so much blood in her.

Miela was right.

Argon watched as the two women slowly made their way to the bathroom, the door closing shut behind them. He looked at Helia, who was slowly drifting to sleep in his arms. She was covered in blood, too, but it wasn't hers. He was so thankful.

"I'll take her," Noiro said softly, extending his arms towards Helia. He saw Argon's troubled face, and could only imagine how scared he must have felt. It was the same way he felt, after all. "I'll get her cleaned up.

Argon nodded gratefully.

After a few moments, Elara and Miela emerged from the bathroom, Miela supporting Elara's weight as they shuffled slowly back to the sitting room. Argon rushed over to them, supporting Elara from her other side, and helped put her down onto the soft couch. Her hair was still wet, and he could smell the scented soap on her skin. She was wearing a loose shirt, probably one of Noiro's, as it was so large on her frame that it hung down to her thighs, and a pair of old pants scrunched up around her legs. He brushed her hair behind her ear. He couldn't help himself.

"Take the medicine," Argon told her, moving his hand to her cheek. Elara closed her eyes, leaning her face into his palm.

"Not now, please," Elara whispered, her voice wobbly as she tried not to put any pressure on her injured shoulder. He couldn't understand why she sounded like she was begging him. He had only asked her. His heart ached at the sound of her pleading; he could only think of how she must have pleaded with Yun Zeru.

Elara pleaded because she knew she would cave in if he pushed. She wanted to have her wits about her. She was afraid.

"Please," he said gently. "For Helia."

Elara bit her lip, and then nodded. Argon brought the bottle close to her lips, tipping it slightly to give her a sip. Elara coughed, feeling the warm liquid slide down her throat. It burned, but it also felt good. Argon pulled her into a tight hug, careful not to put any pressure on her injuries.

"I'm so sorry," Argon whispered mournfully. His voice was thick as he swallowed back tears. "He was after the book... I left it there with you. He must have been watching..."

"It doesn't matter," Elara murmured against his cheek, closing her eyes. "He would have attacked any one of us."

"I love you, Elara."

She could feel herself beginning to relax, but she wasn't sure if it was from the medicine, or from the comfort she found with Argon.

Argon could feel her form begin to relax against him, and he shifted her slowly to lie back down as she drifted to sleep. He gritted his teeth together, turning to look at Miela, who had moved further away to give the two some privacy.

That night would haunt him forever.

Yun Zeru would pay.

He had no doubt that he would do everything in his power to destroy him.

Yun Zeru would pay for hurting his family.

Elara felt stiff. She groaned, moving her neck to the side to release a small crick, and stretched. She moved her hand over a thick, fuzzy blanket that covered her body, and slowly pushed it to the side. She could feel the sunlight slowly filling the room, and her consciousness slowly returned. She squinted one eye open, surveying the room, and slowly propped herself up onto her elbows.

She was in Noiro's sitting room. She looked out the window, and saw it was sunrise.

Or was is sunset?

Elara looked around her, disoriented. How long had

she slept for?

Argon sat in the armchair closest to her, his eyes closed and his chest rising softly as he slept. She felt touched. She wondered how long he had stayed by her side. Never had she needed to lean on someone so heavily, and he hadn't left her.

She looked around.

It was quiet. Where was everyone?

She moved to sit up, grimacing as she felt pain shoot through her shoulder. She put a hand instinctively to where she felt the pain, and her hand met a thick, soft bandage wrapped around her side.

Oh.

The horrible events suddenly came flooding back to her, and she groaned. It felt like a horrid dream. But it was real.

"You're awake."

Elara turned towards the relieved voice. Argon was leaning forward, alert as he rubbed the sleep out of his eyes. He immediately came closer, kneeling on the ground beside her as she sat on the couch, holding her hand tightly to his chest, his eyes searching hers. Was she all right?

Elara smiled, and he smiled back.

"Where is everyone?"

"Out. It's been about a day and a half," he said, anticipating her next question.

She looked down at her lap, nodding. She felt sore, but much better than she had when she first come to Noiro's door that night. "And Helia?" she asked, her voice dropping with concern.

"With Miela and Noiro," he assured. "They should be

back soon, actually."

"Where is everyone?" Elara asked again.

Argon sighed. "They're gathering support," he said. "Rounding up people we've fought alongside with in the future. We need help."

Elara nodded. It was a good idea.

They couldn't simply wait around for Yun Zeru to grow his power and strength, and for him to attack again. She shuddered as she remembered his cold, icy smile.

She never wanted to see such a wretched human being ever again.

"Helia is an Elemental," Elara uttered quietly.

Argon nodded. "We've told Estelle. We needed her insight." He held her hand, as if he were afraid she would disappear if he let go. "It makes sense. Helia's a descendant from Princess Water, after all."

"I don't understand," Elara murmured, looking at their clasped hands and squeezing back. "We tried to test her. Nothing happened. How…?"

"It must have been triggered," said Argon. "Fear. Anger. Helplessness. It must have brought it out in her."

"How?"

"Estelle's trying to get us some more information," Argon replied. "But from what she's found, accounts of Elementals from our line often emerged during some stressful event. An example is my grandmother's mother. She was horribly abused by her husband. Guess how he died."

Elara shrugged, clueless, eyes locked on Argon.

Argon pursed his lips. "He drowned. In water that was ankle-deep. The water kept pushing him down, almost as if it were holding him under the surface. Another example is my mother's cousin. She was hiking up one of Mizar's cliffs, and the ground had given away beneath her feet. She fell into the sea below, but… the sea rose up to meet her. It literally rose high into the sky as she fell towards it, as if it were catching her. She drifted to shore without so much as a scratch on her. There are several more accounts…"

"Like Helia being choked," said Elara quietly, guilt wrapping itself around her organs and tightening roughly inside her.

Argon nodded.

"He knows," Elara continued wistfully. "Yun Zeru knows."

"What?"

"When he saw Helia's abilities. He called her the 'Elemental.' He knows. He'll be after us. He'll be after her."

"We need to move." Argon's eyes blazed furiously. "We need to protect Helia. We'll have you go into hiding, and—"

"Going into hiding won't solve anything." Elara shook her head. "We need to stop him. We need to end this."

"How?"

"We need to go to the beginning. We need the Diadem."

THE BEGINNING

"Why are we here?"

Elara's shoulders shook as a strong breeze blew through her coat. She winced as she felt the wind pierce through her injured shoulder.

Ahead of her walked Estelle and Noiro, followed by Miela. Noiro trod carefully over the stony rubble pathway, his hair blowing back in the harsh wind howling through the cliffs as he led the way. Argon walked closely behind Elara, carrying Helia tightly in his arms. She clung to him, burying her face in the crook of his neck to warm her icy cold cheeks.

They climbed down the steep pathway, the cold, icy winds gusting across the roaring grey sea.

The group walked over to the base of one of the cliffs, quickly huddling inside one of the caves. Elara stepped over the small symbol of Polaris etched into the ground at the cave's mouth.

The Old Archives.

"Noiro. Why are we here?" Elara asked again.

"To see Princess Laelia."

Estelle walked deeper into the cavern, slowly coming to a stop in front of the old, weathered statue cloaked in the darkness of the cave. Argon set Helia down onto the ground, taking her hand. He walked towards the statue, Noiro, Elara, and Miela in tow.

Helia stared at the stone woman in awe. Her long hair flowed from her head and merged into the rocky wall, and her long, stone dress was swept behind her. Elara peered at the woman's outstretched hands, the palms cupped together in a protective clasp.

For a moment, Elara expected to see something appear in the statue's hands. But alas, it was empty, save for a small pool of water collecting in the statue's tight grasp from droplets dripping from the cave's ceiling.

"I don't understand," muttered Miela. "I thought we needed the Diadem."

"We do," said Estelle. "But it would be difficult to get the Queen's Diadem from the castle, wouldn't it? The only way you got it in the future was when the castle was destroyed."

"You're right." Argon nodded. "But that doesn't explain why we're here in the caves."

"This statue was built at the same time Polaris was founded," explained Estelle. "If my theory proves correct, then Princess Laelia had this statue erected herself. Which means it's the most accurate depiction that we have to date.

"Do you think that the statue is hiding something?"

"Maybe," pondered Estelle. "Maybe the Ancient

Princess has something here that can help us."

Elara shook her head, confused. "I don't know what we're looking for. This statue stood here for centuries. If there were anything to find, don't you think someone would have found it by now? What if it's gone?"

"It's not," Estelle replied with a smile, pointing to the statue's head. "The Diadem."

Elara looked at the statue curiously. There was no Diadem on the woman's head.

"I don't see anything," said Miela, echoing Elara's observation.

"Of course not," agreed Estelle. "But it's there. The most accurate depiction of the Diadem."

Elara gave her a long, perplexed look.

"If you think about it, we've only ever seen images of the Diadem," defended Estelle. "The only people who have ever seen the Diadem up close is the royal family themselves. We don't have the luxury of time to go to the castle and demand to see the Diadem. Especially not without having to share everything we know about the future. The war. Yun Zeru. Helia. And even then, how would we guarantee we'd be granted permission to see the Diadem? To see the Queen herself?

"I also started thinking... We've only ever seen the Diadem from the front. Every painting that's ever captured the Diadem has only shown the face of the Diadem. The crowning jewels. The jewels used in the Diadem are well-documented, as well: diamond, emerald, sapphire, and ruby. There is no mention of any other stone embedded into the Diadem.

"We also know that, in the future, we took the Diadem, and we found the Aether Stone. So, we know for a fact that the Aether Stone is in the Diadem," Estelle finished.

"But if there's only diamonds, emeralds, sapphires, and rubies in the Diadem, then where is the Aether Stone?" asked Argon.

"Exactly my question," agreed Estelle. "Like I said, there are hundreds of paintings and depictions of the Diadem, but they only ever capture the face of the Diadem. But what if there was something behind the Diadem?"

Estelle turned away from the statue and looked back at her friends. "Noiro, give me a boost." She clambered up onto the statue, supported by Noiro from beneath, and pulled herself closer to the statue's head.

Sure enough, hidden away from prying eyes, a diagram was carved onto the woman's head, etched deep into the stone crevices. It was impossible for anyone to have seen the etching unless they climbed up onto the statue.

Estelle let out a small whoop of excitement. "It's here," she cried. Noiro wobbled as he tried to maintain his balance beneath Estelle's feet while she stretched up higher to take a closer look.

The carving was simple, almost rudimentary. Estelle traced her fingers against the etching. There was a large ring that encircled the statue's head, with four smaller rings looped together at the front. "Diamond, emerald, sapphire, and ruby," Estelle murmured as she touched the four rings. She gently dragged her finger along the large ring, coming to a stop at the very back of the statue's head. There, a small, jagged notch of a ring lay etched inconspicuously, carved in such a manner that it almost looked like a mere imperfection of the statue, as if a piece of stone had simply cracked away.

But it was there, carved deliberately at the back of the ring.

The Aether Stone.

Estelle clambered back down excitedly, quickly explaining to the group what she had seen.

"You're brilliant, Estelle," Noiro rubbed the back of his neck in admiration. "All this time…"

"It's just like the Ballad said," Estelle squealed. "She hid the other amongst diamond, emerald, sapphire, and ruby. It was in the Diadem all along!"

"So, then, that means—"

"Noiro?"

A deep voice interrupted the group's excited chatter, and they hastily fell silent as they turned around in surprise.

"Professor Neptune." Noiro smiled queasily. Elara felt the hairs on the back of her neck rise, her heart dropping into the pit of her belly in dread. How much had he heard?

"How nice to see you!" Professor Neptune smiled cheerily. "I was just out on my usual walk. Are you here to see me?"

"Er, no," Noiro uttered nervously. The Professor's eyebrow quirked curiously. "I mean, yes," lied Noiro hastily. He could see the gears in the old man's head turning, and his eyes twinkled inquisitively. "We were just taking a walk ourselves, and I wanted to drop by and say hello."

"Of course." Professor Neptune smiled. "Come, please. I believe I have some snacks in my office."

The group looked at each other uneasily. The last thing they wanted to do was to waste more time while Yun Zeru was on the loose.

But they also needed to avoid suspicion.

As much as Elara disliked him, there was no denying that the Professor was an intelligent man. She wondered if he could sense the tension in the air, or the unease that the group felt as they followed him deeper into the cave and down long, stony flight of stairs.

Professor Neptune unlocked the heavy door to the Old Archives and walked through, not paying attention to his guests.

"Please, make yourselves comfortable," Professor Neptune mumbled as he gestured absentmindedly at the seats in his office. He walked towards his desk. A messy pile of paper was strewn about, and he casually began to put them in order. "I just need to tidy up some things."
The group hesitantly walked in, filling the small room. Elara was suddenly very aware of the fact that Helia was exposed, and she exchanged worried glances with Argon. His brow furrowed, echoing back her worry, and they both glanced at their daughter between them. Argon instinctively moved forward, partially shielding Helia from view.

The Professor, finally done with putting away his papers, sat down comfortably in his chair, leaning back and putting his legs up on the desk. "So, Noiro," he began, his beady eyes glimmering in the dim light. "To what do I owe this pleasure? I see you've brought a few more friends this time." The Professor looked inquisitively at Estelle, and then at Helia. He lingered for a moment at the toddler, perplexed.

"She's part of a case I'm working on," Miela volunteered.

"Oh? And what case is that, Captain?"

"I'm not at liberty to say," Miela replied firmly, her tone sharp.

The Professor nodded.

"We just wanted to show my sister around," said Noiro, gesturing at Estelle. "She's visiting from the Ursa Isles."

"I've heard so much about you," Estelle offered politely. "My brother's mentioned you quite often, growing up."

The Professor beamed, his chest puffing slightly with the stroke to his ego. "Ursa Isles, eh?" He leaned back in his chair. "I've always wanted to visit there. Tell me…" The Professor began engaging in conversation with Estelle, who keenly kept up with him.

Elara sat rigidly in her set, her eyes drifting around the office. It was a little messier than the last time they had visited, with some loose sheets of paper lying around the floor, and some tools lying on one of the desks nearby. She looked at the scrappily stacked papers the Professor had put away on his desk, squinting as she tried to peer at what was scrawled on the top sheet of paper.

"Oops," Miela uttered gingerly. Elara tilted her head towards her friend, who had accidentally bumped a folder of papers off of one of the desks with her hip. It was rather cramped with seven people piled up into the Professor's small, cozy office; someone was bound to knock something over.

The Professor, however, hadn't taken notice of Miela's little mishap, still enthralled in his conversation with Estelle about the wonders of the Ursa Isles.

Miela knelt down gingerly, and began gathering the scattered sheets of paper back into the file.

Elara turned her attention to Helia. The toddler was leaning against her body, and she held an arm protectively around her as she balanced the little girl on her lap. Argon had shifted his seat in front of the two, as if to shield them both from view. She smiled fondly at the back of his head, and then back down at Helia, who was quietly observing the ticking dials on display in the office.

Miela drew in a low, sharp gasp. Elara looked at her friend, who was still kneeling on the ground. Her eyes were trained on a piece of paper clutched tightly in her hands, the edges of the paper crinkling in her tight grasp. Miela slowly turned her eyes to Elara, and then to Professor Neptune.

Elara peered over her shoulder, looking curiously at the paper.

A vast diagram of a family tree was mapped out across the sheet. She raked over the names and boxes, narrowing her eyes as she tried to grasp its contents.

Her eyes trailed up to the root of the family tree. She blinked at the familiar name.

Princess Laelia.

What was Professor Neptune doing with the family tree of the Ancient Princess?

She looked at the branches of the family tree, each of them stemming from Princess Laelia's four offspring: Prince Air, Princess Water, Princess Earth, and Prince Fire. She followed the line for Princess Water, stopping at the bottom as she spied Argon's name, with Estelle's listed right beside him. Beneath Argon's name was a small box and a question mark.

Elara felt the blood drain from her face.

Her eyes darted to Helia, and then back to the paper.

Another familiar name caught her eye: Inana Erif.

Elara frowned. What was Inana doing on the family tree?

Elara followed her line back to Princess Laelia, and paused as she reached Prince Fire's line.

Elara's knuckles turned stark white as she gripped the edge of her seat. She glanced at Professor Neptune, and then back at Helia.

They needed to get out of here.

"What are you doing?" asked the Professor suddenly. Elara and Miela snapped their necks up. He stood up slowly, glowering at the two women, and reached his hand out for the paper.

"Why do you have this?" challenged Miela, clutching the family tree tightly in her hand.

"What is that?" Noiro inquired, craning his neck to look at the document.

"It's nothing." Professor Neptune smiled coldly. Argon rose to his feet, his hand at his weapon.

"We need to leave." Miela stood up, her nostrils flared. She glared fiercely at the Professor. "And you're coming with us.

"I don't think so," he replied coolly, still seated. He looked utterly relaxed; pleased, even, like a cat having just caught its prey. "Nobody's going anywhere."

The door flung open behind them, and heavy, leather-clad boots clomped their way into the office.

"Did you find it?" the Professor asked the newcomer, a content smile dancing on his lips.

A deep chuckle rose from behind them. Elara's heart stopped at the sound.

That voice.

Elara gulped, fear trickling down her spine as she turned around.

A tall, broad, silver-haired man strode into the office, clad in a lightweight jacket and thick leather boots. His scarred face stretched into a sinister sneer as he eyed Elara and Helia. His eyes flashed. "The Elemental."

"No…" Noiro breathed, looking in horror at the ominous villain before them, and then at his old friend. Professor Neptune looked back at Noiro, a flicker of guilt flashing across his face. But it disappeared just as quickly as it came, replaced with a harsh, cold glower.

"Never you mind," Professor Neptune snapped. "Do you have it?"

"How could you?" Noiro gasped. "I… I trusted you! All this time!" Tears pricked the corner of his eyes, and he blinked it back furiously. "How could you?!"

"I found it," Yun Zeru replied, ignoring Noiro's outburst. He held up an old book in his hand. Two men accompanied him, and Elara recognized one of them from the break-in. "The girl left it at her home when she took off like the coward she is."

"Give it here," the Professor ordered, still seated. Yun Zeru tossed the book towards him, and he gracefully snatched it out of the air.

"Careful," Professor Neptune tutted. "This here is an old book. Quite valuable, if I'm not mistaken." He looked at Estelle, who was frozen in her spot, horrified.

"Fital's Tales," he continued. "One of the rare items that the Old Archives could never get their hands on."

"Was it worth the trouble?" Yun Zeru scoffed. "You had me find a children's book? How will that help me get it?"

"Did you read it?" Professor Neptune inquired.

"No," Yun Zeru jeered. "I don't do that garbage. I'll leave that to you."

Professor Neptune raised an eyebrow, and then began flipping through the book. Elara lunged forwards in hopes of prying the book out of his hands, but one of Yun Zeru's cronies yanked her back. Another one grabbed Helia roughly by the arm.

Argon howled angrily, lurching towards the two and drawing his sword.

"Ah, ah." Yun Zeru's icy voice cut through. "Move another inch, and I'll slice her throat open."

Argon froze.

Yun Zeru grinned frigidly, his scar creasing at the sides.

"Now, Estelle…" Professor Neptune mused. He swiveled to face her. "You mentioned something about the Ballad earlier. So one of the ballads here holds the key."

Estelle glowered at him silently, refusing to say a word.

Professor Neptune began skimming through the book, and came to a pause at the end. "The Ballad of the Ancient Princess."

For the first time since the group had run into Professor Neptune that day, he stopped smiling, his face dropping to a solemn expression as he began to read.

"Well?" Yun Zeru demanded. "How do we get it?"

Professor Neptune's beady eyes flicked back and forth as he reread the Ballad once again. He remained silent, his finger tapping rhythmically on his chin. "The First?" Professor Neptune thought aloud in a soft murmur. He furrowed his brow, confused.

"Well?"

"It's just like we thought," Professor Neptune finally spoke. "We need to get all of them."

"All of them?"

"What are you talking about?" Noiro demanded. "Get rid of who? Professor... Why are you doing this?"

Professor Neptune looked at his old friend. "Power," he said simply. He turned to Yun Zeru. "To get the Elemental power, we need the First."

"The First? What?" Yun Zeru demanded. "What are you talking about?"

"Noiro, elaborate." Professor Neptune shifted his head towards him.

Noiro glared stonily at him, his blood boiling. He pursed his lips shut, refusing to speak.

"Silent?" Professor Neptune smiled. "Funny. You never were one to stay quiet..." He walked over to the small apparatus in the corner of his office, his hands delicately tracing the gleaming strands of metal that held up the elemental bodies: emerald, sapphire, diamond, and ruby.

The Elemental Dial.

The four stones pulsated slowly, vibrating with energy. Professor Neptune eyed his invention, a clever glint reflecting off of his toothy sneer. "Funny how it only seems to do that when you all are here," he said curiously. He looked at Noiro, and then eyed Argon, Elara, Helia, and Miela.

Noiro gritted his teeth.

"Still refusing to say anything, old friend?" the Professor said, his voice dripping with thick, sickening sugar.

Noiro glared at Neptune.

"All right, I'll tell you, then." The Professor stretched his lips into a smile. "Power. It all comes down to power. The most powerful drivers of the Earth are its elements. Think of all of that... The potential! By harnessing the power of the elements, everything would be in the palm of our hands. Food. Weather. Water. We could conquer the world. Instead of sending men to fight, we would send the elements to do our dirty work for us. Sweep the world with devastating droughts, floods, fires, hurricanes, earthquakes. Destruction. All of that power. All of that might... We could control the world."

Elara's heart sank into the pit of her stomach, the words of the Ballad echoing in her ears.

> *Unbeknownst to the Ancient Princess, on that fateful day,*
> *It was no ordinary stone that fell in her way.*
> *For she had consumed the First,*
> *The key to the Elements in which she was immersed.*

> *Mystified by the First and its power,*
> *She feared what might happen with hands that went sour.*
> *Plagued with fears of her prospering empire falling once more,*
> *She set out to secure the world as her existence's core.*

"You're going to destroy the world," Elara uttered in dismay.

"I'm going to control the world," Professor Neptune corrected.

Elara stared at the man hopelessly. This is what it meant to have the power of the elements in the wrong hands, why the Ancient Princess went to such lengths to hide the Aether stone.

There was so much good that came out of the Aether stone. With the War of Waters having decimated the planet, and humanity pushed to the brink of extinction, it was the power of the stone that brought humanity back. Brought life back.

But there was so much destruction that could be done, too.

Elara squeezed her eyes shut. She wished that that wretched stone had been destroyed.

"I just need the last piece of the puzzle," Neptune murmured. "The source of the elements. The First…"

"It's been lost for centuries," Noiro growled. "You'll never get your hands on it."

"Ah, so you *do* know what the First is." Professor Neptune corked an eyebrow, looking like a pleased cat who finally caught its prey. "You're right, though; it's been lost to the ages. Believe me, I've spent years of searching through the world's mines of precious stones. Raiding people's homes. Collecting old jewels." Professor Neptune sighed. "Nothing."

"Let us go," Elara spoke, her voice harsh and steady, growing tired of listening to the depraved ramblings of the Professor.

"There's no point in wasting any more time looking for something that's lost," he continued, ignoring Elara. He looked down at his old, delicate hands, hardened and wrinkled with time. "I don't have much time left on this Earth, you see. I don't have much more time…And then, I thought, what if I could recreate the First?"

Recreate the First?

He turned his head to Argon and Estelle. "Descendants of the Ancient Princess. Her blood flows through your veins. All I need is your blood to turn into stone. All I need is to get my hands on every last descendant of the Ancient Princess."

Elara's breath caught in her throat. All the pieces fell into place, and suddenly everything made sense. Why Argon was first attacked in the time shadows. The break in. The stolen family pictures. The stolen heirlooms. Why Estelle was so terrified of the Aether Stone falling into the wrong hands, so much so that she slit her own throat rather than give up the secret. Why their mother was hunted and murdered in cold blood.

Why Inana Erif and her family were targeted.

Why so many more were.

Targets. They were all targets.

Every last one of the Ancient Princess's descendants were targets.

"The Tawers. Drain their blood for the Elemental Dial."

Yun Zeru sniggered gleefully and asked, "And the Elemental?" He eyeballed little Helia hungrily.

"Like we originally planned," the Professor crooned. "Get her. Keep her. We'll find more. We need agents to control the elements. Warriors. Who better to use than Elementals?"

Elara's blood ran cold.

Helia.

They were going to take her away.

That's why they were after Elementals.

How many more Elementals were out there? How many more would be captured? Recruited? Brainwashed? Blackmailed? Forced to serve Professor Neptune and carry out his sinister plans of controlling the Earth's elements?

How many would be killed?

Elara felt a lump grow in her throat, and she struggled to breathe as realization sank in.

Was that why she had sent Helia back through time?

Were they trying to capture Helia?

Were they trying to kill Helia?

It didn't matter, now. Elara shook her head, her heart breaking as she thrashed against Yun Zeru's men, trying to break free to save her.

She was going to fail.

"NO," Argon roared, lunging forward toward his daughter. He was held back once more. He struggled with all his might to try and break free, but to no avail.

"Professor, you're wrong," Noiro pleaded with his old friend. "This is wrong. Please. Don't do this."

"Don't you see?" the Professor replied simply. "It's for the greater good. It's for power." He turned his head to Yun Zeru. "Do it now. We need their blood."

"How much of it?"

"All of it."

More of Yun Zeru's men swarmed into the room, holding them captive. Miela struggled against her captor, the blade he held to her throat pressing against the thin skin of her neck, droplets of blood gathering at the tip of the dagger. Argon had two men holding him back, restraining his arms as he tried to wildly break free from their grasp. Noiro was locked in a death grip by another captor, his breath catching in his throat, his eyes bloodshot and watery as he fought for air. Estelle was trapped against the wall by another, her hoarse screams echoing off the walls. Elara struggled against her captor as he roughly held her down, screaming until her throat was raw as Yun Zeru strode over to the toddler and picked her up by her neck, screaming and pleading to be let go.

Was this it?

Elara saw Helia's little legs kick in the air and weakly grasp at the large, grubby hands enclosed around her throat as she was brought closer to Yun Zeru's face.

Elara closed her eyes.

They were all going to die.

She couldn't bring herself to watch.

She failed.

Twice.

Elara cried, large, fat tears rolling down her cheeks as she screamed for her baby. She pushed back against her captor to no avail.

There was nothing she could do.

Professor Neptune just sat back in his seat, outwardly bemused by the entire ordeal.

One by one, the men drew their weapons.

"Drain them all, for good measure," the Professor sneered. "And get the Elemental."

With that, the men drove their weapons deep into each of their hostages' bodies, a horrible crunching sound ripping through them as they twisted the blades into their insides and roughly yanked them out. Elara felt the air gurgle in her airway as she struggled to breathe, a blinding, searing pain overpowering her senses.

Blood splattered onto the floor, staining the marble deep crimson. She felt the hand holding her up suddenly let go, letting her body topple over, falling with a splash into the puddle of blood quickly pooling beneath her. She kept her eyes open, desperately looking for Helia, her head frozen in place.

Was she all right?

Was she hurt?

She caught a glimpse of her baby, and her breath caught in her throat at the sight of her own daughter being taken away from her.

And with that, she breathed her last.

THE SURVIVOR

Screaming.

The only noise that rung through Helia's ears was the shrill, piercing sound of screaming. She spun her head wildly back and forth, her eyes raking over the sprawled out bodies before her. Mama. Dad. Uncle Noiro. Auntie Miela. Auntie Estelle. She didn't understand.

Why weren't they waking up?

Couldn't they hear her?

Couldn't they see her?

Her Mama's eyes were open, unseeingly watching her as she felt big, gruff hands roughly pick her up, as if she were nothing but a ragdoll, and throw her over a sharp, muscular shoulder. Her stomach heaved as it landed hard against the man's shoulder, the wind whooshing out of her lungs. She kicked helplessly against her captor, her small arms reaching out towards her Mama. Her throat was dry and sore, her voice growing hoarse from screaming.

"Mama! MAMA!" she called desperately, flailing and twisting her body as the man's grip tightened around her.

Why wouldn't she wake up?

Her eyes were open.

She could see her, right?

"MAMA!"

Helia squealed as she sailed through the air, grunting as her body rolled against the rough, jagged floor before slamming hard against the concrete wall. Her head banged against the wall, and she yelped in pain. "Wait!" she cried, quickly crawling on her knees towards the thick, iron door. "WAIT!"

The door heavily slammed shut, the sound of the thick lock clicking in place echoing through the small, dark, moldy room.

Her eyes stung as tears began to well up, and she felt the lump in her throat grow thicker. Her body felt tight and sore, her muscles tensing as she scanned the room, eyes barely being able to make out what might be lurking in the dark, hidden depths of her cell. All sorts of monsters prowled in the dark. She needed her night lantern to keep them at bay.

But who could she ask?

The monsters who threw her in here?

Helia shuffled back against the wall, her eyes wild and alert as she searched for something, anything, that could be with her in her tiny room. Cold water dripped periodically from the ceiling, falling onto her head and seeping into her scalp. She shuddered. The smell of mold suddenly overwhelmed her senses, and she felt her stomach twist painfully around her gut. She threw her hands over her mouth, heaving as she retched. The acid from her stomach stung her raw throat, and she grasped at her neck as vomit dribbled from her chin and onto her soiled clothes.

Dirty, fouled, scared, cold.

Alone.

Helia miserably put her head down onto her knees and wailed loudly. There was nothing else she could do.

"Elemental 0001," a brusque man barked.

Helia looked up at the man towering over her tiny stature. His hard face stared sternly at her, his bushy, greying eyebrows hanging heavy over his small, black eyes. She winced, the lights in the bright, white hall were bright compared to her dark, dingy cell. She rubbed her eyes with the back of her hand, and then looked down at the floor.

"Elemental 0001," the man repeated, his voice rising harshly.

Helia looked at him again, confused. What did he mean? She frowned. *Elemental.* That word was familiar. Where had she heard it before? Her Mama's face floated to the surface, and she could vaguely remember the word being used during one of her grownup talks. Helia felt tears gather in the corner of her eyes as she tried to focus hard on her Mama's face. What were the color of her eyes, again?

"YOU," the man boomed, suddenly lunging forward and yanking her arm hard toward him. He snarled, "Listen to me when I call you, you filthy brat."

Helia snapped her head up at him, tears dripping

from her terrified eyes. "I- I…" she stammered. She was confused. Was he calling her? She didn't hear her name. She knew her name.

Auntie Miela walked over, her boots smartly clipping against the Grand Library's marble floors. "Your Mama's smart, kid," she said, also kneeling down to Helia. "My name's Miela. Can you tell me your name?"

"H-Helia," she replied, sniffing as she wiped her cheeks and nose with the back of her hand.

"My name is Helia," she said slowly.

She was sure of it.

Uncle Noiro grunted when he felt one of his knees creak as it rested against the marble floor. "We're going to help you find your Mama, but we need your help. Can you be brave and help us find your Mama?"

Her sobs quieted at his gentle tone. She nodded.

"I'm brave," she said quietly.

"Yes, you are," Uncle Noiro praised. "Now, Helia is a wonderful name, but I bet that's only what your Mama calls you. What do other people call you?"

"Helia," she repeated, confused.

"It's a beautiful name." Uncle Noiro smiled.

Helia's heart ripped apart as the kind words of her beloved Auntie Miela and Uncle Noiro echoed in her head.

"Your name is Elemental 0001," the man's voice thundered. Helia shrunk back.

"I'm brave," she said quietly.

"Yes, you are," Uncle Noiro praised.

"I'm brave," Helia dared, her knees shaking beneath her as she spoke back to the man.

A loud smack sounded, and her cheek stung. Her head reeled back, feeling as if it would almost fall off of her neck. "You're filth," the man retorted, and then laughed. He threw a sack of clothes at her, and she buckled at the weight of it thrown against her tiny frame. "These are yours. You will wear them, wash them, and wear them again."

Helia looked down at the sack and peered into it, wrinkling her nose at the old, dirty clothes. They were made from a rough, scratchy material, and looked like the color of sand. She ran her hand against the fabric, and looked at the man. Her finger traced against the fresh stitching of '0001' on the breast pocket.

"Let's go, Elemental 0001. Your training begins."

Helia's stomach growled.

She was hungry.

She looked at the young uniformed man standing before her, then at the old man clad in a set of deep velvet robes draped across his shoulders, and then finally at the small bowl of water set in front of her.

"I know you can do it," the older man coaxed gently. Helia looked at him uncertainly. His voice seemed kind, but his small, cold, beady little eyes twinkled sinisterly at her.

She would never forget his face.

The face of the man who took her family away.

"I saw her, Professor Neptune," the young man spoke. "We saw her do it when we broke into the girl's house. Yun Zeru attested to that already."

"Nothing's happening, still," the old man replied shortly. He sighed, and then looked at the toddler. "If you make the water move, you'll get some food."

Helia's stomach growled loudly, as if on cue.

She stared hard at the bowl of water, unsure of what to do.

Helia begged the water to do something. Anything.

Come on. Move...

She contorted her face and held her breath, her eyes trained hard on the small bowl.

Nothing.

She looked at the Professor helplessly.

He sighed, turning away and walking out of the room. The young man followed.

"Maybe tomorrow." The cell's iron door slammed shut behind them, and Helia was thrown into the cold darkness once more. The sound of the water dripping from the ceiling plinked against the hard floor, and she shifted away from the small puddle.

Beside her, the puddle quivered, and the drops suddenly froze in place. Her stomach grumbling angrily, she wrapped her skinny arms around her belly, and leaned her weakly head against her knees.

Helia's eyes sprung open at the screeching sound of the iron door dragging against the floor, ripping her out of her fitful slumber. She sat up in her small, hard, lumpy mattress, blinking at the sudden light blaring into her dark cell.

"In you go." A large man tossed a small figure in, their body landing hard onto the ground. The cell door slammed shut again, and the heavy footsteps grew further away.

Helia stared silently at the figure laying on the ground, curled up into a ball and whimpering pathetically.

She cleared her throat, catching their attention. The

whimpering slowly stopped.

The figure uncurled, and slowly stood up. It was a small boy, perhaps around seven years old.

"Are you okay?" Helia asked. She felt silly asking the question. Of course, they weren't okay. No one was okay in here.

He nodded, silently wiping at his eyes.

Helia looked at his shirt, her eyes catching the '0002' embroidered onto his scratchy uniform.

"What's your name?" Helia asked.

"Inigo. Inigo Erif," the boy replied, sniffing.

Helia nodded stiffly.

So, they found another one.

She looked at him dejectedly. "No."

"No?"

"Your name is Elemental 0002," she uttered quietly, turning and settling back into her hard mattress. She closed her eyes, the sounds of Inigo's soft, desolate crying resuming in the darkness.

"Your assignment today." Her superior looked down at her. "Rounds."

"Rounds?" Helia mumbled confusedly. "But my duty today is—"

"Rounds, Elemental 0001."

Helia fell silent and nodded, shuffling behind the man.

"March, Elemental 0001," the man barked, not turning back. "Like in training."

"Yes, Mr. Vega."

Helia quickened her pace, matching her steps to the man in front of her, stomping her feet rhythmically against the ground as they entered into the Elites Headquarters.

She kept her eyes straight ahead, ignoring the other marching squads making their way across the campus as they stared at her.

She was beginning to grow used to the stares. Everyone stared at the Elementals. They were a small group, and easy to spot, with their itchy, sandy brown uniform contrasting against the blue uniforms of the Elites. Her eyes shifted slightly over to the thick plume of smoke rising above Polaris's horizon. It looked like they were putting the Fire Elementals to use again.

Helia sighed softly, looking straight ahead of her as she continued to march behind Mr. Vega. How many years had it been since she was first taken away? Seven? Eight? Helia tried to count the passing seasons in an attempt to keep track of time, but with the slow additions of the different Elementals Professor Neptune was rounding up, and the powerful displays of controlling the Earth's elements, the weather and seasons began to meld into each other into one unrecognizable mess. Winters were periodically replaced with scorching heat, and rain fell from the sky in torrential downpours in an unpredictable pattern. Controlled hurricanes and carefully calculated earthquakes tore through the ground.

Professor Neptune could only find and capture eighteen Elementals, and made sure to wipe out the rest of their families. But the destruction that that handful of Elementals could bring with them shook the world to its core.

Helia turned her head in the direction of the castle, now standing in ruins. She stared blankly at it as she marched forward, her mind flashing back to the horrible scenes forever seared into her brain as she was forced to invade the castle with her comrades. The castle, which had stood over Polaris for centuries, fell to rubble in their two-day siege. The Royal Family was wiped out entirely, swept away in a blazing fire led by the Erif clan. The walls of the castle were swallowed whole by the earthquakes ripped into the ground by the Areth clan, and their enemies were toppled over like twigs in the harsh winds that the Ria clan brought with them.

She, as the only surviving member of the Tawer clan, kept watch over the city's massacre under the watchful eye of General Yun Zeru, forced to drive the survivors into the water and watching them get swallowed into the ocean's depths.

Helia's foot caught over a loose cobblestone, and she stumbled momentarily as she tried to catch herself.

Mr. Vega paid no heed, striding strongly out of the gates of the Elites Headquarters, heading towards the city. Helia arched an eyebrow, surprised.

They were deviating from their usual path for rounds.

She knew better than to question Mr. Vega, however, and kept silent.

She followed Mr. Vega as they marched towards the castle. She hadn't been back there in a long time.

Helia pondered detachedly over the invasion of Polaris Castle. As an Elemental Warrior, she had met her fair share of victims and prisoners of war. Each of the victims who succumbed had their own kind of scream, depending on how they died. The ones who burned had the most wretched screams, their voices reaching peaks of shrill shrieks that rang and pierced through her ears in the most bone-chilling way. The ones who were swept away in hurricanes and forceful gales of wind had their screams taken away from their lungs, their voices swallowed and overpowered by the suffocating howls. The ones crushed under boulders and earth had weak screams, their bodies too weak and quashed by the weight of the Earth to make a sound.

The sound of people drowning, however, stuck with Helia. She recalled the first time she drowned a targeted victim, and expected them to flail and scream in the same way the victims of the other Elemental Warriors had.

To her surprise, drowning was quite silent. When people drowned, all of their energy went into trying to breathe and keep their heads above the water. It was very quiet, with their mouths focused on trying to draw in breaths of air rather than scream, only to fill up with water. They pressed their arms against the surface of the water, as if hoping to hoist themselves out of its depths, but alas, their arms splashed and sank beneath the surface, falling uselessly beside them. Eventually, they grew too tired to fight, and their movements became slower, more sluggish. Their heads dipped underneath the water for longer and longer periods of time, until their heads finally disappeared beneath the surface.

Yes. Drowning was quite silent.

Helia's head lifted as they neared a decaying cottage standing at the outskirts of the fallen castle's walls. It was overgrown with moss and small sprouts of trees, and its roof looked like it could topple over with just the right gust of wind. She looked warily at Mr. Vega as he led her into the cottage's entrance. Her skin crawled as she eyed the back of his head nervously, and her marching slowed.

"Keep up the pace, Elemental 0001," Mr. Vega ordered, not turning his head.

He entered, his tall stature disappearing into the darkness of the abandoned cottage. Having no choice, she followed.

Helia stood in the middle of the cottage, the unfamiliar wooden floors creaking beneath the weight of their feet. She looked to the side, eyeing the toppled over armchairs and overturned tables. The shattered glass of the windows littered the floor, and she heard it crunch loudly beneath Mr. Vega's feet as he paced the cottage.

He looked nervous.

Helia looked at him curiously. In all of her years being commanded by him, she had never seen him look nervous before.

What was going on?

Was it another mission?

Her stomach twisted at the possible proposition.

Helia opened her mouth to ask a question, but caught herself before she could speak.

She knew better than to question her superiors.

She stood, her hands neatly folded behind her back as she silently watched the man slowly walk the perimeter of the cottage.

Thud. Thud. Thud.

Helia's ears pricked, and she frowned, concentrating. The faint sound of another set of footsteps began to draw near.

The hairs on the back of her neck stood up, and she felt a chill travel shakily down her spine.

Who was coming?

"Vega?"

Helia turned her head towards the soft voice.

A woman with long, chestnut brown hair stood behind

her. Her soft, gentle doe eyes looked apprehensive as she quietly entered into the cottage. Her clothes were tattered and torn, and covered in grime and dirt. She looked around sadly, as if she was watching the ghost of someone she had once known drift by her. Her eyes rested on Helia, finally.

"Helia," the woman gasped, and ran quickly towards her. Helia winced reactively, bracing herself for whatever this strange woman was going to do to her. Her muscles tensed painfully, and she held her breath in anticipation for the pain she knew would come.

The woman launched herself at Helia, and, to her utter surprise, threw her arms around her, and squeezing her tight.

Helia stiffened uncomfortably.

What?

"You're safe," she cried softly against her cheek, her breaths tickling the hairs on her ear. Helia remained still, utterly confounded.

Slowly, she closed her eyes, and leaned against the woman's embrace. It had been a long time since someone had held her so.

"We have to move fast, Tami. Do you have it?" Mr. Vega said shortly.

Tami pulled back quickly, and ran over to Mr. Vega. She lifted the strap of an old, tattered leather satchel around her neck, and nodded triumphantly. Helia frowned. Where had she seen that satchel before?

"I have it."

"And did you find… *it?*"

Tami nodded.

"Perfect," Mr. Vega uttered. He looked at Helia, and

beckoned for her to come close.

Uncertainly, Helia walked towards the two.

A small, almost intact stone basin lay on the ground. Vega grunted, pulling the heavy stone structure towards the center of the room. Helia eyed it curiously.

"Elemental 0001. Do you know what this is?"

Helia shook her head no.

"It's a sundial," Mr. Vega grumbled, setting the sundial in place. "Tami, bring *it* here. We need to make sure it works."

Tami rushed towards him and bent down, bringing a small, weathered stone pendant out from the satchel. She placed it in the center of the sundial, and then looked up at Helia. "Helia," she said softly, holding her hand up to her. Helia blinked. It had been a long time since she had heard someone call her by her name.

Helia took her hand uncertainly and knelt down. She looked at Mr. Vega uneasily. She had never seen this side of him before. He looked like a completely different person, his usually stern and harsh demeanor melting away into one of concern and trepidation.

He looked worried.

Helia looked at the two of them, and then at the stone. Tami pulled out a small, battered journal from the satchel, flipping the pages and tracing her fingers against the faded numbers etched into the book. She nodded, mumbling to herself, and then began fiddling with the stone. A faint clicking noise began to emit from her ministrations, and Helia's eyes grew wide as a soft, blue light began to glow from within the stone's center.

"It works," Tami whispered, satisfied. She turned to face Helia. "Helia, I know the world's been unfair to you.

And it's unfair to put you through this all again. It's unfair to ask you to go through this again. But we have no other choice…"

Helia looked silently at Tami, uncertain of what she meant. Go through what again? What was she talking about?

Tami looked at her blank expression, and then shook her head. "Oh, right," she sighed. "You were too young… Too young to remember…" She looked at Mr. Vega.

He cleared his throat, and turned to look at Helia. "We don't have time to explain," he said shortly.

"Explain quickly," Tami snapped, her soft demeanor slipping away as she glared at Mr. Vega. "She deserves to know."

Know what? Helia felt the gears in her head go into overdrive as she tried to piece together the cryptic conversation the two of them were having.

Mr. Vega sighed, and then turned to Helia. "We… We were friends with your parents, a very long time ago. I used to work with your Aunt Miela as a Guardian. She was a good friend of your mother's. I inherited her files, her work, her investigations, and…it took us a long time to get here."

"We had to go undercover," Tami continued. "With the Elites wiping out the Guardians and taking over Polaris, we had to find ways to survive, and to keep watch over you."

Helia shook her head. Keep watch over her? Where were they when she was captured by Yun Zeru and his men? Where were they on those never-ending days of food deprivation and beatings? Where were they during those grueling years of training? During years of abuse? During years of being forced to fight as an Elemental Warrior in Professor Neptune's ruthless quest for world domination?

How dare they.

Anger flared up in her chest, and her hollow, sullen eyes burned furiously with life for the first time in years. She looked at Mr. Vega, and she felt something stir inside her. Uncontrollable rage welled up in her, and she could barely hear their next words.

"We needed to wait for the right time. The right time to make our move. You're old enough now. You can do it. You've done it once before. You're going to bend time. You're the only one who can do it again. It's all on you. Again."

Helia shook her head, beginning to protest. Do what? Bend time? What did that mean?

Marching footsteps began to sound outside of the cottage. Another squad was making their rounds of the castle ruins.

"We're running out of time," Mr. Vega pressed. "It's now or never."

Tami pulled the satchel over her head. "Don't you let go," she urged desperately.

Helia's breath caught in her throat at her words. A fuzzy memory surfaced.

"Listen here," she whispered, still carefully twisting the pendant around itself, the blue glow growing brighter and brighter. "You see Mama's bag?"

Helia nodded her head, still sniffling.

"Take Mama's bag—that's right, good girl. Don't you let go, all right? Whatever you do, don't let go. Keep it safe with you."

"Okay, Mama," said Helia, clutching the satchel tightly. She closed her eyes as her mother pulled her hood over her head, pressing

her lips to her forehead in a strong kiss.

She could barely remember what her mother looked like. She squeezed her eyes shut, trying to recall something about her face. Anything.

"Helia, are you with me?" Tami spoke quickly. The marching footsteps were drawing nearer. She looked down at the glowing stone in the sundial, its blue light growing brighter and stronger with every passing moment.

Tami pulled the necklace around Helia's neck. "I need you to stay with me, and remember everything that I'm saying, all right?" she said, cupping Helia's face between her palms. "Everything that you need to answer your questions is in here. She pointed at the satchel. "Don't you let go of that bag."

"It's up to you to change everything," said Mr. Vega.

Helia looked uncertainly between Tami and Mr. Vega. What was happening? She wasn't ready for this. She didn't ask for this. "How will I know what to do?" she asked, her voice scratchy and shaky.

"You'll know when the time is right," Mr. Vega replied, his voice low in apprehension. "Trust your instincts. Trust your memories."

"What?" Helia shook her head desperately. "I don't understand. I don't—"

Before she could say anything else, the light from the stone overtook her surroundings in a blinding flash, and the world disappeared around her.

Helia blinked, her eyes adjusting to the dim light around her. She wildly looked around. Mr. Vega and Tami were nowhere to be seen. She looked down at the necklace around her neck, now looking like an ordinary stone pendant, and quickly shoved it under her shirt.

She was in the same cottage still, but everything seemed different. Instead of the cold, decaying, stony structure, she was sitting in a warm and inviting room. The toppled over furniture previously strewn about was now arranged neatly in the sitting room. A tray with a few empty mugs sat on the table, and a half-eaten biscuit was on a small plate beside one of the mugs. It was the middle of the day, and the sun was streaming into the window, comfortably warming the room. Outside, she could hear the cheerful chatter of some guards passing by, and she strained her ears to hear what they were saying.

Helia slowly stood up, walking over to the window. Outside, birds tittered delightfully as they flitted from tree to tree, and she spied a plump cook toting a cart of freshly baked bread making her way up a neatly pruned pathway. Her eyes moved along the pathway, to the occasional group of guards and strolling townsfolk, and finally, to the castle.

Her breath caught in her throat.

There it stood, in all its pristine glory, its white walls gleaming in the sunlight. Bright, colorful roses and shrubberies dotted the windows and terraces, and she could hear the faint sound of music streaming from somewhere in the gardens.

It was peaceful.

She had never known peace.

Helia shook her head, breaking herself out of her trance. She needed to focus. She looked down at the old, beaten-up satchel hanging by her waist.

Don't you let go.

She wasn't sure if the voice ringing through her ears

was Tami's or her mother's voice. She concentrated.

What did her mother's voice sound like, again?

It had been so long.

She needed to get out of here.

Helia looked out of the window, waiting for the opportune moment to slip out of the cottage unnoticed.

She needed to find a safe place to properly examine the contents of the bag. Tami had mentioned that everything she needed was in that bag.

And she needed to find out what to do next.

Helia's mouth watered.

In the bustling crowd of the Polaris market, the aroma of freshly roasted chicken caught her attention, and her stomach grumbled angrily.

She was so hungry.

It had been a few days, and she had wandered around Polaris in a daze, utterly lost and confused. She felt like a failure, having already wasted so many days just trying to find food and shelter for herself. She had taken to sleeping in the odd nook and cranny in the outskirts of the town, trying to avoid drawing attention to herself.

She hadn't dared to open the satchel, yet. She needed to find somewhere safe, first. There was too much at stake to have something so important be lost, or at risk of being stolen away from her.

For now, however, Helia's energy and attention was on the fat, juicy roasted chicken on proud display at one of the market stalls.

She didn't have any money.

Her stomach growled.

She reached her hand out towards the chicken, and

then hesitated, biting her lip.

She was so hungry. She closed her eyes, drawing her hand back towards her. She couldn't steal. She couldn't risk bringing any unwanted attention to herself.

"You aren't thinking of stealing that, are you, miss?"

Helia froze.

That voice.

It couldn't be.

She turned around, and sure enough, it was.

Professor Neptune.

Helia gaped at him, her mouth opening and closing like a fish.

It couldn't be that easy, could it?

"Ah- I… I wasn't—"

"One chicken for the miss, please." The Professor smiled at the man working behind the stall. He held out a small handful of coins, dropping it onto the counter. The shopkeeper promptly bagged the chicken, placing the hot parcel into Helia's eager hands.

She looked down at the chicken, salivating.

"Thank—" Helia paused. The Professor disappeared in the crowd. She caught a glimpse of his telltale velvet robe swishing behind him before the crowd enveloped him into its throngs.

Things were looking up.

She knew what to do, now.

She needed to find Professor Neptune.

"Come now, Aileh," the Professor chirped, the heels of his boots clicking smartly against the marble floors of the Old Archive. Helia smirked as he uttered her name.

It was a trait of the Elementals to hide their identities

through anagrams. Tawer. Areth. Ria. Erif.

It was her way of taunting him with the truth, dangling it before his very nose, the Professor utterly oblivious to the truth.

It had been a month, and she had managed to track down the Professor and enlist as his personal bodyguard. Using the skills she learned during her training as a Warrior, she quickly captured his attention and impressed him with her prowess in offense, defense, and vigilance. She was, after all, Elemental 0001.

The very first Elemental Warrior.

They just weren't created, yet.

It was the perfect cover, really. She kept her ultimate enemy and target close, never letting him leave her line of sight, while also having the resources of the Old Archive tomes at her fingertips. She had a safe place to examine the contents of her satchel: Two old, ragged books. She had a place to call home.

"Looks like we have some visitors," Professor Neptune mused, standing outside of his office's door. Helia stood alert at his heels, watching intently. Her blood ran cold as she spied a woman clad in a blue uniform.

An Elite.

Helia shook her head, squinting again.

No, it wasn't an Elite.

It was a Guardian.

Helia stared.

"We were friends with your parents, a very long time ago. I used to work with your Aunt Miela as a Guardian. She was a good friend of your mother's."

She stared at the back of the woman's head, her long braid tied neatly behind her.

Was this her Auntie Miela?

She looked at the woman, who was deep in conversation with the other occupants of the room.

"…Targeting scholars, libraries, and schools is a common tactical move in the military to bring a civilization down to its knees," the woman uttered, her voice hard. "Destroying knowledge rips away the identity and strength of its beholder. Languages have been lost that way. Technology. Culture. Progression. By targeting scholars, you can set back an entire civilization hundreds of years. By erasing knowledge, you can ultimately erase that civilization. It's an awful tactic, but an effective one."

Helia frowned at the woman's explanation, a sinking realization settling in.

Now that she thought of it, Helia had never seen scholars before. In fact, having a whole squadron of scholars working and thriving within the walls of the Old Archive was a foreign sight to her eyes. She listened intently to the conversation, eager to learn more.

"It's been done before?" another woman asked, horrified.

Helia's ears pricked at her voice.

She had heard that voice a thousand times in her dreams. That voice that she yearned to hear for so long. That voice that she had replayed in her head so many times, desperate to hold onto the few shreds of what she could remember.

Mama.

She looked at the woman, craning her neck to take in as much as she could of her. She had dark, long, wavy hair that fell over her shoulders and hung down to the middle of her back. Helia watched as the woman turned her head, and she raced to memorize the outline of her mother's face. The way her nose turned ever so slightly upwards. The curve of her lips. The shape of her chin.

Helia brought a hand up to her own chin, recognizing the similarity they shared.

Professor Neptune strolled in, chiming into their conversation. Helia strode in behind him, standing sullenly in the corner of the room. She was suddenly very aware of how she was standing, and the clothes she wore. Her short, dark, wavy hair was pulled neatly into a low ponytail at the base of her skull, with a few tendrils curling softly around her hard, sunken eyes. She wore a fitted jacket over a smart pair of trousers, her gloved hands folded neatly behind her back as she stood stoically

She saw her mother glance curiously at her, and watched as her eyes darted down to the strap around her ankle, spying the hilt of a small dagger, peeking from under her left trouser leg and furrowing her brow curiously.

"Don't mind Aileh," the Professor waved dismissively at her. "She's got quite the personality"—he chuckled—"but she's quite useful. One can never be too careful…"

Helia surveyed the visitors, trying to memorize each of their faces. Her eyes finally landed on her father.

Dad.

Her face contorted as painful memories began to resurface once more. She struggled to keep her composure, and she trained her eyes on his face. He had dark, curly black hair, and he frequently ran a hand through his curls as he engaged in conversation with the others.

They were so young…

Helia held her breath, looking at her parents. She never thought she would see them again.

She wanted nothing more than to reach out and touch them. Make sure they were real. She yearned to run over to them and be wrapped up in their warm embrace. Her body burned desperately, and it took every bit of power and strength she could muster to hold herself back.

She needed to bide her time, if she was going to do this right. She would save them.

She would save all of them.

Something about today felt different.

Helia could feel it in her bones.

Or perhaps, she was just cold.

She had lost track of how much time had passed since she had gotten here.

Was it too late?

No. Helia chided herself for feeling so antsy.

She needed to time it right.

What was it that Mr. Vega had said to her?

You'll know when the time is right. Trust your instincts. Trust your memories.

Trust your memories.

Helia shook her head. She could hardly remember anything from this timeline. She was simply too young.

She felt used. Like a pawn, a mere instrument, being moved back and forth between time, the world pinning their hopes of peace and being saved on her.

Tami was right. It was unfair.

Helia felt resent bubble up inside of her.

She resented Mr. Vega and Tami.

She resented...

Mama. Dad. Uncle Noiro. Auntie Miela.

Why did they leave her?

Helia bit her lip, her anger battling away with a small wave of guilt.

They didn't leave her. They were taken away from her.

"Keep up, Aileh," Professor Noiro called over the wind. She snapped back to the present, and tread carefully over the foot of the cliff, her boots sinking into the soft sand as she followed the Professor on one of his daily walks alongside the ocean.

They eventually made their way back to the entrance of the Old Archive. Her ears pricked. She could hear a group of people chattering excitedly amongst each other. Professor Neptune lifted a finger to his lips, signifying that they needed to approach quietly. Helia nodded, and followed him as they walked closer to the group of people huddled around the statue hidden in the corner of the cavern.

She watched a tall woman clamber back down from the top of the statue's head, excitedly explaining to the group around her.

The woman clambered back down excitedly, quickly explaining to the group what she had seen.

"You're brilliant, Estelle." Uncle Noiro rubbed the back of his neck in admiration. "All this time…"

"It's just like the Ballad said," the woman squealed. "She hid the other amongst diamond, emerald, sapphire, and ruby. It was in the Diadem all along!"

Helia saw Professor Neptune smile.

She shuddered.

She had seen that sinister smile before.

"Noiro?" he called out, smiling as he watched the

group jump in surprise. "How nice to see you!" Professor Neptune smiled cheerily. "Aileh and I just came back from a little walk. Are you here to see me?"

She sulked behind the Professor, watching his every move.

"Er, no," Uncle Noiro uttered nervously. He shifted uncomfortably as he saw the Professor's smile grow bigger. "I mean, yes. We were just taking a walk ourselves, and I wanted to drop by and say hello."

"Of course." Professor Neptune smiled. "Come, please. I believe I have some snacks in my office."

Helia watched as the group exchanged uneasy glances, and were ultimately coaxed into following them to the Professor's office.

Helia followed behind him, her lean, muscular arm propping the heavy door open with ease. It was then when she noticed the little toddler trotting anxiously alongside the group, her mother's hand reaching for hers and holding it securely, eyeing her warily as the pair walked past her and into the office.

Helia's heart stopped.

It was her.

She could feel her breaths echo in her ears, each shaky breath reverberating through her as she watched her toddle-self walk so steadily with her parents. So safely. So blissfully unaware.

Everything suddenly became clear.

Helia remembered this day.

She could never forget this day.

You'll know when the time is right. Trust your instincts. Trust your memories.

This was it.

This was her chance.

She just needed to strike at the right moment...

Helia watched, her heart aching as she watched her Mama and Dad exchange worried glances, and then both look down at their daughter between them. She watched as her Dad instinctively moved forward, partially shielding her toddler-self from view.

She was loved.

She could see it.

She could feel it.

She felt her insides clench.

Watching her toddler-self receive so much care and love was painful. She felt as if she were in mourning. Mourning for herself, for all the loss she had experienced in her short, miserable life under the Elite rule.

Under Yun Zeru's rule. Under Professor Neptune's rule.

She blinked, catching herself before she could spiral into her thoughts.

She could mourn later.

She needed to focus, now.

She watched as the group before her—her family—slowly realize who Professor Neptune truly was.

What he was planning to do.

Not yet...

She watched as Yun Zeru burst into the room with his men, holding her family captive. She watched as Uncle Noiro pleaded with his old friend, begging him not to carry through with his plans.

Not yet...

She watched as, one by one, Yun Zeru's men began to attack.

She felt herself freeze. She wanted to move, but her eyes darted wildly back and forth between Professor Neptune, Yun Zeru, and their men. Fear gripped her bones, and she retreated into the shell she was beaten into when she was first captured all those years ago.

She couldn't move.

She stood stoically behind Professor Neptune, her empty, hollow eyes seemingly devoid of any emotion. Her Mama looked pleadingly at her, begging her, begging the Professor, begging anyone, to do something. She was screaming, begging for her toddler to be let go.

A faint flicker flashed in Helia's eyes as her Mama's eyes caught hers.

NOW.

An incredible crack began to fracture the marble floor, and the ground trembled and shook beneath their feet. She could hear her Mama gasp as a surge of ice-cold water suddenly began gushing out of the floor, sending her body into a cold shock. Her captor shrieked in surprise as the water seeped into his clothes, the cold sending shockwaves into his muscles, causing them to seize. Her Mama took her chance, pushing back against him and breaking free from his hold, running towards her child.

The water roared and swelled around them, pushing and holding the office door shut, the door shuddering in its frame with incredible force.

They were trapped.

Her Mama snatched the toddler from Yun Zeru's arms, taking advantage of his momentary lapse as he stared around him in shock and wonder. Professor Neptune looked at the ground in awe, and then at the child, who was shaking in her mother's arms and wailing.

Her Mama looked down at the toddler in her arms, backing away from the men. She trembled, and her Mama clutched tighter at her.

"Mama, what's happening?" the toddler wailed as the stormy grey water roared around them.

Her Mama looked down at her toddler again in surprise. If she wasn't doing this, then who was?

Helia turned her attention to the Professor.

Finally. This was it.

She was going to save her family.

All of the rage she felt, all of the anger, the pain, the hurt, the suffering... It was all going to be over, soon. She felt a surge of energy blast from her body, and ripped the water from the ground, throwing everything she had into bringing the cold, unforgiving water and exploding it at the Professor.

Helia held the water into a thick column around him, holding him captive within the watery prison. Professor Neptune clutched at his mouth and neck, clawing silently at an invisible force that seemed to suck the life out of him.

Yes. Drowning was quite silent.

Columns of water began to overtake the captors, entrapping them in watery pillars. The room was suddenly filled with watery pillars, the water swiftly swirling around each of Yun Zeru's men. The men tried to fight their way out of the watery pillars, but the current drew their arms back in. One by one, each of their struggles began to slow and finally cease. Their limbs floated limply, swaying with the waves. Their eyes and mouth fluttered open and shut as the water whipped around their bodies, their corpses dancing in the current.

A horrid, watery ballet.

Unbearably captivated, her Mama found herself frozen, watching in horror as the bodies around them waved lifelessly about.

As quickly as the water came, it seeped away back into the ground, leaving the waterlogged, lifeless men strewn about on the floor.

Helia's eyes rolled back as the water disappeared, and she blinked as she tried to regain focus of her surroundings. She felt drained.

She looked at her Mama, who was grasping frantically for her child, holding her close as she shook, their bodies trembling together as they took in the bodies spread across the floor.

"Regards, from your Elemental Warrior," Helia spat shakily at the Professor's lifeless body, her nose wrinkled in disgust as she poked him with the tip of her boot.

Her Mama stood before her, frozen.

Was it really over?

She could hear a commotion erupting outside of the office, and she wondered how many more men would be coming in soon. The door was still held shut, waterlogged and swollen in place, refusing to budge from efforts of others trying to break in.

How many more of Professor Neptune's men were out there? Yun Zeru's?

She broke out in a cold sweat.

How many people were involved?

No, it wasn't over.

It was far from over.

She watched as her Dad broke forward and ran toward her Mama and her toddler-self, scooping them in his arms and wrapping them in a tight hug.

Her family.

They were safe. For the time being, they were safe.

The rest of her family ran towards them, momentary relief and disbelief washing over their helpless panic and taking over, embracing each other in a tight squeeze.

Helia stood watching the group solemnly.

It all felt so surreal.

Her Mama broke away from everyone, and pulled closer towards her.

She saved them all.

She grasped her hands tightly in hers, and she looked into Helia's eyes. "Thank you," she whispered. "Thank you for saving my family."

Helia's grave façade broke at her words. She turned her head away. "I did it," she uttered softly, pulling her hands away from her Mama's. "I did it…"

With that, she collapsed, deep, heavy sobs wracking through her body, a battered Aether Stone hanging from her neck.

"Aileh?" Elara's voice shook. The room was deafeningly silent, a stark contrast to the horrible screams that only moments ago were reverberating against the old, marble walls.

Helia shook her head, tears streaming down her cheeks. She lifted her head up slowly to meet her Mama's eyes. Her eyes were heavy, glistening with tears as she smiled shakily at the name she had given to herself, hiding her identity in plain sight.

"No," She uttered. She looked at her toddler-self, and then back at her Mama.

She watched as her Mama's eyes darted to the Aether

stone around her neck. Her old brown leather satchel hung around her shoulder, and Helia shifted the bag forwards. Her eyes widened as she recognized her old satchel.

She frowned, confused. "How… How did you get this?"

Helia looked back at her, her eyes wide. She slowly stood back up, her knees trembling in anticipation. She had waited her whole life for this moment. Everything she had ever done, all of the hardships she had faced, all of the loss, all of the grief… It was all for this moment.

"It's mine," she murmured. "You told me to not let go, remember?"

"Not let go?" her Mama spoke softly, confused. Those words sounded so familiar to her. She studied Helia, her eyes raking over the young woman. She stared at the sullen woman, her short, dark, wavy hair messily hanging around her face in damp clumps. Her sunken eyes were hard. They were the eyes that had seen far too much. The eyes of someone who had to grow up far too fast. Far too soon.

Her eyes…

They were hauntingly familiar.

"I promised you I wouldn't let go," Helia repeated, her voice breaking.

She could see toddler shaking in her Mama's arms, and her arms tightened around her comfortingly.

"We have to go," Uncle Noiro urged, interrupting their exchange.

Her Mama shook her head, turning to Uncle Noiro.

"We have to go," he pressed again, his eyes zipping agitatedly at the dead bodies before them. "We need to get to the Diadem before—"

"Wait." Her Mama shook Uncle Noiro's hand off of her arm. She looked at Helia.

"I promised I would keep it safe," she repeated, her voice barely a whisper. Her hand dropped down to the old, battered pendant around her neck. "I've kept it safe... All this time... You died for me. You died so many times over for me..."

Her Mama breathed in sharply.

Take Mama's bag—that's right, good girl. Don't you let go, all right? Whatever you do, don't let go. Keep it safe with you.

"Who are you?" she whispered.

"It's me," said Helia, her voice suddenly firm and true. She looked at her toddler-self, reaching out to touch her arm, and then lifted her head to gaze at her Mama. "It's me, Mama."

THE AUTHOR

Sara Galadari is the author of City of Stars, The Pigeon Chronicles, and The Elemental. Born in Dubai, United Arab Emirates, she often spent her youth visiting libraries and checking out dozens of books at a time (taking advantage of her both of her brothers' library cards as well to cheat the system and check out more books for the week), and aspired to become a writer from a young age. After taking an interest in psychology and exploring the science behind human connection and behavior, she eventually went on to get her Bachelor of Arts and Master of Science in Communication from Portland State University.

When not writing, Sara enjoys binge-watching TV shows, discovering new restaurants, travelling the world, exploring museums, mastering insane rollercoasters, and memorizing choreographies. Sara lives in Dubai with her husband and son.

Printed in Great Britain
by Amazon